Isabelle Broom

The Orange House

T0343544

HODDER &
STOUGHTON

First published in Great Britain in 2024 by Hodder & Stoughton Limited
An Hachette UK company

The authorised representative in the EEA is Hachette Ireland, 8 Castlecourt
Centre, Dublin 15, D15 XTP3, Ireland (email: info@hbgi.ie)

3

A CIP catalogue record for this title is available from the British Library

Paperback ISBN 978 1 399 72112 7
ebook ISBN 978 1 399 72113 4

Typeset in Plantin Light by Hewer Text UK Ltd, Edinburgh
Printed and bound in Great Britain by Clays Ltd, Elcograf S.p.A.

Hodder & Stoughton policy is to use papers that are natural, renewable
and recyclable products and made from wood grown in sustainable
forests. The logging and manufacturing processes are expected to
conform to the environmental regulations of the country of origin.

Hodder & Stoughton Limited
Carmelite House
50 Victoria Embankment
London EC4Y 0DZ

www.hodder.co.uk

Isabelle Broom was born in Cambridge nine days before the 1980s began and studied Media Arts at university in London before a twelve-year stint at *Heat* magazine. When she is not travelling all over the world seeking out settings for her escapist novels, Isabelle can mostly be found in Suffolk, where she shares a home with her two dogs and more books than she could ever hope to read in a lifetime.

To find out more about Izzy and her books, as well as read excerpts, view location galleries and gain access to exclusive giveaways, you can sign up to her monthly newsletter via her website, isabellebroom.com.

Also by Isabelle Broom

My Map of You
A Year and a Day
Then. Now. Always.
The Place We Met
One Thousand Stars and You
One Winter Morning
Hello, Again
The Getaway
The Summer Trip
The Beach Holiday

For my family

I

Violet

It was only when the message arrived that I realised how unprepared I was to receive it.

That's the thing about shock, though, isn't it? Seismic when something happens unexpectedly, worse when that same something was an inevitability for which you stubbornly failed to prepare.

I stared at the words until my eyes stung, the text blurring as I fought to regain focus. Beyond the window, life went on. Traffic ground forwards, bicycle wheels turned, voices carried, and a stiff breeze chased city litter along gutters and into drains. It was all white noise to me.

I've put the house on the market. Thought you should know. H

For the past two years, I'd thought of the two of us as sitting on opposing sides of a chess board, each waiting for the other to make their move. This was his, and now, I knew, it was my turn.

'Violet?'

The door behind me was ajar, and the man now standing in the gap sounded terse as he said my name. I turned to face him, rearranging my features into what I hoped was a contrite expression.

'Sorry.' I glanced towards the phone in my hand, ready to explain, only to falter.

The man – my boss, Robert 'call me Bobsy' Prior – raised an enquiring brow. It was flecked with grey and impeccably neat, much like the goatee a few inches below it. 'Let me guess,' he said, 'another family emergency?' His tone left me under no illusions as to how he felt about that particular phrase, one that I had, admittedly, been unable to avoid trotting out on numerous occasions.

'Not this time,' I told him, trying for a smile. 'It's nothing.'

It's everything.

He nodded briskly. 'I'd like a word in my office.'

'Now?' Panic fluttered. 'But I have that viewing—'

'I took the liberty of rescheduling that.'

He waited a moment for me to register the importance of his statement. Bobsy Prior never rescheduled, not when it ran the risk of negatively impacting customer experience, and therefore business earnings. Whatever he wanted to talk to me about was serious.

Purposefully, he led the way back inside and dolefully I followed. Of the four desks inside our estate agency, only one other was occupied, and when I caught the eye of the young woman sitting behind it, she immediately looked away.

Guilt.

It was an emotion I recognised only too well.

'Take a seat.'

Bobsy's own desk was obscenely tidy, the white laminate surface blemish-free and reeking of furniture polish. Aside from a neatly ordered set of trays – one labelled 'In' the other 'Out', there was little save for a closed laptop and a pot of red biros. On the day of my first interview, I'd sat in the same chair I was perched on now and wondered if I should be worried about what those pens represented, the hint they gave as to the personality of the man in front of me.

'Intuition is always right, because truth is never wrong,' my dad had been fond of saying. One of his many wise proclamations. They had been coming back to me with increasingly regularity, and often I comforted myself by imagining he was in the room with me, whispering them into my ear.

I became aware of a tapping sound and glanced up to find Bobsy watching me, his mouth set and fingers drumming.

'I'll cut right to it, shall I?'

I sat up a little straighter.

'Did you,' he asked, 'or did you not, advise a client against putting in a bid for the house on Tension Road?'

'Which one?' I enquired mildly, though I knew full well.

'The former HMO,' he said, using the acronym term for a house in multiple occupation. The one to which he was referring had been repurposed into a series of bedsits, but now the owner was selling up and wanted to attract those in search of a project, ideally a young professional couple with the time and resource to transform the dilapidated property back into a home. So far, so reasonable, until you considered the price tag.

I sighed. 'Oh, that one.'

'According to Sheena, your exact words to the individuals at the appointment were: "One point two is far too high. If I were you, I'd go in under nine hundred."'

No wonder my colleague had been unable to meet my eye.

'It is too high,' I said. 'Far too high. You know that as well as I do. The vendor's dreaming if he thinks we can get that for him. The roof is rotten, the guttering needs a do-over, and that's before you start on plumbing and electrics. And the garden—'

Bobsy held up a hand to silence me, before launching into a monotonic spiel about 'competitive markets', 'desirable postcodes' and 'surveyor guarantees'. I didn't need to spell out the truth, which was that my instinct had been to protect the would-be buyers from investing in a money pit, and that I'd put their welfare above any thoughts of my own or the business's commission. Bobsy had figured out that much on his own, and he was furious.

'Selling is what we do; it's the job. If you can't stomach that element of the role, Violet, then I'm afraid you leave me with limited options.'

'Such as?'

The fingers continued to drum. 'I think you know.'

'You can't just sack me,' I said hotly. 'That's illegal.'

He sighed. 'If I'm honest, Violet, this latest stunt doesn't represent the most troubling example of your conduct. There is another, far more concerning issue at play here, one which I had hoped we could avoid discussing. If I'm honest,' he said again, a sure-fire preface to another damning indictment, 'I prefer not to dwell on such salacious behaviour. What I'm giving you here is an opportunity – walk away without a fuss, and I won't be forced to take the matter further.'

'I don't know what you're talking about,' I said, though I could feel the heat in my cheeks. How had he found out when I had been so careful? 'Please.' It was close to a whisper. 'I need this job.'

The arrangement of Bobsy's features gave nothing away. He was as blank as the pristine walls of his office.

'And I need people I can trust,' he replied crisply. 'People with a strong moral code. I'm being lenient here. What you have done . . . well, there are legal implications, and I'm sure neither of us wants to go down that path.'

The fact that he was right in his condemnations of me did little to assuage my anger, as it spread through my veins like nettles. I thought again about the message informing me that the house was going to be sold. Not just a house, but a home – our home, the place where life as I knew it had changed, where perhaps the most vital part of it had ended. The shock I'd felt as I read those words had calcified into rage, and it was the latter that brought me abruptly to my feet.

Bobsy rocked back in his seat, seemingly alarmed by the sudden movement.

'I've changed my mind,' I said, continuing to talk over his attempted reply. 'I don't need this job after all. You're right, I'm no good at ripping people off. In fact, I don't know what I was thinking accepting this job at all. You don't need to fire me, because I quit, OK? I quit with immediate effect.'

Bobsy stood up clumsily, his features curled into a scowl, but whatever he chose to say next was inaudible against the ringing slam of the door as I yanked it shut behind me. Crossing to my desk, I snatched up my few possessions, swept past a gaping Sheena, and headed out on to the street without so much as a single backward glance.

2

Violet

Adrenaline kept me going until I reached the park at the end of the road, after which panic took over. Collapsing down on to the nearest bench, I put my head in my hands and tried to stop my legs from shaking.

The hated blazer I'd bought specifically for the job I'd just lost was no match for the chill of the afternoon, late May having presumably decided that sunshine wasn't yet necessary, at least not when it came to the city of Cambridge. Mallorca, I imagined, was far warmer. The small Spanish island boasted an average of three hundred sunny days a year, while England only managed a paltry fifty-nine. I knew because I had looked it up, had done so purely to torment myself, a punishment of sorts for pain caused. My mind and I often played this game, one reminding the other of all the reasons to feel undeserving, ashamed, self-pitying, and it had rendered me weary.

My phone buzzed. It was bound to be Bobsy, terminating my contract of employment in writing, but it could also be something else, another emergency, him . . .

The latter made me check.

The text was from the same person who'd messaged me less than an hour ago, back when I still had a job, a purpose, some semblance of hope. There were no words, only a link to a Balearic Properties website. Steeling myself, I clicked on it, knowing what the photos would show yet staring at them anyway, my heart immobile in my chest as I scrolled down to the description.

Exceptional house for sale in Pollença old town, Mallorca north coast

Loved locally for its quirky turret design, orange walls, and mature citrus trees, this one-of-a-kind property is situated close to the Calvari Steps – one of the most sought-after locations on the island. Lovingly restored by one family over twenty years, it has four bedrooms and three bathrooms set across three levels, with breathtaking views across the town and mountains beyond.

The hillside plot offers the benefits of being close to the town's amenities yet secluded enough to provide an escape from the bustle of tourists. In short, it is the perfect family home, suitable for year-round living or holiday stays – and to see it is to fall in love with it. Viewing highly recommended.

Price on application.

The perfect family home.

Struck by a wave of nausea, I bent double, my head between my knees as I drew in one deep breath, followed by another. I didn't want to be here by myself, not in this state, but I was alone, had never been more so, and it hurt.

I sat up slowly and swiped the screen of my phone, searching through my limited list of contacts until I reached the name I was looking for – someone I knew still cared. She answered on the second ring.

'*Si? Bueno.*'

Hearing my old friend's voice brought me almost to tears. 'Ynes, it's Violet.'

She tinkled out a laugh. '*Cabecita roja!*' she cried – *little redhead* – 'This is a nice surprise.'

A few feet ahead of me, a pigeon had begun to inspect an empty crisp packet, its silvery grey head tilting to the side as if it was admiring its reflection in the foil. There was half a flapjack left over from lunch in my bag, and having taken off its wrapper, I broke it up into pieces and tossed them across the grass. Ynes was chattering away as she always did, sharing snippets of Mallorcan gossip, asking when I would visit, saying that it must be soon, that I was needed, that there were things to be resolved. I had no idea how to answer, and so waited in silence until she said, 'So, why is it that you are calling me? What has happened?'

I swallowed. 'I've done something stupid,' I said, and heard the air-hissing sound of a wince.

'*Háblame*,' she said soothingly. *Talk to me.*

Haltingly, I explained about the buyers I'd put off, the trouble I'd got into as a result of it, and the strident way by which I'd walked out of my job.

I didn't, couldn't, tell her about the other reason I'd been forced to quit.

'You hate this job?' Ynes asked.

'*Sí*,' I mumbled.

'Then why do you care, *cabecita roja*?'

How best to make it clear that I did care, not about the job, but about the salary it provided? I needed money, more now than I ever had before, and the stakes were terrifyingly high.

Ynes, who did not know the full story, remained pragmatic. 'Who needs to work for an *imbécil* like this?' she said. 'It is done now. You will find other work.'

She made it sound easy, but it wasn't – not for me. I had no formal qualifications, no degree, no experience aside from what I'd gleaned during the few years spent working for a business I'd long since abandoned, and no savings.

'Who's going to offer a lucrative role to a thirty-seven-year-old woman who's moved back in with her mother?' I said joylessly. 'Nobody.'

Ynes snorted. 'So, take a holiday.'

The pigeon strutted and weaved, picking through the grass with its beak. I looked up at the pallid sky, tuned into the rumbling growl of cars and buses as commuters idled along rush-hour roads, all of them with somewhere to go, and with somebody waiting at their journey's end. I had neither; no purpose at all other than to be there in case anybody needed me – in case *he* needed me.

'The house is on the market,' I said, to an audible gasp from Ynes.

'No? I do not believe it.'

'I've seen the advertisement.'

Ynes rattled out a stream of Spanish disparagement. 'You cannot let the house go,' she exclaimed. 'This is not the right decision.'

'Isn't it?' I countered, in a murmur so low that she demanded I repeat myself. 'It's the only thing left that belongs to both of us. We can't keep it, not after— I don't want to sell it, of course I don't, but perhaps it is for the best.'

In the beginning, when the future was still unclear, I'd felt the same way as Ynes, the idea of the house no longer being a part of my life abhorrent enough to cause me sleepless nights. But things had changed since then, I had altered in ways I thought impossible, that first mistake acting as a domino to hundreds of others, each one steering me towards this moment, on this bench, trapped, scared, and fast running out of options.

Ynes had begun to mutter under her breath, the rapid Spanish indecipherable. My friend was disappointed in me; she didn't understand why it had come to this, or how I'd allowed it to happen. The only thing I could think of to say was sorry, but it was so worn out, that word; threadbare and desultory.

'It's only a house,' I said meekly, and was rewarded with a snapped '*qué ferte*'.

'Listen to me, *cabecita roja*. I am your friend, and because of this, I will not tell you lies, not even the little white ones. It is better to snip the stem than wait for the petals to drop, you know this.'

Again, I could think of nothing to say.

'Selling the house is a mistake,' she went on. 'One that you will both regret.'

'It's not that simple,' I protested, but Ynes shushed me.

'Life becomes complicated when you complicate it.'

There they were again, the words of my father.

'Whatever you decide to do, sell or not sell, you must talk about it,' she urged.

'I've tried,' I said insistently. 'You should see all the messages on my phone, the emails that go unanswered – he doesn't want to hear me.'

Ynes drew in a long breath, and the exhalation that followed sounded sorrowful. 'Then perhaps,' she said, 'it is time that you gave him no choice but to listen.'

3

Violet

Our first mistake was thinking that love would be enough.

When you build a house, you don't simply stack up a pattern of bricks and balance a roof over the top; you draw up a plan, establish the foundations, and create a home from multiple layers of careful craftsmanship. A marriage is the same; it needs so many components, a solid framework for all that love to adhere itself to before it sets, cement-like, into the elusive happy ever after. Perhaps if Henry and I had spent more time constructing us and less time fixing up our house, we could have made it. In my darkest moments, I pretended to myself that I blamed the place – hated it, even – but I never truly believed it.

Standing proud but unassuming on its steep hillside plot, the once ramshackle abode had sun-blushed apricot walls, barrel roof tiles, and a cylindrical turret with porthole windows, which marked it out as unique amongst its Mallorcan neighbours.

Henry had chosen the name in that typical Henry way of his, settling on La Casa Naranja – The Orange House, to use its less glamorous-sounding English moniker – because that's what colour it was. When I teased him about it, he'd argued that orange was a warm colour, a summer colour, the colour he associated with me, and therefore us. And as I stared up at the rough stone facade now, trying to see it as a stranger might, it was impossible not to feel nostalgic for the two of us as we were then, before everything started to fall apart.

In the week since Henry had sent his message, I had thought of little else, the terse words he had chosen cutting a swathe right through me. When I considered the mess I'd made of my life in England, being here felt like running away, though I knew all I'd done was flee one set of flames for another. There would be consequences to the actions I'd taken, but for now I had to push those fears aside. Focus on the present, avoid dwelling on the past, and remain blinkered to the future.

I closed my eyes and focused on breathing for a few seconds. Below me in the hub of Pollença town, a clock chimed three times. If I concentrated, I could make out the faint scent of trumpet vines, honeysuckle, and the acrid dust kicked up by the endless stream of tourists; the smells of what I had associated, for the longest time, with home. Being back here again had unmoored me, set me adrift in a wash of conflicting emotions.

Giving in to a sigh, I stooped to pick up my small suitcase, using my free hand to push aside the decorative metal gate that separated La Casa Naranja from the street. The patio was tidier than I remembered it being. Terracotta pots were arranged in a neat line along one wall, a broom and pitchfork propped beside them. Aside from a few stray leaves and petals, the smooth grey paving stones were bare, and it looked as if someone had recently weeded between the gaps. Holes gaped in the mud, reminding me of tiny screaming mouths, and I averted my eyes as I made my way to the front door. I was in the process of locating my key when I heard a click, followed shortly by a voice. *His* voice.

'Oh,' said Henry. 'It's you.'

I made myself look at him. All those hours we'd spent gazing at one another, and I could barely bring myself to meet his eye.

'It's me.'

A silence followed, during which we both twitched uncomfortably.

'I wasn't sure if you'd be here,' I said. 'I was told you were on a job in Palma?'

'I was,' he replied. 'I finished this morning.'

'I see. And how . . . How are you?'

I glanced up as I posed the question, my eyes coming to rest somewhere around his midriff. Henry was tall and broad, his form filling the open doorway, and he was dressed in the same tatty overalls I'd seen him wear a hundred times before, the top part shrugged off and the sleeves knotted around his waist. The black T-shirt he had on underneath was speckled with splatters of paint, as were his arms, which he'd folded across his chest. Decorating was the part of his job he relished the least, the task he found the most tedious, but he continued to grit his teeth and get on with it. That was Henry, a doer not a dallier, the kind of man who'd crack a tooth on a steak before complaining to the chef that it was overdone. It took a lot to break through his veneer of affability, but smash through it I had.

He hadn't answered me, and I hesitated for a moment, torn between sadness and bewilderment, unsure of what I should say or do next.

'I didn't think you'd want to stay here,' he said then, glancing over his shoulder into the bowels of the house. 'Thought you might find a hotel.'

I spluttered out an incredulous 'as if'.

'What's wrong with that?'

'Henry,' I said steadily, 'it's June now, and it's Pollença.'

'So?'

'So, I'm not made of money, as you well know. Affording the flight was a stretch, and I had to take the bus up here from the airport.'

I loathed talking about money, and it showed, my frustration leaking into my words, making them sound brittle. I could feel Henry's judgement of me as keenly as I could the sweltering heat of the afternoon.

'If being here is such an inconvenience, Violet, then why come at all?'

He never referred to me as 'Violet' – I was 'Vee' to him, always had been. 'Violet' made it sound as if we barely knew each other.

'Because of the house,' I replied. 'I assumed the fact you messaged me meant you thought we should discuss it properly, but then you ignored all my calls, so . . .'

'So?' Henry shifted position; his arms still folded.

'If you'd agreed to talk to me sooner, we could have organised the sale months ago, before the summer. We might even have had everything sewn up by now – the finances, the asset split, the paperwork.'

'Paperwork' was the word I had chosen to use in place of 'divorce', and I only had to glance at Henry to know he'd understood. It was painful to hold his gaze, and I had to force myself not to give in to the discomfort. In the end, it was he who turned his head away, relinquishing a sad sigh as he did so.

'This was your idea,' I reminded him, stepping forwards. The shade provided by the bougainvillea I'd planted enveloped me, and despite the prickling unease I felt at being so close to him, it was a relief to get out of the sun. Henry unfolded his arms and ran a hand through his hair, which was every bit as thick and dark now as it had been the day we met. I'd long envied the Mediterranean blood that ensured he thrived in this climate while I, with my Anglo-Irish auburn curls and pale skin, wilted.

'You were the one who insisted we split up and divide everything. All the decisions I've made since then have been based on that exact outcome. If we're really going to let this place go,' I went on, trying to sound resolute, 'then I want to be involved. It's my house, too.'

'And what if I've changed my mind?' he said, not looking at me. 'What then, Vee?'

Could he mean that he'd forgiven me?

Henry had gone very still, his eyes focused on the ground. I held my breath as I waited for him to continue, yearning to touch him, fearing what would happen if I did.

'Are you saying that you're having second thoughts about the house?' I whispered. 'Or about us?'

Henry shook his head, and I blinked back tears as the hand I'd raised to grasp his fell limply to my side. I had been foolish to hope; the seed of my longing planted too late; its fragile roots destroyed by his dismissal. It had been a mistake to come here, to see him, to torture myself with reminders of what I'd lost.

'I'll go,' I said, my voice cracking as I reached again for my suitcase. 'You were right. I should have found somewhere else to stay. Ynes will lend me her sofa, I'm sure.'

Henry clenched his fists, frustration contorting his features.

'Don't—' he began, but I was already moving, already at the gate, already running away from the past before it wrapped any more tendrils around me. I'd reached the pathway when I heard another sound, one that stopped me in my tracks, triggered every sense I had, and twisted my guts into a mess of conflicting emotion.

A single word, one I both craved and abhorred.

Mum.

4

Violet

A split second. That was all it took for me to regain my composure and hitch the corners of my mouth up into a smile. I was well practised in the art of what I liked to call 'Mum-terfuge', the ease of which I was able to project a pretence of contentment so deeply ingrained that it had become as natural as breathing.

Turning, I pushed open the gate and dragged my case back across the patio towards my son. He was standing in the space that Henry had now vacated, and though he was tall – taller, even, than his dad – Luke was lean in the extreme. I could see the sharp edges of his collarbones jutting out through the fabric of his T-shirt, the handsome bone structure he'd inherited from my late father half-obscured by the first tufts of a downy beard. Nineteen years old now, not quite a man; a flower that had yet to bloom but was by no means less beautiful in spite of it. And of all the things Luke was, beautiful could be relied upon as a constant.

We didn't hug one another in greeting – my son was not an affectionate person – but he did appear, outwardly at least, to be pleased that I was there. He had still been very young when his myriad behavioural issues began to manifest, allowing me plenty of time in which to learn his tells; study him with the ardent dedication of one who is determined to love. Now, I saw the flicker of something close to pleasure in his deep-set green eyes.

'You look well,' I said, following him inside. 'Nice to see you with a bit of colour on your cheeks.'

Both statements were true, but I'd selected the anodyne compliments with care – a double act of self-preservation, such as a sprinkle of gravel above and below each spring bulb. The latter would be protected from rodents, me from Luke's distemper.

He paused at the bottom of the stairs, his fingers tracing a circular shape across the rail. Each of the individual banisters had been slotted into place by Henry during our second summer here, and the dry scent of reclaimed acacia had permeated the house for days afterwards. Aside from the few pieces of furniture we'd bought at second-hand markets or from Pollença-based friends looking to offload, much of the rest of it was handmade, including the vast olive-wood dining table that dominated the lower part of the house. It was the creation of which Henry was most proud, and he was right to be so.

'I'd usually be burnt by now,' he muttered. 'Probably would be, if Eliza didn't keep nagging me about sun cream.'

Eliza.

Had the stress of the past few weeks somehow made me forget that Luke's girlfriend was coming out to Mallorca with him – or had he simply not told me?

'Of course, Eliza,' I said, lacquering enthusiasm like gloss over my surprise. 'How is she? Where is she? I'd love to meet her.'

Luke squinted at me from beneath his untidy dark fringe. 'Um, wouldn't you rather, you know, get settled in or something first?'

'Oh dear,' I replied, in my highest, brightest 'Mum' tone. 'Is that a polite way of telling me I look dreadful?'

He sighed. 'You look fine, Mum.'

'Because I can go and tart myself up, if you want me to? There might even be some make-up in the bathroom, although it might be a bit dried up. You know how hot it gets in—'

'Whatever you want.'

'I want what you want.'

Too late, I remembered this particular phrase was one that irked him and suppressed a wince as he shook his head and dodged past me.

'Luke,' I cajoled. 'Listen, I'm sorry. I— Wait!'

The saucepans thrummed on their hooks as the back door slammed, and almost immediately, a cramping pain ripped through my stomach. Fewer than five minutes I'd been in his company, and already he was angry with me. It was tempting to retreat; go upstairs and unpack; splash cold water on my face and wait for the anxiety to ebb – but to do so might make him even angrier. Instead, I forged ahead, through the kitchen with its terracotta tiled floor, exposed honey-stone walls, and painted blue worktops, and out into the rear garden, where I narrowly avoided colliding with a very petite, very pretty, and very pink-haired young woman coming the other way.

Mistaking my raised hands of shock for the offer of a hug, Eliza stepped between them and wrapped her arms around me. I became briefly aware of her chin against my shoulder, and the coconut aroma of her sun lotion.

'You must be Luke's mum,' she said, leaning back to take me in properly.

'Please, call me Violet – or better yet, Vee. We don't stand on ceremony in this family.'

Eliza glanced over towards Luke, who was sitting with his back to us on the steps, and I thought I caught the ghost of a frown pass across her features. In a bid to show solidarity, I rolled my eyes and made a small tutting sound, but Eliza didn't appear to notice. She had turned away and was delving through an oversized straw bag. Having extracted a hat, she tossed it in Luke's direction, laughing when it landed askew on his head. I thought about all the times I'd coerced toddler Luke into sun-appropriate clothing, of the punches and kicks he'd aimed my way if I so much as uncapped a bottle of Ambre Solaire in his orbit. He would scream and squirm, and, despairing, I would call on Henry to help. One of us would then clamp down his limbs while the other attempted to smear on the cream, both of us coming away battle-weary, tearful, and often bloodied. Nineteen-year-old Luke did not so much as murmur; he merely grunted a 'thanks' and readjusted the cap so the peak covered his exposed neck.

Eliza: one; Violet: nil.

'You are good,' I told her. 'Looking after him like that.'

She considered this, her grey eyes narrowing a fraction. There was a silver stud in the shape of an arrow pierced through her right eyebrow, and it was on the tip of my tongue to make some kind of light-hearted comment about Cupid. Eliza, perhaps fortunately, spoke before I had the chance.

'I wouldn't call it looking after,' she said. 'I look out for him.'

My smile felt tight. 'Is there a difference?'

'Looking after is something you do for yourself, looking out is what you do for others.'

'But some people can't look after themselves,' I pointed out gently. 'The infirm and the frail or very elderly, and babies and young children, too.'

Eliza wrinkled her nose at a passing bee. 'Right,' she agreed. 'But Luke is none of those things – and neither am I.'

I longed to tell her that it wasn't that simple; not where her boyfriend was concerned. Luke did need to be looked after

– he'd always needed to be looked after – and where his needs were concerned, she couldn't conceivably be a match for me, his mother. I was the person who understood him, better and more comprehensively than anyone else, and there was no doubt in my mind that by the end of their summer together, Eliza would find this out for herself. I didn't have to tell her; Luke would do it for me without even trying.

'Well,' I said, through my rictus grin, 'I'm very glad the two of you have each other, and that you're here with us.'

I took a few steps forwards and reached out a hand to pat Luke on the shoulder. To my intense relief, he didn't flinch, and feeling buoyed, I offered to prepare drinks.

'Gin and tonics? It's about that time – or it is somewhere.'

Luke shuffled to his feet. 'We can do it.'

I started to protest, but he ignored me, lifting an arm to create a space for Eliza to slide into.

'I'll pick some fresh lemons off the tree, then,' I called, as they went into the kitchen, wondering as I did so whether Henry would decide to join us. I wanted to know what he thought of Eliza; if he'd drawn any conclusions about her and Luke's relationship – but I was no longer sure if these types of discussions would be welcomed. Confiding in each other was something that had fallen away a long time ago. You had to have mutual trust in order to confide.

I heard the chink of glasses coming from indoors, Eliza asking if the ice-cube tray had been filled with bottle or tap water and Luke's baritone reply.

'Lemons,' I reminded myself, with a small shake of my head. Verbalising my mental to-do list was a new habit, one I appeared by osmosis to have picked up from my mother. I'd been living with her for five months, having given up the three-bedroom semi in the small Cambridgeshire village that Henry and I had rented together. Affording it alone had eventually proved impossible, as had finding somewhere else to live when I had nothing saved with which to put down a deposit, nor any proof of long-term employment. The day I was compelled to move back in with my mother was undoubtedly the second most galling of my life, and the sooner I could escape, the happier both of us would be. In order to do that, however, I needed money.

A lot of money.

Taking the stone steps two at a time, I hurried down from the back porch to the upper part of the garden, where I discovered to my dismay that weeds had overtaken the carefully curated flowerbeds. Red-hot pokers were doing their best to push through a thatch of needle weeds, and the purple of the lantana petals were barely visible. Bending to pull up a clump of dry grass, I accidentally uprooted a fragile pink daisy, and scolded myself ferociously. All those hours, all that tender care, all for nothing.

I was mildly comforted when I discovered that the cacti beds on the next level down were thriving, and the aloe plant appeared to have tripled in size. Unfortunately, the same could not be said for the majority of my herbs, which had been all but overrun by mint. Mojitos would perhaps have been a more suitable choice of aperitif than gin and tonics, and the plant's fresh scent was heavenly. Weed-ridden it may be, but the garden still soothed me. It was my favourite part of the house for good reason.

Having reached the far wall, I braced myself against the bark of the lemon tree and, finding a foot-hole sturdy enough to take my weight, sprung up from the ground and made a grab for the fruit.

'*Cuidado*!' I heard someone yell. *Watch out*.

My outstretched hand grasped thin air, and I yelped in alarm as my sandal slipped off its perch, sending me crashing sideways on to the wall. There was another shout, and then two pairs of arms were on me, hoisting me on to my feet. I looked up to see Henry, his brow constricted by concern, mouth only inches from my own. Even when I was this close to him, it was difficult to meet his eye, and instinctively I turned away.

It was then that I saw who else had come to my aid.

And my blood froze.

5

Violet

Of all the places I thought I might see this man again, the garden of La Casa Naranja was not one of them. But here Juan was, in all his stubble-coated, deeply tanned glory, seemingly completely at ease with the person who'd banned him from ever again crossing the threshold.

I gaped at him, incomprehension writ large, and struggled for something to say. The word that kept floating to the surface, oil on the water of my inherent British need to be polite, was 'why'.

Why are you here? Why is Henry not reacting? Why is this happening? Why?

I managed to emit a low, sort of murmuring sound.

'Are you OK?' Juan laid a hand across my forehead. 'Hot,' he proclaimed, in thick, heavily accented English. The way he pronounced his 'O's made them sound flayed, as if his throat was somehow stripping the skin from each one on its way out. I stepped away from him.

'I'm fine,' I said, bending my elbow so I could examine the scrape on my upper arm. 'It's a scratch, it's nothing.'

Henry reached up and casually plucked a lemon from one of the lower branches of the tree – one that I'd failed to reach even after scaling the wall.

'Here,' he said, handing it to me. 'You need only have asked.'

The back door opened to reveal Luke, his cursory glance transforming into an expression of delight when he saw who had joined us.

'*Mi amigo*,' cried Juan, jogging up the two sets of stone steps to greet him. Luke abandoned his tray of drinks on the patio table and allowed himself to be pulled into a hug, grinning as Juan clapped him on the back. As I did during every interaction that I saw the two of them share, I tried hard not to envy their closeness, nor the casual way our Spanish neighbour crossed Luke's boundary and found himself welcomed as opposed to rebuffed. There was no doubt that if it pained me to witness this show of companionship, it must be agony for Henry.

'What brings you here?' Luke asked.

Juan hesitated for a moment before answering, his gaze straying to Henry, who was making his way to the patio just ahead of me. 'I am here with a proposition,' he said. 'For your father.'

Eliza chose that moment to fling open the shutters in the bedroom above, a wet bikini top in her hands that she promptly started to wring out. Ducking to avoid the droplets of water, I deposited my lemons on the table and, picking up the knife Luke had brought out on the tray, started to slice them.

'What proposition?' Henry's flat tone betrayed no emotion beyond perhaps mild curiosity.

'A house,' said Juan. 'Here, in Pollença town.'

I took a sip of gin and tonic and winced at its strength.

Henry's face must have registered interest because Juan then clarified the address of his mystery house as being on Carrer de la Garriga, a narrow lane around fifteen minutes' walk from where we were standing.

'It is . . . *un desastre*,' he went on, punctuating the statement with a shrug.

'Is that a good or bad thing?' asked Eliza, who had floated out to join us in a pale green floor-length sundress.

'Bad,' I supplied, at the same time Henry said 'good'. Eliza blinked at us, confused.

'Most people would consider a wreck of a house to be a bad thing,' I told her. 'But Henry isn't most people.'

'You want Dad to do it up for you?' guessed Luke, and Juan beamed at him.

'*Sí*! He is the best, after all.'

I took another sip.

'Antonio heard that it was becoming available, and he arranged for me to make the first bid,' Juan explained. 'It is a gift,' he added. 'For Tomas.'

I could not be sure if I had imagined Henry flinch when he heard his father's name, but at the mention of Juan's son, Tomas, he visibly softened.

'Generous gift,' observed Luke, as Eliza picked up the tray of drinks from beside me and offered it to the three men. 'You go ahead,' she urged when Henry looked as if he was going to refuse. 'I can make myself another one.'

It should really have been me who played host, me who saw to it that everyone was given refreshments, and me who went inside now and mixed a drink for Eliza – but I was loath to leave the unexpected tableau playing out in front of me. Juan not only back in The Orange House, but seemingly in our lives, the past wiped clean as if it were no more than dust on a windshield.

Luke was right – a house was a lavish gift, wreck or not – and by rights, La Casa Naranja should have been his one day. Henry and I had talked about it. Putting down my glass, I tried not to react as my stomach twisted unpleasantly.

'Tomas has outgrown the apartment in Palma,' Juan continued. 'The place is full of Paulina's toys, and soon there will be a new baby.'

'Carmen's pregnant?' I blurted, to which he smiled.

'*Sí. Soy un abuelo.*'

'*Abuelo* means grandfather,' I told Eliza. She'd just returned with a large drink and slid the hand not holding it into one of Luke's.

'I did not think I would be a grandfather twice over at the age of forty-five,' Juan said, with an affectionate lament. He raised his drink as if toasting the absurdity of life and drained it in a single gulp.

'*Salud,*' I said, retrieving my own gin and tonic. Henry, I noticed, had yet to drink any of his.

'So,' said Juan, 'what do you say, my old friend? Will you come and take a look, help Tomas to plan for the refurbishment? It will be a big job,' he added. 'There is money.'

Henry would refuse – he had to.

I jumped violently as someone began hammering on the front door. Luke said he'd go, and a few moments later, a little girl hurtled through the open back door and threw herself against Juan's legs.

'Paulina, *mi muñequita,*' he crooned, hoisting the dark-haired toddler into the air and rubbing his nose against hers.

'*Basta*, Abuelo,' she squealed, writhing as he tickled her.

Luke reappeared with Tomas, who was less classically handsome but more lithe than his father. He greeted Eliza with genuine warmth but offered little more than a faint nod in my direction, choosing instead to bestow his attention on Henry. They had much in common, the two of them, and I could see his arrival was having the desired effect. As soon as Tomas pleaded his case, Henry capitulated, telling Spanish father and son that he'd be happy to inspect their house at the earliest opportunity.

I stole a glance at Luke, but he had moved a few paces away and was listening intently as Eliza whispered something in his ear. Whatever she was saying had turned the tips of his ears the same bright pink as her hair, and as I watched, he dropped a kiss on her collarbone.

Overwhelmed by a sudden urge to cry, I looked hurriedly away. The little girl had grown bored of pulling Juan's ears and was wriggling to be put down.

'Papá,' she said, reaching up towards Tomas. As he levered her into his arms, Paulina found herself face-to-face with Henry, and promptly screamed.

'*Caracortada!*' she cried, repeating the word over and over as she buried her head against her father's chest. Tomas shushed her, soothing and scolding in turn until it became clear she was not going to stop.

'Sorry,' he said, before carrying the near-hysterical girl back indoors.

Eliza was looking at Luke, who'd turned pale. 'What does Caracortada mean?' she asked, and it was Henry who answered.

'It's a word I hear a lot these days,' he said, the flatness of his tone at odds with the wretchedness of his expression. I made myself look at him then – really look at him – at the raw, puckered skin that had yet to heal, the jagged line where flesh had been torn from bone, and the still swollen eye that would never again find focus.

'*Caracortada* means Scarface.'

6

Henry

Twenty Summers Ago

His father had presented him with the key that morning. It had fallen out of the envelope containing his birthday card and landed with a soft clunk in his lap.

Henry had experienced a tightening sensation across his entire body as he held the small brass object up and examined it, his fingers tracing its grooves and edges.

'This is a house key,' he said in Spanish, to which Antonio nodded.

'*Sí*,' he confirmed. '*Tu casa.*'

Your house.

It had not felt real then, and seemed barely plausible now that he was standing right in front of it, staring up at the crumbling walls and boarded windows, marvelling at the sheer size of the place.

'*Un gran reto*,' his father had gravely proclaimed. *A big challenge*. But one he believed Henry was ready for. And if Antonio had faith in him, that was enough to convince Henry that he could and would succeed. But it was going to take a lot of work – a fact that became undeniable as soon as he let himself inside.

The stone staircase opposite the front door was still standing, but most of the banisters were broken or rotted and some sort of plant with dark green leaves had pushed its way through a crack by the bottom step. Paint peeled off walls, light fittings hung bare, and the frayed ends of wires stuck out where sockets had once been. Whoever had owned the house previously had done a thorough job of stripping it down before they left – either that, or looters had come in later and helped themselves to anything of the remotest value. In what Henry guessed was the lounge, he found nothing but a rusting watering can and a pile of yellowing newspapers, and there were no appliances or cabinet doors in the kitchen. Stooping to peel gingerly at the putrid corner of a filthy rug, he was pleasantly surprised to find smooth terracotta tiles below it, most of which appeared to have miraculously survived intact. They represented something, he decided. A point at which to start.

He was about to venture upstairs when he heard what sounded like a squeal coming from outside. Instead of opening the back door, Henry lifted aside what was left of the flimsy curtain strung across the window and peered through the gap. On the far side of the overgrown garden, where the boundary wall curved around the bough of a lemon tree, a leg appeared, and then another, followed by a small, neat bottom, encased in stonewashed denim. The girl stretched a foot down until the tips of her toes were touching the ground, then she let go, landing nimbly on the earth.

Henry had enough time to take in her vibrant red hair and slim, pale arms, before the girl crouched and was obscured by the bulbous paddles of a large cactus. Indecision rooted him to the spot, his fingers immobile on the grotty curtain until it occurred to him that this was his house. The mysterious redhead, whoever she was, was trespassing on his land, which meant he was well within his rights to go and confront her. What would his father say if he could see him now, hiding like a *cobarde* because he was scared of some girl?

Henry looked down at himself, at the T-shirt he'd put on clean that was now flecked with dirt, the cargo shorts with the ripped pocket and the trainers that had seen better years, let alone days. A quick sniff of his armpits reassured him that he had, at least, remembered to put on deodorant that morning – but had he brushed his hair? Henry ran an exploratory hand through it and encountered sticky remnants of gel, but perhaps the girl wouldn't notice. Not that it mattered. She was a trespasser – how could she judge him?

Henry opened the door. '*Hola*,' he called loudly, making his way towards the spot where he'd last seen her. The terrain was so tangled that he tripped twice, and almost stumbled over sideways when what he thought was a solid thicket fell away beneath his foot. The girl was on her haunches in one of the flowerbeds and looked up in alarm as he bore down on her.

'Sorry. God, sorry.' She cowered as if he was about to strike her. 'I was just— I didn't think anyone lived here.'

'They don't – at least, they didn't until about ten minutes ago. Don't worry,' he added, as the girl eyed him dubiously, 'I'm not going to call the *policia* on you or anything.'

'This is your house?' she asked, making no move to stand. 'It can't be.'

Henry folded his arms, head tilting to one side as he considered her.

'Why not?'

'Because you're too young.'

'Is that so?'

'Only lottery winners or rich brats own houses when they're still teenagers,' she said primly. 'Which camp do you fall into?'

Henry smirked. 'Do you really think,' he said, 'that if I'd won the lottery, I'd have bought a place as decrepit as this one? I could just as easily have blown the lot on a Malibu beach house – or better yet, a private island.'

'So,' she mused, shifting until she was in a more comfortable position, 'that must mean you're a rich brat, then?'

Henry laughed. 'Nope. Guess again.'

The girl glanced around disparagingly. 'I think it's safe to assume you're no gardener.'

'That's a fair assessment.'

'And you can't be a pool boy, because there's no pool.'

'Observant.'

'Which means,' she said, beady gaze searching his face for clues, 'you must have climbed over the wall to have a poke around in here, exactly like I did.'

'Oh, so that's why,' he replied, scooting down beside her. 'You broke into my house to poke around.'

'I did not break in,' she said, affronted. 'Not into the house, at any rate.'

'Was it my lemons you were after?' he said. 'Or my oranges?'

'You have those?'

He nodded. 'There's a tree out front.'

She smiled at him then, and Henry felt himself blush as he registered how pretty she was. A scatter of fox-red freckles decorated a petite, open face, the fiery hair falling in soft waves to her shoulders, which he could see had caught the sun. She wore a black vest tucked into her shorts, and a silver chain bore a 'V' pendant that was nestled in the hollow of her throat.

'There's also a much lower wall around that side,' he went on. 'And a gate. Feel free to use it next time you decide to burglarise the place.'

'It's not breaking in if you issue an invitation.'

'Who says I am?'

'Well, aren't you?'

'That depends,' Henry replied laughingly.

'On what?'

'On three things.'

'Only three?' she mocked, moving from a squat to a sitting position in a single, fluid movement. She might be small, but she was toned, and seemed to somehow radiate energy. It came off her in waves, as if she was a thoroughbred at the start of a race.

'If you agree to answer three questions, then I'll agree to let you roam around my garden and help yourself to as many citrus fruits as you want.'

Having thought for a moment, she offered him an elfin hand and he took it in his own, marvelling at the fierceness of her grip as they shook on the deal.

'First question,' she prompted, stretching over to rub the dust from her shoes.

'Your name.'

'Violet. And yours?'

'Henry.'

'That's not very Spanish.'

'Feel free to call me Enrique if you prefer.'

'Are you Spanish?' she asked. 'You don't sound it, but you look like you are – you're very handsome.'

Henry stammered out a 'what?'.

'Don't be all modest about it,' Violet said, her tone matter of fact. 'You're easily a nine out of ten – maybe even a nine point five. It's all about symmetry,' she explained, scrutinising him without a trace of embarrassment. 'Your features are all perfectly balanced, nothing too big or set at a wonky angle, and your eyes are the same goldy-brown colour as Freddie Prinze Jnr's, who everyone knows is the best-looking man on the planet.'

Henry had no idea who she was talking about, but that didn't stop him enjoying the comparison.

'I'm only half Spanish,' he explained. 'My mum's English, and England is where I lived until I was sixteen.'

'And you're now . . .?'

'Eighteen.' Henry allowed himself a small smile of pride. 'Eighteen today, in fact. How about you?'

'Oh, happy birthday to you then. I turned seventeen a few days ago, my mum made the waiters in our hotel sing to me, which was probably the most embarrassing experience of my life to date. Was that your second question?'

He blinked, lost somewhere mid-ramble.

'The age thing?' she said.

'Sure, I guess so.'

'OK, and what's the third?'

'I want to know what drew you into this garden.'

For the first time since they'd started talking, Violet appeared to lose a fraction of her inimitable cool.

'I told you.' She sounded cagey. 'I thought it was just an abandoned old house.'

'That's not really an answer.'

'I would argue that it is.'

'Come on,' he insisted. 'There must have been something that caught your eye.'

She glared at him momentarily, but there was no malice behind it. 'If I come clean, you have to promise not to take the piss.'

Henry raised his palms. 'I wouldn't dare,' he said honestly, and was gratified when she laughed.

'The sad fact is,' Violet began, pulling up a handful of baked grass and scattering it on the ground between them, 'I'm really into plants.'

Henry was nonplussed. 'What's sad about that?'

'A girl called Violet having a secret flower-press hobby? Come on!'

'I think it's sweet,' he said, recoiling at her ferocious 'oi' of response.

'Sweet?' she repeated, practically spitting out the word. 'Don't make me vomit.'

Henry laughed; he couldn't help it. 'OK,' he agreed. 'Maybe sweet is the wrong word – maybe you're simply a geek?'

'Geek is better,' she mused. 'Geek I can live with.'

'Go on, then,' he urged. 'Show me which plant it was that you deemed worthy of trespass?'

Violet fixed her gaze on him, and Henry saw as she did so that her eyes were a bright, grasshopper green. There was so much about her that intrigued him; he could feel himself becoming bewitched by this girl, with her easy wit and rose-bud lips. If only he was bold enough to remark on her beauty, repay the compliment she had so unashamedly bestowed on him, but he worried it would sound disingenuous now, as if he were merely saying it to be polite when in truth he had thought her to be gorgeous from the very moment he set his eyes on her.

'Look over there,' she instructed, 'under the lemon tree. Do you see those pink flowers?'

Henry squinted through the dancing heat. 'The ones that look like frilly bells?'

'Frilly bells,' she scoffed. 'Those are funnel petals.'

Henry shuffled on to his feet.

'Where are you going?' asked Violet.

'To pick you one,' he said. 'For your flower press.'

She started to protest, but he was already kneeling in the dirt, his fingers sliding down the stem of the largest specimen until they encountered soil. With a quick flick of his wrist, the plant snapped, and Henry held it out proudly to an approaching Violet.

'You didn't have to do that,' she said, accepting the flower and cradling it as one might a precious artefact.

Henry gestured towards the base of the tree. 'There are plenty more,' he said. 'Consider it your reward for educating me on funnels.'

'The plant is actually called a whistling jack,' she told him. 'Or you can refer to them as foxglove sword lilies, or even eastern gladiolus, if you want to be boring.'

Henry could not imagine a girl like Violet ever becoming boring, nor standing for it long from someone else. He was struck, then, by an overwhelming urge to impress her, to carry out some sort of daring stunt or dredge up a nugget of profound wisdom. But before he could do or say anything at all, Violet had stepped forwards on to her tiptoes, and kissed him, very gently, on the cheek.

Henry felt his insides turn to liquid.

'What was that for?'

She glanced from the flower in her hands back to him and smiled. 'I just wanted to see if I was right.'

'About what?'

The look Violet gave him then was almost coy.

'About the nine-point-five thing. Turns out I was wrong.'

'Oh?' Henry deflated. 'On closer inspection, am I more of a two-point-six?'

'No,' she said, before adding in the cool, casual way to which Henry was fast becoming accustomed, 'I'd say you're a solid, golden-eyed ten out of ten.'

7

Violet

If it had been up to me, we would have eaten dinner at the house. There were plenty of ingredients in the cupboards, and bottles of locally made wine in the rack – but Luke had been adamant, and I knew better than to refuse him.

Henry had not returned from going to view the house with Juan and Tomas, and I dithered over whether or not to send him a message, telling him where the three of us would be. In the end, I concluded that it would probably be better if he didn't know. Henry had not forgiven me, that much had become abundantly clear during the short time we'd spent in each other's company, and the thought of making small talk with him in as intimate a setting as a restaurant was disquieting. I was more than a touch perturbed, therefore, to find him waiting for us when we arrived, still clad in the same tatty overalls and paint-splattered T-shirt he'd been wearing that afternoon.

'Hello,' I said, in a clipped, formal voice that I'd never used around him before.

He managed a low grunt of reply, before standing up from the table to greet Luke and Eliza. Indecision over what to wear had led me to panic-choose a shapeless sack of a dress the same shade of brown as the underside of a mushroom, while Eliza, in contrast, looked radiant in an abstract patterned jumpsuit, her chin-length bob teased into feathery curls.

'What a beautiful place,' she said, sliding deftly into the seat opposite mine. We had come to Bar Nou, a traditional

Spanish taverna tucked away along a backstreet not far from Pollença's main square, Plaça Major, and been given a table outside. It was a little after eight p.m., and a low-slung sun was busy dropping sunflower petals of light across the rooftops. The air around us hummed with sounds; the clinking of glasses and the tinkle of laughter, while through the open window above us floated a tantalising scent of grilled fish, olive oil, and fresh basil. I hadn't eaten a thing since before my flight that morning, and the two gin and tonics I'd consumed up at the house had left me feeling hollow and edgy.

'We should have called ahead and ordered paella,' I said, as a waiter strode past us with an enormous sizzling pan of the stuff. 'One without any prawns, of course.'

'Are you allergic to shellfish?' Eliza enquired. 'My cousin is – she accidentally ate some crabmeat once and her tongue swelled up to about five times its normal size.'

I felt Henry's gaze on me. 'Nobody's allergic,' I said. 'It's just that Luke dislikes them.'

My son looked up from his menu. 'No, I don't.'

'Yes, you— Well, you used to.'

Eliza shot a glance towards Henry. Was she seeking an ally in case this disagreement turned sour? I didn't want to butt heads with Luke but was confused by his flat-out denial. For so long, and with such dedicated effort, I had made it my priority to learn all his likes and dislikes right down to the most incremental things, and suddenly here he was, essentially deadheading what I'd thought was a perennial truth.

'It's fine if you don't like them,' I went on, ignoring Henry's sigh of frustration.

Luke rearranged himself in his seat; his legs had grown so long that I could see the knobble of his knees above the edge of the table.

'I used to hate them,' he said tersely, 'but that was years ago, when I was a stupid kid.'

'You've never been stupid,' I exclaimed, and again, Eliza and Henry exchanged a look. They were against me, the three of them, the newcomer to our dysfunctional unit having chosen her side of the fence.

A waitress appeared then to take our order, and by the time glasses of wine and water had been poured, a basket of bread deposited, and tiny ramekins of olives offered around, the tense atmosphere at the table had eased somewhat. Having decided to play it safe by saying as little as possible throughout the remainder of the meal, I lapsed into silence and listened as Eliza held court, chatting away about her and Luke's university friends, which of them was dating the others and the various scandals that had occurred during the past academic year. Neither Henry nor I had ever made it to university – him because he'd never wanted to, and me because Luke had come along before I got the chance.

'It's so cool that Luke's in a proper house,' Eliza remarked, stabbing her fork into an asparagus spear that was drenched in butter and crackly with salt. 'Trying to get any reading done in Halls is impossible – I think I'd be failing if I hadn't been able to stay with him most of the time.'

'We were lucky to find that place,' said Henry, who'd chosen padrón peppers as a starter and was using his hands in place of cutlery. 'A builder mate of mine put me on to it, organised a decent rate.'

Eliza nodded sagely, going on to talk at length about the unfair student loan system, and how terrifying a prospect it was to be thousands of pounds in debt before you'd even started out in your career. One of the smartest things Henry and I had done – though the burden of it had fallen mostly on his shoulders – was build a savings pot for if and when our son attended university. Luke had only needed a partial loan to cover tuition and wouldn't have to concern himself with the funding of either rent or utility bills. It was all taken care of by the bank of Dad and, to a far lesser extent, Mum – although I had been the one to furnish the place, treat him to new clothes, bedding, and kitchen utensils, as well as a MacBook Pro. Having complained that his mobile phone bill was eating into his allowance, I had taken over the direct debit for that, too, telling myself it wouldn't be forever, and that his needs took priority.

The decision had been simple to make, the means by which to honour it trickier to navigate.

'I suppose it's good practice,' Eliza allowed, though she sounded unconvinced. 'My parents are very much of the "you're an adult now, so it's about time you learnt how to manage your money" opinion – at least Dad is.'

'I like your dad,' put in Luke, who was shredding a slice of bread. I watched as he rolled small morsels of the dough into balls and tossed them down for the sparrows, a congregation of which had gathered around his seat. 'I think he's a good laugh.'

'You only think that because the two of you like geeking out together,' Eliza teased. 'My dad loves the arts,' she explained. 'I might look like an artist, what with this hair –' she fiddled with her flamingo-pink locks – 'but really I'm a scientist – or trying to be.'

'Remind me of your subject,' I said, though I couldn't recall Luke ever telling me. The fact that he had a girlfriend at all wasn't something he'd announced, more something I'd gleaned from a series of casual name-drops, made by him during calls home. Our catch-ups had gone down from nightly to twice or occasionally only once a week, but I still kept my phone within answering distance at all times. If Luke were to ring and not be able to reach me, it could spark any number of crises.

Eliza had finished her asparagus and put her knife and fork together before replying.

'I'm studying psychology and child psychology,' she said. 'It's a combined course.'

In all likelihood, we had probably read a lot of the same books, though I couldn't say as much in front of Luke. Instead, I smiled, and asked her if she was enjoying it.

'Very much so,' she confirmed. 'It's fascinating. And as much as I joke about my parents, it's down to them that I'm doing this course. We've always been close, you see. Me and my brothers were encouraged to talk about our issues with the family, and so I got used to understanding how all their brains worked, as well as my own. I'm no expert, by any means, but I'm definitely enjoying learning more.'

'She's acing it,' said Luke, sliding a hand over Eliza's. It was strange to see him being so openly tactile, but it was rapidly becoming less so. He'd overcome a lot to get to this point and deserved the affection of a person not bound by blood to offer it. I noticed that Henry, too, had registered their closeness and tried to remember when he'd last laced his fingers through mine – or touched me at all, for that matter. There had been a time when we could hardly bear to be parted, he the solid pergola around which I'd wrapped my vines, whereas now I imagined he'd rather tether himself to a charging bull than come into contact with me.

Excusing myself, I ventured inside to the bathroom, where I splashed cold water across my face and stood for a few minutes with my head resting against the vanity mirror. It was cool in the small space, the air-conditioning unit rattling out a chill from its perch below the ceiling, and I could hear the muffled shouts of a busy kitchen coming through the wall. My reflection stared back at me morosely, dark shadows like ink smudges below eyes heavy-lidded with fatigue. I tugged at my skin, pulling taut the faint lines that seemed to multiply on a daily basis, lamenting as I did so all the hours that I'd spent with my chin tilted up towards the sun, oblivious of its damage. Heartbreak had played an additional role in my ravaging – misery and regret draining my colour, robbing me of sleep, and etching deep crevasses around my sullen lips.

I had no right to feel sorry for myself, not when I considered all that Henry had gone through – what he was still enduring, how he must feel when he looked into the mirror and was confronted with such horrific scars. I had no right at all.

Back at the table, the main courses had arrived.

'You didn't need to wait for me,' I said. 'Wouldn't want your food to go cold.'

'Not much chance of that in this heat,' said Eliza, who was fanning her face with the drinks menu. Someone had topped up my glass, and I sipped the wine gratefully. The street had grown busier in the time I'd been indoors, the running tap of tourists seemingly content to bump along in a chattering stream.

Henry stretched his hands behind his head and cracked his knuckles.

'How was the house?' I asked, and for a moment he looked confused.

'Oh, you mean Tomas's place? A bloody mess. The roof struts are rotten and much of the external stucco has fissures. We're going to need to demolish whole sections.'

'We?' I echoed, and he threw me a disparaging look.

'Juan says he'll help out, but I can't see that happening, even if he and Tomas are trying to keep costs to a minimum.

Unfortunately for them, the house doesn't have a stash of black money under the floorboards – it doesn't have much floor left to speak of, truth be told.'

'Black money?' queried Eliza, pausing in the process of deboning her bream.

Henry pushed some rice around with his fork. 'It's when you buy a house for, say, one hundred thousand euros, but the seller declares less on the deed, marking it down as eighty thousand. They then essentially skim off the difference, usually in a lump sum of cash, and avoid paying as much tax.'

'And this happens a lot?'

'Let's just say, some of the richest people in Mallorca have accumulated a lot of their wealth through black money.'

'Including Abuelo,' put in Luke. 'My grandfather,' he explained to Eliza. 'He's a bit of a property mogul.'

'A bit of' was putting it mildly.

'Oh, so it was it him who gave you the house?' she exclaimed. 'Luke told me you got it as a gift for your eighteenth birthday, but I assumed he must be joking.'

'True story.' Henry shrugged. 'Of course, it was worth barely anything then – it was practically a building site – but now . . .' He let out a low whistle.

'How much?' Eliza sat forwards in her seat. 'Are we talking hundreds of thousands?'

'Try over a million,' Luke said breezily, and Eliza stared from him back to Henry.

'No way?'

'Perhaps even one-point-five, if someone both foolish and rich wanted it enough,' Henry said. 'And in my experience, rich people often are quite stupid.'

The conversation was making me uncomfortable.

'Can we stop discussing money, please? It's just so . . . crass.'

All three looked round at me in surprise.

'Crass?' Henry repeated.

'Yes, crass – and boastful. Not everyone has the good enough fortune to be given a house, Henry. Some people are never given anything; they have to work for it.'

He looked at me through narrowed eyes. 'Are you saying I haven't had to work for what we— what I have? Is that what you're claiming? Well, that's typical coming from you.'

I took a furious sip of wine. 'What's that supposed to mean?'

'You know full well,' he seethed.

'For fuck's sake,' muttered Luke, which silenced us immediately.

'I'll go.' Henry's hand was already reaching into his overalls pocket for his wallet.

'No, I will,' I said, snatching my bag off the back of the chair and digging out my debit card. Placing it firmly down on the table, I recited the pin number, telling them the meal was 'my treat and no arguments'.

'Do you want me to come with you?' asked Eliza, but I waved her away.

'You stay,' I said, offering her a tight smile. 'I'd rather be on my own.'

It wasn't true, not even close, but it was exactly what I deserved.

8

Violet

The balmy evening merged into a sultry night as I wandered aimlessly through Pollença's congested backstreets. I was oblivious to all but my own malaise, and barely registered the expressions on the faces of those I passed. Everyone seemed to be in high spirits, their jovial babble a steady percussion behind the strains of music and song filtering out from restaurants and bars.

It was too late for cicadas, but the swallows still soared, tiny rips in the navy fabric of the darkening sky. I searched for the stars, but only the very brightest were visible, high beyond the warm yellow eyes of opened shutters, dropped diamonds of light.

Storming away from the table had been a mistake, but more than that, it had been out of character. Being me was becoming increasingly difficult, and at times I barely recognised myself as the person I'd once been, that plucky, confident girl who'd shimmied over that garden wall twenty years ago to pick a flower, only to end up finding something far more beautiful, more rare, more vital. When Henry and I had been the sole focus of each other's lives, things had been so much easier. I knew how to love him, I had since the very first moment we met, and had assumed the same natural pattern would follow when I became a mother. To discover I'd been wrong about that had altered the very core of me, twisting me into someone else, a person that neither I nor Henry knew what to do with.

My thoughts were shattered as church bells began to chime, and I pressed a hand against the rough stone wall beside me as I counted. Eight ... nine ... ten. I had been walking in a directionless meander around the town for over an hour. It was time to go back to The Orange House; back home. Stifling a yawn, I made my way to the bottom of Pollença's famous Calvari Steps, weariness overtaking me as I trudged past the towering cypress trees to the halfway point and turned left. From here, La Casa Naranja was only a hundred yards away, and I could see the glow of light from its highest, circular window. Luke's room.

When he was still very young, he and I had pretended the turret was the hull of a great ship, the vast expanse of blue sky beyond our make-believe portholes a fine stand-in for swirling ocean seas. Those hours we spent together in a fantasy of our making were some of my most cherished memories of motherhood. Our holidays here had begun with such frivolity, the three of us unshackled from the everyday pressures of life in England. The house and the island that bore it had continued its annual restoration of us, right up until the moment we became damaged beyond repair.

Rubbing at my eyes, I let myself in and dropped my bag on the dining table. The lounge door was closed, but as I started across the hallway to fetch a bottle of water from the fridge, I heard what sounded like furniture being dragged across the floor coming from within.

Henry. It had to be.

Steeling myself, I pushed open the door.

'Oh, it's— Sorry.'

Eliza let out a gasp as she swung around to face me.

'Shit,' she said, then hurriedly, 'I didn't mean to swear – you startled me.'

I told her not to be silly, falling silent as I noticed the blanket in her arms, the pillow at one end of the pulled-out sofa.

'Is something the matter?' I asked. 'Have you and Luke fallen out?'

'No, no.' She shook her head, pink tendrils falling across her eyes. 'We're fine. Luke's just having one of his, you know, times when he needs to be alone. I'm giving him some space.'

'Is he all right?'

I'd asked the question more sharply than I intended and regretted it when I saw Eliza flinch.

'He's fine – just assimilating.'

'Assimilating what?'

She shrugged awkwardly. 'Tonight, himself, you, life – everything. I don't know exactly. First, he assimilates – only afterwards will he be ready to talk about it.'

'Me?' I pressed. 'Why does he need to assimilate me?'

If Eliza had appeared uncomfortable before, she now looked positively ill.

'Sorry,' she said, picking up the pillow and hugging it against her chest. 'I don't really feel like I should— That is to say, I don't want to—' She gave up, grimacing at me in either sympathy or dismay – I couldn't quite tell which.

'Has Luke said something to you about me?' I persisted. 'Is he annoyed with me about leaving the dinner earlier? He is, isn't he? I did it for him, that's the stupid thing. I left so as not to upset him.'

This half-truth hung stagnantly in the air between us for a few moments before Eliza sat down on the sofa. She could not have made it clearer that she wanted me to leave her alone, but I needed to know more. Luke and his problems were the proverbial itch that I could never seem to scratch enough.

'Are you sure everything is OK between the two of you?' I asked, crossing the room, and sitting down uninvited beside her. 'I know what he can be like.'

She appeared to bristle at this. 'Luke hasn't said or done anything to upset me,' she reiterated carefully. 'Sometimes he needs a bit of headspace. I don't take it personally.'

The implication being, of course, that I did.

'I think I'll go and check in with him,' I said decisively, but Eliza stilled me with a light touch.

'Wait,' she said. 'I really think that you— Oh god.' She started to pick agitatedly at her chipped green nail polish. 'This is so . . . ugh.'

'Circle of trust,' I promised, hating how desperate I sounded. 'You can tell me what he said about me – I'm used to it, and I won't say anything to him.'

'I'm sorry.' Eliza was shaking her head. 'I can't do that. Me and Luke, we trust each other. Trust is important to him, and I can't go behind his back. I'd be breaking a promise if I did, and he'd never forgive me.'

She sounded so wretched at the thought that I put my arm around her, and was surprised when she leaned into me, her head resting gently against my shoulder. The last time Luke had sought out a cuddle from me, he'd still been in primary school, and I was pathetically grateful to Eliza for her willingness to accept the comfort I offered.

'Has he told you,' I asked, 'about his childhood, and how difficult he found his teenage years?'

She nodded but didn't speak.

'You might think that you know him,' I went on, my cheek warm against the side of her head, 'but there's a lot to Luke that I'm betting he hasn't shown you. I've known him for nineteen years, and you've been in his life for . . .?'

'Seven months.'

'Well, then.'

She sniffed, lifting a hand to wipe something off her face, and I wondered if she was crying. It would not have surprised me in the slightest if she was. I'd been on the receiving end of Luke's 'I need to be alone' speeches often enough to appreciate their severity, and I understood how ostracising it could feel when he lashed out.

'I don't think time has much to do with it,' Eliza mumbled.

'To do with what?' I replied, thinking I must have misheard.

'Knowing someone. I think you can know someone completely in no time at all, if they choose to let you.'

An image of Henry strode, unbidden, into my mind, and I shook my head, dislodging Eliza from my shoulder in the process. She didn't look defiant any more so much as tired and, feeling a stab of something close to guilt, I stood up to go.

'You're exhausted,' I said. 'I shouldn't have disturbed you. Can I get you anything? A hot drink? I can make fresh mint tea, if you like, or just some water?'

Anything to ensure she reported back to Luke in glowing terms.

Eliza shook her head. 'No, thank you.'

I turned to go only to immediately spot a pair of feet on the stairs.

A swearword far worse than the one Eliza had used rushed through my head.

'Luke,' I called. 'Wait!'

I ran to catch up with him, but it was no good. Having thundered noisily up the two flights to his turret bedroom, he slammed the door behind him so hard that every fibre in my body vibrated. A few beats of terrible, foreboding silence filled the house, and I was forced to quell a yowl of pain as my stomach contracted into knots. Being Luke's mother had conditioned my body to register a threat, and I was helpless to prevent it from responding.

Not then, not now, not ever.

9

Violet

My mobile phone woke me, the screen lighting up with a message from Luke.

Got bus to Palma. Back late, will eat out. x.

I stared at the single 'x' for a long time, blinking as I calculated how much sleep I'd managed to get. Not enough, was the answer. It never felt like enough.

Staggering out from under the sheets, I went straight to the window and opened the shutters, recoiling at the brightness of the sun. The main bedroom of La Casa Naranja offered a far-reaching panorama of the Tramuntana mountain range that never failed to lift my spirits, but it was the view directly below me that I found most edifying. That of the garden. *My* garden. The beds and borders, shrubs and fruit trees, bird bath and compost bin – all chosen, planted, and nurtured by me. I was proud that sections of it had thrived despite my neglect. The multiple blooms were a testament to my careful planning, the fragrant roses evidence of the nutrient-rich food I'd mixed by hand. I was adept at gardening, taking care of plants came as naturally to me as carpentry did to Henry.

When he and I had launched our home building, repair and refurbishment business, House-a-Home, a little under thirteen years ago, it had been my idea to offer a landscaping service in addition to interior projects, and many of our early clients hired us as a result of it. The two of us would go into a property and make our assessments, Henry within the walls of the house, me out in its grounds, before coming together to draw up a schedule and begin estimating costs. Those early halcyon days of working life had been tough but rewarding, my self-confidence growing upon each job's successful completion. I discovered team management skills I'd been unaware I possessed and had designed our company logo using a basic Canva subscription. At last, it felt like I was good at something, that I was achieving, and when I'd had no choice but to give up the role, I'd cried for weeks.

Stepping away from the window, I rifled in my case for something to wear, then showered and dressed, not bothering with make-up but applying high-factor sun lotion to my face and bare shoulders. Henry's comments the previous evening about La Casa Naranja being worth a potential million euros or more had been playing in a loop in my mind. It was impossible not to envisage how much of a difference that amount of money could make, not only to me but to Luke. Sentimentality would not pay the bills, and so I had resolved to accept what was happening and do whatever I had to in order to ensure it did. With a final, cursory glance in the mirror, I headed downstairs determined to make a start on packing the place up.

There were eggs in the fridge, so I scrambled a couple and ate them out on the terrace with a handful of homegrown tomatoes and black coffee. Usually, at this time of year, I would harvest most of them and make passata, or sun-dry them in batches on the flat patio roof to use in salads. There were high levels of lime in the island's soil that prevented mineral absorption and, as a result, the fruit and vegetables grown on Mallorca tasted exquisite. If Luke hadn't become phobic about the pips when he was a child, I would have incorporated our garden tomatoes into every meal.

I thought again about that single 'x' at the end of my son's message, wondering if he'd forgiven me my transgression of the previous night. I had replied effusively, of course, wishing him and Eliza a fabulous day. These were the steps of our dance, the 'la-la-la-la' hands-over-ears song our particular tune.

Breakfast done, I carried my plate indoors and was in the process of rinsing it under the tap when my phone began to vibrate in the pocket of my dress.

It was my mother.

I toyed with the idea of letting it ring out, then thought better of it. There was always a chance, however minuscule, that she was calling for a nice reason.

'Hello,' I trilled, as cheerfully as I could muster.

'Yes, hello, Violet.'

'Is everything all right?'

'Fine, yes, fine,' she said shortly, as if the question barely warranted a response. 'How are you? How's Luke?'

I considered my answer before replying.

'He's, you know, Luke-ish. His girlfriend is out here with him, and she seems . . .' I hesitated. What was the adjective that best suited Eliza? Opinionated, capable, compassionate, mature? I settled on 'nice'.

'And Henry?'

I raked my fingers through my hair. It was still damp from the shower and would undoubtedly dry to a frizz.

'Violet?'

'Yes? Sorry, trailed off for a moment there.'

'Henry – have you seen him?'

'I have,' I confirmed.

'And?'

'He's . . . you know Henry.'

'Things between the two of you still dire, I presume?'

My mother cut to her point the same way shears might through strands of grass.

'Well, he is at least speaking to me,' I told her. 'Which is something.'

'There's some post for you here,' she said, apparently now done with the subject of my estranged husband. 'I haven't opened it, obviously,' she went on, and I could picture her then, perched on the seat of the ancient telephone table in the hallway, sensible Marks & Spencer blouse tucked into tapered beige trousers. Henry had once described her as 'a porcupine in a smart outfit', which pretty much summed things up. My father, though conservative, had been soft as peat below the surface, his core of kindness cushioning my mother's inherent spikiness. Losing him had also meant losing the gentler side of her, and while I didn't blame my mum for the way she was – grief did all sorts of terrible things to a person – I did miss the old her. But then, I missed the old me, too.

'I'm glad to hear it, Mum,' I said lightly. 'It's against the law to tamper with another person's mail, you know.'

'Yes, yes – no need to be facetious about it.'

'I was joking.'

'Well, don't. A few of these letters have "do not ignore" printed on the front of them.'

Oh.

'Probably nothing urgent,' I said. 'A smear test reminder or something.'

'These aren't from the NHS. They use those special envelopes with the blue logo – we got enough through the door when your dad was ill.'

'Do any say where they're from?'

'There are three,' she said, and I heard the sound of paper shuffling as she leafed through them. 'Two from different companies, none of which ring any bells with me, and another with no stamp or postmark, so it must have been hand delivered.'

A chill went through me as I contemplated the final thing she'd said. Staring out through the kitchen window into the garden, I watched a warbler as it flitted from branch to shrub. The summer Luke had turned five, I'd bought him a Mallorcan birds poster and pinned it up on the wall right next to where I now stood. He'd sit with his small pair of binoculars raised, feet up on the sill, and a look of concentration on his face, announcing each new arrival in that oddly solemn way of his.

'What do you want me to do?' asked my mother. 'Shall I open them?'

'No!' I'd practically shouted. 'Sorry, I mean, don't worry. I'll deal with them when I get back.'

'But they might be important,' she insisted. 'You haven't missed a bill, have you?'

I hesitated. 'No, nothing like that.'

'I suppose you don't have to worry about money, not now you're living with me.'

I closed my eyes, counted slowly to ten. 'I'll be out of your hair again soon,' I said. 'Just as soon as we sell this place. Now, if that's all you needed me for, I should really go and get on with clearing it out.'

'Right, well – do send my love to Luke, won't you?' She allowed a beat to follow before she added, 'And to Henry.'

'I will.'

'And Violet?'

It took all of my effort not to sigh. 'Yes?'

'Try to be nice. Remember what your father used to say? If you can't be nice, pretend—'

'And if you can't pretend, be quiet,' I finished. 'Bye, Mum.'

After she'd rung off, I stood watching the warbler as it dug through the soil and extracted a worm. The creature wriggled in desperation, its urge to survive strong despite the hopelessness of its situation. Unable to bear its final moments, I turned away, sank down into one of the kitchen chairs and, with my head in my hands, proceeded to silently sob my heart out.

10

Henry

Nineteen Summers Ago

Henry hadn't thought it was possible to love a person more than he loved Violet, but he had underestimated quite how powerful it would be to watch her go through childbirth. Violet was bold, he'd been aware of that since the moment he spotted her legs dangling over his garden wall, but now he knew she was properly brave, too.

'Do you want to hold him?' she asked now, her voice still hoarse from screaming. It had been a 'difficult labour' the midwife told him. More difficult than many. And while Violet was fit and strong, she was also small – but never scared, not that. His girlfriend was determined to succeed, and so she did, but it had taken the best part of two days.

'I do want to –' Henry felt himself welling up – 'but I'm . . . What if I do it wrong?'

'You won't.' Violet's weary smile found his. 'Just don't drop him, OK?'

It felt like a relief to laugh, albeit half-heartedly, and Henry wiped his eyes as he approached the bed. It was the first time the three of them had been alone as a family, and he hoped he wasn't messing things up. He wanted Violet to be proud of him, although nothing he could ever do would come close to matching the sacrifices she had made – to her life, her body, her future.

'He's so tiny.'

Violet smiled again as she stared down at their son's sleeping face. There were faint bruises on his temples from the forceps, and his expression was one of quiet fury.

'Maybe I shouldn't,' Henry said, raising his hands. 'He looks comfortable with you.'

'He looks really pissed off,' said Violet, and they both laughed, quietly so as not to wake the baby. 'Poor boy, he's inherited your resting face,' she added, and Henry frowned on cue. 'Come on,' she said. 'You'll have to hold him sooner or later, and now is as good a time as any. Besides, I want to drink that cup of tea the nurse brought in.'

'What if he wakes up and cries?'

Violet winced as she attempted to shuffle back against her pillows.

'Newsflash,' she said wryly. 'He's a baby – I think waking up and crying is basically their MO. That and pooing, and puking, and holding on to your finger with their tiny hand until you forgive them for all the other stuff I just mentioned.'

Henry reached across and brushed a few tendrils of hair off her forehead. Sweat had darkened it to a copper beech hue, while her writhing had swirled the top into an untidy nest. To Henry, she had never looked more beautiful. He wanted to tell her so but felt too choked to speak. The enormity of this moment, and of the decision they had made to keep their baby now so shockingly unequivocal, was at risk of overwhelming him, and Henry looked down to find that his hands were shaking.

He could still recall the day Violet told him she was pregnant. It was the twenty-third of October, and Henry had been working on the house since dawn. Having sourced enough second-hand barrel tiles to fill the gaps on the roof, he had clambered up there only to discover that the wooden panels below were split and cracked, which added not only a considerable amount of time on to the project, but cost, too. He was fast running out of funds now that the peak tourist season had drawn to an end, and his shifts at the Majestic Hotel in Port de Pollença were dwindling. Soon, Henry knew, he would have little choice but to accept a job working for his father, but the idea of that made him uneasy. He loved Antonio; he just didn't like him much.

Violet didn't know how fortunate she was to have, as she put it, 'normal, boring parents'. As far as he was concerned, normal and boring trumped absent and dodgy any day of the week, and even though Henry knew that Violet's dad and especially her mum were wary of him, he still admired them.

Since the first two heady weeks they'd spent together back in late May, Violet had returned to Mallorca twice – once for a long weekend in July, accompanied by her mother, and again for a week at the very end of August. The latter trip had been different to the others because Violet had arrived alone and stayed with Henry in his Pollença studio apartment. They had grown close – closer than he ever had to anyone – and lain awake together until the small hours, limbs entwined on his narrow, single bed, plotting their future together. Henry would finish doing up the house while Violet finished her A levels, then he would rent it out and move to England while she studied for her degree. After that, the two of them would travel the world. Violet liked the idea of volunteering, doing some teaching, perhaps, while Henry simply wanted to build. Where he did it was of little importance, so long as she was there with him.

There was no phone at his apartment, so Henry had got into the habit of calling Violet from the telephone box not far from the bus station. As he dialled, his attention was drawn across the street to a bar, and the two elderly men playing a game of cards on a table outside it. One was smoking a pipe, while the other sipped a glass of what looked to be brandy. His father drank a ton of the stuff, enough of it that Henry often smelt Antonio's pungent breath before he saw him.

'Hello.'

He only had to hear her voice to feel better.

Henry smiled into the receiver. 'I love you, Violet Lupton. I'm saying it now in case I forget to tell you later.'

'Well, I love you, too, Enrique Torres.'

'I've told you before,' he said with a laugh, 'it's Henry – like the Hoover.'

He waited for her to join in with his laughter, frowning when she didn't. '*Qué pasa?*' he asked. *What's up?*

'I'm all right.'

She suddenly sounded a long way from all right, and Henry told her so.

'How did it go with the roof?' she asked.

'I don't care about the roof; I care about you.'

To his astonishment, Violet started to cry. A few minutes passed during which Henry did his best to comfort her, but she seemed unable – or unwilling – to tell him what was wrong. A list of increasingly fraught options lined up in his mind: she was sick, someone in her immediate family was sick; she'd failed an important test, been bullied at college, fallen out with a friend, fallen out of love with him. No, Henry consoled himself, she'd just told him she loved him. It couldn't be that.

'Whatever it is, you can tell me.' Henry fed another two-euro coin into the slot. One of the old men at the table stood up and went into the bar, a trail of pipe smoke curling in his wake.

Maybe she had cheated on him? The thought made him turn cold with dread.

'You'll be cross with me,' she sobbed.

'Of course I won't.' But he would, Henry thought, if she'd kissed someone else. He'd be cross enough to tear the world down.

'I'm so stupid.' Violet had stopped crying and was hiccupping instead, the tremble of fear in her voice unmistakeable. Henry yearned to wrap her up in his arms, tell her that everything would be OK, protect her from whatever it was making her sad.

'You're not stupid, you're per—'

'Pregnant,' Violet wailed. 'Pregnant is what I am.'

'But . . .' Henry trailed off, disbelief making his head spin. They had been so careful. She'd told him she was taking the pill, but he had insisted they use a condom as well, just to be sure, and he had stuck to that rule every time they had sex – every single time except . . .

'Your last night here,' he said.

Violet sniffed. 'It must've been. I was sick the day before, after the gazpacho. I didn't want to tell you in case it put you off me,' she moaned. 'Which seems really silly now.'

'Silly,' he agreed.

'I knew that if you're sick, it can stop the pill working, but I never thought that— I thought we'd be safe. I'm so sorry, Henry. I've ruined everything.'

'No,' he reassured her, 'you haven't. This isn't your fault – it's nobody's fault.'

'You aren't angry with me?'

'Vee, of course I'm not angry with you. How much of a *bastardo* do you think I am?'

'You don't have to do anything,' she said in a rush. 'I can take care of it and—'

'I'm coming,' he said, his decision made in the moments it took him to say the words. 'It might take a few days, but I'll be there. I promise.'

She told him not to, that she would be fine, but Henry was adamant.

'Promise me you won't make any decisions until I'm there?'

'OK.' She sniffed. 'I promise.'

He remembered every word they'd said to each other.

In the hospital, Henry's hands were still shaking, but he did not let it stop him from reaching down and scooping his son into his arms. Violet let out a small, contented sigh, sipping her tea as Henry lowered himself slowly into the chair, his eyes wet and bottom lip trembling.

'I can't believe I'm a dad,' he murmured, glancing up to see tears glistening on Violet's cheeks.

'And I can't believe I'm a mum. Eighteen years old and a parent – definitely a curveball I did not see coming.'

'I'm going to look after you,' Henry said, looking down once again at his sleeping son, taking in his feathery thatch of dark hair and tiny pursed lips, the soft black lashes and delicate little nose, his exquisitely perfect ears, and rounded cheeks.

'You hear that, Luke Christopher Torres?' he said. 'I'm going to look after both of you for the rest of my life.'

11

Violet

I couldn't settle to anything after the phone call with my mother and decided to walk the short distance into town. It was Sunday, which meant market day, and a good opportunity to see Ynes and pick up some of Luke's favourite foods – a gesture of goodwill that I hoped would go some way towards redeeming what I'd said to Eliza. He might have added an 'x' to the text message he'd sent me, but I knew my son. He would chew over what he'd overheard – '*I know what he can be like*' – and bury it somewhere in that head of his, waiting for the right time to hurl it in my face.

It was a relief to escape the emotional landmine of The Orange House and lose myself for a time in Pollença's human slipstream. As well as the usual flock of tourists, the market lured in local residents, too, all of them keen to browse the many stalls or meet up with friends for a coffee in the square.

Beginning at the far end of Via Pollentia, a wide, sun-dappled street overhung by plane trees, I withdrew a small amount of cash and wandered as far as the first fruit and vegetable stall, where I picked up a punnet of white grapes, a couple of striped, plump aubergines, and several glossy peppers, before crossing the road and filling three plastic pots with olives. Luke particularly liked the garlic-stuffed Manzanillas, while Henry preferred the smaller, saltier Arbequinas, so I bought both, plus some plain Gordals, stowing each purchase carefully in my ragged old jute bag.

The sky above the market awnings was a freshly laundered blue, the sun that beat down through it fierce and bright. I paused to buy myself a two-euro cup of freshly squeezed orange juice, before my magpie mind drew my eye to more stalls. But while I tried on rings, gazed at colourful rocks and crystals, and ran my fingers across the fabric of embroidered dresses, I managed not to give in to temptation. Spending any more money than was strictly necessary was a mistake I could no longer afford to make, but browsing was free, and it was a welcome distraction. In the end, I lingered so long at the market it was past lunchtime before I made it to Plaça Major, where I made a beeline straight for my most cherished Mallorcan friend.

Ynes was the owner of Pollença's largest and most successful floristry business, and every Sunday she set up shop in the town's main square. Meeting her by chance during my first ever visit to the island meant I'd known her almost as long as Henry, and the fact that she was closer to my parents' age than mine did not prevent our budding friendship from flourishing. She was, like me, fanatical about plants, and had been instrumental in helping me transform the garden at La Casa Naranja, but she also had a passion for aprons. Today's selection was patterned with lavender and bumblebees, and she'd dabbed on a startlingly purple eyeshadow to match.

'*Cabecita roja*,' she exclaimed, clasping my cheeks in her hands before bestowing a kiss on each. 'Look at you, *la flaca* – you are tiny.'

My plan of disguising my diminishing weight under shapeless dresses had clearly failed to fool Ynes, and she shook her head in dismay as she patted me down like an airport customs official.

'Enough groping,' I joked feebly, moving clear of her roving fingers. 'People will talk.'

'People,' she grumbled. 'I don't care about these "people".'

'You look well,' I told her. 'Love the apron.'

That won me a smile.

'You are unwell,' she said, telling not asking.

I assured her that I was fine, to which she tutted scornfully.

'Fine? Your husband is trying to sell your house without telling you. Not fine.' She waggled her finger at me. 'Everybody here is seeing the advertisement, asking me what is going on, and I have to tell them, "*No sé.*" I don't know.'

'The situation with the house, and with me and Henry, it's complicated.'

'*Complicada*, eh? Of course *complicada*.'

'It's so good to see you,' I said, trying a different tack. 'How's the business go—'

'I even see Antonio, and he ask me: "*Donde esta Violeta?*" He believe you ran away.'

'He really said that?'

I'd known Henry's father would've been surprised by my sudden absence, especially given its timing, but I also assumed that by now he would've been told the full story behind it. To claim that I'd chosen to abandon Henry was so gross an accusation that for a few moments, all I could do was mouth in silent disbelief.

'I told him that he was talking out of his ass,' she said, as I let out a bark of shocked laughter. 'Antonio is always having a mouth like a donkey's ass.' She raised an eyebrow. 'He thinks he is a big chief – pah!'

Leaving me for a few minutes while she served a group of holidaymakers, I loitered to one side, my gaze roaming across her pots, trays and buckets. There were orchids in cellophane, fledgling Bird of Paradise plants, pillar-box-red carnations, and frothy bunches of pastel-hued hydrangeas. I thought forlornly of the weeds that had overtaken my garden, and how long it would take the new owner to restore it.

When Ynes returned, she did so with a small potted cactus. 'A gift,' she said. 'To remind you that things can always find a way to grow – *sí?*'

I didn't want to cry for the second time in one day, and so I said nothing.

'You have missed Pollença?'

I nodded. 'So much. I don't think I realised how much until I got here.'

Ynes reached across and tucked a strand of hair behind my ear. Like most people, she was taller than me, but not by much, which made avoiding her eye all the harder.

'La Casa Naranja is your home,' she said softly. 'Mallorca is your home.'

I shook my head. This island had been Henry's long before he shared her with me, and I couldn't imagine living here without him. If we got a divorce, it made sense that he'd be the one to keep this place, and I would stand aside and let him have her.

A small queue of customers was beginning to form, and having assured Ynes I'd be back, I crossed Plaça Major and followed the lane that encircled the vast, decorative church. There was an ice-cream parlour tucked away down a side street that I knew sold takeaway coffee, but when I reached it, I discovered an estate agency in its place.

Staring in at the house listings, each one a kaleidoscope of golden stucco, terracotta tiles, and blue squares of swimming pool, I searched to see if La Casa Naranja was among them. The original advertisement Henry had sent me had been posted on the Balearic Properties website, but I had no idea if he had circulated it more widely.

I needed to talk to him.

Turning away from the window, my stomach somersaulted as the man himself appeared at the far end of the street. Despite thinking only a moment ago that I wanted to see him, instinct insisted I hide, which I did by darting into a gift shop on the opposite side of the lane. It was from inside there, as I stood half-concealed behind by a display of postcards, that I watched my husband walk right past me.

Another woman's hand clutched tightly in his.

12

Violet

As soon as the two of them were out of sight, I set off back to the house, all thoughts of Ynes and the promised cups of coffee abandoned. My dithering of that morning was replaced by a fervent need to act, to do something, a single thought repeating itself mantra-like in my mind as I barrelled past the hordes of tourists.

The sooner you do what needs to be done, the better for everyone.

Selling would mean an escape from so many of the mistakes I'd made, and now that I knew Henry had moved on with someone else, getting as far away from him as possible was the only thing I wanted to do.

Having stowed the few items of food I'd bought from the market in the fridge and set the cactus Ynes had given me on the windowsill, I retrieved a roll of refuse sacks from the drawer beneath the sink and tore a load off in quick succession. One for charity donations, a second for the tip, and a third for anything I would take back to England. Letting the kitchen door bang shut behind me, I crossed into the lounge area and went straight to the dresser – a hideous mahogany relic that had belonged to Antonio's grandmother, and to which Henry was inexplicably attached. Over the years, it had become a dumping ground for all the detritus of our lives that we no longer used but were unwilling to throw away. Until now.

I sat down cross-legged on the floor and opened the first cupboard, easing out a tatty-looking cardboard box that promptly came apart and spewed a 200-piece jigsaw puzzle depicting an image of Palma Cathedral into my lap. It had been bought for Luke during his puzzle-loving phase, and that had to have been over a decade ago. I contemplated trashing it, but that felt wasteful, so instead I laboriously scooped the pieces back into the box, fastened an elastic band around to keep it secure, and put it carefully in my designated donation bag. There were more jigsaws stacked inside the dresser, and old board games such as Pop-Up Pirate and Hungry Hippos. I could not imagine myself, Henry and Luke ever sitting down as a family to do something as light-hearted as gobbling tiny balls with mechanised hippopotamuses, and so these, too, I decided to give away. In a papery thin carrier bag stuffed down at the back, I unearthed a sketchbook of Luke's early drawings, and lost myself for a time flicking through its pages. He had taken to illustration in much the same way foxgloves do to abandoned churchyards, flourishing over the course of one summer into a naturally talented artist. Rather than create strange creatures from his imagination or draw stick people with bulbous heads, Luke turned to the things around him for inspiration. Among the early efforts in this book were a bank of artichoke plants, lemons in a wicker trug, the grey tortoiseshell cat that used to snooze under our patio table, and Henry's old red jeep, complete with its driver. I touched a finger to the crayon scribble of dark hair, running it down over the pink, unblemished face below. Luke had depicted Henry in sunglasses, his mouth not a semicircle of cheerful red but the straight black line of a frown.

Closing the book, I placed it in the 'keep' sack and got started on the second overflowing cupboard, my hand almost immediately encountering the soft edge of a photo album. I thought I'd taken all of these back to the UK two summers ago, but this one must somehow have been missed. It was an old-style album, with adhesive pages and peelable plastic coverings. Looking inside risked becoming upset, but my glimpse of Henry had pushed me into a 'to hell with it' mood. Flipping open to the first page, my breath came to a sharp halt as I was confronted with an image of myself, pregnant and impossibly young, beaming up towards Henry. His eyes were on me rather than the camera, a tanned hand placed protectively on my swollen bump. I remembered that Ynes had been the one to take it. She'd passed by with some baby clothes and a few bits and pieces, and Henry had asked her if she'd mind capturing the moment. He'd tried to fit us into the frame himself, he told her, but my belly was far bigger than his arm was long. Our shared laughter was clear in the image, the pair of us aglow with happiness and excitement.

I'd seen enough, and putting down the photo album, I stood and left the room, not stopping until I'd slopped a double measure of gin into a glass and topped it up with a small splash of tonic. This time, when I took a gulp, I didn't wince. All I felt was relief at having doused my tears in time, and distemper at my own hot-headedness. There could be no more nostalgia; no more dredging up the past. I would have plenty of time to mourn my marriage later.

The front door opened. I heard it, but didn't move, watching through the gap behind the kitchen door as Henry came into view. He must have spotted the spilled innards from the dresser through the front window, because instead of going upstairs he strode briskly through to the lounge. There was no call of 'Vee' or an exclamation of surprise; Henry remained silent, and when a few minutes had passed and he had yet to re-emerge, I drained what was left of my gin and went in to join him.

'Hello,' I said, from the doorway.

He was kneeling on the rug, head down, the scarred half of his face shadowed by the peak of a blue cap. He turned at the sound of my voice.

'You've been busy,' he said.

'Thought I may as well get a start on things.'

Henry nodded slowly. 'Find anything interesting?'

'Plenty.' I went further into the room. 'Some of Luke's old drawings. I'd forgotten quite how good he was, right from the first time he picked up a crayon.'

A whisper of a smile passed across Henry's lips. 'Another skill he inherited from you.'

'Hardly,' I retorted. 'The only thing I'm any good at sketching is plants. Luke does the flowers and the vase, and the table it's sitting on, and the view through the window behind it. Do you remember the year he decided to draw the Calvari Steps – all three hundred and sixty-five of them?'

Henry made a small noise of amusement. 'He made me count them to make sure he hadn't missed any. I was cross-eyed by the time I'd finished.' At the mention of his eyes, he raised an unconscious hand to the one that was damaged – a gesture that made my heart contract as if pierced. But no sooner had my sympathy been stirred than I remembered the dark-haired woman in the lane, her hand in his, mouth open, skirt swirling, and everything inside me that had softened hardened once again.

Henry picked up the photo album I'd been looking through, and I watched as he turned over the first page, mumbling something I didn't quite catch.

'What was that?'

Henry looked at me with a steadiness that did nothing to soothe my agitation.

'So young,' he said quietly. 'We were just kids.'

He was right, of course, but that did not stop the remark from rankling.

'Well, sorry if I didn't turn out to be world's number one wife and mother.'

'That wasn't what I— Why do you always react like this?' He blew air into his cheeks. 'I mean, what's the point of me saying anything? You always find a way to twist it into an attack.'

I folded my arms. 'If I'm taking offence, it's because you're saying things that I find offensive.'

Henry gawped at me, understandably bewildered. 'I don't want to argue with you,' he said. 'I can't do it. I decided after—' He put down the album and got to his feet. 'You're obviously on top of everything,' he gestured to the mess, 'but please don't throw things away simply because you're in a huff with me. You might not want to look at photos of the two of us, but Luke might someday – or his children.'

'Fine,' I said curtly, picking up the sack I'd been using for charity donations. 'No photos.'

As I continued to haul items out from the dresser, Henry stood and watched. The sorrow that had settled between us felt oppressive – a fog through which my emotions could do little more than stumble. We'd had so much, he and I, and now there were only remnants, scraps of a marriage, wisps of what once had been love. A fuzzy-felt farm went into the bag, followed by a Care Bear teddy and a pencil case full of felt-tip pens, and throughout all of it, Henry said nothing – not until I extracted a blue wooden box.

'Not that,' he said, crouching to take it from me.

'I remember this,' I said, as he slid open the lid. 'It looks good as new still, doesn't it?'

Henry appeared stung as he rocked backwards on his heels, the toy clutched close to his chest. 'That figures,' he said, so dolefully that I almost gave in to my perpetual yearning to reach for him. 'It's been in the back of that cupboard for years. I put it there when Luke . . .'

He trailed off, but I knew what he'd been about to say. Both of us carried wounds from that day, though I saw now that it was Henry's whose ran the deepest.

13

Henry

Eighteen Summers Ago

Two weeks Henry had been away from them. He had done the maths and worked out that fourteen nights amounted to three hundred and thirty-six hours – and he'd pined his way through every single one of them.

It had been Violet's suggestion that he travel out to Mallorca ahead of her and Luke, so that he would have time to make at least a few of the rooms in La Casa Naranja safely habitable for a baby. Both of them had been desperate to see the island again after more than a year's hiatus, but money was tight, and a hotel or even rented apartment was far beyond their financial means. Henry could've asked his father to put them up, but pride prevented him. Antonio had been disparaging to say the least when he heard about Violet's pregnancy, urging his son to reconsider, telling him they were too young to be parents, too inexperienced in the ways of life. It had taken all of Henry's self-possession not to shout back in his father's face. Ironically, the one lesson Antonio had taught him was how not to raise your child.

Besides, La Casa Naranja was still his house – their house, his and Violet's and Luke's – and Henry wanted to make it as good a home for them as he possibly could. Since arriving at the still half-dilapidated dwelling a week after they celebrated Luke's first birthday, Henry had worked on the repairs and refurbishment from dawn until dusk every day, often staying up late into the night sanding, sawing, priming, or painting. He'd sourced a fridge from a restaurant in Puerto de Pollença that was going out of business, paid next to nothing for a sofa and armchair that had been used as display items in one of the shops in the town, and accepted a generous gift of towels, bed linen and kitchen utensils from Ynes. Determined that his son would not have to rely completely on hand-me-downs, Henry spent his nights building Luke a cot from reclaimed olive wood and splashed the few euros he had spare on a selection of toys.

On the day Violet's flight was due, Henry set off for the airport in Palma feeling as satisfied as he could that the house, for the main part at least, was clean, safe, adequately equipped, and ready to welcome his little family.

The first flash of red hair emerging through the crowd in the arrivals lounge caused his heart to expand with joy, and running forwards, he scooped Violet up into his arms.

'I've missed you so much,' he breathed, kissing her cheeks, her ears, her forehead, her wide, smiling mouth.

'We've missed you too,' she said, her gaze dropping to the buggy. 'Haven't we, Lukey? You missed Papá, didn't you?'

Henry squatted down on to the balls of his feet and reached across to stroke his son's cheek, marvelling as he always did at the softness of the baby's skin, the unblemished newness of him. Luke blinked but didn't smile, and Henry tried his best not to be miffed. The poor thing must have been through a lot these past few hours, he reasoned. First time in an airport, first time on a plane, first ever time in Mallorca, unless you counted the months shortly before he was born. He had been conceived on the island – of that there was no question – and that made him a Mallorcan in the truest way, regardless of what might be printed on his birth certificate. It had been the same for Henry himself, and the fact that he and his son now shared this characteristic made him feel closer to the boy somehow. Violet had done the most – carried him, birthed him, breastfed him – so it stood to reason that she'd be Luke's most treasured person. Henry understood that, but he still looked forward to building a bond with his son that was all their own.

'*Vamos*,' he said, taking both Violet's suitcase and the handle of the pushchair. 'Ynes lent me her car, so we don't have to get the bus for once.'

'My hero.' Violet sighed, her hand closing over his. Together, they strolled with their son out into the Spanish sunshine. Henry didn't think he'd ever felt more proud or happy, he wanted to stop every passer-by, turn to them, and say, 'Look, this is my family. See how beautiful they are, how much we love one another.' He would get a loudspeaker and announce his adoration to the world if he could, fly a banner through the skies and shoot a rocket up to the moon – whatever it took to spread his joy. Somehow, he'd ended up with everything he wanted before even working out what those things were, and Henry could scarcely believe how lucky that made him.

'Wow,' was Violet's first word as she made her way cautiously into La Casa Naranja's new and improved lounge. 'We have a sofa?'

'And a chair,' Henry said proudly. 'Give me a few more weeks, and we may even have shutters at the windows, too.' Unclipping Luke's straps, he lifted the baby out of the car seat he'd carried inside, nuzzling his nose against his son's face only to recoil. 'Uh-oh – I think we have a poo-nami situation.'

Violet folded her arms. 'Definitely your turn.'

Using his free hand, Henry fished the changing bag out from underneath the pushchair. 'I'll go up and change him in our bedroom.'

Violet wheeled around from where she had been examining the freshly painted stone wall. 'We have a bedroom?'

Laughing, they made their way upstairs, careful to keep to the wall side. Henry had long since demolished what had been left of the rotted banisters but had yet to source or craft any replacements.

'I put us in the biggest room,' he told her. 'The one that faces the mountains. I thought Luke could have the turret room, once he's old enough.'

'Perfect.' Violet hurried up the final few stairs so she could wrap her arms around him. 'It's all perfect – you're perfect.'

'Hardly!' He laughed, nodding towards another room that had a pile of rubble at its centre and little more. 'But at least the roof won't leak on us any more.'

Having laid Luke down on their bed, a clean towel unfolded beneath him, Henry set about the process of bottom wiping while Violet explored the rest of the house, her coos of amazement filtering through the walls. Luke had watched his mother depart through wide eyes, and now considered his father with open suspicion.

'She'll be back in a minute, buddy,' he soothed, but his son showed no sign of crying. He rarely seemed to, not even when he woke hungry in the night, and Violet had confessed that some of the other mothers she saw at baby groups were at their wits' end dealing with mewling infants. Henry had soon after nicknamed Luke '*chico duro*', which was Spanish for 'tough guy', and was already harbouring fantasies of all the rough-and-tumble games the two of them would be able to play together as he grew. He'd missed out on that phase with Antonio and was keen to right the wrong when it came to his own little boy.

'We're going to have so much fun,' he told Luke now, feeding his chubby arms through the sleeves of a clean Babygro. 'You and me – we're going to do it all.'

Luke remained impassive for a few seconds, then blew a loud raspberry.

'Don't hold back,' Henry joked. 'Tell me how you really feel.'

When Violet didn't return, he carried the baby back downstairs and went out through the half-finished kitchen into the garden, where he found her crouched in the same place that he'd first seen her, underneath the lemon tree.

'The whistling jacks have quadrupled.'

Henry smiled. 'There's a ton more out front, too – they all sprang up against the wall.'

Violet brushed dust from her hands off against her jeans. 'In a minute, darling,' she said to Luke, who having spotted her had stretched out both his arms to be held. 'Mummy needs to check on her herb bed.'

'I'll show him the toys I bought,' Henry said, swinging the now-grizzling baby up in the air to distract him. 'Oh, and I hope you don't mind, but I said we'd have dinner at the Rodríguezes' house tonight.'

Violet frowned.

'The whos?'

'Our new neighbours down the hill. Juan and his – I think it's his wife, although I'm not sure if they're married. Her name's Ana, and they have a little boy a few years older than Luke.'

'How many years older?' she asked warily. 'I don't want him being rough.'

'I think he's about four?' Henry shrugged. 'I'm sure it'll be fine.'

Violet still looked doubtful.

'We don't have to,' he hastened, as they made their way back inside. 'I just thought it might be nice to have friends that are also parents. They might even have some baby things they no longer need.'

She smiled at that, urging him and Luke to 'go and play' while she set about making tea. So much of the stuff they'd accumulated had been donated, and Henry knew they were starting to run low on clothes now that Luke had outgrown the majority of his nine-to-twelve-month items. He probably should have spent the money he'd saved on practical things, rather than the elaborate toy toolbox he was now presenting to his son, but Henry had not been able to resist once he'd seen it. The set contained miniature versions of all the tools he himself used, and he couldn't wait to show his son what each one did, perhaps send him off with his own list of toddler-appropriate DIY tasks to complete. Luke, however, did not seem enamoured with the gift. Having levered open the lid and inspected its contents, he turned and crawled across the lounge to the sofa. Henry watched as he pulled himself up on to two wobbly legs, before stretching a pudgy hand out to his mother's discarded rucksack.

'Peh,' he seemed to be saying. 'Peh, peh.'

'That's Mummy's bag,' said Henry, shuffling over on his knees. 'Look, why don't we play with this hammer?'

Luke took the wooden tool, gnawed at it for a few seconds, then dropped it.

'Peh,' he said again.

'He means pens.'

Violet appeared behind them in the doorway, drying her hands on a tea towel. 'That's what he calls his crayons, because he can't say the word yet.'

'I wanted him to play with the things I got,' said Henry sulkily.

'Lukey,' called Violet, immediately snaring her son's attention. 'Shall we play . . . tools?'

Henry attempted to pass his son the toy hammer again, but this time Luke shook his head.

'Sorry.' Violet grimaced. 'Sometimes you just have to let him decide. He'll make his own way to the toys when he wants them, you'll see.'

Henry forced a smile. He'd so badly wanted to properly bond with his son – especially after two weeks away from him – but Luke could not have made it clearer that he wasn't interested.

'He's just a baby,' Violet said then, as if reading his thoughts. 'It's not personal.'

Henry got to his feet. 'You're right,' he said. 'I'm being stupid as usual.'

'Why don't you practise some walking with him?' she suggested. 'He's getting so much more confident on his feet every day, aren't you, baby?'

Buoyed by her obvious confidence in him, and by the idea of playing an intrinsic part in one of his son's landmark achievements, Henry sat down again and scooted backwards until he was a few feet away from Luke.

'Come on,' he urged. 'Come to Papá – you can do it.'

The little boy half turned towards him, one of his hands still holding fast to the sofa.

'I'll catch you,' promised Henry, opening his arms wide. 'Just let go.'

Luke did let go, and for a few seconds, as he wobbled precariously on his tiny bare toes, Henry allowed himself to hope.

He's going to take his first steps and they're going to be in my direction.

But almost as if he had considered that option and found it lacking, Luke turned away from Henry, shutting him out, and wobbled across the room towards his mother.

14

Violet

Henry turned the little wooden box over in his hands.

'The day I gave him this – or tried to,' he corrected bitterly, 'was when it started.'

'When what started?' I asked, though I knew full well. Henry sighed before replying, as if each of his words was a leaden weight.

'You and Luke, shutting me out.'

We'd had this argument so many times. I closed my eyes, steeling myself for the wash of pain that always followed in the wake of his accusations.

'I was his mother,' I said, through clenched teeth. '*Am* his mother. I was at home with him while you were working – he barely saw you. I know it wasn't fair, but that was the situation. I was his port in the storm of babyhood, so it stands to reason that he favoured me over you in the beginning. He didn't shun you any more than I did.'

'You both did,' he said, with conviction. 'From that day onwards, when it became clear to all of us that I was not the father he wanted, Luke began to withdraw – and you let him. You encouraged it.'

I put my head in my hands and rubbed them across my face. 'He. Was. A. Baby.' I'd spoken as if each word had a full stop and saw immediately that it hadn't landed well. Henry glared at me but didn't reply.

'I wanted nothing more than the two of you to find common ground,' I insisted. 'It was you who refused to compromise. Seriously, Henry, this tale of woe you've concocted isn't wholly fair. You're talking about our first summer here as a family – Luke didn't even show so much as an inkling of an issue until he turned five. His only crime back then was to be keener on his crayons than playing pretend-fix-the-house. Are you sure it wasn't you who took against him, not the other way around?'

When he still didn't say anything, I went back to my task of clearing out the dresser. I was always calmer when I had a practical task to complete, and would probably have boxed up every possession in the house before pausing to wallow.

Henry left the room but returned shortly afterwards with two bottles of water, one of which he put on the floor beside me.

'Better for you than gin,' he said, and though I tutted, I accepted it was true.

The silence between us stretched, the only sound the chirping of the birds outside in the trees, and the low murmur of distant voices. It wasn't uncommon to look outside and find tourists at the gate, their cameras raised to capture our unique turret.

'You know,' Henry said presently. 'There was a time when we had conversations that weren't about Luke. I can still remember some of them, even if you can't.'

'Of course I can. During those first few months after we met, I'd make lists of all the funny things that happened to me during the day so I could tell you about them on our evening calls.'

He made a small noise of bemusement. 'You and your lists.'

'I used to think: the longer the list, the longer I can keep him on the phone.'

'Silly. I never wanted to hang up. Back then, when I was here and you were there, it was so hard.'

'It was,' I agreed. 'But it was also exciting, wasn't it?'

Henry's eyes slid towards the photo album. 'We were so young,' he said again.

'Young and in love,' I replied. 'More fool us, eh?'

He smiled sadly. 'More fool us.'

The energy that had swarmed during our short altercation had gone, and in its place was the same sorrow as before, quiet and brooding. *I'm sorry*, screamed my brain, but my mouth remained shut. I had not forgotten the woman, how it had felt to see her hand clasped in his.

'Have you met anyone?' I blurted, unscrewing my bottle of water. 'I mean, since . . .'

'This?' he asked, motioning to his face. 'What do you think?'

Don't lie to me, Henry. Please don't lie to me.

'I think if you had, you wouldn't tell me.'

'Have you?' he said challengingly, the heat in his tone making me shrink into myself.

'No!' I was nettled by the mere suggestion. 'But if I had, I'd tell you.'

Henry gaped at me. 'You're unbelievable.'

'Well, you literally are,' I retorted. 'I don't believe a word you say.'

Henry was gearing up for another scathing remark when the sound of voices floated in through the open window. We turned to each other, bound together, albeit fleetingly, by our shared apprehension. I recovered quickly, and by the time Luke and Eliza let themselves in and came to join us, I had scrambled to my feet ready to greet them.

Luke looked from me, to Henry, to the overflowing bags of his old toys. His frown lines were deeper than they rightly should be in someone of his age – but then, the same could be said for all three of us.

'Are you throwing everything away?' he asked, and it was impossible to tell if he was annoyed by the idea, or indifferent. I hurriedly explained about the three-bag system.

'Do take a look through it all, if you want to,' I added. 'See if there's anything you want to keep.'

Eliza peered around him, pierced eyebrow lifting when she saw the mess I'd made. 'Ooh, is that a photo album? I'd love to see some baby photos of Luke. He always tells me there aren't any,' she added, 'but I know that can't be true.'

I registered Henry's slight flinch.

'There are some,' I said, not wanting to muddy waters that were already decidedly murky between myself and my son. 'Do you mind if Eliza takes a look?' I asked him.

Luke took in his girlfriend's pleading expression. 'Whatever.'

'Yay!'

'What about the rest of the stuff?' I asked. 'Any toys you want, or games?'

He didn't reply.

'Luke?'

This time Henry had spoken. He still had the toy toolbox, and now held it out in front of him, offering it to his son for a second time. I watched as an understanding of sorts seemed to pass between them, and then Luke looked away.

'Throw it all away,' he said. 'I don't want any of it.'

15

Violet

I didn't see Luke or Eliza again until the following morning.

They found me where I'd been since shortly after dawn, out on the patio with my bare feet propped up on the wall, a battered gardening book open on the table next to me beside a pot of fresh mint tea.

'Where's Dad?' Luke asked, stretching his long arms above his head. His hair was ruffled, and behind him, Eliza rubbed sleep from her eyes.

'Not here,' I said, unable to elaborate further.

Luke's expression hardened a fraction. 'Well, did he say when he'd be back?'

'He didn't, sorry. I should have asked him.'

Why did I always feel the need to apologise?

'Did you need him for something?'

Luke glanced over his shoulder at Eliza. 'I was hoping he'd give us a lift.'

I lowered my feet to the floor so I could pivot around and face him properly.

'Right now?'

'Yeah, I mean, soon ideally. We've been invited to spend the day on Antonio's boat. He called just now; said we should meet him over in Port de Sóller after breakfast.'

'We can get the bus,' put in Eliza, who was twirling a lock of hair around her finger, but Luke pulled a face. I understood his reluctance. Port de Sóller was a popular location, and it was likely the buses would be packed with tourists. My son did not do well with crowds and having taken the bus down to Palma and back yesterday, I was doubtful he'd up to facing a similarly stressful journey so soon.

'I can drive you,' I said. 'I'll ask Dad if I can borrow the jeep. I'm sure he won't mind.'

Luke looked unconvinced. 'You reckon?'

'Sure,' I replied breezily, exuding far more confidence than I felt. Picking my phone up from the seat beside me, I swiped away an email notification – the third in as many days from my bank – and tapped out a quick message to Henry.

'Right,' I said, readying myself to stand. 'Can I get you both some breakfast? You must be starving, and I picked up some lovely—'

My phone pinged. *Keys are on the hook*, was all Henry had written. No kisses from him. I held it up so Luke could see.

'Cool,' he said, at the same time as Eliza rushed out a 'thank you'. 'I'd better let Antonio know –' Luke added, big thumbs dancing across the screen of his own phone – 'that it's you coming with us, instead of Dad, in case he . . . you know.'

I thought I did. On account of my conversation with Ynes – who, I realised with a stab, I still had to call and apologise for running out on – I knew Antonio had some strong opinions where I was concerned, and I doubted the old man would pass up an opportunity to make his feelings known. It was an inkling that was proven correct a few moments later, as a reply came through to Luke's phone saying that yes, of course I was very welcome to join the party, and that he was 'eager' to see me after 'so long'.

Chalking this up as the first passive aggressive strike of what I feared would be a very long day, I fixed a rather grim smile on to my face and set about preparing breakfast.

There were three separate routes that ran from Pollença down to the south-west seafront village of Port de Sóller, and I decided – perhaps unwisely, in hindsight – to take the one that wound up through the mountains, thinking that it would provide far better scenery than the inland highway. I had forgotten, however, about the millipede ribbon of cyclists that would be clogging up the roads, not to mention the plethora of coaches, minibuses and hire cars.

'I'm so sorry about this,' I said, as we found ourselves trapped in a bottleneck of traffic for what felt like the tenth time. From the back seat, Eliza, who'd wriggled her top half free from the seat belt in order to drape her arms around Luke, told me not to worry.

'I had no idea Mallorca had so much forest,' she observed, as I negotiated a wince-inducing bend in creaking first gear. 'There are more pine trees here than in Lapland.'

'Sadly, less than there should be,' I said, nodding towards several stumps. 'It snowed heavily here in March last year, and a million trees came down. I read that the roads up here were closed for over a month while they cleared all the debris away.'

Eliza let out a low whistle. 'Poor things.'

Luke said nothing. His attention was on the road, jaw set and eyes watchful. I tried to concentrate on manoeuvring the jeep, but the sight of the felled trees had shaken me. That was what misery did, made you self-indulgent. These fallen spruces had nothing to do with the failure of my marriage, and yet I saw them as a metaphor relating to Henry and me, as if the destruction of nature could be somehow compared to that of love.

Once we had skirted around the old village of Lluc, with its vast, ornate monastery and lumbering tour buses, the way became clearer, and the tension in the jeep lessened as we finally began to make some progress.

'Do you want to stop at Cúber?' I asked Luke. 'So Eliza can see the view?'

He considered, seemingly indifferent. 'Sure, yeah, whatever.'

The car park that lay adjacent to the observation deck was full, as I'd feared it would be, so I dropped the two of them off and drove back along the road until I found a place to pull over. The air was moist beneath the canopy of leaves, and I swatted at hovering insects as I walked, my bag swinging at my side. The lake everyone stopped to admire at this spot was man-made, but no less beautiful for it, and on a clear day such as this one, the surface of the water was a smooth, cerulean blue.

I located Luke without any trouble. He was at the far end of the fenced deck, and easily a head taller than most of the assembled tourists.

'Hey.' I touched a hand to his back. 'Where's Eliza?'

He pointed to the path below, and lifting my sunglasses, I squinted down until I saw a dot of pink hair.

'She went to take photos of the sheep,' he said fondly. 'She really loves animals.'

'You used to be scared of sheep,' I told him. 'Do you remember when me and Grandad took you to Wimpole Farm during lambing season?'

He shook his head.

'Well, we did. We thought you'd be fine with the baby sheep, but if anything, they frightened you more than the big ones. Perhaps it was their unpredictability – all that leaping around.'

'I was a wuss,' he said solemnly, though not without humour.

'You were . . . cautious. Sensible, some might say. Animals are, after all, still animals. You can't trust any of them one hundred per cent. Look at what happened to that man who fed a wild hippo every day, or the bloke who tried to live as a bear.'

'Those are pretty extreme examples.'

'I guess so.'

'And you don't have to do that, you know.'

'Do what?'

Luke turned to look at me, brow furrowing from the glare of the sun. 'Defend my weaknesses. You do it all the time.'

I was stung, and my voice when I replied betrayed it. 'They're not weaknesses.'

Luke gave in to a sigh. 'OK, Mum. Whatever you say.'

'That's just it, though,' I persisted. 'I am your mum, so of course I'm going to think the best of you. You might choose to interpret the – let's call them hesitancies – you had as a child as some sort of flaw, but I prefer to see them as an exercise in self-preservation. So many little boys take unnecessary risks growing up, and I was glad you never did.'

'Not never,' he cut across me, the volume of his voice creeping up a few notches. 'What about the time—'

'Oh look, here's Eliza!' I cried, rushing over to greet her as she reappeared on the steps just below us. 'There you are. Were the sheep friendly? I'm sure they hang around here purely to beg food off all the tourists.'

And on I blathered, my stream of chatter obliterating Luke's attempt to dig up the past. I did not want to talk about the day to which he'd been alluding, not with him or anyone else. Given the chance, I would scour it from my mind completely. Yank it out by its roots and treat the earth below it with glyphosate, thus ensuring I never had to think about it again. Because while there were many things that I'd be willing to do for my son, to support, protect and nurture him, I did still have exceptions. And dredging up memories that would do nothing but cause pain was chief among them.

16

Violet

We reached Port de Sóller as church bells began to chime eleven, each of us hot, dusty, and in dire need of a cold beverage.

While Luke and Eliza went in search of soft drinks, I wrangled with the ticket machine in the car park before we all set off along the seafront promenade towards the harbour, side-stepping the multitude of visitors that had lined the street to wave at passing trams. The orange carriages that ferried folk up and down the hillside were as synonymous with Sóller as their yellow cousins were with Lisbon in Portugal. A good number of passengers packed into the seats waved through the open windows as they trundled past, and I was touched to see even Luke raising a tentative hand of greeting in return. Eliza was in chipper mood; smile wide beneath the 'Mallorca' bucket hat she'd put on and chin tilted up towards the sun. The blistering heat of the day was being tempered somewhat by the breeze rolling in across the water, but my skin still prickled with it. Luke had dressed sensibly in an oversized T-shirt and loose boarder shorts, while Eliza, whose skin was olive and less susceptible to burning, was defiantly exposed in a bandeau top and minuscule shorts.

It took the three of us longer than I'd hoped to find the boat, Eliza and I falling behind as Luke led the way through the maze of vessels moored in the harbour, swearing under his breath. It was a relief when the diminutive form of Henry's father eventually came into view in the distance, his arm a blur as he urged us to hurry.

'It's my fault,' I called, by way of a greeting, ready to take on any blame that might be dished out by our host. 'I insisted we take the scenic route.'

Luke muttered something unintelligible as he bent to remove his trainers.

'Come, come,' said Antonio, stepping back as we made our way across the narrow gangplank and dismissing my apology with a flick of his wrist. 'There is sangria.'

'Ooh,' enthused Eliza, who'd hooked her flip-flops over one finger. 'Liquid brunches are my favourite.' She proceeded to go into ecstasies about the modest-sized yacht, admiring the polished deck floors, chrome fixtures and gleaming white surfaces. 'I feel like I'm on an episode of *Below Deck*!'

Antonio absorbed the praise as greedily as a sponge would a bowl of water, chest puffed out and grin swarthy. There was a roguishness in his manner that was so at odds with his son's straightforward and strait-laced nature that I often wondered at how closely they were related. Henry regretted the fact that he hadn't been able to forge any kind of relationship with his father until he was in his teens, but in my mind, it was a bullet dodged. Antonio's dominant personality could easily have seeped through into his second-born son's, and I doubted I'd have fallen so in love with Henry had he been anything like his bulldog of a dad.

'Lucas!' he bellowed now, grabbing his grandson around the waist and hoisting him into the air. Given the fact that Luke was six foot, four inches to Antonio's five foot nothing, the pair of them looked utterly ridiculous, and my heart went out to my son as I saw colour flood into his cheeks.

'Put the poor boy down, Toni,' I chided, which did little but encourage the older man. Antonio tightened his grip until Luke turned almost puce, his flailing arms becoming increasingly urgent as he wriggled to free himself.

'Toni,' I said again, this time with less humour. 'You're hurting him.'

Antonio laughingly let go, dropping Luke abruptly so he staggered and almost fell. Eliza's nervous giggle tapered off and hurrying forwards, she tried to steady him.

Luke, however, brushed her hands irritably away. 'I'm fine,' he said, through gritted teeth. 'Don't fuss.'

Expecting her to meekly retreat, I was shocked when Eliza tutted. 'If that's what you want,' she said, with all the calmness and poise I lacked. 'But you know I was only acting on an instinct to help you – it wasn't fussing.'

I waited for him to snap back at her, wrench his arm free and storm off the boat. But Luke merely smiled sheepishly. 'You're right, I'm sorry.' He pulled her against him, murmured a 'thank you'. I gaped at him – at both of them. Luke had never apologised for his outbursts; as far as Henry and I were concerned, he was allergic to culpability.

Blissfully unaware that his actions had very nearly caused a storm of yacht-sinking proportions, Antonio strode across the deck and patted Eliza happily on the head, in the manner one might to a dog that had just mastered a new trick.

'She has you on the tight leash, *sí*?' he said, and to my utter astonishment, Luke actually laughed. *Laughed.*

'Best way to keep her close to me,' he said, to which Antonio slapped him gleefully on the back. I groaned inwardly as I looked on. Luke was doing what he always did when confronted with the forceful disposition of his Spanish grandfather and turning into a more manic version of himself. The shift wouldn't be noticeable to many, his tells subtle enough for even Eliza to miss, but they were obvious to me. I steeled myself for the physical reaction I knew was imminent, and sure enough, felt a stabbing in my stomach that I only managed to mask because Antonio had begun leading the other two away. Giving myself a moment to breathe through the pain, I went after them, around the narrow edge of the boat towards the main deck.

Having shooed us all on to a wraparound leather banquette and pushed a jug of sangria and several glasses in our direction, Antonio went up to the bridge and, moments later, we felt a rumble as the engines started. The yacht's bosun, Diego, who was seventy if a day and had the wrinkled, tarnished skin of a walnut, showed remarkable agility as he hurried from stern to bow, fastening ropes and yelling instructions through a radio to the other members of crew, two Spanish twenty-somethings who looked too alike not to be brother and sister. I watched them go about their tasks as my own anxiety whirled, wishing I had a physical job to occupy my restless limbs.

Eliza took her hat off and shook out her pink hair. She had made short work of her sangria and was already in the process of helping herself to a second glass. I was finding it was diffi-cult not to keep checking on Luke, and although he seemed content enough, his expression serene and shoulders relaxed, I could hear the faint tapping of his sock-clad foot against the deck.

'Are you OK?' I asked, leaning in so Eliza wouldn't hear me. 'We can go back if—'

He shook his head once, mouthing a barely perceptible 'no', and I shrank back against the seat. Port de Sóller was spread out behind us, a scatter of Battenburg-hued buildings against a backdrop of mountains and sky. Boat masts bobbed and keened on their moorings, the vanishing harbour a giant pincushion cut through with swathes of lights. As the yacht chugged gently out past the swell, the horseshoe curve of the bay rose up to see us off, the lighthouse at its tip eliciting an 'ooh' from Eliza. Where she recognised a beacon of hope, however, I saw only a symbol of my own loneliness, and immediately felt ashamed. This spiralling pattern of perpetual doom had to stop. Feeling sorry for myself was not going to change anything.

I stood up and made my way to the edge of the deck, wrapping my fingers around the railings as I peered down at the churning froth of water below. The wind whipped up my hair and tossed droplets of spray across my bare legs, the roar of the engines loud enough that if I screamed, there was a chance nobody would hear me.

'Mum!'

It was Luke, and sensing from his tone that it wasn't his first attempt at getting my attention, I hurried back to the table just as Antonio reappeared.

'Diego has taken over the controls,' he explained. 'I thought that we could go to the beach at Escorca, perhaps with some stops for swimming along the way?'

That, we all agreed, sounded nice. Many of the coves along the section of coastline he'd suggested were only accessible by boat, and likely to be less crowded than those connected by road. As we sailed on, Antonio fired questions at Luke and Eliza in his trademark scattergun way, cajoling and teasing until he got the answers he wanted. Within half an hour, I'd learned a lot more about their relationship than I could ever have hoped to glean through my own conversations with Luke. He was not receptive to my questions, no matter how anodyne, and having found myself at the receiving end of caustic knockbacks too many times to recount, I'd concluded that it was better to wait, and hope, and be satisfied with the few morsels of information I was tossed. Being afraid of your own child was unthinkably dreadful, but it was where I'd ended up, nonetheless.

It didn't come as a surprise that Eliza was more open than Luke, but I was shocked when she admitted to Antonio that yes, she and Luke did plan to move in together officially once the new term started, and that of course they'd discussed the possibility of marriage and children.

'We're very much on the same page,' she said earnestly.

'Becoming a parent is an extremely big responsibility,' Antonio replied, extracting a segment of orange from the sangria jug and sucking it thoughtfully. 'It is better to wait until you are older, past the age of twenty-five.'

'Oh, for sure,' Eliza said and glanced at Luke. 'Neither of us want to be old parents either, though.'

I cleared my throat. 'Define old.'

'My mum was forty-two when she had me, and she ended up going through the menopause while I was going through puberty. That wasn't ideal.'

'At least she had wisdom and experience on her side,' put in Luke. 'Better to be well prepared than unprepared.'

The leather squeaked beneath me as I shifted in my seat.

'*Sí.*' Antonio nodded sagely. 'You cannot be a parent if you are still a child yourself.'

'You can if you have no choice,' I said, only to immediately regret it. The three of them stared over at me expectantly, waiting for me to elaborate. 'I'm not saying I was forced into having you.' I turned to Luke. 'Just that you weren't planned, as such. You were a surprise – a very nice surprise. My happiest accident.'

'How old were you?' asked Eliza.

'Seventeen when I fell pregnant, eighteen when Luke was born. Henry was nineteen.'

'No way!' she exclaimed. 'That means my mum is old enough to be your mum.'

'Probably best not to point that out to her,' I joked weakly, and Eliza laughingly agreed.

'Why did you?' interrupted Luke, head down and attention focused on the ice he was swirling around in his glass.

'Why did I what?'

'Keep me?'

Although I'd had an inkling what he was going to say, hearing him ask the question made my heart contract as if squeezed.

'I was healthy,' I said. 'I loved your father; my parents were willing to help us – there was no reason not to keep you.'

'You must have wanted to, as well?' This came from Eliza, and I got the impression she'd prompted me not out of curiosity, but because I should have said it myself. She was right – it was the first thing I should have said.

'Yes,' I agreed. 'Of course I did, more than anything. I was scared, as you'd expect given my age, but once I came around to the idea, I was happy. We were so desperate to meet you, your dad and me,' I told Luke. 'I can't even tell you how much.'

It was not the whole truth, but close enough to be convincing.

Or so I hoped.

17

Henry

Seventeen Summers Ago

The wheels of the buggy snagged on a tree root, and Henry clenched his teeth. The last thing they needed was for Luke to wake up again, not when they'd spent the best part of an hour strolling up and down the waterfront trying to get him off to sleep.

Violet had crouched down and was making soothing noises, her hand on their baby's chest. Luke squirmed, stretched, and set his features into a frown, but his eyes remained blessedly closed.

Henry let go of the breath he'd been holding in. 'Close one,' he whispered, as Violet smiled wearily up at him. She was exhausted – they were both exhausted. Henry could no longer recall a time when he hadn't been worn out to the point of collapse.

'It's just a phase,' Violet's mother was fond of saying. 'No baby is easy.'

That might be true, Henry always thought, but he'd be willing to bet that their baby was more difficult than most. For the first year of his life, Luke had slept, as the old saying promised, like a baby, and he'd barely cried either. That had all changed in the weeks after they'd brought him home from his first Mallorca visit, and he and Violet had looked on in horror as their cherubic little boy changed into a screaming, writhing ball of potent fury.

'What does he have to be angry about?' Henry would often exclaim, as his son clawed and scratched and sobbed in his arms. 'He has everything. A safe, comfortable home, parents who worship him, grandparents on hand to help, food, toys, games, attention.' So much attention. More than Henry, who'd been raised by a single working mum, had ever received during his formative years.

'He always gets like this after we spend time with your dad,' Violet said now, rubbing at her eyes as they continued on along the path. It was nearing six in the evening, and the sunlight speckles on the water had faded from silver to gold. Pine trees swayed gently above them, long branches trailing like giant's fingers into the sea below; down on the shoreline, birds picked and chattered.

Henry did not want to upset her, so he waited a few moments before replying, trying his best to quell the surge of irritation that had flared in his chest.

'Antonio gets him so worked up,' Violet went on. 'All that rough-housing and throwing him up into the air – Luke hates it.'

'He was laughing the whole time,' Henry protested.

Violet made a scoffing sound.

'He was!'

'Because he was scared, not because he was enjoying it.'

She always did this – made out that she knew what was going on in their son's head, even if his actions contradicted it.

'I think you worry too much,' he said, quietly so as not to goad. 'Luke's only two.'

'I'm aware how old my son is, Henry.'

'I know, but—'

'And of the two of us, I'm the one who spends the most time with him. I know him better than you do, and I know when he's putting on a game face.'

If she'd been trying to hurt him with this comment, stewed Henry, then she'd be able to put a tick in that particular box. Did she not see him out from dawn until dusk every day, putting in the hours on his apprenticeship at the building yard so he could work his way more quickly up the ranks? Was she blind to the fact that he was doing whatever he had to in order to support them, saving every spare penny so they could move away from her parents' house and get a place of their own?

'I don't want us to argue,' he said, defaulting, as usual, to the role of peacekeeper. 'Please, Vee.'

Henry could tell she was still annoyed with him, her anger simmering just below the surface of her set jaw. Violet's moods were like waves, tempers that swelled from barely there ripples to crashing froth in minutes, leaving trails of destruction in their wake. Henry's were more solid, but constructed slowly, each argument they had representing another hammered-in nail.

'I'm just so tired,' Violet said, with a sigh that made her sound almost as old as her mother, who Henry was sure must be at least sixty. Violet had confessed that her parents tried for a long time to have her, and he'd often wondered if the reason why her mum was so hard on them now was because she harboured some jealousy towards her daughter for conceiving Luke so easily. He'd never mentioned it to Violet, though. It would only upset her, and Henry figured they had enough to contend with already.

'I'll take him tonight,' he promised. 'We'll sleep downstairs, so you don't hear him crying.'

But Violet was shaking her head. 'He needs me,' she said dejectedly. 'He won't settle with you.'

Despite all his efforts, Henry felt himself bristle. 'He might, if you'd only let me try.'

'No.' She was adamant. 'I wouldn't be able to sleep anyway, I'd be too worried about him, and there's no point in both of us suffering.'

They walked on for a while in silence, past beachside restaurants teeming with sunburnt tourists, souvenir shops overflowing with stacks of inflatables, and cocktail bars belching out cheesy pop tunes. Henry watched a group of guys approaching a table of girls of around his age and envied them their fun. None of those people had to concern themselves with sleep training, or weaning, or which brand of nappies were the most absorbent; their lives were about frivolity and living in the moment, not sterilising bottles and competing for early nursery places. When Violet had told him she was pregnant, Henry had been so sure that keeping the baby was the right thing to do – so much so, that he'd flown to England and made his case to her – but very occasionally, in his darkest and most wrung-out moments, he questioned if it had been the right decision. Violet had told him emphatically that they were too young, and he had made her trust that they weren't. He, Henry, had done this, and so he must be the one to make everything all right.

'Whatever you think is best,' he said, taking one hand off the buggy and wrapping it around her shoulder. Violet melted gratefully into him, her body warm against his, and despite the exhaustion, the residue of their row, and all his worries about the future, Henry felt a stirring of desire.

'If we get home without waking him, we might even have time to . . . you know,' he said.

Violet gripped him tighter. 'Sounds good to me,' she said.

Their eyes met, an understanding passing between them, and a moment later they had set off at a jog, both laughing as they dodged and ducked around tourists, children, Port de

Pollença residents walking their dogs, never letting go of each other's hand. The bus came into view ahead of them, its red bulk tantalisingly close.

'Hurry,' urged Henry, quickening his pace, and dropping Violet's hand so he could gesture to the driver to wait. Narrowly missing a seagull that was busy devouring a pizza slice, Henry barrelled on, reaching the stop just as the bus began to move. '*Esperar*!' he called. *Wait*. But when he turned to reach for Violet, there was no sign of her. The driver threw up his hands impatiently and, cursing, Henry waved him away, turning as he heard a man's voice.

'*Hola*! Hey, Enrique,'

It was Juan, his arm raised and usual wide grin in place. The two men greeted each other in Spanish, and Henry explained about the missed bus.

'So, you get the next one,' Juan said. 'Come and have a drink.'

Looking over his neighbour's shoulder, Henry saw the unmistakeable red hue of Violet's hair as she headed into a nearby bar.

'Ana is there,' Juan explained, adding with a glance at the pushchair, 'with Tomas.'

Henry did not want to sit and drink *cerveza* with their friends, no matter how jovial they were; he wanted to take his beautiful girlfriend home and make love to her.

'One drink,' he said eventually, reluctantly, and followed Juan across a crowded outdoor terrace. Rihanna was singing about her umbrella, and he wished she wouldn't do it quite so loudly. There was little hope of Luke staying asleep long in here and, once awake, he might not go down again for hours.

'There you are,' said Violet. 'You ran off.'

'To catch the bus,' Henry replied stiffly, careful to keep his fixed smile in place.

Tossing her mane of long dark hair over one shoulder, Ana stood up from her seat to greet him, a stack of bangles sliding down her slim, tanned arms as she kissed each of his cheeks. Five-year-old Tomas was in the chair beside her and held up a toy car for Henry to see.

'Lamborghini,' he enunciated carefully, as Juan beamed down at him with pride.

'*Increíble*,' said Henry, unable not to recall the set of wooden vehicles he'd brought home for Luke only to have them rejected.

'Vroom, vroom,' yelled Tomas, as he pushed the car backwards and forwards across the tabletop. Ana smiled at him indulgently, rolling her eyes as Tomas almost sent his glass of orange juice flying before turning her attention towards Luke.

'Sleeping – lucky you,' she said, adding in an undertone, 'They are terrorists when they get older.'

'Luke won't be,' Violet responded instantly. 'He's never shown any sign of being rough or boisterous.' It wasn't strictly true, and Henry detected a hint of annoyance in her tone. Juan had gone inside to fetch each of them a drink, and he watched as Violet's eyes strayed after him. She'd always got on better with Juan than Ana, whereas for Henry, the opposite was true.

'How are you?' Ana asked him now, sticking to English, Henry presumed, so as not to exclude Violet. When he told her they'd been out with his father all day, she visibly softened.

'Ah, Antonio – such a brilliant man.'

'He is?' came Violet's surprised reply.

Ana turned to her, nonplussed. 'If Antonio had not given Juan a job, we would have nothing,' she said. 'When we met, do you know that he was a fisherman? Can you imagine it – the stink of him?'

Violet seemed affronted, but Ana merely laughed, her fingers searching the table.

'I have told my brain that I do not smoke any longer,' she said, tapping her temple, 'but my hands have not, how do you say it, received the memo?'

Henry, who had dallied with the habit for all of two months when he was sixteen, nodded sagely.

'Vroom!' shouted Tomas, only to be shushed by Violet.

'Sorry,' she said, as Ana sat back and folded her arms. 'I just . . . I thought he was going to wake Luke, and we're at our wits' end with his poor sleeping, aren't we, Henry?'

'Tomas could sleep through a hurricane,' said Juan, who'd returned with a tray of drinks. Putting a beer down in front of Henry, he passed Ana her red wine then presented Violet with some kind of multicoloured concoction, complete with pineapple wedge and pink paper umbrella.

'What is it?' she asked, reaching for the straw.

'A hanky panky.'

Violet giggled, and Henry caught Ana narrowing her eyes. The irony of Juan presenting his girlfriend with the one thing that he, Henry, had been hoping to share with her tonight was not lost on him, and picking up his bottle, he drained a third of it in a single gulp. Juan took the seat next to Violet's, stretched his arm around the back of Ana's chair, and began telling them a joke about two nuns that Henry had heard a hundred times before. It did not translate well into English, but both women laughed regardless, Violet rocking forward in her seat. Music blared, voices rang out, and a ruddy-faced woman wearing a sequinned cowboy hat screeched as she tripped over in the street outside.

Henry was fairly sure that if he lay down here on the sticky, drink-stained floor, amid all the chaos and noise, he would still be able to sleep. Any hope he'd harboured about having sex with Violet had gone, as had his desire. All he wanted was to go home and rest, and having made up his mind, he got to his feet.

'We can't go yet,' protested Violet, blinking as she looked up at him. 'I haven't finished my hanky panky.'

Juan bellowed in delight just as Ana, who was becoming impatient with the non-stop 'vroom, vrooming' of her son, made a grab for the little Lamborghini. Tomas shrieked, snatching away his prized possession only to lose his grip on it. There was an agonising pause as each of them followed the trajectory of the small metal object in mute horror, and then, with a heart-cleaving scream Henry knew would haunt him forever, the toy car collided hard with Luke's peacefully sleeping face.

18

Violet

'You've missed a bit,' I said, reaching up to wipe a blob of sun cream from Luke's face.

'I can do it.' He veered backwards out of reach. 'Just tell me where?'

'On your nose.' I wrinkled my own. 'And your chin – and under your eye, where your scar is.'

The faint white line where Tomas's toy car had done its damage all those years ago was still visible; the first crack in the veneer of my friendship with Juan's now-ex-wife, Ana. Even after her son had injured mine, it still felt as if I was the one being judged, and it irked me how she always made a point of lavishing Henry with attention, the implication being that I was neglectful, that he deserved better. I guess I had to admit that she'd been right about the latter.

We'd dropped anchor not far from the main beach at Escorca and having waited the requisite time for our simple lunch of Mallorcan salad, grilled langoustines, bread, and aioli to settle, Eliza and Luke were now going to brave a swim. I watched from the upper deck as first she and then he, albeit less enthusiastically, clambered down the metal ladder and dropped into the clean water. The boat had its own inflatable slide, which the younger members of the crew were busy setting up, while Diego kept an eye on the two in the water.

Antonio patted the seat beside him and flashed me a congenial-looking grin.

'Come,' he said. 'Sit. Talk to me.'

'What do you want to talk about?' I asked him warily.

'The house,' he said, without preamble. 'I do not think you should sell it.'

As I sat down beside him, a small 'huff' of irritation escaped my lips. 'It wasn't my idea, it was Henry's. Maybe speak to him?'

Antonio fished a packet of cigarettes from the front pocket of his open shirt and lit one, closing his eyes in satisfaction as the first drag filled his lungs. I fanned the smoke away, but he didn't look remotely contrite. Being or saying sorry wasn't Antonio's style; he was a man well accustomed to being pandered to by others. I took a moment to study the craggy outline of his face, the strong nose and closely cropped grey hair. He was still handsome, despite his advancing years, though in a classic rather than noteworthy way. It must have galled him to father a son as exceptionally handsome as Henry, upon whom everyone showered praise. Or used to.

'Maybe I want you to speak to him,' said Antonio, resting his cigarette on the edge of a terracotta ashtray and removing his mirrored Ray-Bans. Having picked up one of the heavy cloth napkins left over from lunch, he set about polishing each lens in turn, lifting them up to the sun every so often to check for smears. I heard Eliza shout something, followed by the deep rumble of Luke's laughter, and smiled despite myself. There had been a time when I wondered if my son would ever go near the water again, and he'd have been justified in deciding not to.

'He is better?' Antonio asked.

The sunglasses were back in place, and I saw my own reflection as I turned to face him, warped and ungainly. I didn't need to ask who 'he' was.

'Getting there,' I said, although 'better' wasn't quite the right word. Luke had not recovered from who he was as a person, that was implausible – he'd just grown more adept at handling himself.

'And you?'

'Me?'

'You are better?'

'There's nothing wrong with me.'

Antonio took a long drag of his cigarette. 'You must fix this . . . thing,' he said, waving an expansive arm. 'This thing between you and my son, it cannot go on.'

The casual way in which he referred to the seismic change in both Henry and my circumstances was typical Antonio, though it also gave me pause. Talking to Ynes had made me wonder how much, if anything, Antonio knew, and this appeared to confirm that it was very little. Henry may blame me, but he hadn't told anyone else that he did. That had to mean something.

Antonio was twirling his hand in the air now, a conductor with a stick of tobacco instead of a baton. 'You love him, he loves you, yada, yada,' he said. 'Whatever you think is the problem, it doesn't matter more than that, more than love.'

'Henry's made his mind up,' I said slowly. 'It was his decision to split up and he was the one to list the house. He won't change his mind now, not when I— Not when it's all been decided,' I finished lamely.

'What did you do to him?' He had asked the question quietly, his tone almost menacing in its intensity.

Another yelp filtered up from the water, and I heard Luke call to Eliza, telling her the slide was up at last. It was my excuse to go, end this awkward conversation, tend to my boy, and turn my back on this man who seemed determined to provoke me. I was saved instead by the buzz of my phone ringing in my bag, and having snatched it up triumphantly, I hurried away into the glossy interior of the yacht.

'Yes, hello?'

In my haste to escape Antonio, I'd blithely overlooked the fact that it was an unknown number calling.

'Hello, Violet.'

I went very still. 'What do you want?'

'That's not very polite,' the caller said mockingly. 'Aren't you going to ask how business is going?'

'That's of no interest to me,' I hissed, raising a hand to shield my lips from view. 'I told you in my message that I can't help you any more.'

A tutting sound followed this declaration, as if I were a child who needed scolding.

'We had an arrangement. I help you; you help me – remember?'

'Things change,' I said. 'You'll get what you're owed. Soon, I promise – but I can't do the other stuff for you any more.'

'Can't?' asked the caller. 'Or won't?'

'Both,' I said defiantly, though from the drawn-out sigh that followed, I knew it had been the wrong thing to say. All I had done was goad when I should be placating.

'This deal we made, you agreed to the terms. It is non-negotiable.'

'You're not hearing me,' I said insistently, pacing up and down on the polished wooden boards. 'The decision has been made for me. I'm not even in England any more, I'm in—'

'I know where you are. When are you coming back?'

'I . . . I'm not sure. But when I do, I'll have what I owe you.'

'Do you mean money?'

My confirmation was met with brittle laughter.

'You're going to have to do better than that, Violet. A deal is a deal.'

I started to argue, but my throat had turned dry. I clutched the phone more tightly against my ear as he reiterated his demands, dread dripping through me like acid.

'Do we understand each other?'

'Yes,' I whispered, and again, 'yes.'

Antonio had come into the cabin and stopped right behind me, an empty glass in his hand that he held up with an enquiring look. I shook my head, resisting the temptation to shoo him away on his own boat, and watched him pad like a panther over to the bar. Having unscrewed a bottle of brandy, he poured out a generous measure, then reached down for a second glass.

The call ended and I went across to join him, sinking down on to a stool and putting my head in my hands.

'You are upset.'

'I'm not,' I lied, the word muffled by my hair, which had fallen forwards over my face.

'You look as if you have received bad news,' he said, and for once, his concern felt genuine. Antonio was right, it had been bad news, but not the kind that comes as a shock. I had tempted fate into motion, and now it was catching up with me.

'It's fine,' I said, making myself look up and smile at him. 'It was my mum, calling to complain about something the neighbours have done. You know how she can be.'

Antonio opened his mouth to reply only to be distracted by Eliza, who had appeared on the deck outside, soaking wet in a bright green bikini with her pink hair slicked back. There was no sign of Luke and, for a second, panic gripped – the echo of a response that had altered the very shape of me.

Antonio must have been studying me; I saw the crease of discernment cross his brow.

'Maybe I will have a drink after all,' I said, shaking my head at the offer of brandy and asking for something non-alcoholic. Out on the deck, Eliza was posing for photos at the top of the inflatable slide, contorting her body into preposterous positions to make Luke laugh. Everything was clean – the sky, the glistening water, the polished surfaces of the sleek yacht, even the tonic in my glass – but inside, I felt putrid. Through the grubby residue of the phone call, Antonio's question stood out in stark relief: '*What did you do to him?*' Overwhelmed by a need to unburden myself, resolved suddenly to tell Antonio the truth, I put down my glass and took a long, steadying breath. But before I could speak, the older man started coughing. Really coughing.

'Toni,' I exclaimed. 'Are you all right?'

He was bent double, one hand on the counter and the other pressed to his chest. The cigarette he'd been in the process of lighting dropped to the floor. Hurrying around to his side of the bar, I thumped him gently between the shoulders, then again with more force. Antonio's cheeks and neck were a livid puce, his eyes bulging behind the sunglasses that had slipped down his nose. I was on the verge of shouting for help when he finally gained control. The spluttering stopped, and he stayed where he was for a few long minutes, breathing heavily and wiping tears from his cheeks.

'Ice,' he croaked. 'I choked on the ice.'

'What ice? There wasn't any ice in your glass.'

'Yada, yada,' he wheezed, waving me away.

'Toni,' I began, but he was already striding away from me, back into the sunshine to join the others. Shaking my head, I crouched down to retrieve his dropped cigarette and saw something else on the floor, a sight nobody ever wanted to see.

Multiple splatters of bright red blood.

19

Violet

We made it back to Pollença as the sun was beginning to set, its golden light spread like honey across the baked clay roof tiles of the old town. La Casa Naranja seemed to glow as if smouldering, the outside walls still warm to the touch.

There was no sign of Henry, but I knew I had to see him, that what I had to tell him couldn't wait.

'Do you mind if I pop out?' I asked Luke. He and Eliza were halfway up the stairs, his hand in hers as it always seemed to be.

'Sure,' he said, the word stretched out by a yawn. 'We were thinking of having a lie-down before dinner anyway.'

'I'll prepare something for you as soon as I get back,' I promised. 'Won't be long.'

'M'kay.'

I went out of the house and turned left, avoiding the Calvari Steps in favour of a more meandering but less crowded route. The vast hillside that rose up behind the town had been thrown into shadow, its golden-walled monastery poised like a curl of candied fruit at its top. Like many of Pollença's streets, Carrer de la Garriga sloped downward from top to bottom, but it wasn't as narrow as those on the outskirts, and the dwellings here were taller. I followed the sound of grinding machinery until I reached a tumbledown property bordered by a high metal fence, beyond which I could see a mini excavator, several wheelbarrows piled with rubble, and a stack of rotten planks. Having negotiated my way through a gap where a boundary wall must once have been, I stepped gingerly across the messy front yard and peered into the gloom of the house. A cement mixer stood prone next to a roll of stained carpet, and on the far wall was Henry's beaten-up old radio, tuned into a local island station.

Having called his name a few times to no avail, I ventured further inside until I came to the stairs, craning my neck to see up to the second floor, from where I could hear the whirring sound of machinery. Having decided the steps looked safe enough, I hurried up, being careful to keep to the wall side.

I found Henry in the room nearest the top of the stairs; his back to the doorway and ear defenders strapped on over a yellow helmet. He was cutting wood to length with a circular saw and didn't see me until I'd moved right round to stand in front of him.

'Hey,' I mouthed, my hand raised.

Henry started in surprise but recovered quickly. Stretching out a booted foot, he flicked off his power tool at the wall.

'Jesus, Vee,' he grumbled, staring around the room as if searching for something. 'Here,' he said, removing his defenders and passing across the helmet. 'Put this on.'

I pulled a face. 'Is that really necessary?'

'It's not safe in here,' he said shortly, glancing up towards the ceiling. 'The roof still isn't sound. I'm waiting on materials.'

'Sorry,' I said, grimacing as the top of my head came into contact with the sweat-soaked inside of his hard hat. 'I was shouting, but I guess you couldn't hear me?'

'Nope.'

There was a beat of silence, during which we stared at each other, and then Henry motioned to the door.

'Let's go downstairs. There are some beers in the cooler, and I must be about due a break.'

Once we were outside, I removed the helmet and propped it on the handle of an old broom. Henry frowned as he squinted up at the purple-tinged sky.

'It's getting late,' he said. 'Must've lost track of time.'

'I hope the Rodríguezes are paying you well for this,' I remarked, thanking him for the bottle of beer he'd just used his teeth to open.

'Just the going rate for mates.'

'It's a big place,' I observed. 'A lot of work for one person.'

'Tomas has been here on and off.'

'Just Tomas?'

'Juan looks in but doesn't get his hands dirty.' Henry grunted in bemusement. 'Probably worried about chipping his manicure.' He ruffled his hair, took a tug of beer.

I tried not to look at his scars.

'That's your father's influence,' I said. 'Don't you remember how much he used to tell me off for having dirt under my nails? Every year for Christmas, he bought me gardening gloves, and every year without fail, I'd say thank you, then put them in a drawer with all the others.'

'Should've given them to the second-hand shop,' said Henry.

'Surely just one of each pair,' I joked, and was rewarded with a real smile.

'Hard to believe he used to be a fisherman,' he mused.

'Who, Antonio?'

Henry fixed me with a look. 'Juan. Perhaps it was his years spent catching things in nets that helped him ensnare my father's good favour.'

'Is that what he did?'

'I assume so.' Henry shrugged. 'You know how charming he can be.'

'I should have asked Antonio today,' I said, swigging more beer.

'Ah, yes.' Henry brushed sawdust off his bare knees.

I'd found a clear patch of earth to sit on while he'd perched himself on the closed lid of his cooler. I could see a glimpse of pale upper thigh where his shorts had ridden up and ached to touch him.

'How is the old cockerel?' He'd long referred to Antonio in this way, often using the Spanish '*gallo viejo*', and I'd always agreed it felt like an apt comparison.

'That's actually why I'm here,' I said haltingly. 'Why I came to find you. Something happened today on the boat.'

Henry tossed his head back and sighed deeply.

'Oh god, what now? He didn't do or say something to upset Luke, did he? I've told him so many times not to mention the height thing.'

Antonio's mocking of both Henry and Luke's tall stature was a stand-up routine both had grown weary of long ago, but that did little to deter the old man.

'Not really,' I replied, 'although he did pick him up and spin him around.'

'Christ.' Henry looked aghast. 'He's a braver man than me.'

'He was OK in the end,' I said, explaining briefly about Eliza, and how she hadn't stood for Luke snapping at her.

'Christ,' said Henry again.

I wanted to say more, fill him in on our son's apparent plan to get married and have children one day, the casual way in which Eliza had discussed them living together, as if they had it all worked out – but all that could wait. It had to.

'That was all fine,' I said, 'but later on, after we'd all had lunch and the kids were swimming, Antonio had a funny turn. One minute he was fine, then suddenly he had this coughing fit—'

'He does smoke like a soldering iron,' interrupted Henry.

'I know, but this was . . . different. He coughed up blood.'

Henry paused with the bottle of beer halfway to his lips. 'Blood? Really?'

I nodded. 'Sorry. I thought you'd want to know. I did try to ask him about it afterwards, find out if it was a new thing, or a one-off, but he refused to give me a straight answer, just told me it was nothing.'

'That isn't like him.' Henry was looking thoughtful. 'He never shies away from the truth usually, no matter how brutal it is, and he relishes people making a fuss of him.'

'You should talk to him,' I said.

'Hmm.'

'I really don't think this is a "hmm" situation – what if he's seriously ill?'

Henry shook his head. 'I'm sure it's nothing,' he said. 'If he was sick, he'd have found a way to use it to his advantage by now. That's what he does.'

'I don't agree.'

'Well, he's not your dad.'

'No,' I said. 'I don't have a dad. Mine died because he got sick and didn't tell anyone.'

The tears came then. Six years, and it still hurt. Six years, and the guilt continued to choke me. Henry listened to my quiet sobbing for a moment, and then, with a sigh, he stood up and came to sit on the floor beside me.

'Sorry,' I said, using the hem of my dress to wipe my nose.

Henry brushed his knuckles against my knee, such a small gesture of kindness but one that made me want to weep all the harder.

'I'll talk to him,' Henry said. 'To my dad. I promise – OK?'

He had made promises before only to break them, but that had been then.

This was now.

'I just wish he'd lived long enough to see Luke as he is now,' I whimpered. 'I can't bear that he died in the midst of it all. Those years were . . .' I trailed off, suppressing a shudder.

'Your dad always had faith in Luke,' Henry reminded me. 'He said that everything would work itself out in the end. Wasn't one of his little sayings something about believing in tomorrow?'

'Your present situation is not your final destination,' I intoned.

'That's the one.'

'God, I miss him.'

Henry's hand hovered over mine, but he withdrew it without making contact.

'And not only him,' I whispered.

'Vee . . .' There was a warning note in his voice.

'Don't you ever think it's ironic?' I asked. 'That we stuck it out through those first two years living with my parents, through the stuff that went on when Luke started school and all the years where it felt like we were crouched in the trenches, waiting for a bomb to go off – all that only to give up when it seemed like he might be OK after all?'

'Giving up wasn't what happened,' he said. 'You know that.'

He'd raised a hand unconsciously to his face as he spoke, a gesture that muted any further argument I'd been preparing to make. The fact remained that if it hadn't been for my actions, my selfishness, my stupidity, then Henry would not look the way he did now. I wanted forgiveness and he needed someone to blame – it was a stalemate past which there was seemingly no forward path.

'I'm sorry,' I whispered. I had said the words to him so many times, each apology a pebble tossed against a mountainside of resentment. Henry closed his eyes, took a breath, and opened them again.

'It's getting late,' he said, picking up my empty beer bottle. 'Will you be OK for a minute while I go and lock up the tools?'

I nodded as he stood.

'Henry,' I said, addressing his tanned calves. 'Take this.'

I tipped the broom holding the hard hat out towards him. 'Thanks.'

I sat in silence, eyes down and cheeks wet, watching as he walked away. My limbs were leaden, immobilised by self-pity, my heart hard as stone. I wanted to burrow through the dirt and hide, take root in the dark and wait for the rain. I could regrow, start again, take all that I had learnt and mould it into something more durable.

But I would have to do it alone. Without him.

'Henry, wait!'

I scrambled to my feet, kicking up dust, ready to follow him, to talk to him, to beg him if necessary. But I was too late.

On the far side of the yard, the metal gate was lifted to one side, and a man appeared in the gap.

Juan.

20

Violet

'*Buenas noches*,' was how he greeted me, raising a hand as I brushed dust off the back of my dress.

Dressed smartly in soft grey chinos, white polo shirt, and a pair of tan-coloured deck shoes that looked fresh out of the box, Juan made his way over and leant forwards to kiss me on each cheek. I found myself assailed by the woody scent of his aftershave, as well as something more astringent.

'I can smell the ocean in your hair,' he told me, to which I smiled faintly. Did he know I'd spent the day on Antonio's boat? It was likely.

'Henry's inside,' I said, and Juan glanced towards the house. 'But don't go in there without a hard hat on or you'll get told off.'

'I am on my way out to dinner,' he explained, unhooking his sunglasses from between the buttons of his shirt. Like Antonio, he favoured Ray-Bans, though this pair did not have mirrored lenses. He didn't put them on, just turned them over in his hands.

'So, you thought you'd pop in on the way past and check on progress?' I guessed.

Juan nodded. 'Paulina has been asking me when her new bedroom will be ready,' he said, beaming indulgently at the mention of his granddaughter. 'She is impatient, the same as me.'

'There are worse traits.'

'And probably, I have all of them,' he said, though I knew him well enough not to be taken in by his show of self-deprecation. I cast my mind back to the first time I'd met him, as a new mum barely out of her teens, recalling how the confident and strikingly handsome Spaniard had seemed so much wiser, steadier, and more comfortable in his skin than either me or Henry. Both of us had been happy to be swept beneath his wing, and I'd been pleased when the two men formed a bond over those first few summers. Juan's friendship had meant a lot to Henry, just as it had to me.

When the latter emerged from the interior of the house a few minutes later, there was a tense kind of smile fixed across his face. He and Juan greeted each other with little more than a nod, and I hovered awkwardly on the periphery, waiting while they discussed building materials and schedules.

'I can't see it being ready until at least September,' Henry said, his tone matter-of-fact. When the two of us had founded our business, we'd made a pact to always be honest with our clients when it came to timeframes, even if doing so led to disappointment.

'Better they start with moderate expectations we can exceed, rather than vice versa,' he'd said, which I'd learned was a typical Henry way of seeing the world. When I'd told him I was pregnant, he hadn't promised anything more than he was able to. There was no big declaration, he'd simply arrived at the front door of my parents' small house in Cambridge, sat the three of us down in the lounge, and put forward a plan of how he and I would raise our baby.

'I'll have to move in here,' he'd said, and I'd watched the colour drain from my mother's cheeks. 'Sooner the better, so I can establish myself in a job.'

He would work as hard as he could, earn as much as he possibly could, do whatever he had to do in order to support the baby that I was still, at that stage, in two minds about keeping. I wanted to go to university, to travel, to be selfish for a little bit longer. I had none of the faith and commitment that seemed to come so naturally to Henry and was ashamed of myself for it. I didn't want to let him down, nor risk losing him. It was easier to slip into the tailwind of his enthusiasm and let it carry me right through to term.

He had no idea how close I'd come to choosing a very different future for myself. Neither of them did.

'I should get off,' I told them. 'I promised the kids I'd cook.'

'The kids,' echoed Henry, shaking his head. 'Don't let them hear you call them that.'

'I still think of Tomas as *mi pequeño*,' Juan said with a low chuckle. 'They will always be our little boys, eh? No matter how big they get.'

'If Luke gets any bigger, we'll have to take the roof off the turret,' I joked, turning to go. 'Should I save a portion of dinner for you?' I asked Henry.

He scratched behind his ear. 'No, thanks. I'm— I have other plans.'

The woman in the street, her hand reaching for his, glossy hair swinging.

'Oh.' Even speaking hurt. 'I guess I'll . . . The keys for the jeep are back on the hook.'

'Thanks.'

He couldn't appear to meet my eye, but Juan had no such qualms.

'Shall we walk together?' he asked, tucking the arm of his sunglasses back between his shirt buttons. 'I am going the same way.'

This would be bound to annoy Henry.

'Why not?' I smiled at him. 'It will be good to properly catch up.'

I strode away and heard Juan murmur something to Henry before he hurried after me. Having negotiated the makeshift fence, we headed along the darkening street, close but not near enough to touch. Now that the sun had properly set, the sky was a deep violet, its surface aglow with the promise of stars.

I waited until we reached the corner before I spoke. 'Are you really going the same way as me?'

Juan raised a single, trimmed eyebrow. 'It is Pollença,' he said expansively. 'Every street leads to every other street.'

'Does that make us mice in a mouse run?'

'Why don't we say marbles?'

'I'm not sure I have many left,' I said, and he gave me a rather crooked smile, the meaning lost on him.

'I heard about the house.'

'Are you going to lecture me about it, too?'

We had reached Plaça de l'Almoina, a small square with an ornate fountain in its centre, Pollença's symbolic rooster standing illustriously at its top. Holidaymakers filed past in a blur of noise and colour, bumping against us as they went. Juan put his arm around my shoulder to shield me, ushering me forwards out of the scrum.

'To sell?' He sucked air through his teeth. 'It feels so . . . final.'

'It's the best option for everyone concerned,' I said robotically. 'Henry has moved on, and I need to do the same.'

Juan's dark eyes narrowed.

'What do you mean "moved on"?'

'Moved on as in seeing someone else,' I said, attempting to sound casual about the fact, as if the mere thought didn't rip my insides to shreds. 'I saw them together.'

Juan looked as if he didn't believe me.

'I did,' I insisted. 'She has long dark hair and they were holding hands.'

'Have you asked him?'

I shook my head slowly. 'Not my place.'

Juan made a tutting sound. 'He is still your husband, *sí*?'

I agreed begrudgingly that he was, 'on paper'.

'So, you can ask him whatever you want.'

'Hmm,' I said, unwilling to confess my real reason for avoiding the subject. If I did what he was suggesting and raised the topic of this woman with Henry, then I ran the risk of having him confirm my worst fears. As things stood, I only suspected he was romantically involved with someone new, I didn't know for sure, and knowledge like that had the power to crucify me. I wasn't sure if I was strong enough to bear it.

Juan touched a hand to the crook of my elbow, drawing me across to the doorway of a restaurant kitchen. I looked up at him, taking in the familiar curve of his nose, the fullness of his lower lip.

'You used to talk to me about all the things happening in your life,' he said. 'You can still trust me.'

I shook my head, and he let out a low hiss of frustration.

A bin bag was hurled out through the open door, and I only just managed to hop out of the way in time.

'That was a bit close for comfort,' I said, leading the way across the lane and through the puddles of light spilling down from shop windows. I was restless in his company, itching to escape, though I knew to admit as much would bruise his ego.

'Are you talking about the rubbish,' he asked, 'or me?'

I chuckled. 'Can it be both?'

'Violet.'

The way he said it, enunciating each syllable, stirred something in me, the faint trickle of a feeling that had long since run dry. He put a hand on my arm to still me, and this time I sighed under the strain of it, of him, of all my diverging emotions.

'You don't need to worry about me.'

I don't deserve your concern.

'I can find out,' he said urgently. 'About this woman that you saw. There are people who will know, and I can be . . .' He paused, searching for the English word.

'Discreet?'

'*Sí*, discreet. Nobody will know who is asking, and this way, you can be certain.'

There was no need to ask him why he was willing to do this for me – I knew why. We all had an agenda, that self-interested part deep inside, and who was I to judge Juan for following his? I told him to go ahead, shutting down my fear with a nod, telling myself that the truth would do as promised and set me free.

Because if Henry had fallen in love with someone else, then we really were over.

Finished, broken, done.

21

Henry

Sixteen Summers Ago

They had slept with the shutters propped open, and Henry awoke to the sound of birdsong, a smile reaching his lips as he rubbed grit from his eyes. Violet lay beside him, pale lashes fanning freckled cheeks and red hair spilling out across the pillow. He watched her chest as it rose and fell, marvelling at the love that bloomed in his own.

A glance at the clock on the bedside cabinet told him it was late, a few minutes from eight a.m., and there hadn't yet been so much as a murmur from Luke. It was always this way on their first night back on the island, La Casa Naranja enveloping the three of them in welcome. This place was theirs; the only solid thing Henry owned. Even the old Ford he drove in England had been given to him by Violet's father, and Christopher Lupton had steadfastly refused any offers of payment. Henry greatly needed a car and accepted it in good grace, but he still felt indebted whenever he drove it. They were all still living under the same roof, and the older Luke got, the more paraphernalia he accumulated. What had once been a neat and orderly abode now creaked under the strain of art supplies, jigsaws, and wooden learning toys; endless piles of folded washing and stacked packets of night-time nappies. Despite both their combined and tireless efforts, three-year-old Luke was still getting to grips with the concept of toileting – a problem that caused no end of clashes between Violet and her mum.

'Sometimes, you have to be cruel to be kind,' she'd insist, but her approach did not work with Luke. If anyone pushed him, he shoved back.

Loath to wake Violet but unable to resist touching her, Henry stroked a slow finger along her arm, nuzzling in close as she started to stir. The selfish thread inside him had been tugged by desire, and he was delighted when Violet responded to his kisses by sliding her leg over his.

'Morning,' she murmured, her sweet breath hot against his throat. Henry put his hand on her waist, pulled her to him.

'I love waking up here,' she said, speaking through a smile. 'With you.'

'Me too.'

'I wish my parents would agree to come, see how much it's changed, how beautiful you've made it. I don't think I can stand another row with my mum about selling.'

'I get where they're coming from,' Henry allowed, dropping a kiss on her collarbone. 'If we sold, we'd have the money to buy somewhere in England sooner and be out from under their feet.'

'We've offered to rent somewhere about a million times,' she pointed out, arching against him like a cat. Henry hooked his fingers under the bottom of her pyjama top and eased it upward, watching with pleasure as his lazily grazing thumb made Violet shiver. Four years they had been together, and she could still reduce him to putty. Henry felt almost stupid with lust, the galloping pace of his heart at odds with the stealth with which his fingers explored her. The top was dropped to the floor, his hands seeking her small, high breasts. He kissed each of the stretch marks left there by pregnancy, loving her all the more for having them, perpetually in awe of her body and what it had given them.

'I'll talk to them again,' he promised. 'Convince them it's time that we move out.'

'You'd do that for me?' she teased, easing down his boxers. The leg that was draped over him curled and tightened, drawing him in. Henry closed his eyes.

'I'd do anything for you,' he murmured. 'I'd even sell this place, if you asked me to.'

Violet's bright green eyes widened. 'You would never do that!'

He chuckled. 'I might.'

Violet put a hand against his chest and pulled back, unhooking her leg.

'Henry,' she said sternly, waiting until she had his full attention, 'I would never ask you to sell this place. I love it here; I can't imagine our life without our beautiful orange house. Losing it would be like losing you or Luke – it's unthinkable.'

He could see she'd upset herself and rushed to reassure her. 'I would give up everything else I own before I let this place go,' he said, wrapping her up in his arms. 'And I know that doesn't amount to much yet, but I'm doing my best. I'm trying every day, for us and for our future.'

'I know you are.'

She kissed him properly then, tugging at his hair, tasting him, needing him. Henry swam a few glorious lengths in pure sensation, then slowly he pulled away from her.

Violet, breathless, blinked at him. 'Where are you going?'

Henry grinned as he clambered up on to the mattress. 'Not far,' he said, leaping naked to the floor. He had plans to build an en suite next to their bedroom, but for now they had to make do with the main bathroom a few doors down. It took him less than a minute to run there and get what he needed, but as he turned to go back, an idea came to him.

Smiling broadly, his precious cargo clasped tightly in one hand, Henry made his way along the landing to the room at the far end and flicked on the light.

The little bed was empty.

'Luke?' he called, venturing further inside. He checked behind the curtains, under the bed, inside the wardrobe; he wrenched open drawers and threw aside toys. Running out into the hallway, he crashed into Violet, who was clad in just a towel.

'Where's Luke?' he said, stepping around her and shouting his son's name over and over. Violet joined in, her voice lilting and sweet at first, then louder and more frantic. The turret was unfinished, the door always locked, but Henry fetched the key and checked inside regardless, swearing in earnest as a splinter of wood went into his toe.

'I can't find him anywhere!' Violet's shrill cry filtered up from the ground floor.

'Check the garden,' Henry shouted back, limping back into their bedroom where he pulled on his boxers. There was no time to worry about shoes. Taking the stairs two at a time, Henry reached the front door as Violet clattered through from the kitchen, her face as white as the towel she was still clutching around herself.

'I don't understand,' she sobbed. 'Oh, Henry – what if someone's taken him?'

'No!' he yelled, with such ferocity that she quailed. 'Sorry, sorry!' He rushed across, held her for the briefest moment, felt the rush of her heart against his chest.

'I'll find him,' he promised, trying to break free, but Violet clung to him.

'You're not going anywhere without me.'

The haze of the morning had yet to clear outside, and the sky was muted by cloud. Henry did not feel the stones underfoot, nor the scrape of the latch as he pushed through the gate. Instinct told him right, but Violet ran left, and after a moment's hesitation, he went after her, hearing her cry as she reached the road.

'What is it?' he called, terror making him lightheaded so that he half staggered around the corner. Violet was there, kneeling on the asphalt, a small dark-haired boy wrapped tightly in her arms.

'Oh thank god.' Henry gave in to tears as he knelt down, enveloping them both in a bone-crushing hug.

Luke squirmed. 'Get off, Daddy. You're hurting me.'

'Sorry.' Henry forced himself to let go, blinking away yet more tears as Violet set about examining every inch of their son, his boy, his baby.

'I think he's OK,' she said, her well-practised 'Mum' voice noticeably shaky. 'I can't see any marks on him.'

Luke was clad only in a nappy, his pale body so small and vulnerable.

'What were you thinking, little man?' Henry asked, ushering the two of them back to the side of the road. The truth sat loud but unspoken between him and Violet, how close they had come to never getting Luke back, to life as they knew it being over.

'You mustn't run off like that,' Violet chided gently, crouching so she could look Luke in the eye. 'Mummy and Daddy were scared when they couldn't find you.'

'Cat,' he said, and Violet glanced up at Henry.

'That bloody stray,' she muttered. 'He must have followed it.'

'How did he even get out through the door?' said Henry, who could remember turning the key in the lock himself the previous night. 'Did you know he could let himself out?'

Violet bristled. 'Of course Mummy didn't know,' she said, addressing Luke rather than him. 'Silly Daddy, asking such a silly question.'

'What's that?' Luke was pointing at the small velvet box in Henry's hand, the one he had fished out of his washbag before discovering that his son was missing. Henry was momentarily confused to see it there, and then he smiled.

'Now that,' he said, getting down on one knee, 'is a very good question indeed.'

Violet's eyes were wide as she realised what was happening, then she raised a hand to her mouth, almost losing her towel in the process.

'I was trying to create a perfect moment,' he said, giving in to a laugh. 'But I guess this will have to do.'

'Why has Mummy gone all pink?' asked Luke.

'I don't have much to offer you,' Henry went on. 'Nothing except a crumbling house, a better locking system for all the doors, which I'll get cracking on with today, and, oh yeah, my total and absolute devotion.'

She reached for his hand.

'I know we're young, and broke, and still trying to work out who we are, and that there's so much about life that I don't know yet, so many lessons I have still to learn, but there is one thing I am sure about, Violet Lupton, and that is my love for you. You're my best friend, an amazing mother to our three-going-on-thirteen-year-old son, and you inspire me every day. I can't imagine my life without you in it, and I know that will never change. You're all the clichés, every single one of them. You complete me, you make me a better man, you make me feel whole – all of them, all the cheese, every corny line from a romance novel, every searing note of a love song, all the poems and teddies clutching hearts and funny feelings in your pants.'

Violet had begun to laugh through her tears. 'At least you're wearing pants,' she said.

Henry looked down at himself, then back towards her, crouched there in her towel, their beautiful baby boy pulled close in beside her.

'This is me,' he said simply. 'Laid almost literally bare, all the pieces of me asking all the pieces of you to be each other's forever.

When he opened the box, the ring inside it glistened.

'It's not a real diamond,' he said. 'But I figured you more than make up for that.'

'I love it, it's perfect. And I don't need a precious stone,' she told him. 'All I need is you two, and our summers here together. That's all I want forever – our life and us, exactly as we are right now.'

As if on cue, Luke put his head on one side and said, very clearly and without preamble, 'I did a poo.'

'Exactly as we are right now?' repeated Henry, as the two of them lapsed into laughter. 'Are you sure about that?'

Violet took the ring from its box and slid it on to the third finger of her left hand.

'I'm sure,' she said, leaning over to kiss him. 'It's all shits and giggles with us, isn't it? And what could be better than that?'

22

Violet

In the days that followed our conversation in the rubble-strewn garden of Tomas's Pollença home, Henry and I barely spoke. He was up and out of the house before I woke, then back long after dinner. On the few occasions I'd waited up for him, a hopeful bottle of wine open on the patio table, a plate of food covered in cling film in the fridge, he'd done little more than grunt 'goodnight' at me before disappearing off upstairs. But as much as those interactions saddened me, they were preferable to the alternative – him not coming home at all. I hadn't heard anything from Juan about the mystery woman, but the anticipation was making me jumpy. Every time my phone beeped or buzzed, I snatched it up instantly, only to baulk at the sight of an unknown number, or a text instructing me to call. I was close to breaking point, the growing tension making me nauseous, my nerves set on edge.

When I opened the door after breakfast on the fourth day to find Ynes waiting on the step, I almost wept with relief.

'*Cabecita roja*,' she said, dragging me towards her with such gusto that my chin ended up buried somewhere in her bosom.

'No Enrique today?'

'No,' I said, as I righted myself, and proceeded to fill her in briefly on my estranged husband's recently errant behaviour.

'It does not have to be this way,' she said, pushing a Tupperware box of home-made empanadas into my hands. 'Eat these, *la flaca* – skinny girl – and then fix your marriage.'

'You make it sound so easy.'

We went through the kitchen and out into the garden beyond, where Ynes busied herself with deadheading an antique rose while I pinched out the side shoots from a tomato plant. It was what we'd always done, worked side by side, talking while we pruned, dug, and watered. Our friendship had been nurtured in this garden, and the familiarity of it, of the two of us together, soothed me now.

'I've missed this,' I told her. 'Missed you.'

Ynes started to answer, then winced.

'Thorn?' I asked, and she nodded, cursing under her breath as a bead of blood oozed from the top of her forefinger.

'Nature is a cruel mistress.'

'A bitch,' Ynes agreed, sucking her finger. 'But this is why we love her, *si*?'

'Why do you think that is?' I mused, as Ynes extracted a pair of gardening gloves from her apron pocket. It was the same deep-green colour as the dress she wore beneath. 'That as humans, we're programmed to love the thing that hurts us the most.'

Ynes looked at me shrewdly. 'When Manuel left me, I thought the fire of that pain would devour me,' she said, bashing her palm against her chest. 'But the flames died down; I am stronger now.'

'You were so young,' I said, remembering the tale as she'd told it to me not long after we met. She and Manuel had defied the wishes of their parents to marry in secret, only for him to be lured away by someone else not three years later. Ynes had explained pragmatically that he'd grown impatient at her failure to conceive, yet I knew without needing to hear the words how much agony that must have caused her. My relationship with Luke might well be a complicated one, but the thought of not having him at all was untenable.

'*Si, solo una bebé*,' Ynes concurred, with a sly grin. 'An excuse to never grow up.'

The two of us were still giggling when Luke appeared around the back door. Clad only in boxers, his hair was a slept-in mess.

'*Chico hermoso*,' crooned Ynes, clapping her gloved hands together. 'Look at you!'

'Probably best not to, considering I just woke up,' Luke replied dryly.

'Shall I make you and Eliza some breakfast?' I offered. 'I can pop out and get some—'

'No, no – don't worry.' Luke ran a hand through his fringe, pushing it off his forehead. 'We'll get something in a bit.'

'Did you need me for anything else?' I hurried out. 'The washing you gave me is done, I left it folded on the landing.'

'Is Dad here?'

I felt my face fall and, with some effort, hoisted a smile back into place.

'He left early. Work. You know what he's like when he's on a new project.'

Luke nodded, but he didn't say anything.

'If there's something you need, then—'

'It's fine, Mum.'

'I can call him if—'

But Luke had gone, thankfully not slamming the back door behind him. I waited, knowing it would only be a matter of seconds before Ynes spoke.

'Your boy is a man.'

I hadn't expected that. I'd assumed she would chastise me for being so eager to please him, or for not reacting when he'd interrupted me mid-flow. I turned away from the house to face her, taking in the dark bun streaked with grey, her soft, lined skin and kind eyes. My friend might be forthright, but she was also fair, and the most generous person I knew, both with her time and her emotions. She'd always loved my boy, had never wavered in her adoration, not even in his most difficult years. The two of them shared an understanding, a bond of mutual respect that I knew was lacking between myself and Luke. I'd have felt envious of anyone else, but not Ynes.

'Sometimes, I look at him and see only the little boy he once was,' I confessed. 'To me, he still has that vulnerability. I can't seem to shrug off this need to mother him all the time.'

Ynes shot me a bemused look. 'You believe that it wears off one day, this "need to be a mother"? That you will one day stop – poof!'

I plucked another tomato stem, clumsily so the fruit came loose and dropped to the ground. I stooped to pick it up, using my thumb to wipe the dirt off its pale green surface. It was not ready to eat, would likely upset the balance of my anxious stomach, though I loathed the idea of it going to waste.

'I thought it would get easier as he got older,' I said. 'That he would need me less.'

'And that is not happening?'

I sighed, not wanting to lie to her. 'OK, that I would need him less.'

'Ah.' Ynes studied me for a moment, then she took my hand. The rubber coating of her gloves was coarse, her fingers firm as they gripped me. She didn't speak again, didn't try to coax or second guess, she simply held on to me, waiting while I worked out what it was that I was trying to say. The truth was there, but I couldn't reach it, not quite, and perhaps sensing that a rope had begun to tug inside me, Ynes let go of my hand.

'He is better,' she said, though with more uncertainty than I was accustomed to hearing from her, as if she were testing the word out, rather than settling on it.

'I think so,' I said with a shrug. 'I hope so.'

'There have not been . . .?'

I shook my head and she smiled rather grimly.

'Nothing like that – not yet anyway, but I can sense it there, his temper, frothing away beneath the surface. Being in the same house as him, even this house,' I went on, glancing around with a sigh, 'feels like living with a grenade. The pin has been pulled out, and we're all waiting for the bang.'

Ynes put her head on one side. 'But you stay?'

'But I stay,' I agreed solemnly, helplessly. 'He's my son.'

'And Enrique? Where is he?'

'Working,' I said, to which she rolled her eyes theatrically.

'Hiding,' Ynes corrected. 'You are the matador, and he is *un cobarde.*'

I blinked at her, not understanding.

'A coward,' she said, punctuating the word with a terse flick of her wrist.

I should have defended Henry, but it felt nice, for once, to have an ally. Bad cop parent was a role I'd never wanted – it had been foisted on me by my own reluctance to push back. Luke needed someone to side with him, even when he was being impossible, and more often than not that person had been his dad. I'd sleepwalked into it, not grasping how much of a routine we'd got into until it was too late, until I was trapped in a part I'd never read for. When it came to being a mum, I considered myself an understudy at best. If I'd been better, perhaps Luke would have been too.

'You should not let him do this,' Ynes said, drawing me out from my deep, brooding well. 'I do not believe that what happened could be so bad, so bad that all the blame has been given to you.'

I hadn't told her everything. My shame had prevented me.

'I deserve it,' I said, hanging my head. 'Henry's accident . . . it was my fault.'

Ynes shook her head violently. 'Were you driving the car? No.'

'You don't understand,' I said wearily.

Another tomato hit the ground by my feet, and this time I swore in frustration as I bent to retrieve it. My face grew suddenly hot, my chest tight. Ynes was scrutinising me, I could feel the weight of her gaze and glanced away, unwilling to meet her eye. A dark shape passed across the kitchen window, and I heard the sound of voices.

'I should go and see if they want help with breakfast,' I said, relieved to have an excuse to scarper.

'Violet.'

I exhaled slowly, turned. Ynes was looking at me pityingly, which was almost worse than the judgement I had been expecting. Sympathy of any kind was liable to unmoor me, and I smiled through the tears that pressed to be shed.

'You must stop,' she instructed. 'All this blame. It is not fair, it is not right.'

'But—'

'But? But nothing. It is time to be selfish.'

'Who, me?' I laughed at the absurdity of such a sugges-tion, but Ynes's expression was pure steel.

'If the men can be selfish,' she said archly, 'so can you.'

23

Violet

Ynes's words of misguided wisdom continued to prod finger-like against my temples for the remainder of the morning, and by the time Luke and Eliza had finished eating and were chasing around ideas of how to spend their day, I was more than ready for a distraction.

'How about we go to Alcúdia?' I suggested, as Eliza helped me clear away the breakfast plates. I'd cooked the dropped tomatoes in the end, gently frying them in olive oil, fresh oregano, and a generous twist of black pepper, and had two scraped-clean plates to show for it.

Luke glanced up from the table, at which he sat hunched over his phone.

'Sure, yeah,' he said. 'Whatever.'

'His enthusiasm knows no bounds,' I murmured to Eliza, and was pleased when she let out a laugh.

Henry, for once, had commandeered the jeep, so the three of us made the thirty-minute journey by bus. The small town of Alcúdia was in the north of the island, its oldest part encircled by meticulously restored high medieval walls. Having crossed from the bus stop to a grand stone archway, we strode beneath it and found ourselves in the shadow of Sant Jaume church. I was not religious, and neither was Henry, although Antonio often extolled to us both the merits of Catholicism. As far as I was concerned, he could keep the idea of an omnipotent Almighty, and I would settle on admiring the buildings created in His honour.

'Wow, it's stunning,' said Eliza, who was wearing a white dress that set off her ever-deepening tan. Gold hoops gleamed at each ear, and she'd twisted her short pink locks into a minuscule bun. 'I love how the stonework looks like a flower.'

'That's the rose window,' I told her. 'And the church itself has been integrated into the city walls.'

She nodded, awed into a silence that proved contagious. The air was dense with a heat so heavy that even the palms above us were still, and the sun that sought us out did so with an intensity that scratched. Luke had put on his usual tent-sized T-shirt and jersey shorts, sneakered feet huge at the end of pale, hairy shins. The combination of his exquisite bone structure and height coupled with her colourful hair and piercings ensured that a fair amount of attention was drawn their way, but while Eliza seemed aware in the way that many young women and girls are, Luke appeared to be oblivious. He either failed to notice or cared not about the curious gazes of those we passed as we weaved our way through the shady backstreets.

'I thought it'd be busier,' he said, turning to Eliza. 'Maybe we could do that thing?'

'That thing?' I echoed.

'Luke wants me to pose for some photos so he can use them for a portrait,' Eliza said, sounding mildly embarrassed.

'I've tried to draw her before,' he said cagily, 'but I can never get it quite right.'

'I've told him it's probably my fault,' she teased. 'On account of being so asymmetric.'

'No, you aren't,' Luke and I chimed in unison, as he pulled Eliza towards him. I was still growing accustomed to this tactile side of him and averted my gaze as he bent to kiss her. Henry and I had been the same once, constantly pawing at each other, but the intimacy we shared had tapered off as Luke's struggles worsened.

I mulled this over as we continued to explore, Eliza finding new things to remark upon at every turn. The papery thin petals of the bougainvillea were 'reminiscent of Matisse's cut-outs'; the pots of flowers on steps and windowsills 'nature's fireworks'; and the mottled walls 'so like sourdough, I want to cover them in slices of avocado'.

'Dad used to go into a trance-like state whenever we came here,' I said. 'Do you remember, Luke?'

'Yeah.'

'He'd run his hands across the walls and stick his fingers into the gaps, puzzling how it all fitted together, working it out, and telling us at great length how good the design and building techniques must have been for it still to be standing.'

'Alcúdia is a celebration of craftsmanship and vision,' quoted Luke, pulling off an accurate impression of Henry at his most impassioned.

Eliza trailed her fingers over the coarse texture.

'My dad would put old sections of wall into art galleries if he could,' said Luke. 'He puts more merit into buildings than he does anything else.'

'We all see beauty in different things,' I allowed. 'For your dad, those things are most commonly made from bricks and mortar.'

'I see beauty in people,' mused Eliza. 'But by that I mean their idiosyncrasies and unique ways of seeing the world, not what they look like. My parents taught me that a body is just a body – a vessel for the soul, and I agree with them. What makes us human is on the inside, not the outside.'

'You should say that to my dad,' muttered Luke, as we skirted past a vast cactus. 'He's been so, I don't know, weird since the— since his face changed.'

'Poor man,' said Eliza, while I silently reeled. 'I'm so used to the scars now that I barely notice them.'

'Give him time,' I managed to say, though it was difficult through the churn of misery that had become my insides. 'It's been less than two years, and the whole thing must have been deeply traumatic for him.'

'And he is still very handsome,' Eliza said, to which Luke shrugged noncommittally.

I nodded. 'People would remark on how good-looking he was all the time when we first met – often complete strangers. I had such a complex about it in the early days. I assumed people wondered what a man of his calibre was doing with a freckly imp like me.'

Eliza scoffed good-naturedly.

'But then you were born and all that changed,' I went on, turning to Luke. 'You became the one who got all the attention, all the old ladies hurrying over to cluck at you in your pram and tell me how gorgeous you were.'

Luke stared straight ahead, a stony look on his face. I had meant what I'd said to be taken as a compliment but had somehow strayed yet again on to conversational turf that he'd rather I'd left untrodden. It was so hard to know what to say, and I had become an expert in getting it wrong.

'What about you, Luke?' Eliza said, coming to my rescue. 'What do you see beauty in?'

He thought for moment, a muscle twitching in his jaw. 'Truth,' he said at last. 'Although I see a lot less of it than I'd like.'

My immediate response to this was a shocked 'oh', and when I looked at Eliza to gauge her reaction, I saw that she, too, seemed lost for words. Luke felt as if he was being lied to – that point he'd made loud and clear – but was it me he was taking a pot shot at, or Eliza? I found it hard to imagine it was the latter option. I thought about what Eliza had said to me, when she'd spent a night on the couch.

'Me and Luke, we trust each other. Trust is important to him.'

Those two were mutually honest, but I had lied to Luke many times. Never out of malice, only to shield him, protect him from himself and, yes, sometimes to protect myself from him. Did that make me an ugly person, or a desperate one?

'Shall we get an ice cream?' Eliza suggested, the brightness of her tone at odds with my sullenly contemplative thoughts. We had wandered from the dusty backstreets into a wide square, which was bordered on every side by colourful awnings. An ice-cream shop, complete with predictably long queue, was in the corner farthest away.

'I'll go,' I offered, keen to escape, but Luke cut across me.

'S'all right,' he mumbled. 'Dad lent me some euros this morning. Pistachio, right, Mum?'

'The greener and nuttier the better.'

I watched him lope away, bony shoulders hunched and hair flopping forwards over his eyes, relinquishing a sigh as I leant back against the nearest wall. Eliza stood a little to one side, fiddling with the hem of her dress.

'Is he happy?' I asked, and saw her eyes widen in surprise at the question. I hadn't known I was going to ask it until I did.

'I think happy is too simple a word,' she replied cautiously. 'Luke is . . . complicated, and he's anxious a lot of the time. I think he'd need a different brain to be happy, in the traditional and simplistic way. I don't mean it as a bad thing,' she hurried on. 'I like that he's a deep thinker, that he's considered and measured in the way he responds to things, you know?'

'He's always been anxious,' I said, trying for a smile. 'Though I think he fought back against it for a long time.'

Eliza nodded in understanding. 'I know what you mean,' she said. 'When I met him, like, the first few times we spoke, he used to pretend he was happy all the time, and it was really weird. He was almost manic sometimes. I remember asking him if he was on something.' She laughed softly at the memory. 'But of course, he wasn't. You know he hates drugs?'

'I know he's distrustful of them.'

'Totally,' she agreed. 'He's too smart to put any pharmaceuticals into his body.'

'You're right,' I said, somewhat mechanically. 'He is.'

'I called him out on it,' Eliza went on, pulling a loose thread from her dress and twisting it around her finger. 'The fakeness. I told him to stop acting and be himself, even if that meant being quiet, or subdued, or even rude. I knew I liked him, but I didn't want some pretend version of him, I'm not about that. It took him a while to dismantle all those walls he'd put up, but slowly he started to show me the real him.'

'He always seems so angry with me,' I said, staring past her towards the throng of people congregating in the square.

Eliza dwelled on this for a moment. 'He's not angry,' she said. 'Sad, maybe.'

'Oh god.' I pressed a hand to the side of my face. 'That's even worse.'

'It's natural to be sad when something bad happens. I hope you don't mind me saying, but you and Henry both seem sad to me and . . . one sec,' she said, stepping away. 'Oh, Luke's calling me. Do you mind if I—?'

'You go,' I urged, as she hovered on the spot. 'I'll try and find us somewhere to sit.'

Even if I'd no qualms about pinching one of the many café tables, that option was out of the question due to the sheer number of tourists, and the square had little in the way of benches. Eventually I came across another of Mallorca's many estate agent's, which offered the double benefit of being closed and having a low, wide windowsill on which to perch. A couple that looked to be in their early thirties, well dressed and highly polished, were peering through at the listings, and I scooted across so as not to block their view.

'These are nice, but far too small,' I heard her say, to which the man agreed they were, 'a bit on the pokey side'.

'And most have pools,' she went on. 'Daddy says the upkeep is a nightmare.'

Curiosity got the better of me. 'Sorry, I didn't mean to eavesdrop, but am I right in thinking you're on the hunt for a holiday home?'

The man turned first, a smile of polite solicitude above a pressed pale-blue shirt. His hair was startingly blond, almost white, while the woman – who I assumed must be his wife, given their matching gold bands – had the carefully high-lighted locks of someone who spent numerous hours in a salon.

'Do you work here?' she enquired eagerly, her face falling when I shook my head. 'I'm afraid we're becoming a bit of a nuisance for the agents,' she confessed. 'Our list of specifica-tions is extensive, and nobody's shown us anything yet that's up to the mark.'

'Which area are you hoping to buy in?'

'Oh, Pollença. Absolutely,' the man put in adamantly. 'Used to visit as a boy, always promised myself I'd get a pad there one day, and now, here we are, aren't we, Mags?'

'I fell in love with it the moment Malc brought me here,' she gushed. 'Do you know it well?'

I stifled a smile. 'You could say that.'

'You don't happen to know of anyone selling a house, do you? Ideally, we'd want at least four bedrooms, a garden, parking, nice views.'

'And no pool?'

Mags tinkled with laughter. 'No pool,' she confirmed. 'You'd think it would be easy, but we've been made to feel as if we're asking for the proverbial moon on a stick. I just know, and Malcolm feels the same way, that the house of our dreams is here – we just need to find it.'

I stood up from the windowsill, wiped the dust from my dress, and beamed at them.

'As luck would have it,' I said, looking from one to the other, 'I think you just did.'

24

Violet

I made it back to The Orange House less than an hour later to find Henry ensconced in the kitchen, a large sandwich in his hands and a mess all over the worktop.

'Hello,' he said, through a mouthful, as I bundled packets of ham and cheese and half a tomato back into the fridge. Then, 'I was going to do that.'

'No time,' I said, wiping a cloth over the surface I'd just cleared before rinsing it out under the tap. 'Are you done with that?' I swiped the mug from beside him before he could answer and tipped the dregs of his coffee into the sink.

'Where's the fire?' he asked, more bemused than annoyed.

I didn't answer, instead heading out through the open back door to the nearest flower bed, where I snatched up a handful of wild berry echinacea. Back in the kitchen, I fetched a vase from one of the cupboards, added water, hurriedly arranged the flowers, then took it out and placed it on a low table near the bottom of the stairs.

Henry followed me out, still holding his sandwich.

'What are you . . . What's going on?'

'Is your bed made?'

'Eh?' He gawped at me.

'The bed, in the spare room, is it made?'

'No, but—'

I left Henry mid-sentence, racing up the stairs two at a time, tidying first his room before venturing, albeit more reluctantly, into Luke's lair. I needn't have worried, however, because aside from a rolled-up pair of socks under the chest of drawers, there was little out of place. Luke was notoriously slovenly, so I had Eliza to thank. The master bedroom was immaculately clean, cushions arranged just so, and shutters open to show off the view of the mountains. Having given the en suite a cursory glance, I hurried back out on to the landing and straight into Henry.

'There's mustard on your T-shirt,' I told him, and he frowned.

'So?'

'I'm just saying.'

'Is the king on his way over for a cream tea?'

'What? No.'

'You're behaving as though he might be.'

'I just want the place to look nice.'

'Where's Luke?' he asked, one hand propped on the banister.

'I left him in Alcúdia with Eliza.'

'Is he OK?'

'He's fine. Not happy, apparently, but definitely not doing drugs, so that's something.'

'You're doing that thing where you talk in riddles,' he said.

'I need to get past.'

I tried to go around him, but Henry wasn't budging. On the wall behind him there was a framed photo of us, taken when Luke was around six. We were on Antonio's old boat, the smaller one he'd used mainly for fishing, and Luke looked solemn in his lifejacket, bottom lip protruding. He'd still yet to master the art of smiling for the camera.

'We need to talk,' Henry said, his tone switching down a gear.

'About your dad?' I replied, doing my best not to let my frustration show. 'Did you speak to him? Is he all right?'

'No, and yes, and I'm not sure, but I think so.'

'Right, yes, good,' I murmured, my mind on other, more pressing matters. Aim for three o'clock was what I'd told Malcolm and Mags – but what was the time now? Henry wasn't wearing a watch and I'd left my phone downstairs, but there was a clock in our bedroom.

'Where are you going now?' he called, as I retreated along the corridor.

Ten to three. I still had to check the downstairs loo.

'Violet, for pity's sake.'

He was in the doorway, blocking my exit, hands raised as if about to reach for me. I became suddenly aware of the bed – *our bed* – looming large only metres away. When I woke in the night, I often reached out in the hope he'd be there, my subconscious still trapped in the version of my life I hadn't burned to the ground.

Taking a few steps backwards, I pressed my hand to my chest, felt the pounding of my heart, too hard, too frantic, and sat down heavily on the edge of the bed.

'I really don't have time to talk right now,' I said in a small voice.

'There's always time to—' he began, only to be interrupted by a loud knocking.

They were early. Having moved aside to let me pass, Henry fell into step behind me as I raced towards the front door.

'Hello,' I said cheerfully, ushering our potential buyers inside. 'This is my ... Henry. Henry, this is Malcolm and Mags. They're looking for a house in Pollença and, well, we're looking to sell one.'

Malcolm offered his hand and gave a stoic Henry's a vigorous shake. 'We've only seen the front and we're huge fans already,' he said.

Mags, who was wearing a very new-looking sun hat complete with green gingham bow, went one step further than her husband by greeting me with a hug.

'The citrus trees, the wrought-iron fences, that turret,' she enthused. 'It's all magical.'

'Come through.' I flapped a hand in the general direction of the lounge, letting them go in ahead of me. 'It's a bit bare in there because I've been clearing everything out, but you'll see that it's a good size.'

Mags went into ecstasies over the terracotta floor tiles, while Malcolm fired questions at us about wiring, TV aerials, and how good the Wi-Fi signal was.

'Hoping to install a virtual golf room – can't neglect the old swing practice.'

Henry answered most enquiries in a short, achingly stiff manner, all the time trying desperately to catch my eye over their heads. I ignored him.

'We'd need to do a fair bit in here,' Mags said, when we trooped into the kitchen. 'All this wood feels slightly oppressive, don't you think, Malc? Was it like this when you moved in?'

'It wasn't much more than a shell when we moved in,' Henry said. 'I built all these cabinets.'

Mags turned very pink. 'Oh, I see. Well, it's very nice. The blue reminds me of the sea. It's just not my style, that's all.' She tittered. 'I prefer something a little shinier.'

'I bet you do,' muttered Henry.

'Carpenter by trade, are you?' enquired Malcolm, noticing Henry's tatty overalls and heavy boots for presumably the first time.

'Builder, joiner, restorer, electrician, plumber,' I told them. 'Henry can do anything.'

'Except make things shiny,' he intoned.

Mags started to giggle nervously. 'Gosh, I really didn't mean to offend. It's just been such an exciting day, meeting Violet completely by chance when we'd almost given up hope, coming here and discovering your incredible home. I mean, how can you bear to part with it? I don't think I ever could.'

'That's a very good question,' said Henry. 'Violet, do you want to take this one?'

'Why don't I show you the garden?' I blustered, practically pushing them out of the back door. 'Help yourself to lemons!' I trilled, waving as they took the steps down from the upper patio. 'I'll make us some refreshments.'

'What the hell, Violet?'

Henry, I realised, was seething.

'What?' I replied, extracting a bottle of white wine from the fridge. There was only enough left for one glass, so I'd have to top them up with sparkling water. 'We needed a buyer, I found us one.'

'And invited them here without even asking me?'

'It all happened really fast. They were keen to see it, and I thought, why not? We're not exactly inundated with offers.'

'That's because it's not on the market yet.'

My hand shook as I poured the wine. 'But the advert— I saw it.'

'I retracted it,' he said. 'I thought you knew that.'

'How could I have?'

'Vee,' he went on, choosing to ignore the question, 'this is mad. We can't sell La Casa Naranja to people like that.'

'Shh,' I hissed. 'They'll hear you.'

'I don't care.'

I slammed the bottle down on the worktop hard enough to make the glasses ring. 'What do you want from me?'

'Me?' he exclaimed. 'I want us to discuss this properly, like adults.'

'It's a bit late for that,' I snapped, turning my back on him, and ferrying the drinks outside.

Mags was on the patio. 'Thank you.' She accepted the watered-down wine and took a sip, recoiling slightly but recovering well. 'Malc is busy scrutinising your tomato plants.'

'They come free with the house.'

She smiled. 'It really is lovely. Can I ask what kind of price you were thinking?'

A big question: one I'd thought about endlessly but had no definitive answer for.

'We'd have to seek advice on that score,' I said. 'But it will be in line with the market.'

'So, around the two-mill mark?'

Two million euros.

The ground seemed to slant away from me.

'Like I said, we still need to work out the specific details.'

'Well, do make sure you let us know ASAP,' she said breezily. 'Early birds.'

I wasn't sure if I relished the idea of this house, nor Henry and I, as worms that Mags and Malcolm hoped to gobble. But then again, if we had to let it go, why not simply sell to the highest bidder and to hell with what came next?

From inside the kitchen, I heard the fridge door open and a hiss as Henry opened a can of beer.

'Did you have any other questions?' I asked, as Malcolm trotted up the patio steps.

'I did want to ask you something,' said Mags conspiratorially. 'About your ... husband, is he?' She leaned in, and though I feared what was coming, I did nothing to stop it. The door behind us opened a crack, Henry emerging just as Mags uttered the words: 'What on earth happened to the poor man's face?'

25

Violet

'Henry, wait!'

He didn't wait. Instead, he slammed his way out of the house with such ferocity that I feared all the windows would shatter.

'I need to go after him,' I said to a decidedly scandalised Mags and Malcolm. 'Just leave your contact details on the side and close the door behind you when you go.'

While I didn't exactly relish the idea of two strangers poking around unchaperoned, I was more fearful of the state Henry would work himself into if left alone to brood.

Hurrying out across the front garden, I got on to the street beyond just in time to see him reach the corner and hesitate for a moment before heading uphill, away from the town. There was a spot he liked to go, not far from El Calvari chapel, where a grove of olive trees stood like guards against the hillside. Deep at its heart was a clearing, a small pocket where you could lie flat on the ground and stare up at the sky.

'You found my hiding place,' Henry said, not ten minutes later, half turning as I approached. He was sitting cross-legged on the ground, the can of beer nestled in one of his discarded boots.

'I'd have known my way to it blindfolded,' I said, ignoring the voice in my head that urged me to kneel down behind him, wrap my arms around him, pull him close.

'If you want this place to stay a secret, you have to stop telling people about it.'

Henry grunted. 'You're the only one I've told.'

My mind strayed unbidden to the woman I'd seen him with, the relief at knowing he hadn't yet shared this place with her was palpable.

'Can I sit?'

'Knock yourself out.'

'You'd probably prefer that.'

He took a swig of beer and eyed me with disdain. 'Then I'd have to carry you back up the hill, and between you and me, I'm not sure I've got the strength – not after a morning spent propping up roof joists.'

'You need an apprentice.'

I regretted the comment as soon as I'd made it. Henry had taken on an apprentice, a young lad, Barney, from a college local to us in Cambridge, who'd found the education system tricky to navigate. One of the many support networks we tried and hopelessly failed to get Luke to engage with put us in touch with him, and Henry had offered him a slot on his team shortly afterwards. Of course, that had all fallen into disarray the summer before last, and though House-a-Home had continued to limp along, fulfilling pre-booked projects using temporary staffers, losing his mentor had come as a huge blow to Barney. Upon learning that Henry planned to stay in Mallorca indefinitely, he had quit and was now working in a pub. I'd seen him there one day by chance, during a leaving drinks for a colleague at the estate agency, and had been shocked by how deflated he was, how sad and small.

Henry must have been thinking about Barney as well, but for whatever reason – guilt, perhaps – he didn't mention him. Instead, he just shook his head.

'I'm sorry,' I said, arranging myself quietly on the ground next to him.

'For?'

'For not warning you about Malcolm and Mags.'

Henry made a gesture of acknowledgement.

'And I know they're a bit –' I looked sideways at him – 'much, but Mags mentioned two million euros to me as if it was nothing. Two million, Henry – think what that would do for Luke's future – we'd be able to set him up in his own place, mortgage-free. Remove all the additional stress from his life.'

He considered this, taking a long drink of beer to buy himself some time.

'Is that really what's best for him? What he wants?'

'Isn't a home and a stress-free life what everyone wants?'

Henry shrugged.

'Have you ever asked him?'

'Have you?'

I sighed. 'Why must we always do this, Henry? Play this game of tug of war with our son as the rope?'

He dropped his chin to his chest. 'I don't know.'

'I want what's best for him. It's all I've ever wanted.'

'And you think I don't?'

'No.' I let out a bleat of frustration. 'I just wish our ideas of what was best for him were aligned. They used to be, when he was little, remember?'

Henry picked at a spot of dried paint on his overalls. 'I always imagined that Luke would inherit La Casa Naranja one day,' he said. 'I wanted to hand over the key to him, just like my father did for me.'

We had discussed this precise scenario many times, the first being not long after Luke was born, when my parents gave me a lump sum to ensure my name was added to the deed. 'An early inheritance,' my dad had called it, and Henry, who'd been considering giving the house up due to spiralling costs, had been only too happy to accept. He had always thought of it as our home, he'd said. All the money did was make it official. We both wanted it to stay in our family – but that had been before.

'You were the one who listed the house,' I said quietly.

He grimaced. 'I know. I was angry when I did that.'

'Are you still angry?'

I willed him to look at me, but he didn't. Couldn't.

'I'm sad, Vee.'

I felt myself crumple. 'Like father, like son,' I said. 'Eliza told me earlier that Luke is sad as well. I guess that makes three of—'

'Why don't we wait?' he said, suddenly hopeful. 'Hold on to the house until Luke has finished his degree at least?'

I shook my head, cringing as he threw up an exasperated hand.

'Why not, Vee? He's a student – he doesn't need a bloody house of his own yet. He doesn't even know what he wants to do, where he wants to live, who he even is.'

'That's all very well,' I said, staring not at him but at the dry earth. 'But the fact remains that the house is our only shared asset. If you still want to get a divorce, we need to split everything, and that means selling.'

'Shared asset.' He practically spat the words at me. 'You sound like a lawyer bot.'

I remained silent while Henry raked through the ground with his fingers, stoic in the midst of his agitation.

'Do you not think you've taken enough away from me already?'

I took a deep breath.

'Why are you so desperate to sell all of a sudden?' he persisted. 'Why now?'

'I live in my mother's house,' I said stonily. 'I sleep in my childhood bedroom.'

'So, move out.'

I laughed at that, but without humour. 'Have you any idea what it costs to rent a place in Cambridge? A house with enough space for Luke, should he need it? I can't very well go into a flat share with a load of students. And work is . . .' I trailed off, unwilling to admit I'd all but been sacked. He thought so little of me already.

'If it's just money you need, I can help. The business can give you a loan.'

A torrent of self-loathing surged through me. 'I don't want to rely on handouts from you any more, Henry; I want my own money in the bank, and to be able to make a bloody decision about what to buy without having to run it past you – or anyone else. I want some bloody autonomy.'

Rather than dismiss me, Henry listened, his jaw working as cogs turned in his mind. I found it astounding that he was still willing to be receptive to me at all, and my body slackened into despair as I considered yet again what I'd lost, who I had hurt. I hated that there was a barrier between us; I hated that I was no longer allowed to touch him, comfort him, love him.

'I'm not like you,' I mumbled. 'I don't have a career, or a skill set. I never got the chance to get good at anything.'

'You do have skills,' he countered, draining the last of his beer. Froth spilled out from the can over his stubbled chin, and he wiped the back of his hand across his face. I studied him for a moment, saw how the scarred flesh had pulled the left side of his mouth down in a permanent scowl, a fixed point of sorrow I was helpless to cure.

'I never wanted to stop working for our business,' I said, needing him to know, wanting him to understand.

'House-a-Home, it was everything to me. Having to leave and go back to being trapped at home all the time broke my heart, but it wasn't like I had any choice. There was never any question that I would be the one to make the biggest sacrifice.'

Henry's eyes were wide as he turned to face me. He looked genuinely shocked.

'Is that really how you remember it? Because what I recall is us not having a choice. I didn't want you to be stuck at home either, but one of us had to be out earning and you'd made it very clear to me many times over who the better parent was. Can you honestly sit here now, Vee, and tell me that if I'd offered to be the one who spent ninety-nine per cent of their time with Luke, you'd have been fine with it?'

I could not, as he well knew.

'Jesus, Vee, I know it was hard for you, but it was tough for me, too.'

If I spoke, I would cry, and I didn't want to cry again, not in front of him, not when he had suffered so much pain because of me. I looked around us at the olive trees, each so strong and salient, and wished I could be more like them; weather every storm and come back stronger; grow a new branch and put out leaves every spring, no matter how harsh the winter had been. But unlike the roots surrounding us, which were grounded deep in the earth, I had rooted myself in the love I shared with Henry, and that had all been ripped apart.

'It's still hard for me,' I said quietly. 'I feel like he's a missile and I'm the target he's locked onto, and all the time, I'm waiting for him to be fired.'

Henry nodded grimly. 'I know what you mean.'

But did he really? Had he ever had a physical reaction to our son? An ache that brought him almost to his knees?

'You asked me just now if I've talked to him as if that's an easy thing to do. Haven't you noticed how Luke hates any mention of the future? Any modicum of pressure to make decisions. What if he's never able to tell us what he wants? Do we hold on to the house and continue to struggle financially because there's a chance he might one day want it?'

'I'm not struggling financially.' Henry sounded nonplussed.

I clenched my teeth. 'No, of course you're not, because you live here, rent free, and you work full time. I don't have those options; I have to stay in England and—'

'Why?' he interrupted. 'Why do you have to stay there?'

I looked at him sharply. 'Because our son is there. He might be at university, but he still needs a bolthole in case he . . . in case things go wrong; he still needs to know that one of us can be there in a few hours.'

'He needs those things?' countered Henry. 'Or you do?'

'For god's sake, he's only nineteen. It wasn't so long ago that we couldn't leave him unsupervised at all in case he harmed himself.'

The truth landed hard, and I saw the flicker of hurt as it passed across Henry's scarred face. The sun had moved as we'd been talking, and the clearing was bathed in warm light. I could hear the chirp of cicadas in the trees, the faintest whisper of wind.

'I'll do a deal with you.' Henry cleared his throat. 'I'll agree to sell La Casa Naranja to those frightful people if you tell me the real reason you want me to.'

I sat up a fraction straighter, wariness making the hairs stand up on the back of my neck.

'You know why. I just told you why.'

'No, you told me lawyer speak, but I know there's something you're keeping from me – another piece to this puzzle that you won't –' he frowned – 'or can't tell me.'

I started to argue only to be silenced by a look.

'I know you, Vee,' he said. 'I've known you a long time. You can be honest with me.'

I shook my head, unable to speak, defiantly not meeting his eye.

'Whatever it is,' he said, inching closer to me, 'we can sort it.'

There was a hole in one of his socks. I could see the nail of his big toe, smooth and pink with health, and burned with the need to touch it – touch him. When I didn't answer, Henry raised a gentle hand to my cheek. A long moment passed where neither of us spoke or moved, and then, very slowly, I edged away from him.

'There's no big secret,' I said, and the lie was like acid in my throat. 'I only want the money I'm entitled to so I can move on with my life and you can move on with yours.'

'And that's what you want, is it?' he said. 'To move on?'

It was the very last thing I wanted.

'It's not as if I have a choice, is it?'

This was his chance to save us; find a way to forgive me. *Say yes, Henry. Please say yes.*

'No,' he said, calm and solemn. 'I guess you don't.'

26

Henry

Later, Henry would tell people it was the incident with the digger that did it. Before that day, he'd only had an inkling that his son was not like most children, an inherent sense that there were fissures below the surface of his serious little boy.

Violet had planned every stage of their garden with meticulous detail, working out what to plant, consulting Ynes on where to separate beds, and figuring out how to ensure that everything thrived during the months that she wouldn't be there to tend to it herself. Everything had been sketched out in her careful hand, and she'd come to Henry for help with the bigger structural jobs, such as adding steps and creating a rockery. For the first week of their summer sojourn on the island, she'd painstakingly uprooted and stored every plant she wanted to save, digging deep into the ground to ensure fragile roots weren't damaged, and unravelling their delicate strands with her fingers. Any robust weeds or flowers that were at the end of their natural life, she allowed Luke to pick. He had inherited his mother's love of the outdoors as well as her treasured flower press, which he was clutching as Henry watched him come cautiously out through the back door. Every other child of five he encountered seemed to travel at a set speed of full throttle, often cannoning off whoever or whatever happened to be in their way. Luke was different, he was guarded, and would shy away from any kind of game that incorporated a surprise or chase element.

'What's that?' he asked now, in the high, imperious tone that reminded Henry of Violet's mother. His son was pointing towards the small excavator that had just been delivered, its angled arm and clawed base raised in preparation for work.

'That's a digger,' Henry told him, remembering what Luke's nursery teacher had told them about explaining how things worked. Luke, she'd said earnestly, worried less when he understood better, and so Henry took the time to talk the little boy through exactly what the machine would do, and why he had decided to use it in the garden.

'Would you like to ride on it with me?' he asked.

Luke squinted up at him, gaze watchful below his tangle of dark hair. 'I'm not sure.'

'It'll be fun. You can sit on my knee.'

Luke shook his head.

'Please,' Henry cajoled. 'I think you'll like it when you see what it can do. Mummy will be so proud of you,' he added, knowing this would go a long way towards convincing his son to at least consider saying yes. They may not have much in common, the two of them, but basking in the glow of Violet's adoration was very much a shared desire.

'Come on,' he said, holding out a hand for Luke to take. 'We'll get in the digger and call up to Mummy, so she sees us out of the window. You can wave to her.'

After what felt like an interminably long pause, Luke relented. Putting his flower press down carefully on the low wall of the patio, he took Henry's outstretched hand and allowed himself to be led down the steps towards the digger. Henry lifted him up into the seat, wriggled the keys out of his shorts pocket, then climbed in behind.

'Ready?' he said.

Luke nodded obediently and, having done a quick final check, Henry fired up the digger's engine. It spluttered, rumbled, and then roared to life, the little cab vibrating as the starter motor whirred. Glancing up towards the house, Henry smiled as he saw Violet's head appear at one of the upstairs windows, her expression one of delight.

'Look, Luke – there's Mummy. Why don't you give her a wave?'

But Luke didn't move. He was rigid, Henry realised, frozen in horror. Peering round, he saw the whites of his son's eyes, the pallor of his skin, the open slash of his mouth. Sensing that something terrible was about to happen, Henry made a grab for the keys – but he wasn't fast enough. Luke shot up and began to scream, his arms and legs thrashing as he writhed to be free. Henry took a fist to one eye, an elbow to the groin, bellowing with pain as he attempted to gain control of the hysterical child. He heard Violet shouting, then glimpsed a blur of red as she flew out through the back door towards them. Luke lurched forwards, his head narrowly avoiding a large lever and hitting the panel of buttons beside it with a sickening crunch. The digger continued to tremble as the engine growled.

Violet wrenched open the door of the cab, her hands grasping for her son.

'Turn it off, for god's sake,' she cried.

'I'm trying!' Henry yelled back, fear and guilt making him sound angrier than he felt. Luke was still in a state, and as Violet stepped up to try and reach him, she received a punch in the throat.

'Hold him,' she croaked, blinking back tears. Henry did as instructed; wrapping both his arms around Luke and clamping him as tightly as he dared against his body. He could feel the frantic racing of his son's heart, the heat of his anger, and felt close to tears himself. Violet was making soothing noises, her hands stroking Luke's hair. Henry met her eyes and saw his own fearful bewilderment reflected back.

'What were you thinking?' she hissed at him.

Henry released his grip a fraction and allowed Luke to slither out of his grasp. The boy's hands reached immediately for Violet, and gathering him up into her arms, she crooned, 'It's OK now, baby. Mummy's got you.'

Frustration was mounting inside Henry.

'I didn't force him,' he told her. 'I gave him the option. He wanted to have a go.'

Luke shook his head against his mother's shoulder.

'You can't coerce him into being like you,' Violet scolded. 'You know he doesn't like loud noises and rough games.'

'A digger is hardly a game—'

'You should have checked with me,' she insisted.

'But he wanted to,' Henry said again, and once more Luke defied him.

'Too loud,' he whined. 'Don't like it.'

Violet hugged him tighter. 'Don't worry, darling. You never have to hear it again.'

'And how's that going to work?' Henry exploded. 'We need it to get the garden done. Your garden!'

'We can do it without the digger.'

'Vee . . .'

'Fine. Then me and Luke will go to the beach instead. Would you like that, sweetie? We can take the buckets and spades?'

'How is this a good lesson, though?' Henry persisted, following Violet across the garden as she carried a still-whimpering Luke back to the house. 'You're just teaching him to run away from the things that's he's irrationally scared of.'

'You think we should lock him in there and tell him to put up and shut up, is that it?' she stormed.

'Now you're being ridiculous.'

Violet stopped at the bottom of the patio steps, and Henry moved in front of her. He was all set to continue their row until he took in the dark smudges under her eyes, the listlessness of her gaze, the concern that was etched across her features. All she was doing was trying to protect their child, and he was being cruel.

'Sorry,' he said, shame making him droop like one of Luke's picked flowers. 'I'm an idiot. You're right, I should have waited for you. I thought it would be a fun surprise.'

'We don't like surprises – remember?' Violet's tired smile indicated that by 'we', what she actually meant was 'Luke'. Henry had not forgotten; he should've known better than to push against a boundary firmly drawn.

'I'm sorry, little Mister,' he said, crouching so he could look his son in the eye.

Luke turned his face away and buried it against Violet's chest.

'Did you hear that, baby? Daddy said he's sorry.'

Nothing. Not so much as a murmur. Luke may as well have hit him again, thought Henry. The pain of this was on a par with that.

'You two go,' he told Violet, levering himself back to a standing position. 'Head to the beach. I'll stay here and do everything I need to with the digger, and make sure it's gone before you get back.'

'Thank you,' she said, beckoning for him to lean over so she could press her lips briefly against his. 'And don't worry about Luke, I know just how to cheer him up.'

Henry stood and watched the two of them go, a mess of conflicting emotions tumbling inside him. But of all the things he felt in that moment, the one that struck him hardest was the relief.

He was glad that she had taken their son away because it offered him a break from the permeating, all-encompassing worry that had become such a stain on their lives. And no matter how vile he knew this made him, there was nothing Henry could do to deny it.

27

Violet

The scent of cooking onions roused me from my stress-induced stupor, and I pushed myself up into a sitting position. There was a dent in the pillow where I'd buried my face, and smears of mascara on the white cotton. Crossing into the en suite, I grimaced at my reflection in the mirror before using a wet tissue to wipe my eyes.

It smelled as if the onions were burning.

Picking up my phone as I left the room, I made my way downstairs, paused for a moment, then put the handset screen-side down on the hall table. The calls were becoming so frequent that the cursed thing had begun to feel like an enemy. Each time I picked it up, I was confronted by a new demand, another warning, a missed call, a voicemail instructing me to make a payment.

I had so far ignored all of them.

Feeling anxious was a state I'd long grown accustomed to, and rather than tackle this new set of problems head-on, I merely absorbed them. What were a few money issues against the mess I'd made of the rest of my life? Who cared about debt when I'd already lost most of the things, and people, I cared about?

Avoiding my mother's calls was a trickier prospect, though I'd managed to stall her by firing off a series of vague messages about 'showing buyers around' and 'speaking to lawyers'. If she believed I was doing something to better my situation, she'd worry less. Although in truth, of course, I was doing nothing. Henry and I had settled into an uneasy stalemate since he'd laid down his ultimatum, neither one of us mentioning the potential sale of the house or Mags and Malcolm, whose messages I'd also steadfastly ignored over the past two days. So many people needing so many answers from me, and I could offer nothing satisfactory to any of them.

'Something smells good,' I said, pushing open the kitchen door to find Luke and Eliza standing together by the stove. There was a large frying pan spitting away on the hob, the blackened remains of what were once edible onions welded to its surface.

'I think we may have the heat up too high,' said Eliza, in a careful tone that made me glance more closely at Luke, notice the rigid set of his jaw, the hardness in his eyes.

'It's fucked,' he snarled. 'It's all fucked.'

'I'm sure it's not,' I cajoled, as Eliza took an involuntary step backwards. So many of Luke's blow-ups began with something like this, an incidental mishap that most people would simply laugh off. The trick was not to exacerbate the problem whilst simultaneously acknowledging that his response was valid. I had described it to Henry once as walking a tightrope, telling him that 'as long as you focus on the end point, you'll get to the other side safely'. That was the theory, in any case.

'Onions are notoriously fond of burning,' I said, peering around him and down into the pan. 'What is it you're making?'

'Paella,' Eliza told me. 'Or trying to.'

I took in the pile of chopped tomatoes on the worktop, the jar of saffron and freshly plucked bay leaves.

'You know,' I said, 'if you really want to create an authentic Spanish paella, then it needs to be cooked outdoors, over an open fire.'

Luke switched his gloomy attention from the burnt onions to me.

'What?'

'You've seen how they do it down at the beach bars. Why don't we do the same? I'm sure between the three of us, we can cobble something together. It'll be fun.'

Luke chuntered. 'A fire? In here?'

'Well, in the garden preferably.'

He frowned, considering. 'All right.'

I experienced a whooshing sensation as the tension left my body.

'You two start,' Eliza said, unhooking her bag from the back of a chair. 'I need to pop out. We forgot garlic,' she said, gesturing to the heap of ingredients. 'I'm guessing that's pretty much a non-negotiable?'

'Correct,' I said. 'It's one of the essential components of the *sofrito*. No *sofrito*, no paella. And this,' I added, taking the frying pan off the hob, and marching it over to the bin, 'is far too small for our culinary needs. We're going to need a bigger dish.'

Having scraped off the offending onions and given Eliza a list of all the other bits and pieces we'd need, Luke and I ventured outside to Henry's tiny work shed, where we discovered an old wok with a broken handle, and a rusty metal tripod we could balance it on. Having picked a spot in the overgrown vegetable patch a good distance away from any trees, I set about clearing a large patch of earth while Luke lumbered off to gather some stones, which he arranged in a circle on the ground. As luck would have it, Henry had already cut and stacked a decent amount of firewood for the indoor wood burner, and there was a box of kindling sticks in his shed.

'You can do the honours,' I said to Luke, passing across a box of matches. His fingers shook as he readied one against the strip, uncertain suddenly, his eyes flicking to mine in search of reassurance. I nodded.

'Go on. If the house burns down, it's on me.'

He gave a snort of laughter. 'You're weird, Mum.'

It was one of the kindest things he had ever said to me.

With the pan beginning to warm on the flames, I chopped more onions while Luke tackled the peppers.

'Why do you hold them like that?' he asked, as I curled the tips of my fingers out of harm's way.

'Because knuckles are harder to nick with the knife,' I explained, and was touched when he moved his own hand into the same position. Despite the heat of the late afternoon, it felt like a comfort to have the flames crackling so close to us. There was something so evocative about the sound, and I found myself relaxing into the simple pattern of slicing and dicing. Luke, too, appeared to have mellowed, his head down and mouth slightly open. I loved him in these quiet moments, when I could allow myself to believe there was peace inside him, even if it was a fleeting glimpse.

'Right, time for oil,' I said, pouring a generous glug directly from the bottle into the wok, which fizzed appreciatively.

'Onions now?' asked Luke, but I shook my head.

'Give it a few minutes to warm through first, then we'll need to keep an eye on them, stirring continually to make sure they don't stick.'

Luke shuffled along the wall on his bottom until his trainer-clad feet were level with the edge of the makeshift firepit.

'Since when did you know so much about cooking?'

I cocked my head to one side, raised my eyebrows. 'Well, I like to think preparing dinner for you and Dad every night for years on the trot taught me a few things.'

He considered this, the implication behind it perhaps occurring to him for the first time, as a moment later, he asked, 'Did it ever bother you? You know, doing everything, around the house and stuff?'

The oil was beginning to smoke, so I tossed in the onions.

'Your dad did his share of household chores,' I said. 'But he was often held up at work, so it usually made more sense for me to take care of dinner. I didn't mind.'

I had minded him being late, though. I had minded that very much.

'Did you ever consider being a chef?'

I was so surprised by the question that I laughed.

Luke looked at me nonplussed. 'Then what did you want to be when you were a kid?'

'A world-class gymnast. Here, give the onions a stir.'

'Ha ha,' he intoned, as I passed him a large wooden spoon.

'Seriously. I was pretty good, I'll have you know. Nowadays, I'd have more chance of sprouting wings and flying to the moon than I would have of executing the perfect backflip, but when I was a teenager, there was no stopping me.'

'What did stop you?' he asked, as the pan spluttered and smoked.

'Oh, I grew out of it,' I said casually. 'It was never going to be a real job.'

'Grew out of it. By that, do you mean got pregnant with me?'

'Can't it be both? Obviously, it's not a good idea to do cartwheels when you're expecting a baby.'

Luke didn't smile. 'Why didn't you go back to it after I was born?'

He was focused on his task, eyes not on me but the food, and though his tone was casual enough, I suspected this was not a conversation he was a hundred per cent comfortable having. This desire he had to delve into my past, to understand who I was as a person rather than simply his mum, was new. We were both navigating uncharted territory here, and treading cautiously was a must.

'I suppose I could've tried again once you went to nursery, but by that time we'd started planning the business. I was always far more passionate about plants than I was about being a gymnast anyway.'

'And what about now?' he asked. 'Do you really enjoy working at the estate agent?'

I had yet to tell him that I'd lost my job, and for a moment, I fumbled for something to say that wasn't an outright lie. 'I don't hate it,' I said slowly. 'But ideally, I'd prefer to be doing something else.'

'Like what?'

'Like what I used to do, designing and maintaining gardens for people.'

'That made you happy?'

'It did, yes – the happiest.'

And there it was. Simple, painful, truth.

'So, do it again,' he insisted. 'I know you and Dad dissolved the business pretty much – he told me. But you could start up something new – a venture that was all your own.'

I was shaking my head.

'Why not?'

'It's not the right time.'

It was a cop-out answer, and Luke knew it.

'I still don't get it,' he muttered, going back to his stirring. 'You and Dad. I don't get what went wrong. You used to be so –' he waved a hand around, searching for the right word – 'close. Like, finish each other's sentences close. When me and Eliza started doing that, I knew she was, like, the one. Because it reminded me of you and Dad.'

He raised his eyes, catching mine before I had time to glance away, and for a moment we were locked together, each willing the other to say more, share more, open up more, but neither of us had time. The back door had opened, Eliza emerging, followed closely by Henry, the latter's eyes widening when he realised what we were doing.

'You're just in time,' I called by way of greeting. 'These onions are crying out for some garlic.'

Eliza skipped down the steps to join us, a carrier bag in her hand that she swung towards Luke. He stood up to kiss her, the fingers not holding the wooden spoon mussing up her rose-coloured hair. A warmth stole through me at the sight of them, and I saw the same softening in Henry's features, too, as he made his way more slowly towards us.

There was something about being in this garden with him, in almost the exact spot we had seen each other for the very first time, that calmed me. If the scene was being shot for a movie, it would be in soft focus, the camera zooming in to capture the gentle pattern of leaves stirred by breeze, the lackadaisical path of a bee as it moved from one bloom to the next, fuzzy legs turned a dusty yellow by pollen. It represented more than simply the start of our love story; it had become our refuge, the place we found one another again in the hardest times, each soothed by the familiar scents, the uncompromising sturdiness of the trees, the heat of perpetual sunshine. What little faith I had that fate would look kindly upon us again was peaked out here. I found that I could almost believe it.

'What do I do with this, Mum?' Luke asked, extracting a bulb of garlic, and peering at it as one might a tarantula.

'Remove the cloves but leave them in their skins,' I told him. 'We'll toss them in with the onions, get a lid on the pan, and give them ten minutes or so to roast up nicely.'

'Yes, chef,' he quipped.

'Will you join us?' I said to Henry, unable to stop the cadence of my voice rising.

'*It's a good day,*' *I wanted to tell him. A good Luke day. Don't miss it.*

I read his answer in his features before he'd even uttered a single word.

'I have a . . . thing. It's . . . I can stay for a bit. I really just came out here to give you this.'

I stared at the phone in his hand. My phone.

'It was ringing when I got in, and there are some messages, I think. Don't worry,' he added, as I took the handset from him. 'I didn't read them or anything.'

There was only one message, and it was from Juan: *Are you available tonight?*

This could only mean one thing.

I can be, I typed back, rapidly calculating how much time it would take to finish the paella, eat it, and not seem as if I was being rude by slipping away.

Meet me at U Gallet, 10pm. I have some information for you.

'Everything OK?' asked Henry. 'You look—'

'Fine,' I interrupted. 'All fine.'

'You're not going to say who it was?'

'Oh, you know,' I said, feigning indifference as I slipped the phone into my pocket. 'It was nothing. Nobody.'

28

Violet

The venue Juan had chosen for our meeting was one of the busiest in Pollença, and I had to practically fight my way through a throng of drinkers in order to reach him.

'I arrived early,' he said, when I asked how he'd managed to secure us a space, and patted the cushion beside him. U Gallet was cave-like inside, with mottled stone walls, candles in jars on the tables, and a long, underlit bar. Juan had taken the liberty of ordering us a bottle of Tempranillo, and he poured some out as I shrugged off my cardigan. I'd felt bad for sneaking out of the house without telling Luke where I was going, though he and Eliza had sloped off upstairs with his laptop as soon as we were done eating, saying something about watching a film. I hadn't needed to worry about what to tell Henry, because having hung around long enough to politely sample our actually very successful paella, he'd made his excuses and headed off into the night.

'*Graçias,*' I said to Juan, as he clinked his glass against mine. My fingers were clammy, and the stem of the glass slipped as I went to take a sip, splashing blood-red droplets of wine against my bare thigh.

'Ach.' Juan licked a finger and dabbed at the spillage. There had been a time, not all that long ago, when I'd have thought nothing of such a gesture, but tonight his casual pawing of me was discomforting.

'How are you?' he asked, as I readjusted my position to put a few extra inches between us.

'Fine,' I lied, putting down my glass. 'Why did you want to see me? Is it about Henry? Did you find out the name of the woman he's seeing?'

The corners of Juan's mouth drooped. 'Can we not have a drink first? We are old friends after all.'

I took three large gulps of wine in quick succession. 'See,' I said. 'Drinking.'

Juan chuckled good-naturedly. 'Always with the jokes,' he observed. 'You are still as funny as I remember.'

'And you're still just as pleased with yourself.'

'Oof!' He put a hand to his chest as if I'd struck him. 'You are angry with me.'

He hadn't posed it as a question, but it was obvious he was expecting an answer.

'I'm not angry,' I said, mellowing a little as the wine began to take effect. 'At least, not with you, not any more.'

'Ah,' he said, grin widening, 'now, I think we are getting to the egg of the pudding. You are not angry with me, which means that you must be angry with—'

'Nobody,' I said, before he could say Henry's name. 'Except myself, perhaps.'

He put a hand on my arm, and I moved it away, not looking at him. The wine was going down too easily, and though I knew it was foolish to keep drinking, and that turning to alcohol in times of stress was becoming a concerning habit of mine, I said nothing when Juan topped up my glass. A young Spanish couple were trying to cram themselves into a vacated seat beside me, but there was barely room for one person, let alone two.

'Watch it,' I snapped, as the girl trod down hard on my sandalled foot; her apology drowned out by the bellow of her drunken boyfriend.

'Remind me why you chose this place again,' I grumbled, but Juan merely laughed.

'It reminds me of being young,' he said. 'Do you remember when we all used to come here together, Tomas playing with his toy cars and Luke with the colouring-in books?'

I smiled faintly. 'That was a long time ago.'

'Not so long.'

'Our boys are men now – Tomas is a father himself.'

'And Ana is an *abuela*,' he replied, sounding gleeful.

'How is Ana?' I asked.

Juan pulled a 'who cares' face.

'Don't you see her any more?'

'Not so much – she is in Palma, always with her friends. On the days that I go to visit Tomas and his family, she stays away from the house.'

'That must make you sad?' I pressed.

Juan reached for his wine and took a far more modest sip than the ones I'd been throwing back.

'Am I unhappy that my marriage is ended? *Sí*. Do I think that it could have been saved? No. Ana is better without me – we are both happier.'

'And you have no regrets? You wouldn't go back if you could, do everything differently?'

He shrugged. 'Some, perhaps. But altogether, no. You cannot change what has already happened, you can only try to learn from the foolish decisions you make.'

'Amen to that,' I drawled, raising my glass.

Juan got up to visit the bathroom, and afterwards I watched as he sauntered over to the bar, not mingling with the crowd of tourists but propping himself at the service end, where he leaned across and spoke genially to the bartender.

'Vi-o-let!' he shouted, so loudly that I cringed. 'Are you hungry?'

I shook my head, mouthing a clear 'no' across the room. I'd eaten more than enough of the paella to keep me full for days, if not weeks.

Juan returned to the table with two full shot glasses in hand.

'What are these?' I took one and sniffed it.

'Tequila,' he announced. 'So we can pretend that we are young again.'

'I refuse to drink to that,' I said, then made him laugh by tipping the lot down my throat. I knew it was reckless, that I was beginning to feel less inhibited by the second, but there was also something irresistible about being bad for once. Juan always had been a person who could tempt that side out in me.

'You were right,' I told him, leaning back against the wall as the barman put a plateful of assorted cheeses, meats, olives, and breadsticks down on the table in front of us. 'It's actually quite nice to feel young again, even if I will regret it in the morning.'

Juan plucked a grape from its stalk, and after a moment, I opened my mouth, letting him feed it to me.

'I think perhaps that you and I, we got old too quickly.'

'Having children will do that to you,' I replied. 'The day Luke was born, I aged at least fifteen years – how about you?'

'With Tomas? Twenty,' he proclaimed with mock solemnity. 'But do you ever imagine what your life would be like if you never had a child?'

'Of course,' I said, as he peeled off a slice of chorizo. 'I asked Henry that question once, but he refused to answer, said it was unhealthy to dwell on impossibility.'

Juan rolled his eyes. 'If everybody thought this way, nobody would play in the lottery.'

'True!'

'And many books and movies would not exist.'

I affected a shudder. 'Doesn't bear thinking about.'

'Maybe it is for the best that you and Henry . . .' He mimed snapping something in two.

'Why?' I said testily. 'Because he's a realist and I behave like an ostrich?'

For a moment, Juan looked confused, and I was forced to explain what I meant about burying my head in the sand. The moment he got it, he responded by laughing, but I found that I no longer could. We'd cycled back around to me being angry with myself, and my mood had soured accordingly.

'Henry is not the only man in the world,' Juan said, with slow emphasis. 'There are other men; a different choice for you.'

His hand settled on my knee, and I stared down at it, the noise of the bar a low hum that seemed to reverberate in the air around us. Queasiness churned in my stomach.

'Did you find out?' I asked. 'Who she is – the woman I saw with Henry.'

Juan gave a nod. '*Sí*. I know.'

I drew in a short, sharp breath. 'And?'

His hand was still on my knee, hot fingers pressing against my flesh. I stretched my leg further beneath the table, releasing myself from his grasp. Juan made a 'pfft' sound and moved his hand to the plate of food. I watched as he picked up a cube of Manchego that was dribbling in oil, not caring that I'd offended him.

'So, who is she?'

I tapped my foot against the floor, my frustration mounting as he took what I perceived to be an inordinately long time to finish the rest of the cheese. Only when the platter was empty save for a single, curved pepper, and Juan had dabbed a napkin to the corners of his mouth, did he finally deign to reply.

'Her name is Bo.'

'Bo? What kind of a name is Bo?'

'She is working at La Residencia, the big hotel in—'

'Deià, yes. I know where La Residencia is. I had my wedding there, remember?'

Juan raised an eyebrow.

'How did they meet? Is it serious? What does she do there? What is she like?'

He leaned away from me. 'She is there only a few months, organising events and things like this, but I don't know how she and Henry were introduced.'

I was about to launch into a second rant when I noticed someone waving at me from across the bar. It was Mags, I realised with a lurch, coming towards me with Malcolm not far behind.

'I need to go,' I said, standing up and clambering over Juan. 'Right now, I need to get out of here.'

The candle on the table was knocked flying, and the woman who'd trod on my foot shrieked as hot wax splattered across her legs. Keeping my head down, I ducked around the crowd, keeping half an eye on Mags and Malcolm to make sure I wasn't about to collide with them, before squeezing my way through to the bar. Juan had followed me, and I heard him protest loudly as I asked for the bill.

'Just let me,' I said, pressing my credit card against the machine. There were two short beeps, and the word 'declined' flashed up on the screen.

'That doesn't make sense,' I whined, as my heart plummeted down to my ankles. 'Let me try again.'

After a second failure, Juan reached over and used his own card, reassuring me not to worry as he ushered me towards the door. Hearing someone, presumably Mags, call my name, I grabbed his hand and towed him out into the street, urging him to hurry.

The night air was fresher than the fuggy warmth of U Gallet, and lights blazed at every window we passed. Instead of going back towards The Orange House, I dragged Juan towards the main square, taking each cobbled lane at a run. It was so ridiculous, *we* were so ridiculous, that I was overcome by a helpless desire to laugh, eventually coming to a breathless stop in a narrow alleyway stacked with plant pots. Juan leant against the opposite wall, far less puffed out than me. The hot sting of humiliation prevented me from meeting his eye, even when he reached across to cup my cheek.

'You are beautiful, Zorra,' he said, and when I didn't immediately pull away, he stepped closer. Zorra was the Spanish word for 'vixen'; only once before had he referred to me by that name.

'Don't,' I said, but either he didn't hear me, or he chose not to listen. At the precise moment it dawned on me that he was going to try and kiss me, and before I had time to react, a shadow fell across us and two people came into view at the end of the alley. One of them was a woman with long dark hair, impossibly slim legs, and a furious expression.

The other one was Henry.

29

Henry

Twelve Summers Ago

Four years to the day since he had got down on one knee in only his pants and asked Violet to marry him, Henry found himself waiting for her beneath a gazebo festooned with flowers. She was already his wife – they had taken care of that at a registry office in Cambridge two weeks ago – but privately Violet had confessed that she wouldn't feel properly married until they'd exchanged vows in Mallorca, and Henry had smiled widely at that, because he couldn't have agreed with the sentiment more.

Thanks in large part to the persuasive power of his father, they had secured La Residencia hotel in Deià for both the ceremony and the party that would follow, and Antonio had taken it upon himself to invite almost everyone he'd ever met – or so it seemed to Henry. He cast an eye over the rows of guests, searching the faces for those he recognised. Ynes, who had helped Violet with all the floral arrangements, gave him a discreet thumbs-up from underneath a startingly enormous hat, while Ana smiled thinly from her seat between Juan and Tomas, the latter of whom was busy devouring a rocket-shaped ice lolly. Luke was inside with Violet's mother, the plan being to bring him out only at the very last minute. They couldn't be sure how he would react to so many strangers, although when Granny Lupton had suggested that perhaps it was wiser for her to take him somewhere else for the day instead, both Violet and Henry had refused. They were his mum and dad, and it was important to them that Luke be there to witness such a special moment in his parents' lives.

There had been troubling incidences at school, reports of Luke snatching things from other children and once even biting another boy; wandering off during group story time and refusing to engage in group activities. Noise sensitivity was still an issue, but they were managing it with child-size ear defenders, and Luke knew he could ask to sit in the 'quiet room' if he felt overwhelmed by the chaos of the classroom. This he did, more frequently than his teacher deemed strictly necessary, often taking a stack of books with him, or whatever art tools were his current favourite. Crayons had rapidly been rejected in favour of pastels, and there had been a mildly concerning black felt-tip pen phase, during which he'd drawn only large human heads with crocodiles inside them – but lately, he'd switched to simple pencils and paper. Violet had encouraged him to draw a card for Henry's birthday the previous month, and she'd later told him that Luke had mulled carefully about what he was going to do for days before he started. The resulting picture, of La Casa Naranja complete with turret, stray cat, and orange tree, had been framed and hung in pride of place on their bedroom wall. Every time Henry looked at it, he found a new and thoughtful detail to admire. For all his problems, nobody could deny the fact that his son was talented.

'This is his way of telling you he loves you,' Violet had explained. 'He finds pictures easier than words.'

As far as Henry was concerned, there could have been no greater gift.

Hearing footsteps, he turned to see his father approaching. Antonio had dressed to impress in a pale cream linen suit and emerald silk shirt, which was open at the neck to reveal a thatch of wiry dark hair and a thick, gold chain.

'My stupid giant boy,' he said affectionately, clapping Henry hard on the back.

'*Hola*, Papá.'

'Are you happy?' Antonio asked, beaming with pride as he surveyed the wedding that he had so generously helped fund. Henry assured him he very much was.

'A house, a business, a son, and soon a wife – you have done well, *gran chico*.'

Antonio rarely, if ever, praised Henry, and he was taken aback by the genuine pride in the older man's tone. Their relationship had always been one of gentle goading from Antonio's side and festering resentment on Henry's, so it made a pleasant change when they were able to converse on a more adult level.

Henry checked his watch. Violet was running late.

Antonio made a show of standing on his tiptoes to readjust his son's bow tie, and several guests laughed in appreciation. Having batted him away, Henry squinted along the make-shift aisle and saw the reflection of the sun in the hotel's glass patio doors as they were pushed open. This must be it, he thought with a thrill, she was on her way to him at last. Antonio had caught on, too, and having given his son's grey morning coat a final readjustment, he hurried down the steps and took his seat in the front row.

Henry heard the bells in the village of Deià chime as the music began – 'And Roses And Roses' by Astrud Gilberto – his whole body tingling with the thought of seeing Violet in her dress. She hadn't worn it to the registry office in Cambridge in the end, telling him she preferred to save it for today, and while Henry had thought she looked lovely in the cream trouser suit from Next, he knew he was about to be bowled over, and grinned as he heard several gasps float up from the guests.

But then, a murmuring sound filtered through the banks of chairs, one that caused the hairs to stand up on the back of his neck. Something was wrong. Turning, Henry saw his father-in-law Christopher approaching, his cheeks aflame and suit crumpled.

'What is it?' Henry met him halfway along the aisle. 'What's happened?'

'I can't . . . we can't,' Christopher was barely coherent. 'We need help.'

From the corner of his eye, Henry saw Ynes get to her feet and make her way along the row, apologising in Spanish as she stepped on the toes of guests in her rush to reach him. Antonio, too, had risen, the smile that had been fixed falling as he reached the assembled group. They were all talking at once, and Henry couldn't hear, couldn't think.

He looked at Christopher. 'Take me to them.'

The older man led the way towards the hotel, and Henry followed, ignoring the expressions of enquiry on the faces of those he passed. Antonio was only a few paces behind, Ynes at his side, her hat removed and clutched in both hands. They clattered up the steps and in through the open door, Henry's polished brogues tapping loudly against the polished wooden floor of the lobby. A bank of sofas was arranged in a semicircle not far from the reception desk, a vase full of lilies making the air smell pungent and sweet. He never had cared for the scent, found it cloying, and after today, he would not be able to bear it.

Violet's mother, Eleanor, was kneeling on the floor, her face scarlet as she struggled to contain his squirming, screaming son. Henry wanted to rush forwards and pull Luke away from her, respond to the boy's increasingly desperate cries to 'let me go, Granny'. He hesitated, unsure of what to do or say, glancing around until he saw another figure, this one cowering, her face turned away, shoulders shaking.

Violet looked as if she'd been attacked by a rabid dog. The plaited halo of her hair had been pulled out on one side, and the delicate lace sleeve covering her right arm had been torn. Henry crouched down in front of her, saw the livid scratches that criss-crossed her chest, the pink mark on her cheek that was starting to bruise.

'Don't worry.' She braved a smile as Henry examined her injuries, feeling as he did so a hot and fierce anger tearing through him. 'I'm OK, really,' she said, though her bottom lip trembled. 'Dad, I told you not to fuss. I'll be fine in a minute. I just need to— I'll be OK.'

Christopher Lupton's watery blue eyes connected fleetingly with Henry's, and in that moment, he understood exactly who was to blame.

Luke.

As it dawned on Henry what must have happened, his son broke free from Eleanor, pushing the older woman so hard that she fell sideways on to the floor. Christopher stumbled towards her with a shout of dismay, Antonio swore, and Violet cringed against Henry. Luke barrelled over, fists flailing, mouth agape, and threw himself at his mother, clinging so tightly that she cried out in pain. Henry saw his small hand creep up to her hair and tug, his fingers pulling, teeth clenched in determined fury.

'Stop it,' he bellowed, more forcefully than he ever had before, his voice cracking open with fear and confusion. He grabbed Luke's arms, but the little boy was strong, and Violet screamed as more of her hair was ripped out. The harder Henry gripped, the rougher Luke became, his legs kicking out and his rigid body convulsing like a beached fish. Violet's gold hoop earring was torn away, and Henry saw blood trickle down her neck.

'You're hurting her,' he shouted. 'Luke, you're making Mummy bleed. Stop it – just stop it!'

His son growled, and it was a guttural enough sound to make Henry recoil.

Antonio stormed forwards, his hand raised as if to strike.

'Don't!' screamed Violet. 'Leave him.'

Even now, in the midst of such a maelstrom, she cared only about Luke's welfare. Henry bit down hard on his lip as angry tears flared. Antonio had swung around and was stalking away, grumbling to himself. Luke had begun to wail; still he held tight to Violet, angry but scared, terrified of his own outburst and powerless to stop it. Ynes, who had been standing silently to one side, stepped forwards and placed a tentative hand on the boy's quivering shoulder.

'*No la toques,*' she soothed. '*Toma mi mano.*'

Don't touch. Take my hand.

She repeated the words, her tone soft and singsong, a lullaby of persuasion. Luke's shudders lessened, and eventually, his vice-like grip began to ease, the small arms falling to his sides, the chin dipping to his chest. Ynes scooted down until her nose was level with his, and whispered something Henry did not catch. The little boy nodded, then his face collapsed into sobs.

'It's my fault,' murmured Violet, through a mess of running make-up. 'I should have known he would react badly to seeing me look so unlike myself. It scared him.'

'Scared him?' Henry grunted. 'Jesus Christ, Vee – look at the state of you.'

She started to cry.

Ynes was ushering Luke away now, Henry heard mention of ice cream.

'He didn't mean it,' Violet stuttered, her hand shaking as she wiped her eyes. 'He didn't mean to hurt me.'

'But he did!'

'Yes, but—'

'But nothing, Vee. He is out of control. We need to do something, see someone, we can't put it off any more. This isn't something that's going to go away on its own.'

She was shaking her head, tears dropping on to the pale satin skirt of her beautiful dress, ear stained red with blood, weals across her chest where Luke had dragged his nails through the flesh. Christopher looked ashen, his arms full of his still-weeping wife, while Antonio glared down at them, twitching with impotent fury, eager to get on with the ceremony, look after his guests, be the centre of attention. It was all wrong.

'This is supposed to be the happiest day of our lives,' Henry said despairingly to Violet, and was surprised when she responded with a broken-sounding laugh.

'And so it will be,' she said.

He sighed, rubbed a hand across his jaw.

'Listen to me, Henry.'

He focused his gaze on her, stared into eyes that were puffy and veined with red.

'Everything is going to be OK. This was just a blip, a silly tantrum. Luke is fine, will be fine, we'll be fine, all of us. I promise.'

Henry wished he could believe her, put his faith in those assurances and trust that she knew better than him.

But he couldn't, wouldn't, and didn't.

30

Violet

I leapt away from Juan as if he'd stung me.

'Henry,' I said, unable to disguise my shock.

'Violet,' he replied coolly, from the end of the alleyway.

He looked smarter than usual, in a fitted shirt and pale jeans, his dark hair falling over his eyes. For a moment, I saw Luke, but it was only a flash of similarity. The sullenness, perhaps? The distrust.

The woman standing next to him, who I knew now was Bo, folded her arms. There was a deliberate gap between them, I noted, and a small bubble of hope inflated inside my chest.

Juan stepped towards them, hands raised placatingly, and said a few words in Spanish that I missed. Bo glanced from him to me and rolled her eyes, while Henry watched on in silence, not saying anything until Bo turned and spoke to him. I caught the gist, picking up '*esposa*', which meant 'wife', and '*pelirroja*', the word for 'redhead'. All three were talking as if I wasn't there and, unsurprisingly, it rankled.

'Hello,' I said, loudly enough that Bo broke off mid-sentence. She looked more disappointed than cross, and as I drew closer, she retreated, unwilling to mirror my polite smile with one of her own. Putting a brief hand on Henry's arm, she murmured a few words in a low hushed tone, before turning on her heel and striding briskly away.

Henry sighed, shaking his head as I went to speak.

'Not now, Vee. I'm too tired. We'll talk tomorrow.'

As he started to walk away, Juan reached across an arm, blocking my path.

'Excuse me.' I rounded on him. 'What do you think you're doing?'

'Come on, Violet.' The way he drew my name out, lazily rolling his tongue over every vowel, made me seethe. 'Let us go, have another drink.'

My voice, when I'd recovered it, sounded hoarse. 'No,' I said. 'I'm grateful to you for finding out, you know, about Bo. But it doesn't mean I want you to . . . That we are . . . Oh, for god's sake,' I moaned, losing patience with myself, with him, with the situation. 'I just need to go.'

Juan didn't try to stop me, nor did he give chase, but he did issue a parting comment.

'Your marriage has ended, Violet. You must accept it. The sooner that you do, the better it will be for everybody.'

I didn't see any point in bothering with a response.

Henry hadn't said where he was going, but I guessed it would be towards La Casa Naranja, back to his cocoon, where we'd been happy until I'd sullied it; until the course of our lives had become mired by stress and trauma. I broke into a run, catching up with him a few yards from our front gate. The house was in darkness save for the turret window, which burned bright as a polestar against the blackness of night.

'Wait,' I said, hot and breathless. 'What you saw, in the alleyway just now, it wasn't anything.'

Henry turned, frowned.

'Juan, he . . . I think he thought that I wanted him to . . . But I didn't. I don't.'

He was wearing aftershave, a new scent I didn't recognise, and a dart poisoned with jealousy shot through me.

'Who was that woman?' I asked, a self-sabotaging part of me needing to hear it from him.

Henry hesitated for a moment before answering. 'Her name is Bo. She works at La Residencia.'

'Do they still have weddings there?'

I hadn't meant to sound spiteful, but his expression told me I had.

'I guess so,' he said evenly. 'Given that it's Bo's job to organise most of them.'

I waited for him to continue, swatting away a hovering mosquito in irritation. It had been Henry who taught me the difference between the males and females, the latter being the only one of the two that fed on blood. I felt like a bloodsucker now, the person responsible for draining all the gaiety from the man I cared for so deeply.

'Are you in love with her?'

It was a bold question, and Henry's response was a short bark of laughter.

'What?'

'Do you love her? It's simple enough.'

In truth, of course, it was anything but – love being the stickiest, trickiest question of all.

Henry looked at me steadily. 'No, Violet, I'm not in love with her. We've been on three dates, tonight being our last.'

I pictured the sour look on Bo's face, the contemptible way she'd scrutinised me.

'Last?'

'I didn't think it was fair to keep seeing her. I thought that I was ready to, you know, but as it turns out . . .' He trailed off, hands splayed open in a 'that's that, then' gesture.

'That you're not?'

'So it would seem.'

'Henry,' I began, only to fall silent. I hadn't known what I was going to say, only that I needed to say something, to show him that I understood because I felt the same way. The idea of being intimate with someone else – anyone else – was abhorrent to me, and I burned with shame as I recalled the way I'd allowed myself to bask in Juan's attention only an hour ago.

'Well, for what it's worth, I'm glad,' I admitted. 'And I know that makes me a selfish, vile person, but it's not as if you don't know that about me already.'

Henry's lips twitched, but he didn't smile.

'I saw the two of you together, you and Bo, not long after I arrived. I should've said something to you about it, I know, but I felt like it wasn't my place. I didn't want to annoy you any more than I already had, and then I mentioned it to Juan, and he said he'd do some digging for me, find out who she was and if you and she were serious.'

His gaze found mine then, sudden, sharp.

'I know, I know.' I shook my head, staring down at the ground. Weeds were sneaking through the cracks in our boundary wall, their roots leaving tiny pathways through the cement. Over time, water would get inside, and the foundations would start to crumble, the weight of the stones becoming too much for the structure to bear.

'That's why I was with him tonight,' I went on. 'I didn't want to be, I felt like I had to be, I needed to know if you and her were . . . If you really had moved on.'

Henry went to rub his chin, only to flinch as his fingers came into contact with his scars. He was still learning how to live in this new body. I'd gone through a similar experience during and after pregnancy, though I knew the two were incomparable. I had chosen to have Luke; Henry had not volunteered to be mutilated.

'I did like Bo,' he said simply. 'She never looked at me pityingly, the way you are now,' he added. 'I can take intrigue, shock, even disgust – but pity?' He shook his head. 'No, that's not for me. It makes me feel weak.'

'You could never be weak,' I implored, my hands twisting together as I fought the urge to reach out to him. 'You're so strong, you always have been – I'm the weak one.'

'Jesus, Vee – what's this we're doing now? Some sort of competition to discover which of us is the worst human being?'

'We both know the answer to that one.'

Henry groaned. It was all he seemed to do when confronted with me.

'We've both done bad things,' he said. 'Stupid things.'

'Dangerous things.'

The word had slipped out thoughtlessly, and straight away I wanted to snatch it back. Instead of replying with a barb of his own, however, Henry merely took a long, deep breath.

'That was it, wasn't it?' he said. 'That was the moment, that day.'

I toyed with the idea of lying to him, but there was no point.

'There were lots of moments,' I said. 'From both sides, but yes, I think that one was the worst. I tried to move past it, but I couldn't. Not for ages.'

We fell into a brooding silence, each of us ushered back into a past we'd have done anything to erase. Henry looked haunted; stricken – and it was terrible to behold. We never had been able to share the pain of that day, and I wondered if now, at last, there might be a way.

'Can I?' I said, opening my arms. 'For Christ's sake, Henry, I just want to hold you, if only for a moment.'

He clenched his hands into fists and shook his head, refusing to look at me.

'Please.' I moved towards him, desperation funnelling courage. 'It's me. I'm still me.'

When he looked at me again, I saw doubt in his eyes. 'Are you, Vee?'

'I am.' I nodded furiously. 'I promise you, I am.'

Henry shoved both his hands into his pockets; the signal could not have been clearer.

'What about all the secrets?' he asked. 'The stuff you're refusing to tell me.'

Defeated, I allowed my arms to fall limply to my sides. It had grown darker in the time we'd been talking, our hushed tones muffled by the humid night air. I looked up towards the porthole window. It was still aglow, bright gold like a dropped penny, and if I could've wished on it, I would have. Everything I wanted was tied up in decisions I'd made in the past, things I did that I yearned to change, but Henry and I knew better than most that what is done cannot be undone. Altering the future was my only option, and for that to work, I had no choice but to tell the truth. I owed Henry that much, and yet my impulse was to delay. When his phone started to ring, its shrill tone cutting a swathe through the tense atmosphere, I was so relieved at the interruption that I almost wept.

He squinted at the screen for a long time before answering, his intrigue turning rapidly to shock, and disbelief.

'What it is?' I asked, my mind going automatically to Luke. But he was upstairs in his room, safely ensconced with Eliza. Wasn't he?

'Henry.' I was insistent. 'What's happened? Tell me.'

He said nothing, just stared at the handset, his mouth drooping open, eyes wide.

'You're scaring me.'

He didn't respond.

'Henry, what's going on?' I demanded, grabbing his shoulders, shaking him, trying to bring him back to me. When he finally spoke, the words weren't so much sounds as rasps, although one was unmistakeable.

Antonio.

31

Violet

A massive heart attack.

A statement nobody ever wanted to hear, but one that Henry had no choice but to accept when his older half-brother rang with the news. When he then repeated it to me, the ground seemed to shift, the alcohol I'd so willingly tossed down my throat in the bar churning unpleasantly in my stomach.

'Is he—?'

There was no need to finish my sentence; his face told me all I needed to know. Antonio was dead.

'No,' I gasped. 'I can't believe it. When?'

Henry blinked at me, dumbfounded, the hand that wasn't clutching his phone shook violently. Even in the semi-darkness of the lane, I could see that his face was devoid of colour.

'Mateo couldn't get a flight tonight,' he said. 'But he said he'll be here as fast as— Shit. Sorry.' Staggering forwards a few paces, he steadied himself on the low wall.

I rushed to put my arm around him, no thought other than to comfort. I was reeling, whereas Henry was barely coherent, his wild eyes darting in every direction as he muttered to himself; reactions that reminded me acutely, cruelly, of Luke.

Luke. I would have to tell him Antonio had died, that he'd now lost both of his grandfathers. The thought turned me cold.

'Come inside,' I said to Henry. 'You need to sit down.'

He allowed me to help him over the threshold and into the lounge, where I lowered him on to the sofa and fetched a generous measure of brandy. Having stared down at it for a few seconds, he raised his anguished face to mine.

'This smells like my dad,' he said, and started to cry.

Feet sounded on the stairs, and moments later Luke appeared in the doorway.

'Hel— Oh. What's going on?'

I hesitated for a moment, torn between husband and son, taking in the shock on Luke's face as he registered his father's distress. The hateful, selfish part of me wanted someone else to take over, a doctor or a kindly distant relative, anyone who could offer rational calm. But Henry was not capable of speaking, so that only left me.

'I'm afraid there's been some bad news,' I began, quailing at the way he immediately tensed. 'Antonio has . . .' I paused as Eliza came into view behind Luke, pink hair askew, piercings glittering in the muted light from the lounge's only lamp. He didn't turn to greet her, nor did he respond when she put both her arms around his waist.

'Has what?' he demanded, with such force that it jolted me. Henry got to his feet and began to pace up and down, a hand covering the destroyed half of his face. The shock and grief had worked like an accelerant on this, most acute vulnerability; he might have been with us, his family, yet he could not bear us to look at him. I saw Eliza's hands tighten involuntarily as Luke asked his question again, bellowing the words into the room.

I couldn't help it, I cowered away from him.

Henry stopped pacing.

'He's dead, all right?' It was close to a snarl. 'Antonio is fucking dead. Am I making it clear enough for you? Are the words getting through that screwed-up head of yours?'

'Henry!' I said furiously, as Luke recoiled, his features a mess of sudden anguish. 'Don't listen to Dad,' I begged. 'He's in shock, he doesn't know what he's saying.'

Eliza's face crumpled, her arms no longer on Luke but wrapped tightly around her own shoulders. I could see the whites of her knuckles.

'You're scaring Eliza,' I cried, as Luke advanced into the room, not stopping until he was nose-to-nose with Henry. They squared up to each other, a match in height but Henry so much broader, the thickness of his arms making Luke's look like twigs, the glass of brandy still clutched in one hand.

'What are you going to do?' he taunted. 'Hit me like you used to do to your mother?'

'Henry, please!' I was crying, great wracking sobs I couldn't control. 'Stop it.'

Luke was trembling all over, his lips bunched into a scowl, fists clenched.

'How?' he hissed, his spittle landing on Henry's scarred face. 'How did he die?'

'A heart attack,' Henry said, his voice every bit as rigid, each word inflicting a fresh blow. 'I suppose you wish it had been me instead.'

Luke flinched but didn't reply, his eyes narrowing as Henry continued to glare at him.

I heard Eliza whimpering and fought the urge to rush over and comfort her. I couldn't risk taking my eye off the other two – not even for a second.

'It's not Luke you're angry with, Henry,' I pleaded. 'Stop this now, both of you.'

'Oh, but I am angry with him,' said Henry, the menace with which he spoke eliciting another frightened moan from Eliza. 'I know we'd all rather pretend I wasn't, but for some reason – hell, I don't know, perhaps because my dad just died

– I wonder if it's not better to be honest for once in this family.'

Fear had rooted me to the spot. All I seemed capable of doing was mouthing in horror, a voice repeated in my head over and over.

Stop it, stop it, stop it.

Henry took an aggressive swig of his brandy. He didn't often drink liquor, and it showed. Almost immediately, he began coughing and was forced to break eye contact with Luke. I hoped it would go some way towards defusing the situation, but if anything, both men seemed angrier to have been interrupted. I kept waiting for Eliza to say something – do something – but she was as terrified as me. I needed to intervene more forcefully; it was my job. But still, I couldn't seem to move. Pain snarled in my gut, the urge to flee overwhelming.

'Antonio wouldn't want this,' I said. 'He'd hate seeing the two of you fighting.'

Henry laughed without humour. 'Oh, is that what you think?' he said, speaking very slowly, making sure to enunciate every syllable. 'I happen to disagree. My father has been telling me for years that what Luke really needs is discipline and proper boundaries. Ever since our wedding, in fact.'

'Oh, for heaven's sake.' I could feel the heat rising in my own body, defensiveness pushing aside any residual fear. 'You're talking about our son, Henry – he's a human being, not a dog that keeps peeing on the carpet.'

Luke briefly closed his eyes, uncurling his fingers only to clench them tightly into fists once again.

'But that's just it, isn't it? That's all we do, Vee. Talk about our son, consult so-called experts, read books, go over his problems, what to do about them, how we can help him cope. It's like a broken bloody cement mixer, churning on and on.'

'Shut up!' I almost screamed. 'Just shut up.'

I could see Luke was deflating, the burst of adrenaline that had sent him striding across the room had dissipated, and he looked all of a sudden impossibly fragile. I took in his bony knees, messy hair, and mismatched socks, and saw only innocence.

'This isn't Luke's fault,' I said, though it was barely a murmur. 'Henry, look at me.'

He didn't – or couldn't – comply, but he did at least take a step back, raising his glass to his lips for another swig of the brandy.

'Come on.' I stretched a hand towards Luke, wanting to tow him away. If I could get him on his own, I could explain; reason with him, tell him that his dad didn't mean what he said, that it was wrought from pain, not truth. But Luke didn't want to be led from the room, and calmly but firmly removed my fingers from his arm.

'I think we all need to take a breath,' I said hurriedly. 'We've all had a big shock. Why don't I make some tea? We can all sit down and—'

'Mum.' Luke's tone was pure ice. 'Just stop it. You're trying to make everything OK,' he pointed out, eyes never leaving his father's. 'But they're not. Antonio –' he paused as his voice wobbled – 'he's gone.'

I wanted to shout, to beat my fists against his chest, shake him. I could feel it then, the potent fury that coursed through Henry, the frustration we had both suffered for so many years, each of us trying to keep it hidden from the other. And it wasn't just us – Luke carried it, too. It had simmered below the surface since he was a child, and all I'd ever done was suppress it. In him, and in myself.

'Luke?' Eliza had found her voice at last, though she didn't sound like herself. Taking a few paces forwards, she came to a stop a short distance behind him, close enough that he'd know she was there, but not near enough to be within striking distance. She was wearing a Minnie Mouse pyjama set and, like Luke, looked startingly young. The fact that she was being forced to witness this was unbearable, and when she stole a glance at me, I tried my best to muster up a semblance of a smile.

'Let's go upstairs,' she begged him. 'Or out for a walk? Get some air?'

Luke didn't respond, but his shoulders lowered a fraction. The fight was going out of him, the mist clearing, though he was still wary of what his father might do.

Henry, too, looked wretched. Unable to stop crying, he kept bringing up a fist to his cheeks and wiping the tears roughly away. His pain was palpable, and it cleaved my heart to see him in this state.

'I think that's a good idea,' I said falteringly. 'Eliza's right. We're all upset and—'

Henry turned on me. 'Don't you dare.'

'What?'

'Don't you dare speak for me.'

I was taken aback by his venom, the implied threat behind his words.

'I'm just trying to—'

'Protect Luke? Gloss over anything nasty or difficult? I know. It's what you do best.'

For a moment, I couldn't respond. His accusation had left me winded.

'I'm his mother,' I whispered. 'That's my job.'

'And you're *my* wife,' he said, voice cracking with despair. 'But you didn't protect me.'

Eliza pulled Luke away, her arms around his waist as she guided him out of the room. He was complying, but slowly.

Reluctant to leave me alone with Henry, or unwilling to miss the showdown we were on the verge of having? All I wanted was to stop.

'To love and to cherish,' Henry said acidly. 'That was it, wasn't it? The promise you made.'

I bit back my tears.

'What I want to know,' he sneered, 'is which one of those you were practising when your tongue was down Juan's throat? Was it loving, or cherishing?'

I heard Luke's intake of breath, Eliza's scandalised gasp, and then it all came hurtling out – the fear, the pain, the fury, everything I'd been battling to hold back. I flew at Henry, fists raised, screaming at him to 'shut up, shut up, shut up'. He did nothing to avoid the pathetic blows I rained down on him, standing immobile while I sobbingly ranted. I was aware of nothing but my own torment, heard only the cries coming from my own lips; all my restraint had gone, I was a creature of pure emotion, a beast unhinged, until finally, mournfully, I slid wretchedly to the ground.

32

Henry

The day started out typically enough. Breakfast on the terrace – toast, eggs and tomatoes for himself and Violet, Rice Krispies with all the milk drained off for Luke – followed by the usual half-hour of gentle cajoling, as each of them took it in turns to tempt their son into doing something other than sitting in his bedroom all day.

Henry was keen to get out of the house. He'd been forced to abandon the overhaul of the spare bedroom that he'd begun when they arrived a few weeks previously due to a hold-up on materials, and the knowledge of the mess, and the unfinished plastering, itched at him. Violet had found him in there twice, just staring around in search of a task, and told him off for being 'obsessed'.

'It will all get done eventually,' she said, rubbing at her eyes. 'This is supposed to be our relaxing time.'

She was right, he knew, but relaxation was not a state that came naturally to Henry. He was less agitated when he was busy, whereas Violet seemed to have become almost drunk on sleep. Luke, for the most part, was quieter and more subdued in Mallorca than England and, like them, he relished the break from the everyday pressures. Getting him to school on time had become a battle they lost more often than not, and in the days before term ended, Henry and Violet had been summoned into the primary school Luke attended for a meeting. The teacher was sympathetic, but also practical, warning them that if not dealt with properly, their son's tardiness could soon mutate into a full-blown refusal to attend school at all. That was all very well, Henry had thought bitterly, but other than manhandle Luke from beneath the duvet and into the classroom, his options were limited. Violet, of course, preferred a softly-softly approach.

'If we make an issue out of it, he'll only get worse. At least he is still going in.'

Sure, Henry had brooded, but for how long?

It had taken him months after their wedding to persuade Violet that speaking to a professional was the right step to take, but while the GP had listened, frowned, and asked Luke a series of questions, she hadn't been able to do much else other than refer him to the local centre for addiction and mental health. A letter was written, and they had waited, and waited, and waited. When Luke was eventually seen almost three months later, the counsellor spent less than fifteen minutes deciding that their son was deemed 'low risk' and advised Henry and Violet to go private.

'We're stretched far too thin,' he'd explained lamentably. 'Demand far outweighs resource, and we have youngsters that we have to prioritise. Luke has some behavioural issues, but we don't deem him to be a risk to himself or others.'

For Henry, who'd been the recipient of endless punches and kicks, and seen their house smashed during Luke's terrifying bouts of rage, it felt like an exceptionally cruel dismissal.

'Get some help,' was what well-meaning people suggested, and every time he heard it, Henry had stop himself from shouting back, 'How?'

There was no help, they were alone in their misery, and the sense of helplessness that brought felt overwhelming. Upon

Violet's insistence, Henry had agreed not to discuss their son's ongoing issues over the summer holidays and focus instead on the three of them spending time together as a family. Luke, however, had apparently not got the memo.

'What about Sóller?' Violet suggested now, her eyes meeting Henry's over their son's bowed head. Luke was using the back of his spoon to squeeze yet more milk from his soggy cereal and did little other than grunt in response.

'You used to love riding the tram,' she went on, glancing at Henry for help.

'Mum's right,' he said, picking up the mantle. 'The driver used to let you ring the bell, don't you remember?'

Nothing. Not so much as a murmur.

Henry tried again.

'Alcúdia then? We could get ice cream for lunch.'

Luke shook his head morosely.

'Magaluf?'

That got his attention. Luke's chin came up and he fixed Henry with a quizzical stare.

'Yeah, why not?' Henry said. 'Line the shots up, go to a foam party.'

Violet tutted.

'Dad's being silly,' she said. 'Nobody is going to do any shots.'

'What's a foam party?' asked Luke, and Henry laughed in spite of Violet's exasperation.

They all looked up as a voice carried over the garden wall, bidding them good morning in Spanish. Violet, who'd been standing with her hands on the back of Luke's chair, rushed through the house towards the front door, and soon enough, Juan had joined them on the terrace. He had come with a proposition.

'I am taking Tomas fishing,' he declared. 'In Cala de Deià. And we wondered if you would like to come with us?'

'All of us?' Violet said brightly. *Hopefully*, Henry thought darkly. He had noticed the way their Spanish neighbour casually flirted with his wife, always finding excuses to touch her, and he wished Violet wouldn't lap the attention up so eagerly. He didn't see the man as a threat, so much as a mild irritant, but he had to hand it to Juan – when it came to getting through to Luke, the Spaniard beat Henry hands down. His son had sprung out of his seat and was jumping up and down on the spot with such glee that it was impossible not to feel grateful.

'Of course, the invitation is for all of you,' Juan agreed, laughing as Luke began to zoom around the patio, arms stretched out as if he was a plane about to take off. It was the most animated he'd been in days, and Violet beamed as she watched him.

'Thank you,' she was saying to Juan over and over. 'You're our guardian angel.'

That was, Henry mused privately, a bit of an overstatement.

They travelled down to Deià in two cars, Henry's old red jeep creaking on its wheel bearings as he navigated the hairpin turns of the mountain roads. Luke sat strapped in the back, his pale limbs sticky with sun cream. For once, he hadn't put up a fight when Violet guardedly produced the bottle, and Henry was hopeful that perhaps a figurative corner had been turned that morning as well as the literal ones. This summer could be the one where everything changed for the better, his son finally shrugging off the anger and anxiety and becoming the person Henry knew he had it in him to be – a happy little boy with a positive soul, a child who strode confidently through life instead of cringing in the shadows. It was all he and Violet wanted, and all they ever seemed to talk about.

★   ★   ★

It felt nice to be back in Deià, with its jumble of golden houses that always felt to Henry as if they'd been snatched from the pages of a history book. He had fond memories of the place, from his and Violet's wedding – which began so strangely but had ultimately become a wonderful day of shared love and laughter – to the lazy afternoons they'd spent here when Luke was still very young, wandering the narrow hillside streets with a punnet of strawberries propped on the back of the pushchair between them, juice-stained fingers entwined, sweet kisses exchanged. Glancing across at Violet, he saw that she, too, looked serenely contented, her bare arm diving up and down through the rushing air beyond the open window, red hair rippling across freckled shoulders. A free spirit again, if only for a precious few moments. Henry saw her every day, at home and out doing jobs, across the dinner table in the evenings and tucked in next to him in bed at night, yet it never felt like enough. His love for her had always been this way: intoxicating, passionate, urgent, all-consuming. Even when he was mad at her, he adored her beyond measure.

Henry's mood remained buoyant as he steered the jeep through Deià and followed the road down through the olive groves to the coast beyond, parking up in a shady spot right beside Juan's flashy Mercedes. Tomas, thirteen now and as boisterous, strapping and loud as nine-year-old Luke was cautious, small, and quiet, exploded from the car and started tugging at Henry's door, urging him to hurry.

Violet, laughing, headed around to the back of the jeep, and hauled out her cavernous beach bag, in which she'd somehow managed to fit three towels, an assortment of buckets and spades, a large blanket and lunch for everyone.

'All good?' Henry asked Luke, as his son clambered slowly out of his seat and tugged down his baseball cap. It was one of those with an extra flap at the back to protect the neck, though Luke had insisted on wearing it sideways.

He nodded, cowed as he often was in the presence of Tomas, who Henry guessed he yearned to impress. There was something undeniably magnetic about the Spanish teenager, with his easy confidence and wide grin, that drew people to him. Ana had once confided to Henry that she feared for the broken hearts her son was destined to leave in his wake once he started dating. He was such an incorrigible flirt – a trait, no doubt, that he'd picked up from Juan, who was now unpacking fold-up chairs, fishing tackle and a clanking bag of wine bottles from his boot.

'For the *señoras*,' he said to Henry, a glint in his eye as he added conspiratorially, 'to get us into the good books.'

Ana, who'd heard this last comment as she paused to refasten the buckle on her sandal, rolled her eyes and murmured something unintelligible under her breath. Tossing her long dark hair over one shoulder, she put a hand on Henry's arm.

'Shall we run away together?' she said teasingly. 'It would teach this *tonto* a lesson.'

Henry grinned as he admired her smooth tanned skin and wide shining mouth.

'Maybe in another life,' he said, feigning disappointment. 'In this one, I am very much a taken man.'

Ana pulled a face, then laughed good-naturedly before calling over to Violet.

'I hope you realise how lucky you are, *mi amiga*.'

Luke was pulling at Henry's sleeve.

'Can we go?'

Juan passed him a small metal box.

'You,' he said, tapping the peak of Luke's lopsided hat, 'can carry the worms.'

It was a short, dusty walk from the car park to the cove, and Juan led the way, Tomas bounding along in his wake. Violet had fallen into step beside Luke, the tin of bait held gingerly, as if it might explode at any moment, while Henry brought up the rear with Ana. Despite setting off relatively early, they discovered that the rocky shoreline was already littered with holidaymakers, and Henry saw Luke stiffen as he took in the crowds.

'Let's go and get a Coke,' he said, hurrying forwards to steer his son into the nearest of the two tavernas, but Luke didn't budge. Henry looked to Violet, his perpetual 'what shall we do?' expression being met by one of exasperation.

'Luke!' Juan yelled, from the top of a wide, concrete ramp. 'The boat is here.'

The small vessel to which he was now gesturing looked decidedly rickety, its wooden hull scratched and faded. Henry thought it might once have been red, but the paint had long since flaked off, leaving behind only the faintest suggestion of colour.

Tomas had swung his stocky legs over the side and was busy stowing the fishing lines and a cool box beneath the bench seats, while Juan fiddled around untying ropes.

'Aren't we going to eat first?' called Violet. There was a nervous tremor in her voice to which Henry had become well accustomed.

'It'll be fine,' he told her, addressing Luke at the same time. 'Juan's been taking boats like that one out since he was a kid.'

'I don't know.' Violet looked unsure. 'I thought it would be . . . I don't know, bigger . . . sturdier.'

'Luke's not scared; are you, mate?'

Henry had never called his son 'mate' and could not fathom why he'd chosen to do so now. A 'mate' was someone you went down the pub with on a Friday night after work, not your ashen-faced nine-year-old son. Luke was considering his reply when Violet interrupted.

'You don't have to do anything you don't want to, honey. If you'd rather stay on the beach with me and Ana, then that's fine. Or we could go for a hike back up to the village?'

She always did this; laid out multiple options and allowed Luke to choose. It happened on every single day trip, at every mealtime, and on all the rare occasions when they sat down together to watch a film. When Henry had raised the issue, asking Violet why she allowed their son to dictate most, if not all, of their decisions, she'd argued that it helped him feel in control.

'It doesn't matter to us as much as it matters to him, so why do you care?'

And Henry had been forced to admit that he didn't know. But he did care, it bothered him – had always bothered him. So often it felt to him as if he and Violet were the children in their family, while Luke, from his lofty perch of power, had somehow become the adult.

'Mum's right,' he allowed, as his son continued to stare glumly towards the multitude of colourful beach towels, sunbathing couples, and noisy families down at the water's edge. 'You could miss out on the fishing trip, but I think that would be a shame, especially since Juan expressly invited you.'

He was manipulating him, Henry knew, but wasn't Violet guilty of the same exact thing? Each of them had developed their own unique way of communicating with Luke, and this just so happened to be his. He deliberately avoided his wife's stony glare as he continued his process of coercion.

'Go on, do it for me. I've barely seen you these past few days.'

'Henry . . .' Violet's tone had a warning edge to it. 'If he doesn't want to, then—'

'It's OK.' Luke turned to face his mother. 'I'll go in the boat.'

Before either of them could reply, he had stalked past Henry and joined Juan, passing across the bait tin before clambering up and over the bow. With his stick-thin pale legs, spindly arms, and wide, startled eyes, he looked as vulnerable as a stranded duckling, and Henry felt a surge of protectiveness flood through him. Turning to Violet, he bent and pressed a kiss against her rigid cheek.

'I'll look after him,' he said. 'I promise.'

He and Juan took one side of the boat each before steering it down the ramp into the shallow water.

'Life jacket,' he said, once he'd leapt in over the side, snatching one up and passing it across to his son. Luke, who had chosen a seat right at the front, shook his head.

'I don't like the sound it makes.'

Henry gritted his teeth into the approximation of a smile.

'It's for safety, mate, so we can't have any silliness.'

There he went again with that word: *mate*.

Luke folded his arms. 'No.'

Henry was about to argue back when Juan put a big warm hand on his shoulder.

'It is OK,' he said. 'Look at the water, it is like a well today.'

'That's not the point,' Henry said, but again, Juan was insistent. Lowering his voice, he murmured, 'Do not make a big deal out of this. It will only upset the boy. Let him come around to the idea on his own.'

'You sound like my wife,' Henry grumbled back, which only served to make the Spaniard's lips spread even wider. Glancing back towards the beach, he saw Violet and Ana laying out the picnic blanket, the latter having already stripped down to a gold bikini. She was softly edged and voluptuous, while Violet was petite and more athletic.

Realising that he might be enjoying the view a bit too much, Henry turned his gaze quickly away.

'How far out are we going?' he asked Juan, who was manning the rudder. The outboard engine purred as it propelled the small craft forwards, a moderately loud yet unobtrusive sound that did not seem to have fazed his noise-averse boy.

'Not far,' Juan replied. 'If we stay close to the rocks, we may be lucky enough to find *calamar* – perhaps even *pulpo*.'

Henry could not be sure, but he thought he saw Luke suppress a shudder.

Tomas, meanwhile, had stood up and was rummaging around by his father's feet.

'Did you bring the traps, Papá?'

'*Siéntate*,' Juan snapped coarsely. Sit down.

Tomas sat, but not before he'd caused the boat to wobble precariously. Henry's hands reached instinctively for Luke but, outwardly at least, the boy appeared unfussed by the kerfuffle. He was gazing silently out towards the horizon, that quivering blue gradient where sky met sea. The latter was almost turquoise today in its intensity, and clear enough that there could be no doubt as to how deeply it ran. Henry loved the ocean, but he'd never been a particularly strong swimmer. The land suited him better, and it was when both his feet were firmly placed upon it that he felt most at ease. Now that they were out here, the shore far enough away to render individual faces a blur, Henry questioned the reason why he'd been so insistent that they come. He and Luke could have been happily ensconced in the shade, sipping an ice-cold fizzy drink at this very moment, and instead they were out here, bobbing along in the full sun, about to sit unmoving for hours on end in the hope of catching a fish they could just as easily have ordered from one of the beach tavernas. It was as he registered this regret that everything went suddenly, and catastrophically, wrong.

Tomas, still sulking from his father's scolding, decided to cheer himself up by opening the bait tin and extracting a long worm, which he promptly tossed at Luke. Henry watched it land on the back of his son's T-shirt, and saw his hand come around to remove it. A beat passed that was probably no longer than a second, but which would, over time, feel to Henry as if it had spooled out in agonising slow motion, after which Luke's expression turned from one of surprise to horror. Crying out with a mixture of shock and rage, he launched himself off the bench seat and flew at Tomas, fists flailing, mouth a gaping roar. The teenager yelped in alarm and dodged to one side just in time to avoid being struck.

'I'm going to kill you!' Luke screamed, his unbroken voice high and shrill and fierce with intent. Henry staggered on to both feet and the boat lurched in the water, sending him crashing to his knees. Tomas shouted a warning, but as he did so, Luke lost his balance. With a sickening thud, he fell backwards and cracked the side of his head on the wooden hull.

'Watch out!' Henry cried, struggling to get up as the boat swung violently around. One moment his son was there, slumped on the deck, and the next he was gone, over the edge to be stolen by the sea. Henry blinked, unable to believe what had happened, the enormity too much for his brain to process. By the time it did, and he was scrabbling forwards on all fours, Juan had already dived off the side of the boat.

Henry heard a keening sound coming from the shore. Violet must have witnessed the whole thing, and she was powerless to do anything other than react. Tomas was crying as he repeated the word 'Papá' over and over, and Henry felt hot tears begin to well in his own eyes. He was torn by indecision, not knowing if should jump off the boat or not, fearful of abandoning Tomas and scared of what might happen if he didn't, petrified of the sea and of his own inability to save his son, hateful and frightened and useless and— Henry gasped as a head broke through the surface, followed by a second. Juan's thick arm was tucked under Luke's chin, the other cutting through the water towards the boat.

'Here!' Henry stretched out both his arms, grasping his son's shoulders then sliding both hands under them. With Juan pushing from below, he managed to pull Luke out of the water and into the boat, where he lay, silent and sodden, among the mess of fishing tackle and coiled rope. Henry had done first-aid training at work, but had yet to put it into action, and now found that he couldn't remember where to start.

'Help!' he shouted, desperately, as Tomas heaved his father back over the side. Juan was panting with effort, but unlike Henry, he didn't hesitate. Reaching Luke's side in less than a second, he knelt and put an ear to the boy's mouth, then tilted his head back, pinched his tiny nose between thumb and forefinger, and brought his lips down over his mouth. Henry could hear Violet's screams, the lapping of the waves, the silent sobs coming from the shuddering teenage boy by his side, and then, mercifully, the rasp of a choking cough. A terrible coldness gripped Henry as the truth settled over him, bringing with it an avalanche of shame.

All he had done, all he'd been capable of doing was to sit, and wait, and watch, as another man, one far better and braver than him, breathed life back into his son.

33

Violet

The only thing I wanted to do in the days after Antonio died was hide. Not only from the brooding watchful gaze of my son and the smouldering ball of distemper that had become my estranged husband, but from myself. So much of what had happened could be blamed solely on me, and while I was hurt by Henry's betrayal, of the way in which he'd made it clear that I'd been the one to stray, I also understood it. What I was finding far more difficult to forgive was the way he'd spoken to Luke, the manner in which he'd confronted him, and the caustic remarks he'd made about him being 'screwed up'.

The wounds inflicted by father on to son during those moments would leave scars – of that, I was certain. Luke would dwell, and he would suffer, and then, eventually, he would blow. It was only a matter of time, and no amount of hiding away would change that.

News of Antonio's death spread rapidly through Pollença, and when I ventured out of the house on the morning of the second day after it happened, I discovered Ynes in the lane outside. She was clutching a frothy bunch of pink peonies wrapped in brown paper, and a carrier bag that strained under the weight of foil-covered dishes.

'*Cabecita roja*,' she said sorrowfully, enveloping me in a rather moist hug. The trudge up the Calvari Steps from the centre of town had left a sheen of sweat on her skin, and there were bright blue mascara blotches under her eyes.

'I am very sorry.'

She pulled back to look at me, the paper around the flowers crinkling as she gripped the top of my arm. There was concern etched across her features that made me want to curl up into a ball at her feet and weep. When I'd called my mother the previous day to tell her the news, she'd reacted more with bewilderment than sympathy.

'Was he ill? He always seemed so energetic.' Then, 'Did he have a younger girlfriend, someone pushing him to do too much?'

And while I'd never have expected her to fly out for the funeral, I was hoping she'd be, at least in part, concerned about my well-being. Unlike my mum, who I felt had viewed me differently ever since the day I told her I was pregnant with Luke, Ynes treated me as if I was something fragile, one of her delicate blooms that required careful handling – and I needed that. Perhaps more at this moment than any other. And so, I let my Spanish friend see my tears; hold me to her chest and stroke my hair. We stood together in the lane that way for some time, while the ignorant sun poured liquid gold puddles across the rooftops.

'Sorry,' I said after a time, lifting my head and wiping my eyes. 'I've cried all over your apron.'

Ynes's dark eyes crinkled. 'I have many more.'

'Do you want to come in?' I asked, gesturing towards the house, but she shook her head, taking my hand and leading me over to the boundary wall.

'Sit,' she instructed.

I sat.

Ynes lowered her bag of meals to the ground before easing herself down beside me.

'How is Enrique?'

I shook my head and she grimaced.

'Ah. And little Luke?'

I smiled at that. Of all the words a person could use to describe my son, 'little' was not one of them. Unsure if she'd know what I meant by 'subdued', I settled instead on 'quiet'.

Ynes nodded. 'Death is harder for the young.'

I thought about my mother in the weeks after my father died, haunted, broken, and angry enough to spit fire. I'd wanted nothing more than to tear down the world with her, but one of us needed to remain strong. And I had Luke. Falling apart was an impossibility. I'd envied my mother her raw and unequivocal grief. While she had burned white hot, I had smouldered, hiding my sadness behind practical tasks, and saving my silent tears for the few moments each day that I was alone. I knew I should be encouraging Luke to let out his own grief, but the cowardly part of me could not bear to face him, not now he knew what I had done. My betrayal.

'It doesn't feel real,' I murmured. 'Antonio was so . . .'

'*Grande*,' Ynes intoned, adding with a chuckle, 'He would enjoy hearing us talk like this about him.'

The hint of a blush crept across her cheeks as she said it, and I stared at her, my brow arched in enquiry.

'You and Antonio?'

She smiled. 'A long time ago. But you must not tell this to anyone.'

'I won't – but why the big secret?'

She leant in, lowering her voice conspiratorially. 'My papi is eighty-four, but he would still—' She slapped the back of one hand against the palm of the other. 'He has not forgotten what Antonio was like as a boy, always in trouble, misbehaving, fighting.'

'Boys and their troubles,' I said with a sigh, although it wasn't a universal truth, not when I considered what Henry had been like when I'd met him. His determination to do the right thing by me, and by us, and the willingness he had to love and be loved, could perhaps all be attributed to Antonio. Not because the older man had set good examples, but because he'd demonstrated to his second-born son what not to do. However, while being a supportive partner had come naturally to Henry, it was undeniable that fatherhood had proved trickier. He wore the role as he might a suit off the rack; it looked good on him but didn't fit quite as well as it should have.

'Women are no better,' Ynes said, punctuating her words with a dismissive sniff. 'We are all –' she whirled her hands around her head – '*loca*.'

'You can't say that!' I exclaimed, but she shrugged.

'When you are as old as I am, you can say whatever you like.'

'In that case, I'm looking forward to it.'

'Ach,' she scolded. 'You are still *una bebé*.'

'Does it get any easier?' I asked, wanting her to say that it did, to tell me everything would be OK, that all the worries I had now would seem trivial one day. But Ynes never had been one to play the game of make believe.

'Not easier,' she said, putting a soft, reassuring hand over mine. 'But things, they do change. Life moves on, people grow up and start to make their way into the world.'

'And people die,' I said, to which she smiled.

'*Sí, cabecita roja*. And this is OK. Death is with us, in the earth and the trees, the wind and the sea. Those that we love, they do not cease to be when they leave us.'

My mind went to Henry; the feelings I had for him like knotweed, forever destined to grow no matter how many times they were uprooted.

'Is there anything you need?' Ynes asked. 'Anything that I can bring for you?'

I nudged the carrier bag of food with my foot and smiled. 'I think you've outdone yourself already but thank you.'

I didn't want her to go. Having her there made me feel safer; she was my buffer against the hardships of the world. Ynes got to her feet, and I tucked each of my hands underneath my thighs so I wouldn't be tempted to cling on to her. We both turned at the sound of feet on the lane, my heart dropping as Malcolm and Mags came into view.

'Oh,' said Mags, all brightness and good cheer. 'Is now a good time?'

I gawped at her.

Malcolm blinked uncertainly. He was impeccably turned out as usual, in ironed shorts and a polo shirt with the collar turned up, while Mags looked pretty in a tiered pale-pink maxi dress that could have been modelled on Ynes's peonies.

'We don't mean to be a nuisance,' he began, pausing as his wife rushed forwards, nodding her agreement.

'We really don't,' she said ardently. 'We just love the house so much, as you know and, well, we didn't want to go without making that point clear.'

I could almost feel Ynes's intrigue as it burned through me.

'You're going home to England?' I asked, but Malcolm shook his head.

'Just heading out on a chum's boat for a week or so, doing a bit of sailing, some snorkelling perhaps.'

'Right.'

'But we'll be back soon, won't we, Magsy?'

'This time next week,' she agreed, sounding so hopeful that I glanced away.

'Sorry,' I said, my eyes on the ground. 'There's been a death in the family, so we're all a bit ... Everything is on hold.'

I braced myself against the flurry of 'oh my goshes' and 'how awfuls' and 'you poor things', during which Ynes remained silent, arms folded across the front of her apron.

'We'll know more by next week,' I promised them. 'I'll talk to Henry.'

Not that he'd say much back.

The sun had moved around and had me in its glare, scratching at me with its jagged rays. I raised a hand to shield my face, then turned it over to wave farewell to Malcolm and Mags. They headed back the way they'd come, dragging their feet, each throwing a last, longing look up at La Casa Naranja.

Ynes waited until they were out of sight before she spoke. 'They want to buy the house.' It was not a question.

'*Sí.*' I sighed. 'Very much so.'

'And they can afford to do so, a young couple like that?'

I pursed my lips. 'Apparently.'

Ynes huffed under her breath, before sitting down once again beside me.

'Antonio had money,' she said. 'Plenty of money. You will not have to sell now, I don't think.'

But any inheritance would be Henry's money. Not mine.

I could hear my mother's voice, her words from the previous day's phone call as clear as if she'd been standing right in front of me: 'There are more letters, Violet – they're not going away. You need to do something about them.' And then there were the calls I'd ignored from unknown numbers, the empty funds in both accounts, the credit card with its balance far exceeded.

The despair.

The desperation.

The disgust.

And then there was the other problem, the deal I'd made with a person I should never have let myself trust, who may now never relinquish their control over me.

I couldn't tell Ynes; I was too ashamed to admit the extent of it, but I did manage to share a sliver of truth.

'I don't want to sell the house,' I told her. 'But we have to – don't you see?'

She squinted at me, not understanding, wanting to sympathise but being unable to do so without knowing more.

'Henry—' I stopped. It was too painful, the truth – it stole the air from my lungs.

'*Qué?*' she asked gently. I closed my eyes, squeezed them shut, the texture of the wall rough beneath my hands. Saying it felt impossible, yet somehow, I found the words.

'Henry doesn't love me any more.'

34

Violet

The blow-up I had predicted happened two hours after the funeral.

I had watched Luke closely throughout the day, noticed the muscles twitching in his jaw, the tremble in his fingers, which he kept knotted together in his lap, my gaze on him rather than the procession of mourners. Antonio's eldest son, Mateo, had worked in a shift pattern with Henry, each man taking their turn sitting with the body of their father at the *tanatorio*. Unusually, for a Spanish burial, it had taken place seventy-two hours after death, partly to allow Mateo's wife and children to fly over from their Dubai home and join him, and also because of some disagreement over the family's niche tomb site. I had gleaned all of this not from being told, but by listening through the walls of the house to Henry's increasingly frustrated telephone conversations. When I'd come across him in the kitchen, not long after one such call, helping himself to what was plainly not his first beer of the day, I'd tentatively asked if there was anything I could do to help. Henry had glared at me for a few seconds, then stalked out without a word, slamming the door behind him.

The ceremony had been well attended, which would've pleased Antonio, with many guests openly weeping as the coffin was brought through. Juan did not attempt to hide his grief, and every time he let out another noisy sob, Henry's shoulders stiffened a fraction more. I didn't want to dwell on whether our Spanish neighbour was crying over the loss of a friend, or the fact that Antonio's untimely demise had rendered Juan's job as his right-hand man immediately redundant. It was easier to avoid him, but it troubled me that Luke chose to do the same. He and Juan had shared a unique connection ever since the latter had saved him from drowning, and it was one I'd assumed was important to both of them. If Luke lost an ally in Juan, it would be my fault. Everything, it seemed, was my fault.

In keeping with tradition there was no wake planned, Mateo apparently deciding that the traditional *rosario* gathering in nine days' time would provide ample space within which to celebrate the life of his father.

'I want us to have a party the likes of which Papi would be proud,' he told me, as we huddled together in a patch of shade outside the church. Despite being clad in a dark suit, Mateo seemed impervious to the scorching heat of the afternoon, whereas I had sweated right through my linen shift.

'Let me know if there's anything I can do,' I told him, and he smiled briefly in acknowledgement before turning away to speak to Henry in hushed, rapid Spanish. I was too exhausted, too sad, and too full of dread to linger any longer in town, but it was with trepidation that I made my slow way back towards La Casa Naranja. I'd seen Luke and Eliza leaving the church and hoped beyond reason that they'd chosen to go somewhere other than the house.

'Hello?' I called as I crossed the threshold, only to recoil as a resounding crash rang out, followed by a guttural roar.

Luke.

Ignoring the stress-response stab of pain in my stomach, I hurried past the stairs and made my way through the open door into the kitchen. Eliza was cringing against the far wall; hands up in front of her face, clearly terrified. Broken pieces of crockery littered the floor, and a carton of milk had been upended across the worktop. Luke had his back to me, shoulders hunched and arms dangling loose at his sides, and when he turned to look at me, I experienced a flutter of panic.

'I'll clean this up, shall I?' I said, trying my best to remain calm.

In answer, Luke picked up a second mug from the draining board and hurled it hard against the back door. Eliza squealed, her fear bringing me up short.

'Well, that was idiotic,' I snapped, my voice rising into a shout as he made a grab for the teapot. It was part of a set that Ynes had given me, and I loved it.

'Don't!' Eliza screamed, as splinters of handle and spout skidded across the tiles. 'Stop it.'

But her pleas fell on stubbornly deaf ears. Luke had gone to a place where neither of us would be able to reach him, far into the crimson mists of his own fury and grief and, like any caged or stricken animal, all he was capable of doing now was fighting his way out. Ducking under one of his flailing arms, I held my own open to Eliza and she flew into them, closing her eyes in fright as I wheeled around and ushered her quickly from the room.

'Go down the hill, back to the church, and find Henry,' I told her. 'Run!'

She didn't need telling twice, and was out of the front door seconds later, a blur of black and pink hurtling past the open window. I stationed myself in the hallway, feet planted wide and firm to stop my knees from trembling, and tried not to shout as more sounds of smashing rang out from the kitchen.

'Where is she?'

Luke was suddenly looming over me, shoulders hunched, lips curled.

'You need to try and calm down,' I said, in as level a tone as I could muster.

'Eliza?' he shouted, thundering up the stairs two at a time. I waited a moment, then followed him, reaching the landing as he came storming back down from the turret.

Stay calm. Exude calm. It's fear that's manifesting, not aggression.

'She's not here,' I said.

Luke paced towards me with enough aggression to unsettle me, make me flail, stumble, and clutch the banister for support.

'If she breaks up with me because of this, I'll fucking kill myself.'

I could not halt the tears that greeted this, most hateful threat, and bit down hard on my lip until I tasted blood.

'I'm sure she won't do that. She loves you.' The last words came out strangled as he pushed his way past me, and I pressed myself against the wall for a moment, giving my heart the chance to stop shuddering. I heard the back door open, and then an ominous scraping sound, followed by the unmistakeable shattering of glass. I was gripped by panic, but somehow found my feet, which felt leaden and clumsy below me. I half ran, half fell down the stairs, catching sight of yet more destruction as Luke charged towards the lounge.

'No!' I screamed, grabbing a fistful of his shirt. It was the one I'd ironed for him that morning, a fleeting snapshot of normality in a day that had morphed rapidly into a horror film. Luke shook me roughly away, sending me sideways into the small hall table. A vase of flowers I'd placed there teetered for a second or two, before dropping off the edge, and I watched as a shoal of broken glass and murky water spread across the floor. Luke, who was clutching a large shovel, aimed a kick at the table's flimsy wooden legs and sent it flying against the opposite wall.

'Stop it!' I yelled, my will to remain calm abandoned. 'Stop destroying my house.'

Adrenaline surged through me, obliterating the pain in my gut. I was no longer scared but angry; my limits exceeded, and lines crossed. He was doing what he always did, what I had allowed him to do ever since my wedding day. But I wouldn't stand by and bear witness while he tore the house apart – not this place, not our home.

Luke raised his shovel; he wanted me to cower, perhaps even to fall to my knees, but I couldn't give him that power. I made myself look at him, my eyes fixing in on his, deep-set pools of the darkest green, and flashing with malice.

'This isn't you,' I whispered.

His lips began to quiver, and he pulled them taut, scowling at me as tears brimmed.

'Luke,' I began, but he shook his head, his temper refocusing. Stalking away from me into the lounge, he swung the shovel round and brought it down hard on the big dresser, splintering first the cupboard doors and then the shelves above. I put my hands over my ears, unable to move, knowing it was pointless to intervene, and watched as my son rampaged and smashed and roared.

Then, suddenly, Henry was in the room, his hands on the shovel, the two of them locked together in a silent duel. Luke seemed to crumple, his knees giving way as he folded in against his father, clinging to him as he'd once clung to me as a baby, asking him to help, to make it stop. Henry's eyes were wet, but he did not let go of our son.

'I know,' he said. Not 'it's OK' or 'you'll be all right' or 'things will get easier' – none of the platitudes I had pedalled out time and time again – simply 'I know'.

I know it hurts.

I know it's not fair.

I know you don't mean it.
I know you're sorry.

When I had told Henry just days ago that he was strong, I had meant it. He'd always been stronger than me when it came to Luke, thicker-skinned when the insults were being hurled, more resilient to the physical blows. Where I'd made excuses, Henry had pushed for solutions, demanding we try whatever we could, no matter the cost. Owning up to the fact that your son has problems would be hard for anyone, and it had taken me longer than Henry to get there. In protecting myself from the facts, I had driven a wedge between us, insisting that he treat Luke the same way I did, with cotton wool and a caring face, and never once giving any merit to his suggestions because I believed that I, as his mum, knew better. I'd made a mess of everything, and for what? Luke hadn't needed me in this, his hardest moment, he had wanted someone else, someone he could trust to be honest even if the truth was unsavoury. Once upon a time, I might have resented this new closeness between them, and it was a relief to discover that I didn't. Not remotely.

Henry might have lost his father, but in those moments, as he cradled a weeping Luke in his arms, there was no doubt in my mind that he had gained back a son.

35

Henry

Nine Summers Ago

'Why don't you pop out into the waiting room for a moment, Luke, while I speak to your mum and dad?'

Henry dredged up a smile from somewhere and offered it to his son.

'Go on,' he said, bending to sift through Violet's bag until he located Luke's Nintendo 3DS. 'See how many levels you can pass on Pokémon.'

The handheld gaming device had been a gift, bought by Henry for Luke to say sorry for the incident on the boat, and it had gone a long way towards improving the way his son treated him. A shameless ploy, he knew, but if it worked then who was he to argue? Violet had not been keen on the idea, worrying that it would distract Luke from his drawing. Now that their son refused to attend school, art was one of the only subjects she could get him to do willingly from home, and lately even that had become a battle. It wasn't that Luke was disinterested in learning; he was simply scared to try.

The psychiatrist, Dr Mukherjee, waited until Luke had closed the door behind him, then placed his hands flat on the desk. It was a Balmoral style, Henry noted. Dark chestnut and polished to a shine. Given what this man charged by the hour, it was little wonder that his office furniture was high-end.

As she often did in uncomfortably quiet situations, Violet

began talking, asking the psychiatrist if he was planning a summer holiday.

'We'd usually be away in Mallorca by now,' she told him. 'But we put it on hold this year to see you.'

'I'm sorry that it took until now,' Dr Mukherjee said. 'I understand that things have been difficult.'

They had told him about the fruitless referrals, the waiting, the threats made by the attendance officer in relation to Luke's continued absence from school. The latter had made it clear that they needed a doctor's note if they were to avoid a fine or worse.

'It's been horrible,' said Violet, and hearing the wobble in her voice, Henry reached across and took her hand. 'Everyone seems to think that all Luke needs is a good telling-off, but that doesn't do any good at all. We've tried being cruel to be kind, and we've tried just being kind, but nothing works. He's so angry all the time.'

Dr Mukherjee nodded. 'It is fear that's manifesting, not aggression,' he said. 'Luke is suffering from depression and anxiety.'

Violet emitted a sob and Henry, too, found himself suddenly overwhelmed. For years, they had tried to make people understand there was more going on with Luke than just bad behaviour. To have their concerns justified, for a medical professional to confirm it so matter-of-factly, felt revolutionary.

'He is highly intelligent,' the psychiatrist continued sagely. 'But also sensitive, emotional.'

Violet was nodding. 'Yes,' she said. 'That's exactly it. He feels everything so deeply.'

Dr Mukherjee nodded. 'There is a suggestion, perhaps, of some autistic traits,' he continued patiently. 'But not enough for me to say definitively that he has autism.'

Was that a good or bad thing? Henry wasn't sure.

'What can we do?' he asked, needing a practical solution, an action, something he could fix with his hands or tools. 'I've tried to get him into sports, you know, something to help him work off his aggression, but he's not interested.'

'Luke's not the type,' put in Violet, dropping Henry's hand, and folding her arms. 'He's a quiet boy, he doesn't like rough and tumble.'

'Unless it's with us,' Henry added. 'Or the fixtures and fittings of the house.'

Violet shot him a look.

'Home is a safe space,' Dr Mukherjee said smoothly. 'I am afraid we all let down our guards in our homes, and Luke is no exception. For him, normal life, as we would think of it, is very hard. He must pretend that everything is hunky-dory in order to maintain control, but of course, it is not, and so that control is lost. Anxiety of this nature is often very destructive, but what he does, he cannot help. It's important to understand that. He is not choosing to lose control; it frightens him to do so.'

A silence fell as they took this in.

'It frightens us, to see him in that state,' said Henry. Violet, he knew, would have gone a step further and said that Luke himself frightened her, but she was too proud to admit such a thing.

'We're worried he'll end up seriously hurting himself,' she said.

'Or someone else,' put in Henry, then seeing the hurt expression on his wife's face. 'It's true, Vee. When he's in a furious state, having a full-on meltdown, he doesn't seem to have any concept of who or what he's damaging – he just reacts.'

'I understand,' said Dr Mukherjee. 'Nobody wants anybody to be physically hurt.'

'Exactly,' agreed Henry, as Violet sighed in exasperation. 'It's not a criticism, Vee – I'm just trying to be honest here.'

She ignored him, turning instead to the doctor. 'My husband spends far less time with Luke than me,' she said. 'He works long hours, and since Luke has been learning from home, I've had to be there full-time. I see him all day, every day.'

Only by the smallest flicker of a grimace did Dr Mukherjee express his dismay upon hearing this information. Henry wasn't sure if it was the working he disapproved of, or Violet's unnaturally intense relationship with their son. Either way, their family dysfunction was undeniable. Again, he asked his question.

'What can we do?'

The psychiatrist steepled his hands and tapped his fingers together. His fingernails were very neat, his spectacles rimmed in gold, the serious eyes behind them narrowed in concentration.

'There are some drugs we can try,' he said, reeling off two long names that Henry immediately forgot. Violet, of course, missed nothing.

'Isn't fluoxetine another name for Prozac?'

'It is one of what we call SSRIs,' he confirmed. 'Selective serotonin reuptake inhibitors, and we have found they work well as a combination with CBT, or cognitive behavioural therapy. The medication will have a good influence on mood and emotion, and through the therapy, we can work on teaching Luke how to recognise and manage these periods of crisis.'

Henry was triumphant. At last, they had found someone who was talking sense, providing them with the means by which to make real changes. As far as he was concerned, Dr Mukherjee had just earned every one of the five hundred pounds Henry had paid for his time. When he glanced over at Violet, however, he saw that she was chewing her thumbnail, deep frown lines etched across her brow.

'What is it?' he demanded. 'What's the matter?'

Violet cringed at the harshness of his tone. 'I'm just not sure if he'll agree to take any medication.'

Henry snorted in disbelief. 'Then we'll make him.'

'Mr and Mrs Torres—' the doctor interrupted, but Henry hadn't finished.

'We'll talk to him, explain all the benefits, beg him to listen, bribe him if necessary.'

'Henry, stop.' Violet was shaking her head. 'We're not going to bribe him.'

'Whatever it takes,' he said, speaking over her. 'We do whatever it takes to make him better, get him back in school, help him be normal.'

Violet turned beseechingly to Dr Mukherjee. 'Tell him,' she pleaded. 'He always does this. He never listens.'

Henry felt his cheeks grow very hot. They weren't here for marriage guidance. The psychiatrist, to his credit, did not lose an iota of his inimitable cool. Having regarded each of them for a few quiet moments, he settled his hands in his lap.

'If Luke is keen to try the treatment,' he said. 'And it would never be forced on him – that is not an option. But if he agrees, then it will still be some time before we see a noticeable improvement. Every person is different, and every person responds to therapy differently. With a condition such as this, I cannot simply place a pin along a piece of string and say, that is it, this is how long it will take. Luke will have to learn how to live with his depression and anxiety disorder, how to manage it. We can help; we cannot cure.'

Violet smiled faintly as if this all made sense, as if she'd been expecting it, and her acceptance prodded at Henry, goading him until he was forced to look away from both of them. Pushing back his heavy wooden chair across carpet deep enough to paddle in, he started to pace the room, chuntering to himself.

'I'm sorry,' Violet said, apologising not to but on behalf of him, just as she did so often for Luke, whenever he said or did something poisonous. She not only took on the blame for her own perceived shortcomings, but everyone else's as well. The only real thing she blamed him for was Luke's accident on the boat, and though she claimed to have forgiven him, Henry knew that her anger still festered. It was like a virus, eating away at their relationship from the inside out, and he didn't know what more he could do to make it up to her, and to Luke. He was at his wits' end.

'Can we please just agree that we'll try?' he said, coming to a stop behind where she was sitting. 'Try our best to do what Dr Mukherjee here suggests and convince Luke that it's in his best interests.'

Violet turned in her seat, not quite meeting his eye. 'Of course we can. I never said I wouldn't try.'

She sounded convincing enough, thought Henry. So why was it that he couldn't quite bring himself to believe her?

36

Violet

Luke and Henry remained where they were for some time, the two of them, not moving from where they'd sunk slowly to the floor. Luke wept, but silently, almost meekly, his eyes tightly shut against the carnage he'd caused. I met Henry's gaze for the first time since our awful row of a few nights ago and felt an understanding of sorts pass between us. We were back at an impasse, bonded once again by our child.

I found Eliza in the kitchen, and while she readied mugs for tea, I swept the floor. Beyond the boundaries of the house, all was still, quiet save for the tempered drone of crickets, and the distant purr of a passing plane.

As well as destroying several items of crockery, Luke had smashed out the glass panels in the door and pulverised a jar of shells that he and I had been adding to since his first summer on the island. Having cut up a cardboard box, I unearthed a roll of parcel tape and covered the gaping holes. Mercifully, the wooden frame was intact, which would make adding new panes of glass far easier. I knew that within a few days the job would be done, Henry having quietly and efficiently seen to it without fuss or performance. It had long been the routine back in England – our son would break things and Henry would fix them. The material things, at any rate.

The door into the kitchen opened and Luke walked into the room, his face blotchy and eyes bloodshot. My instinct was to pull him into my arms, but I knew better than to attempt it.

'Eliza made tea,' I said, and he offered her a sheepish smile.

'Cool. Dad had to make a phone call.'

'Shall we go outside?' Eliza suggested, two steaming cups in her hands.

Luke glanced uncertainly towards me, and I nodded in encouragement.

'Sure,' he said. 'All right.'

Stepping carefully over the full dustpan, he made his way out on to the patio, followed closely by Eliza. I heard the drawn-out exhalation of a deep sigh, and the scrape as one of them pulled out a chair. It was wrong to eavesdrop, but I felt rooted to the spot, the cardboard I'd stuck over the door providing too good a barrier to resist hiding behind.

It was Eliza who spoke first. 'I've never seen you like that.'

Luke's response was a tired sounding 'hmm'.

'I mean, you told me that you used to lose your temper, lose control, but I didn't realise how bad— Never mind.'

'It's all right,' he muttered. 'When I get like this, it is bad. Bad is the right word to use.'

'Is it?' she began, only for her words to stall. 'I mean, do you have any control at all, or is it . . .?'

'Intentional?' he replied. 'No. It feels as if someone else has taken over my motor functions, my mood, my reactions. It's pretty horrible, you know?'

'I can't bear the thought of that,' she said quietly. 'How frightening it must be for you.'

Her compassion was touching, but I couldn't help but feel chafed by it. Eliza had seen her way straight through to forgiveness before the – quite literal – dust had settled. My sympathy for Luke was front and centre, but there were other, more unsavoury emotions at play. I was scared for him, but I was also scared of him; angry that he suffered in this way, but angry that I suffered as a result of it and worn out from all the years I'd spent as a hostage on the unstable helter-skelter of his mental health.

'It's been ages since I, you know, lost it this badly,' Luke went on. 'I thought I was on top of it, and I am, most of the time. I could feel myself slipping down these past few days, since Antonio –' he paused to take a steadying breath – 'since the news, since my dad had a go at me.'

I closed my eyes against the memory of those words. *That screwed-up head of yours.*

'I should've known what to do,' said Eliza, sounding upset. 'I just stood there.'

'Don't be so hard on yourself,' I wanted to call through the door. I'd known Luke for nineteen years and I still didn't know what to do when he got like this.

'There's nothing anyone can do,' Luke told her, more solemn than sullen. 'It's on me to sort myself out, not you – not anyone else.'

'But that's so . . . I don't know . . . lonely,' Eliza pointed out. 'There must be help out there.'

'There is,' he conceded. 'My parents, they tried everything. I saw doctors, counsellors, this nice Indian psychiatrist dude, even a hypnotherapist. I was prescribed medication, first when I was around nine or ten, then again, a few years later, but I never took it. I didn't want to. I'd been online by then and read a load of stuff about how they make you feel numb and lazy, and that I'd be at risk of gaining a ton of weight. It was all there on forums and blogs, and I guess I wanted to think the worst, because I was scared, and I wasn't ready to accept that there was anything wrong with me. I went to one CBT session and thought it was a load of rubbish, but I probably should've tried harder, you know? I thought I knew better than all of them.'

I only realised that I was crying when the tears dripped on to my hands. At some stage during their conversation, I had lowered myself down on to the terracotta tiled floor, and I stared now at the slanting pattern of sunlight streaming in through the one intact window.

'It's not too late,' said Eliza cautiously. 'You can try again, go back to the doctor.'

It was as though I heard the shake of Luke's head when he replied. 'I want to do this my way.'

'I get that,' she allowed, 'but you know you can't let something like this happen again, don't you? And I know, I know,' she went on, as Luke started to argue, 'I know you say you can't control it, that it controls you, but you also say you can feel it coming. And if that's true, then you can learn to control it. Tell me, I'll help you – we can work on it together.'

I wiped my cheeks, pressing my lips together hard to muffle my sobs.

'My mum used to say that to me,' he said, so faintly that I had to inch closer to the door in order to hear. 'But being around her, it makes me ... I dunno, it's like a trigger or something. Like, I've already disappointed her before I've even said a word. She's always so fake with me, pretending that everything is OK and that whatever I do, it's fine, when I know it's not, I know it's bloody awful, I know that.'

He was becoming worked up, and I felt myself tense, my body so finely tuned to his moods, the threat of volatility. I understood what Luke meant by 'trigger', because for a long time, I had been triggered by him, too. The two of us falling into a rut of mutually destructive behaviour. All this time, I'd thought I was the best person for him, when in truth, I could well be the worst. At the wedding, it had been Ynes, not me, who'd managed to calm him. That awful day on the boat, Juan had been the one to console him as he spluttered, coughed, and convulsed with shock. Today, it had been Henry he'd needed, not me. I had only made him worse.

'Your mum loves you,' Eliza was saying, managing to soothe where I would only agitate. 'She'd do anything for you.'

Again, I marvelled at her maturity. She may have mocked her parents for being older than most, but their positive influence on her was clear. Henry and I hadn't had any choice but to make it up as we went along.

'I know,' Luke said listlessly. 'But at some point, she started doing nothing at all for herself. I mean, look at her and my dad. They keep telling me it was a mutual decision to split up, but I know it was me who broke them, me who came between them.'

I stared at the cardboard, stunned by what I was hearing.

'You can't blame yourself for what's going on with those two,' said Eliza, sounding almost wily. 'There's the whole Juan situation to consider.'

Shame hit me afresh, dousing me like an acid bath.

'That's probably my fault, too,' grumbled Luke. 'I kind of hero-worshipped him for years, used to hang out at his place a lot, which meant Mum did, too. Dad was always off working, keeping busy,' he added bullishly. 'It's what he does when he's stressed about something, and because of me, he was always stressed about something.'

'It's not your fault,' Eliza assured him, and I sent up a silent prayer of thanks to her for being so fair, so unequivocally in Luke's corner, for being his person. He needed her more than I'd allowed myself to acknowledge. It was time to stop being envious of their connection and start applauding it, and in the meantime, work on resetting my own relationship with Luke. The dynamic had to change, but it wasn't going to be easy to implement. I would require help, and there was only one person I wanted to ask.

As the thought came to me, so the man came into the room, his expression creasing into one of concern as he spotted me crumpled on the floor.

'Shh,' I whispered, crawling on my hands and knees towards him. 'They're outside.'

'Right,' said Henry, making no attempt to speak quietly. I winced as the back door creaked open and Eliza and Luke reappeared.

'Hey,' I said brightly as I shot up from the floor, taking the empty mugs from them and dropping them in the sink. 'I can do these, you two feel free to go, erm, do whatever it was you were going to do.'

Luke glanced at his girlfriend. 'We thought we'd go and lie down for a bit,' he said. 'Been a long day.'

'Good plan,' said Henry, stepping aside to let them pass.

I waited until the floorboards above us creaked with the sound of their footsteps before turning to face him.

'Thank you,' I said, as he opened the fridge to retrieve a beer, then changed his mind and picked up one of the cups of tea still on the side, ferrying it to the microwave.

'What for?'

I fidgeted on the spot, tucking one foot behind the other, folding and unfolding my arms. 'For coming back when the alarm was raised, for stepping in when I was unable to, for calming Luke down.'

Henry frowned. 'You don't have to thank me for being his dad.'

'I know. But I'm grateful. I couldn't reach him, and I lost my cool entirely. I'm useless.' I groaned and proceeded to reel off my failures. Henry said nothing, then moved to the back door and examined the botch job I'd done with the cardboard.

'Not bad,' he mused. 'Clean break, too – that'll make things easier.'

'What's the verdict on the dresser?' I asked, and he grimaced.

'Firewood.'

'Eeek.'

'I think it might be teak actually, but you were close enough.'

'Funny. Did Luke say anything?'

Henry opened the microwave and retrieved his tea. 'Not much,' he said, and then, 'Bloody hell! How many sugars are in this tea? It tastes like candyfloss.'

'Just the one, and really nothing at all?'

'If you're asking me if I know what the catalyst was, then I can't tell you, although I'm guessing the funeral had a lot to do with it. The reality of seeing a coffin and knowing what's inside it – that's enough to upset anyone.'

'And how are you feeling?'

'Me? Oh, you know, peachy.'

'I'm sorry, I just—'

'Just what?'

'Forget it,' I said, stepping around him so I could access the drawer where we kept the bin liners. Pulling out the roll, I tore a couple off and shook them out.

'I'm going to clear up what's left of the dresser.'

Without giving him time to reply, I went through to the lounge, where I dropped to my knees and began extracting splintered chunks of wood.

'Could have been worse.' Henry had followed me from the kitchen, and as I turned, he knelt down beside me.

'I don't see how,' I said.

'Could have been the dining table.'

'He did break the small one in the hallway,' I told him. 'Wasn't that one of the first pieces you made?'

Henry mulled this over. 'I think so. Probably why it fell apart so easily. Don't chuck that!' he said, as I went to bag what was left of one of the doors. 'There's still a hinge on there – I can use that.'

'Waste not want not,' I intoned, earning myself a smile of approval.

'One of many things your father and I agreed on.'

My father. His father. Our fathers.

'God, Henry, I'm so sorry about Antonio.'

He reached for a rubbish sack. 'I know,' he said. 'I know you are.'

We fell into a silence that for once felt welcome. There had been so much noise, and I wanted a chance to digest everything I'd heard Luke and Eliza discussing. The two of us cleared the mess from the lounge and then the hallway, Henry carefully wrapping every shard of broken vase up in newspaper, while I mopped up the water with an old beach towel. After a while, Eliza came down to let us know that Luke had fallen asleep and that she, too, was going to get an early night. I understood. We were all wrung out from the events of the day.

Nobody wanted to eat, but I made a plate of sandwiches anyway, thick slices of cheese topped with a generous helping of Ynes's home-made salsa; a bowl of tortilla crisps and cut-up segments of orange.

'I was hungrier than I thought,' Henry said afterwards, as he carried his empty plate to the sink. 'Do you fancy a proper drink?'

'No.' I shook my head. 'Can't face alcohol, but thanks anyway.'

'I might,' he said, pointing towards the back garden with the neck of his beer bottle. It felt like an invitation of sorts, but the last thing I wanted was another conversation that sparked into an argument. Instead, I said goodnight and made my way upstairs.

Having peeled off my dress, I left it on the floor and went through to the en suite in just my underwear, turning on the tap before splashing cold water across my face. It got into my eyes, and blinking furiously, I bent over the basin, rubbing until I could see once more. When I raised my head again to the mirror, I jumped in fright.

Henry was there, standing in the open doorway, watching me.

37

Violet

I started to speak, but he raised a finger to his lips.

'Hush,' he murmured. 'Don't say anything.'

I swallowed.

The tap was still running, and as I stood, stock still but with my heart hammering, Henry strode across and reached behind me, turning the faucet down to a trickle. I could feel his breath, warm against my throat. Droplets of water were running from my hairline down the sides of my face, where they dripped down on to my chest. Without taking his eyes off me, Henry picked up a towel and began to dab them away. His touch, though soft, was deliberate; and I wanted to pull the rough material from his hands so I could experience the sensation of skin against skin, those fingers that had explored me so entirely, turning me liquid with the merest graze. I started to speak, but again, he shushed me, this time by pressing his forehead against mine. The towel dropped to the floor, and for a moment, his hands hovered, one on either side of me.

He was still wearing a shirt and smart trousers, but his feet were bare. Keeping my gaze level, I raised my hands and began undoing his buttons. Henry watched on as if entranced, composed but paralysed.

'What are you doing?' he murmured, though he made no move to stop me.

'Undressing you,' I said, sliding a finger along his exposed collarbone, then down, my knuckles trailing through the dark hair on his chest. As my hands reached his stomach, the strap of my bra slipped from my shoulder.

'Oops,' I breathed, making no move to put it back. Henry lowered his eyes as my hands worked his belt buckle.

'Vee.' It was almost a whimper.

I unfastened the button of his trousers but left the zipper in place. His need for me was restrained, but one movement from me would unleash it. Instead, I brought my hands up behind my back and snapped open the clasp of my bra, letting it fall between us. He didn't protest when I moved forwards to pull the shirt from his shoulders, nor when I allowed my breasts to press against him, but when I moved my fingers lower once again, he seemed to flinch. There was so little barrier now, sensation a promise that thrummed with want, my own for him and his for me.

'Are you sure?'

He'd posed the question before I had the chance, and my answer came easily.

'Yes.' I said the word not only with my voice but my eyes, my lips, my breath, my whole body. Henry hesitated, eyes widening with what felt like wonderment, and then his hands were on me, pulling me against him, and his mouth, searching and seeking, tasting, and gnawing. He bent his head and sucked at my breasts until I cried out with pleasure, his fingers finding the waistband of my knickers and yanking them down as he kicked his way out of his trousers. There was no part of me he didn't reach, no pocket he wasn't probing, the two of us a tearing mess of mutual longing. I snaked my hand through our tangle of limbs, wanting to find him, to close my fingers around the hardness and guide him into me, but Henry pulled away, lifting me by my bottom on to the edge of the basin and dropping to his knees.

The back of my head collided with the mirror, and several of the bottles I'd propped above the cabinet came crashing down. I registered no pain, because Henry had opened my legs and buried his head between them, his fingers jabbing as his tongue flicked back and forth. There was no time to feel anything other than rapture, great soaring waves of it that flooded my body with heat. Dazed, I fell limply into his arms, aware of little more than the thudding of my heart and the heaviness clouding my mind as he carried me through to the bedroom.

Laying me down on the mattress with infinite care, he stood back to remove his boxer shorts, eyes never once leaving mine as I smiled up at him. It was my turn to devour him as he had consumed me, but when I shuffled up on to my knees, he shook his head. Henry wanted me properly, fully; I knew it because I yearned for it, too. For him, inside me, the two of us united as one, the rightness of it, of us together.

'Come here then,' I breathed.

He did not have to be told twice.

It was many hours later that we finally broke apart, sweaty and satiated. Henry rolled over on to his back, one arm flung out across the pillow, the hand of the other tightly grasped in mine. We hadn't spoken much, save for whispering well-practised phrases to each other during our lovemaking, and now the silence came like a blanket.

I decided to start with a compliment. 'That was nice.'

Henry paused in the process of wiping his brow. 'Nice? Is that all you've got?'

'Fine.' I squeezed my fingers against his. 'It was nicer than nice. How about lovely?'

'Lovely? That's a bit PG, don't you think?'

'Well, how would you describe it?'

'Hot,' he supplied. 'Scorching.'

'You make it sound as if I was feeding you spicy chicken wings.'

'It was finger lickin' good.'

'Very funny,' I droned, laughing as he pulled me towards him. When I raised a hand to his cheek, however, Henry jerked his head away.

'Sorry.' I faltered, unsure of myself.

'No,' he said, expression turning suddenly grave. 'I'm sorry, it's a reflex. I'm still getting used to the idea of someone other than me touching it.'

By 'it', he meant his scars.

'Can I?'

He bit down on his lip. 'All right – but here, let me.'

Lifting my hand, he guided my fingers to his jaw, closing his eyes as I traced the puckered flesh that spread from there to above his cheekbone. The surgeons had done their best, but the damage he'd sustained had been extensive. The corner of his lip remained a deep, bruised purple, and I could see the faint pink line where doctors had stitched his ear back in place.

'Does it hurt?'

His fingers closed around mine. 'Not any more.'

'Do you ever think about it? I mean, obviously you do, but . . .'

Henry looked at me steadily with the eye that was still fully functional. His other drooped in its socket, cursed to gaze forever downwards.

'Less frequently than I used to.'

'What about the other dreams?' I murmured, nestling myself more closely against him. For many years after Luke's near-fatal accident on the boat, Henry had suffered from terrifying nightmares, often thrashing himself and me awake in the small hours.

'I still have them, occasionally.'

I had been so angry with him on the day it happened, and for so many of the days that followed. It had trickled out of me for years, the resentment at what could have been like a slow poison.

'I still think about it all the time,' I whispered.

'The fishing trip?'

'The accident. It's stuck on a loop in my head.'

Henry stroked my cheek, gazing at me for a moment before turning away with a reluctant sigh.

'Where are you going?' I asked, as he scooted into a sitting position and lowered his feet to the rug.

'To the spare room.'

I sat up, wounded by his words. 'Why?'

Henry reached for his discarded boxers. 'I need space to think.'

'About what?'

He rubbed a hand through his hair, agitated by my badgering. 'It's been a long day – a long and difficult day. We both need to sleep.'

'That doesn't answer my question.'

Henry disappeared into the en suite and closed the door behind him. I heard the toilet seat being raised, the sound of the flush and the tap running. When he came back into the bedroom, the rest of his clothes were bundled up in his hands.

'We can talk in the morning,' he said. 'I have to be up early, there's a meeting with my father's *albacea*.'

'His what?'

'The executor of his will.'

'Oh. It's not— I thought it would be Mateo?'

Henry shook his head slowly. 'Apparently not. He asked Juan to do it.'

'You're joking?'

I could see that he wasn't. 'What the hell? So, Juan is who you're meeting?'

'So it would seem.'

'What about Luke?' I said, not caring that I was tearing open the laceration we'd gone some way towards healing over the course of the past few highly charged hours. 'He needs you here.'

I need you here.

'I'll only be gone for an hour or so.'

He was being so rational about it all, about the prospect of inheriting an enormous amount of wealth and property, not to mention the fact that he and I had just crossed the boundary from bitter adversaries to passionate lovers once again. Getting to my feet, I ran across the room, cutting Henry off at the door that led out on to the landing and wrapping my arms around his neck. I was still naked, and I felt the vulnerability that came with it, this show I was making of giving myself over to him so entirely. The dynamic of our relationship had always been balanced, and I knew as I begged him to stay, to hold me, to kiss me, to make love to me 'one more time', that I was throwing us off kilter.

'This isn't you,' he said, as he gently but firmly prised away my hands. Guiding me backwards until my calves connected with the bed frame, he lowered me slowly down. 'Get some sleep. For me. I promise we'll talk tomorrow.'

I slumped. 'Well then, goodnight, Henry.'

He waited until he was through the door before he turned, a faint smile on his lips that did not quite reach his eyes. To me, it felt a lot like pity; only a little like love.

'*Buenas noches*, Violet,' he said.

And then he was gone.

38

Henry

Eight Summers Ago

The bell above the door of Ynes's floristry tinkled as they pushed their way through into the shop. Luke, who for once had woken in a communicative and happy mood, charged ahead, and scooted around the till. There was a clatter as he ran through the colourful beaded curtain covering the door to the back room – or, as Ynes liked to call it, '*el estudio*'. It was where she arranged her bouquets, repotted her plants, and took the cuttings that she would later press into Violet's eagerly waiting hands.

Henry heard the older woman's call of greeting and allowed himself to relax for a moment. There weren't many people that he and Violet felt able to leave their son with, but Ynes was very near the top of the list. She genuinely enjoyed Luke's company and wasn't remotely fazed by his propensity to shut himself off from the world at times.

'I like having a protégé,' she told them. 'And I also believe that it is good for a boy to be bossed around a little bit, eh?'

Henry had glanced at Violet then, expecting her to take offence, but she'd merely smiled and wished her friend the best of luck.

'Pah,' Ynes had retorted. 'A real woman makes her own luck.'

Luckily for her – and for Henry and Violet – Luke's early fascination with flower pressing had not waned as he grew, and now, aged eleven, he was more than content to spend a day helping out in the shop. Ynes appreciated the fastidious way he worked, how he took his time neatly lining the hanging baskets and chose the right size carnation to fill the gaps in a box. Henry admired it, too. It made a pleasant change to have a reason to celebrate his son.

'Remind me, where it is you are going today?' said Ynes, as she leaned over to kiss Henry on each cheek. '*Muy guapo*,' she added, tapping a finger against his nose, and Violet rolled her eyes.

'He'll get a big head if you keep telling him how handsome he is.'

Ynes raised her shoulders in an exaggerated shrug.

'It is not my fault. I can only tell you what I see.'

She was wearing a shiny pink apron over a green patterned dress, and Henry thought that if he kept staring at her long enough, a picture might start to form as it did in the *Magic Eye* puzzle books Luke liked so much. His son and Violet only had to squint for a few seconds to find the hidden image, but it took Henry hours. Or it had, the one and only time he'd bothered to try.

'We're going to a furniture warehouse,' Violet told Ynes. 'You know, that big one on the outskirts of Palma. One of Henry's builder friends told him there's a whole heap of damaged items going for cents, so we're going to take the jeep and see what we can find. We'll only be a few hours,' she added hastily, and Henry thought it was probably more for Luke's benefit than that of their laid-back childminder. Ynes, predictably, waved Violet's assurances away with the flick of a ring-adorned hand.

'Do not hurry,' she said. 'I have plenty of jobs that will keep this *hombrecito* busy.'

'Bye, Luke,' Violet called, and got only a vague mutter of reply.

She was quiet for the first part of the journey, preferring to stare in contemplative silence out of the window as the jeep chewed up the miles of sun-baked asphalt, her hand resting lightly in Henry's lap. It was mid-July, and the sky was a cloudless blue, the earth below it cracked, and the grasses daubed beige by heat. Henry drew in a breath that tasted like baked tarmac and dust and pressed his foot down harder on the accelerator. As if stirred by the growl of the engine, Violet blinked sleepily, and turned from the view to face him.

'He'll be OK today, won't he?'

Henry took her hand, squeezed it. 'Better than OK. He'll be happy.'

She nodded, perhaps wanting rather than allowing herself to believe him. Henry wondered why she'd asked the question at all if his answer would make no difference to her.

'I'm really worried,' she said, 'about him starting secondary school.'

Henry was worried, too. It had taken the two of them, several teachers, and a determined team of support staff the best part of a year to get Luke resettled into his primary class, and now, just as they were beginning to see tentative improvement, he was facing a new and far more daunting gauntlet. Luke didn't like change, he detested noise, and he abhorred being around new people. It was going to be the biggest challenge he – and, by extension, they – had yet to face.

'I feel the same way as you do about it,' Henry allowed. 'But we have the whole summer to prepare him.'

An irritated exhalation of breath greeted this. 'Yes, but I want him to enjoy the holidays. It's not fair for us to put pressure on him.'

'Life is full of pressures, though,' Henry began, trotting out the line he had used on so many previous occasions.

Having the same discussion time and time again was taking its toll on their relationship; the love they shared crumbling; a once-glorious palace that was slowly being taken by the elements of frustration, distrust, and exhaustion. Henry's fingers began to tap the steering wheel.

'He's only a child,' Violet went on insistently. 'Our child.'

As if he didn't know that; was not aware of the fact during every conscious moment.

'Fine.' Henry gave in. He always gave in. 'I'll not so much as say the word "school" until we're back in the UK. I'll pretend it doesn't exist.'

Violet removed her hand from his lap. 'We're almost there,' was all she said.

The furniture store, at least, proved to be a good distraction. Within minutes of stepping from the searing heat of the mid-morning into the cool air-conditioned interior of the warehouse, Henry felt the sourness of his mood begin to sweeten. It smelled of sawdust and varnish, horsehair, and paint, all the scents he associated with the work that had become so intrinsic. When Henry was out on a job, he was the boss. There was no second-guessing or asking for permission, there was just doing: glorious, worthy, captivating doing. Working made Henry feel as if he had a purpose.

Having left Violet examining a range of designer bed frames that they neither needed nor could afford, Henry strolled through the open doors at the back and into a lumber yard, where he quickly selected a range of planks, some broken, mismatched chairs, and a flimsy-looking bookcase. With a small amount of skill and care, he could restore them. The thought alone acted like sandpaper against the roughened edges of his soul. Henry was proud that he had yet to encounter anything he wasn't able to fix.

Well, countered an internal voice, *almost anything*.

Once he'd loaded his purchases into the back of the jeep, the planks poking up through the open roof like teepee poles, Henry wandered back inside to find Violet.

There was no sign of her in the bed section, nor by the wardrobes. Distracted by a murmur of voices, Henry glanced up and saw that a swift had somehow flown inside and was darting across the high ceiling, its small body little more than a smudge as it dipped and dove around the fluorescent lights. He never saw these types of birds in England, only sparrows and pigeons, the occasional inquisitive robin. When Luke was still a toddler, Violet had taken him to feed the ducks down by the River Cam almost every day, a pastime he'd enjoyed until a swan decided to peck his ankle.

Henry squinted across the warehouse, scanning for a flash of red hair, and at last, he saw her, experiencing as he always did a lightening sensation in his chest. No matter how much he and Violet bickered, he still loved her with an intensity that had the power to move him. It was the foundation around which every other facet of their life together was built, and Henry believed in its strength. He had to.

'Found you,' he said, coming to a stop behind her.

Violet, to his surprise, was looking at nursery furniture. 'Isn't this crib gorgeous?' she enthused, all trace of her earlier impatience gone. 'Do you think it's hand-carved?'

Henry crouched to examine the softly rounded bars, and the intricate floral pattern on each of the end boards.

'I'd say that's likely, given the price,' he said. 'Pinewood, too, so it'd be easy to paint.'

'Shame we don't need one.' She shrugged and went to turn away, but Henry stood, taking her arm.

'What if we did?'

Violet looked at him askance. There were dark circles under each of her eyes, her skin pale after months of tepid British spring. 'What do you mean?'

Henry drew her towards him, his hands snaking around her waist. She had got so thin, he thought absently; he could feel the jut of her ribs through her T-shirt.

'I mean, why don't we buy the crib and start trying for a new somebody to use it?'

Violet went very still. 'You want another baby?'

'Yes.' As he said it, Henry realised it was true. 'I do. Don't you?'

Violet was looking at him as if he'd just suggested a picnic on the moon.

'It'd be great,' he continued, albeit warily. 'We might have a little girl this time – a mini version of you! Or another boy, a pal for Luke – it might be good for him.'

Henry knew it was shameless of him to use their existing child as a bargaining chip, but suddenly, in that moment, nothing felt more important than getting Violet onside, and the lure of life improving for Luke was a guaranteed vote winner.

'But what about me coming back to work?' she asked. Providing that Luke settled in at secondary school, as they hoped he would, the plan had been for Violet to pick up where she'd had no choice but to leave off, designing and curating the gardens of the houses Henry worked on.

'You still could,' he assured her. 'At least for a while, then take a few years off after the baby's born. It's only a small hiccup,' he added, sliding his hands up and cupping them around her face.

'A small hiccup,' she repeated, in a voice that promptly drove a nail through Henry's unfailing optimism.

'Yeah,' he said uncertainly. 'Wouldn't it be worth it?'

'Because we've done such a great job with child number one,' she drawled.

He took a step back, flummoxed by her acerbity.

'Luke isn't the way he is because of us,' he said quietly. 'You know that.'

'Do I?' Her eyes were full of tears now – hot, and defensive. 'I don't know, Henry. That's what everyone tells us, but what if they're only saying that to be kind? What if it is something in us? What if I did something to him?'

'Of course you didn't.' He moved to comfort her, but Violet shook him roughly away.

'We can't have another baby,' she said flatly. 'It's too much of a risk.'

But we could get it right this time.

Henry didn't let himself say it, knowing she would likely hate him if he did. He wasn't sure if he even believed it, but he wanted to. Didn't they deserve another chance?

Violet's bottom lip was wobbling; he ached to comfort her, but every time he tried, she shied away. Looking up towards the ceiling in frustration, Henry saw the swift above him, still trapped in a tragic dance as it bashed furiously against the warehouse roof, looking for a way out.

'It's different for you,' Violet said then, her voice small. 'You always wanted Luke.'

He felt himself stiffen. 'So did you.'

But Violet was shaking her head. 'No.' It was close to a whisper. 'And that's why – don't you see?'

Henry stared at her intently. 'See what?'

'What if Luke is the way he is because ... Because ...' Violet looked at him, stricken.

Henry felt ice in his veins. 'Because what?'

She took a deep breath. 'Because there was a moment when I didn't want him at all.'

39

Violet

I didn't think I'd be able to sleep after Henry left the bedroom, but almost as soon as I closed my eyes, slumber crept in and snatched me away. I slept more deeply and dreamlessly than I had in months, only waking when my phone, which had ended up on the floor, started to buzz with an incoming call.

Opening one eye, I read the name on the screen and groaned.

'Hello, Mum.'

'They're taking the car.'

'What?'

I sat bolt upright, so fast that the room spun.

'Your car, Violet. There are some men here with a tow truck. They say they're from the dealership. Where is the paperwork? Oh, heavens, the neighbours have just come outside – I'll have to call you back.'

'Mum!' I cried, but she'd already hung up.

Stabbing at the phone as I pulled on a pair of gardening shorts, I listened while the call rang out and my mother's voicemail picked up.

'Ring me back,' I commanded, then baulked as I noticed the time. It was almost eleven. How had I stayed asleep so long? Having located a vest top and scraped my sex-knotted locks into a toggle, I hurried along the landing and down the stairs. There were no signs of life save for two crumb-coated plates on the kitchen worktop, and as I glanced towards the boarded-up back door, I was reminded sharply of the previous evening; of the tears and the breakages, the fear and the pain, the sensation of Henry's lips as they roved across my body.

The phone rang again.

'Mum, thank god – what the hell's going on?'

'I couldn't stop them.' She sounded thoroughly ruffled. 'Peter next door says that because you've paid less than a third of the original agreement, they can seize the vehicle without going to court.'

'That sounds right.' I sighed, opening the fridge door only to close it again.

'I told them there must be some mistake. That they must have you confused with another Violet Torres.'

'Because there are loads of those around.'

'Well, then, they have the wrong address.'

I could have gone along with the lie, but what was the point? There had been so many lies, and I was tired of them, tired of trying, tired of pretending.

'Mum, listen to me. They took the car because I haven't been paying for it. Not for months. In fact, I'm surprised they didn't come and get it sooner.'

'Why on earth not?' She was edging closer to anger, and for once, it was justified.

'I had to prioritise other things.'

'Like flying off to Spain for a lovely holiday, I suppose?'

A lovely holiday.

I crossed to the sink and began to wash the plates, the handset clamped by my shoulder to my ear, my movements mechanical. A throb was beginning to radiate from my temples, a heat burning through me that couldn't be blamed on the temperature outside.

'Violet, are you still there?' Her voice sounded tinny and far away.

'I'm sorry,' I said. 'I know it must be embarrassing, having such a feckless daughter.'

She didn't appear to have heard me, or if she had, my words hadn't registered.

'This is what all those letters are about, aren't they – unpaid debts?'

'I'm sorting it out, Mum. It's just going to take a few more weeks. But, until then, I don't suppose that you could lend me a bit? Just a few hundred.'

'And where am I going to conjure that up from? I'll have to get equity release on this house,' she went on shrilly. 'Bail you out. Mr McCabe says it's worth a lot more than your father and I paid for it you know. He told me we made a wise investment, that if I ever sold, I should let him know and he'd give me a good price. I might have to take him up on it, because I tell you one thing, Violet, I won't have the bailiffs here. I refuse. What would people think?'

She had worked herself up into such a state that I had to shout her name repeatedly in order to get through to her.

'What did you say?' I said urgently. 'About Mr McCabe?'

She sniffed. 'He knocked on the door a few days ago, looking for you. I recognised him as an associate of Henry's and so I invited him in for a cup of tea.'

The tiles below my feet seemed to tremble.

'And?'

'And it was as I said. He said I was sitting on a moderate fortune, and that he'd be very happy to help if I ever decided to sell up. Very nice man. What's his given name again, Colin?'

'Corbin,' I intoned, picturing the man as I did so, hearing the menace behind his outwardly jovial tone as he'd reminded me that 'a deal is a deal'. I had stopped responding to his texts and no longer answered when he called – was it any real surprise that he'd sought an alternative way to reach me? The message was loud and abundantly clear: I know where your mum lives; I can get to her whenever I want.

'Corbin, that's it,' went on my oblivious mother. 'Very nice man.'

I heard the sound of voices in the hall, then Eliza appeared in the kitchen, Luke a few feet behind. He was clutching a potted flamingo lily wrapped in cellophane, which he thrust towards me.

'Oh, how wonderful,' I said, accepting the plant. Then, 'No, Mum, not you. Listen, don't worry about the –' I turned away, lowering my voice to a murmur – 'other stuff. I'll make sure everything is paid off soon, you have my word. I have to go now, but I'll call you. Soon. Take care of yourself, OK? Be safe.'

'Grandma's on the warpath,' I said as I ended the call. Luke busied himself by looking everywhere but at me.

'Eliza thought you'd like it,' he muttered.

'We both did,' she interrupted gallantly. 'And Ynes sends her love.'

The three of us fell silent as a low rumble signalled the arrival of the jeep in the road outside. I opened one drawer after another, searching in vain for scissors to remove the cellophane, before selecting a carving knife from the block to use instead. I was in the process of watering the lily when Henry strode into the room.

'Oh,' he said, stopping short. 'You're all here.'

Touching a hand to Luke's arm, checking his son was calm, he took a glass from the cabinet and filled it from the tap, not once looking in my direction.

'How was the meeting?' I asked, taking my new plant to the table, and positioning it in a spot where it would benefit most from the morning light.

Henry shook his head.

I caught Luke's eye, saw a question there. 'What meeting?' he said.

When Henry didn't immediately answer, I filled in the details I knew, explaining about the will but leaving out the part about Juan being executor.

'And?' he pressed. 'Dad?'

Henry put down his glass. 'There's a sum for you.'

Eliza gave in to a tentative smile, but Luke remained impassive.

'Right.'

'It's being held in what amounts to a trust,' Henry went on. 'And I'm afraid it's in there until you turn twenty-one.'

I experienced a rush of gratitude towards Antonio.

Luke said nothing, and after a beat or two, Henry continued.

'I can't give you an exact figure, because it may change due to various investments, but it's somewhere in the region of five hundred thousand.'

Eliza's gasp of astonishment matched my own.

'Five hundred thousand euros?' I said, and Henry took a deep breath.

'At least.'

Luke had yet to respond. He was staring at Henry as if waiting for the punchline.

'That's ... well, wow. Enough for a house, or a business start-up. How incredibly generous of Antonio,' I said.

Henry cleared his throat. 'There's more.'

'Oh?'

I had been the one to reply, but he had the undivided attention of everyone.

'Well, for starters, Mateo gets the villa, the boat, and the family share of the business. There are cash gifts for a few staff, those he was closest to –' Henry shot me a look

– 'including Juan. He's inherited a ten-thousand-euro lump, as well as the car.'

'I don't understand,' I said. 'Why so much to Mateo? He doesn't even live here.'

Henry looked nonplussed. 'Spanish tradition decrees that most assets go to the eldest child. That's not me.'

'No, but—'

'And I wouldn't want the business share,' he added firmly. 'Mateo is a better fit.'

Given that Antonio had been a property developer and Henry was a property restorer, it made little sense to me that Mateo, a neurosurgeon who lived full-time in Dubai, had been deemed the obvious successor. As if I'd spoken my concerns aloud, Henry added, 'He'll probably sell – or stay on as a partner in name only.'

'What do you get?' asked Eliza, who'd slithered into her usual place under the nook of Luke's arm. It was as if the blow-up from the previous night had never happened, and I was relieved to see zero sign of any lingering unease on her part. It would help Luke, to know he could trust Eliza implicitly, and it helped me, too. Henry was tapping his hands against the edge of the worktop, a sure sign he was agitated.

'The office,' he said, to which Luke and I both frowned. In all the years I'd known Antonio, he'd always worked from his sprawling hillside mansion here in Pollença. Seeing our confusion, Henry went on, 'There's a place in Palma, the ground floor of a house in the old town. It hasn't been used as anything other than a dumping ground for decades, but apparently Papá still owns it. At least, he did. It's mine now.'

'You should contest,' I blurted. 'The will, I mean – surely Mateo can see how unfair it is?'

Henry was shaking his head. 'I got this place, remember? La Casa Naranja is my inheritance.'

It was impossible to miss the look he threw Luke's way, the hope he'd harboured that his son would accept the keys for this house one day, and thus continue the tradition.

'But it makes no sense,' I insisted. 'I can't believe Antonio would've left you so little of real value.'

'But he did.' Henry's rebuttal was concise, confident. 'The only things I value more than this place are you and Luke.'

I had been ready to say more, but his words abruptly halted mine. Henry looked uncomfortable, as if he'd let slip a secret that wasn't his to share.

'We should visit the office,' said Luke, from beneath an acre of dark fringe. 'Check it out, see what's there.'

'Sure,' Henry agreed. 'When do you want to go?'

Luke looked down at Eliza, who smiled encouragingly. 'What about right now?'

40

Violet

The first key Henry produced opened a door that led straight into a cobbled courtyard. There was a single flight of stone steps leading up to the left, a long, low bench on the right, while towards the rear I could see a bank of potted plants and several wrought-iron tables and chairs. Everything was immaculately clean, and the space felt blessedly cool after the hot drive down from Pollença.

'Have you been here before?' I asked, as Henry stared around.

'Once, I think, when I was a teenager. I seem to remember my mother bringing me here to parade me around in front of my father, so he'd agree to give her money.'

I guessed Henry must have put a call through to his mother in Bali to let her know that Antonio had died, and wondered if it would be to him that she made her next plea for money. Not that I could talk . . .

'I thought you said the office was borderline derelict,' said Eliza, and Henry turned momentarily to face her, his mouth set in a grim line.

'I've been told it is,' he replied. 'We'd better go and take a closer look.'

He took off across the courtyard, leaving the three of us to follow in his stead, presently coming to a stop in front of another door, this one smaller and far grubbier than the one we'd come through from the street. Once open, it emitted a putrid scent of rotting vegetables, and Luke raised a hand to cover his nose.

'One sec,' said Henry, heading inside as Eliza made a gagging sound, then returning a few minutes later with a tied-up rubbish sack.

'Mini fridge,' he explained, holding it aloft. 'Whoever unplugged it didn't bother to empty it first. I've opened all the windows, so the smell should clear pretty quickly.'

Eliza nodded, eyes watering with the effort of not throwing up, and Luke took a few steps back, giving the bag a wide berth.

'I might just . . . Shall we go and get some cleaning stuff?' he suggested.

Eliza nodded furiously. 'Yes, good idea, I'll come with you.'

'Take my wallet.' Henry fished it out from his back pocket and passed it across. 'Bring back some snacks as well.'

We watched them go, fingers entwined, and bodies pressed together, and heard the clank of the heavy outer door closing behind them.

'Should we have asked them to get pegs for all our noses?' I said mildly. 'How bad is it?'

Henry smiled rather ruefully. 'Remember that guesthouse in Great Yarmouth, the Easter before Luke turned four?'

I shuddered. 'As bad as that?'

Henry clenched his teeth together. 'Worse.'

The office, as it had allegedly once been described, consisted of a single square room plus a broom-cupboard-sized bathroom complete with toilet and minuscule basin. I lifted the lid to find brown, stagnant water festering in the bowl, and hurriedly closed it again. The electricity was off, and each of the windows opened out into a narrow lane packed with more tall town houses, meaning barely any natural light filtered in. It was dingy and dank, sad and unloved, and I noticed that even Henry, who prided himself on transforming properties not dissimilar to this into beautiful, liveable spaces, looked downcast by the state of it.

'I wonder why he kept hold of this place for so long,' Henry mused, running his finger along the top of a rickety old desk and disturbing years of dust in the process.

'For storage?' I suggested, only to lever open a filing cabinet and find nothing save for a few empty document folders inside.

There was a framed photo on the desk, and Henry picked it up, using his thumb to wipe the glass clean. I saw the lift in his shoulders, the twitch of his lips.

'My great-grandparents,' he said, passing it over. 'Raimundo and Valentina.'

I'd heard talk of the couple before from both Henry and his late father but had never seen them, so it was with some eagerness that I examined the picture.

'That's their wedding photo,' Henry said, coming to stand beside me and pointing to the long veil that was draped over the seated woman's shoulders. Like me, she had chosen to wear a garland of flowers in her hair for her nuptials, though unlike me, nobody had attempted to claw them off before the pictures were taken. The man standing beside her was strikingly handsome.

'He looks like you,' I told Henry. 'Same eyes. And that expression is pure Luke.'

'Do you think I should grow a moustache like his?'

'All the better to tickle people with.'

Henry laughed faintly. 'Perhaps not, then.'

Unsure of what to say in reply, I was relieved when Luke and Eliza reappeared, bringing disinfectant, dusters, more rubbish sacks, and several tubes of crisps with them. Having gone into mild ecstasies over the black-and-white photo of Raimundo and Valentina Torres, Eliza set about polishing the frame, while Luke and I emptied a sheaf of old papers from a desk drawer and began to flick through them.

'Anything interesting?' asked Henry, through a mouthful of salt and vinegar Pringles.

'Looks to be building insurance and various completion documents,' I said, squinting to make out the scribbled Spanish words. 'Antonio's signature is on a lot of them.' I thrust a few sheets towards him, and Henry examined them briefly, forehead a concertina of lines.

'All these are dated from more than twenty years ago,' he said. 'Surely we can bin them?'

I had no idea, and so merely shrugged, but Luke looked thoughtful.

'You should probably keep everything relating to house sales or deeds,' he told us. 'Just in case.'

Henry considered. 'I'll give the lot to Mateo,' he decided. 'Let him choose.'

I left Luke and Eliza to put the paperwork into an old box file and continued exploring the rest of the office space, wrinkling my nose at the dust motes that hung in the air. A small potted cactus had thirsted to a crisp just below one of the windows, and a map of the island hung loose from its corroded Sellotape fastenings. Lifting some ancient cushions from a long, low table, I brought them to my face and was promptly choked into a coughing fit by the dank smell.

'Are you all right?'

Henry had rushed over and was hammering my back.

'Here,' he said, when I'd regained control of my breathing, and passed me a bottle of water from the bag of supplies. Then, 'Oh, what's this you've found?'

Squatting down, he ran a finger over the top of what I had assumed was a table but what I could see now was actually an intricately carved wooden chest.

'Cedar,' said Henry, lowering his ear to the lid and giving the side a quick tap. 'And seems to have all its original iron fittings. If I had to guess, I'd say it was eighteenth century.'

'If you say it is, I'll happily believe you.'

'They come up every so often in house clearances over here,' he said, as Luke and Eliza came to join us. 'Sell really well at auction.'

'For how much?'

Eliza had asked the question, which fortunately meant I wouldn't have to. The subject of money was a tetchy one between myself and Henry, and I didn't want to be accused by him of reducing everything to its cash value. As it was, his eyes raked over mine before he answered.

'It's hard to say, but I've seen them go at auction for around two thousand euros.'

'Is that all?'

Luke sniggered, but Eliza looked nonplussed. 'It's three hundred years old – perhaps even more. It should, by rights, be priceless.'

'I agree with you.' Henry smiled at her. 'But there are a lot of them around – availability dilutes worth. Only the rarest things fetch the highest prices, it's why original artwork always tops the bill. There's only one *Mona Lisa*, after all.'

Luke was looking at his father with new respect. 'I didn't know you were into art,' he said.

'Oh, you know,' Henry feigned indifference. 'I've picked up a few things over the years, eavesdropped on yours and Mum's conversations when you thought I was asleep in front of the telly.'

He had? This was news to me as well.

'Why didn't you ever say?' Luke asked, and at this, Henry looked sheepish.

'Because it was your thing. I didn't want to get in the way.'

A loaded silence followed this, which Eliza eventually broke by sneezing several times in quick succession.

'There's so much dust in here,' she sniffed. 'I'm going to keep polishing.'

I glanced at Luke; his deep-set eyes unreadable behind the mop of his dark fringe, then down at Henry, who was tugging ineffectually at the padlock on the chest.

'I wonder if there's a key somewhere in here,' he mumbled, more to himself than us, although I told him I'd help him hunt for it regardless. I was halfway through a second, smaller filing cabinet, when the outer door was pushed slowly open.

'*Hola*,' called a male voice.

Henry stood up.

The visitor, who was small and wiry with tufts of white hair and half-moon spectacles, introduced himself as Ignacio before explaining that he owned the rest of the building.

'I knew Antonio when he was a boy,' he said in English, appraising Henry before remarking, 'You are very tall, not like him at all.'

'My mother was a giant,' Henry replied soberly, and the man wheezed out a chuckle.

'Come,' he said, beckoning with a wizened hand. 'We must speak about business.'

Throwing a mystified glance over his shoulder, Henry followed the man out into the courtyard. I could hear the murmur of their voices as I continued my fruitless search for the padlock key, unable to discern much of what was being said. When Henry came back a few minutes later, he seemed happier somehow, lighter.

'That's one problem solved,' he said, pouring a stack of crisps into his hand.

'He had the key?' I asked hopefully, and for a moment, Henry looked confused.

'Oh, you mean . . .? No, nothing like that. He just wanted to know if I'd let him rent this place. His daughter is taking over the house and has plans to turn it into a hostel. They want this office as a sort of lounge area for guests, somewhere they can socialise, and they're prepared to hire me to do the refit.'

'Sounds like a win-win,' said Luke, and Henry smiled.

'I thought so, too. I was never going to do anything with this place – it may as well be given a new lease of life.'

'A second chance,' enthused Eliza, and again, Henry's roving gaze settled briefly on me. Having finished his crisps, he glanced around.

'Now that I know the place will be gutted in due course, I say we leave most of the mess where it is. It'll all end up in a skip in a few weeks anyway.'

'Most?' I echoed, as Henry wiped the crumbs from his hands onto the front of his overalls.

'Everything except the paperwork and the chest,' he said. 'We're taking that with us.'

Luke carried one end and Henry the other, each stepping carefully over the line of plant pots in the courtyard while I locked the office door behind us. Eliza led the way, issuing instructions as she went – 'watch out for the Monstera'; 'don't trip over the step' – and we made it back to the jeep without incident.

'Shit,' said Henry, as he propped his end of the chest against a raised knee. 'The car keys are in my pocket – can you?'

I was ready to retrieve them for him, but as Henry readjusted his position, Luke somehow lost his grip on the chest, which teetered for a second before crashing down sideways on to the cobbles, its lid crunching open as the centuries-old wood splintered apart. Eliza let out a wail, Henry cursed, but I made no sound at all. Any words that might have come were caught fast in my throat, trapped behind the shock that had settled itself there the moment my brain took in what my eyes were seeing. The chest had not been padlocked for no reason; it had been secured to protect what had been hidden inside.

Bundle after bundle of tightly rolled banknotes.

41

Violet

There looked to be close to a million euros, as well as a letter addressed to Henry. I had been the one to find it, the slim white envelope sliding between my fingers as I bent to help the others stuff the money back into the broken chest.

'Here,' I said, offering it to Henry. For a moment, he just stared at it, then snatching it from my hand, he folded it in half and shoved it deep into the pocket of his overalls. It was clear that as far as he was concerned, the priority was getting the cash off the street before someone noticed; the letter would have to wait.

Nobody spoke again until we were all back in the jeep, Luke in the passenger seat with Eliza behind him and me beside her. Henry had gone very pale, his jaw working as he chewed over his shock and, what, excitement? It certainly wasn't an every-day occurrence to discover a real treasure chest, and when I made this point, Luke grinned in amusement.

'I always did think of my father as a kind of pirate,' said Henry. 'I think if he could have got away with flying a Jolly Roger from the boat, he would have.'

'What do we do with it all?' I asked. 'I mean, shouldn't we take it to a bank?'

Henry turned around in his seat. 'No, not yet – not till I know where it came from.'

'We do kind of know,' I said, glancing towards the remains of the chest. 'It can only have been Antonio's money, and he clearly wanted you to find it.'

Henry shook his head, both hands gripping the steering wheel. 'I want to know where he got it,' he said. 'Whose money it is really.'

The compulsion to plead with him was strong, but I forced it down. Did he not see what this money could do for us – for me? If La Casa Naranja was worth the two million euros that Malcolm and Mags were willing to pay for it, then my share amounted to half that. Now that Henry had this cache of, well, cash, he could afford to buy me out, meaning the house would not have to be sold. It was a simple fix to a sticky problem and, as far as I was concerned, made perfect sense.

Henry had begun to tap his foot against the bottom of the jeep, his head lowered towards his hands as he considered his options. Luke glanced from Eliza to me, the three of us exchanging a 'what now?' look.

'Henry,' I began, only to be interrupted by the engine firing up. 'I thought we were staying in Palma for dinner?' I said hesitantly, although in truth, I was glad of an excuse to miss it. As much as I loved the tapas and extensive wine selection at our family favourite La Boveda, I didn't have the funds to pay for either – not even close. Then again, it would've been nice to spend time wandering through the backstreets of the old town, past wooden doors and brightly painted shutters, artful graffiti, and sculptures, as well as perusing the craft stalls clustered opposite the harbour. I'd never known Palma not to throb with people, and to lose myself among the crowds, if only for a fleeting few hours, would perhaps have been a tonic of sorts.

'Can't.' Henry tooted the horn, startling a group of tourists who'd idled into the road. 'Need to stash this lot somewhere safe.'

Barely giving the passers-by time to reacquaint their shoes with the pavement, he accelerated forwards, the jeep's brakes squealing in protest as we circumnavigated a small *plaça* and powered out on to the main road. I watched as the capital fell away behind us in all its distinguished splendour, turning my gaze to greet the vast blue carpet of the Balearic Sea as we beetled along the waterfront.

Almost as if he sensed my yearning, Henry let out a low whistle.

'Apologies,' he said, addressing the car at large. 'We can come back on another day.'

The others told him not to worry. They'd been here a few times already, having taken the bus down from Pollença, and Eliza had done 'all the touristy stuff I wanted to do'. 'I much prefer Pollença anyway,' she said loyally, and Luke smiled to himself.

The further we drove out of the city, the harder I was finding it to focus on anything other than the stack of banknotes, my mind unhelpfully doing sums and presenting me with enticing facts. Each of those bundles, it whispered, comprises twenty thousand euros; one of those would go a long way towards solving your problems, two would wipe them out. Who would it really hurt if you took them? Wasn't this fate's way of ensuring that everyone got what they needed? Luke has his inheritance from Antonio, Henry has his share of the house, plus the business. It's not fair if you're the only one to end up with nothing at all.

Or was it? Hadn't I ended up exactly where I deserved? An image of Henry from the previous night came to me then – his body above mine, his moan of pleasure as we moved together, the flick of his tongue against the hollow of my throat. During those moments, the rest of the world had fallen away, our desire too ferocious a component for even bitterness and resentment to beat. He had forgiven me, or so it had felt, and I'd wanted that feeling of relief to go on indefinitely; had hoped that a vestige of his mercy would survive the dawn, and that we would at last be able to try again.

It was with a certain amount of reluctance that I clambered out of the jeep an hour later, legs stiff and throat parched, unwilling to face whatever was coming next in this strangest of sultry hot days.

'Wait here a minute, will you?' Henry tossed me the keys. 'Guard the mon— jeep. I need to get something.'

Luke and Eliza offered to stay with me, but I shooed them towards the house. Henry was back within a few minutes, an empty canvas bag in his hands.

'Where are you going to stash it?' I asked, as he scooped up the bundles.

'I'm not one hundred per cent sure yet,' he admitted. 'I was thinking the loft, you know, that small space above the turret, but—'

'But?'

'What if that's not secure enough?' He frowned. 'What if there's a fire?'

'It's survived this long,' I pointed out. 'And unless you have a friend with a vault we can borrow, I don't see what choice we have. La Casa is our safest place.'

'You're right,' he agreed, pulling across the zip before lifting the bag from the jeep. 'Whoa, that's seriously heavy.'

'Let me have a go.'

He stepped back and I took hold of the leather straps.

'Bloody hell, it really is,' I said, teeth gritted as I heaved it off the ground. 'I suppose we should be grateful that he didn't collect it all in two-euro coins.'

'There's probably another hoard of those somewhere else – under the floorboards of the boat perhaps? Buried in his back garden.'

'Maybe he put a treasure map in with the letter.'

Henry raised a hand to his pocket. 'I should read it.'

It was obvious he found the prospect daunting, that he was primed for further disappointment or upset. Other than the initial bout of grief that had spewed out of him so devastatingly the night Antonio died, Henry had remained outwardly impassive about the loss of his father. And while I'd wanted to broach the subject on multiple occasions, events had conspired against us. All I yearned to do now, as he stood turning the envelope over in his hands, was comfort him.

'I'll stay with you,' I said quietly. 'I won't read it, if you don't want me to, I'll just be here, in case.'

He didn't say anything for a while, nor did he raise his eyes to mine. A stray cat stalked out from where it had been sheltering in the shade of the low wall and rubbed its scrawny body against my ankle. I should feed it; take it inside and pour a bowl of milk, scrape some tuna from a tin on to a dish. Heat scratched and leaves stirred, a moped engine growled into life, leaving in its wake the sweetly cloying scent of gasoline, thick in the dry air.

'Shall we go into the garden?'

I glanced up. There was a beseeching undertone to his words, and I thought I could understand why. The garden had always been where I went to feel protected, connected, and to have my soul nurtured – but I hadn't guessed that Henry hankered after those feelings, too. Now, as I led the way around the side of the house, I wondered how I could have overlooked his affection for the space we'd both had a hand in creating. I had planted in beds that Henry dug, picked fruit from the trees he'd pruned, admired the distant mountains from pathways laid down by him, and all the while I'd selfishly deemed the area mine.

In silent consent, we followed the steps down until we reached the spot beside the wall, not far from where the fuchsia blooms of the gladiolus pushed proudly through the soil every year. The first flower Henry had ever picked me I had pressed behind glass. I still kept it propped beside my bed, a faded yet no less beautiful reminder of the delicate nature of love. I wished we had endured as it had.

Henry waited until we were settled, then he slid a finger under the flap, tore through the envelope, and cleared his throat. There was a single sheet of paper inside, messy blue scrawl covering one side of it, and I watched as he scanned what was written. It was all in Spanish, and his lips moved as he read, sounding out the words, making sense of their meaning.

'I knew it,' he said, tapping the page with his finger. 'It's black money,' he said. 'Ill-gotten gains. The profit he creamed off the top of every dodgy deal he did over the past ten years.'

Black money. We had discussed it, the four of us, joked about it during that first awkward dinner we'd had on the evening I arrived. It felt like a lifetime ago.

'Can you face reading it to me?' I asked, not really thinking he would.

Henry frowned, then nodded, and having straightened out the letter, he started to speak:

For my beautiful giant boy,

I am confident that you will be the one to find this, and I want you to know that I have saved it here for you. Do not be angry that the house and the business have gone to Mateo. It is the proper way of such things, and he will do what is right.

Now, I must be truthful and confess that I write this letter knowing I will not live to be an old man. I have been ill for some time. The doctor told me that I must stop doing the things that bring me pleasure, but I cannot exist in a life of rules and boundaries. That has never been my way. It is why I have saved this black money for you; I have it because of the fact that I refuse to obey the rules. Do not feel ashamed of your father; understand that he did not ever wish to do harm.

You are not similar to me, Enrique, and yet we are the same. When I look at you, I see the man I could have been, but I guess that you must think of me as a lesson in how not to be. Our path has not been a straight one, but what is a journey without hills and mountains? I have tried to challenge you, never lie to you, and always, my son, fiercely love you and—

Henry broke off, lowering the notepaper and wiping his eyes against his shoulders. Without waiting for permission, I stepped forwards and put my arms around him.

'It's OK,' he said, easing away from me. 'I'm all right – it's just reading it aloud is hard. I'm being stupid.'

There were tears in my eyes, too. 'What is a journey without hills and mountains?' I murmured. 'I'd no idea Antonio had it in him to be so poetic. I thought my father took the lead when it came to making profound statements, but it turns out they were both at it.'

He smiled a watery smile. 'I still miss Christopher,' he said.

'And Antonio?' I managed, though it was hard to get the words out.

Henry relinquished a weary breath, before glancing again at his father's words. Defiant to the last, cheerfully unrepentant, and stubborn as ground elder, Antonio had, in the end, focused on the thing that mattered more than any other. Love.

'Yes,' Henry said, and for a split second, as he smiled at me, I saw a glimpse of the boy he'd once been.

'But I wish more than anything that I didn't have to.'

42

Henry

Six Summers Ago

For the first time since he had let himself into La Casa Naranja on his eighteenth birthday, Henry did not feel comforted to be within its familiar walls. In truth, he was overwhelmed by an urge to escape.

It had not been an easy journey. Hell, he thought, it had not been an easy year.

Turning at the stomp of teenaged feet on stairs, Henry watched his son disappearing from view, and braced himself for the resounding slam that would follow.

Make that thirteen years.

Violet trudged into the hallway, a shambling mess of despair, and made her way into the kitchen with the bags of food they'd bought on their way here from the airport. Henry watched on in silence as she stacked ten packets of instant noodles into a cupboard. Luke was going through one of his 'picky phases' and was refusing to eat much else.

'He'll catch scurvy,' Henry had warned his wife, only to be swiftly rebuked.

'Don't be so ridiculous – it's not the sixteenth century.'

In the end, he'd bought some vitamin C tablets and begun crushing them up to stir into his son's morning cup of tea. If Violet knew, she'd be furious – not because he was slipping supplements to their son on the sly, but because he'd dared to undermine her role as 'Mum'. Henry was no longer trusted to take care of his own child – that much had been made clear to him ever since the incident in the fishing boat. Where once the phrase 'I love you' had been what he and Violet said most often to one another, now all Henry seemed to hear from her was a terse 'I'll do it'.

I'll tidy his room.

I'll do his dinner.

I'll talk to him.

I'll take him to that appointment.

She did not appear to need, nor want, any assistance from him. Henry wished he didn't feel so bitter. Violet had lost her father only a few months ago, her grief making her retreat even further inside herself, and he knew that it was his responsibility to support her. If only she would let him.

'Can I help?' he asked, going to stand beside her at the worktop. Violet was holding a box of teabags in her hands, staring at them as if she'd forgotten what they were.

'What?' she replied vaguely, with a half-turn in his direction.

'Help,' he reiterated. 'With the shopping.'

'Yes,' she said, though shaking her head. 'I mean no. It's fine. I'll do it.'

Henry gritted his teeth.

'It's so hot,' she said absently, stepping around him to open the fridge, into which she put the teabags, her purse, and three tins of tuna.

'Why don't you go upstairs and take a cool shower?' he suggested obligingly. 'I can do all this.'

'No.'

'Vee—'

'I said, I'll do it. I'm just hot, that's all. It's July and we're in Mallorca. A cool shower isn't going to change matters.'

Having closed the fridge, she filled a glass with water and pressed it against her forehead. Unable to stand the tension any longer, Henry left her to it and busied himself with taking the cases upstairs, unpacking the few clothes and toiletries he'd brought, and changing from his jeans into shorts. Pausing on the landing, he craned his head into the stairwell that led up to Luke's turret bedroom, drawn as he so often was by an unsettling concern that his son might be doing something self-destructive. Hearing nothing, Henry crept closer, the floor creaking under his weight.

'Who's there?' demanded a voice, and Henry, to his shame, tiptoed hurriedly away. Increasingly, he found dealing with Luke difficult, the need he had to love and protect clashing with the helplessness of not being able to do so. In the aftermath of his beloved granddad's death, Luke had gone on a rampage through their rented terrace, smashing his fist through the airing cupboard door, kicking out several banisters, yanking down the blind in his bedroom and throwing his mum's collection of potted ferns through the bathroom window, where they broke into smithereens on the driveway below. Grief manifesting as anger, an understandable and even predictable response, especially from a boy who struggled to control his emotions, and yet knowing this made it no less painful to witness. The neighbours had called the police, who'd murmured sternly about a possible charge of criminal damage, while Violet had sat on the carpeted floor of their new front room and wept. Henry had been the one to placate and appease, the person who'd taken time off work to make the necessary repairs, and the husband who'd been pushed away when he tried to offer comfort. Having locked himself in his bedroom for the best part of two days following the incident, Luke had re-emerged as if nothing had happened, remarking amiably on the fact that term time was almost at an end, before asking Violet if he could have some money to buy art supplies.

Henry had watched from his position halfway up a step-ladder while she rooted through her handbag and handed over two twenty-pound notes.

'What?' she'd said, when Henry had made a 'really?' face behind Luke's departing back. 'He needs it for school.'

'It's not that.'

'Then what?'

Henry leant over, speaking to her in the hushed, urgent tone that had become his 'serious voice'. 'He didn't even say sorry.'

Violet's cheeks flushed. She was so defensive, curled tight like a ball of elastic bands. 'Didn't you see him?' she hissed. 'He's stable again. I'm not going to risk ruining that by getting at him.'

'I'll just get back to fixing everything he broke then, shall I?' Henry scoffed, to which Violet had merely rolled her eyes. There was very little fight left in her, but any fire she did have was being kept in reserve for him, not Luke. The unfairness of this made Henry crackle with irritation.

'We need to go back to the airport,' was how Violet greeted him when he returned to the kitchen. Everything she'd put away in the cupboards was spread out across the work surfaces, along with the contents of her handbag. Henry pushed a finger through the mess of old hair ties, stray tampons, a brush trailing red hairs and a half-finished packet of Rolos. Would she think of him when it came to eating the last one?

'Why?'

'I've lost my purse. I must have left it on the plane. I had it when we boarded, I remember putting the luggage stubs in there, but now it's gone. What if someone's taken it? I had everything in there and—'

'Vee.'

'What?'

'Open the fridge.'

She gawped at him.

'Seriously, open the fridge.'

'I'm not going to open— What are you doing?'

Henry had done it for her, and now stood pointing at the very thing she'd been searching for, trying his best not to laugh.

'Oh, come on,' he chided. 'Even you must see that it's funny?'

'To you maybe,' she stormed, snatching up the purse but leaving the tuna and teabags.

Henry folded his arms. 'You think I put it in there?'

'Well, didn't you?'

'No! I watched you do it, you Nelly.'

'Then why didn't you tell me at the time?'

She might well be riled up, but so was he, and this time, Henry was not prepared to back down.

'Oh, I don't know, Vee, let me think. Maybe because you would have bitten my head off like you always do.'

She harrumphed. 'I don't.'

He stared at her. 'OK. If you say so.'

'I'm not doing this,' she snapped, and promptly flounced from the room, slamming the door behind her so hard that it set the pots and pans ringing. Like mother like son, thought Henry sourly, as he checked to make sure the wooden panels were still fully intact. Feeling gloomy, he went into the rear garden, where he paced the length of the small patio, tugging beer from a bottle and grumbling to himself. The sun beat down with the relentless cheer of a drunken party guest, while cicadas sang their clacking tune in the trees. It was a sound he associated with home, one that by rights should have soothed him, but Henry found it impossible to settle. As much as Violet's behaviour was frustrating, he couldn't stand it when the two of them argued, and as much as it irked him to admit, Henry would rather lose a row than perpetuate a bad feeling for the sake of scoring a point.

Putting down his beer, he went upstairs.

There was no sign of Violet in the bedroom, nor was she in either the main bathroom or the en suite. Henry opened the window at the end of the landing so he could scour the front garden and lane beyond, but there was nobody. Steeling himself, he knocked on Luke's bedroom door.

Nothing. Not so much as a 'go away'.

Henry knocked again, this time with more determination, calling out as he did so, 'Luke, is Mum in there with you?'

When he still received no answer, he turned the handle and went inside. His son's suitcase was open on the floor, a sketch pad tossed on to the desk along with a half-empty bottle of Lucozade Sport. They'd only been in the house for an hour, but already the scent of worn socks permeated the space. Henry would've opened the porthole window but knew his son would react angrily to any sign of intrusion. Assuming he must instead be in the small shower room, Henry edged towards it, using a finger to push the door ajar.

Nothing.

The two of them must have done a flit while he was stewing in the back garden, and the realisation of this caused a lava-like surge of indignation to rise up in his chest. Racing back downstairs, he located his mobile phone and put a call through to Violet. She didn't answer, but a few moments later, a text arrived.

Luke wanted to see Juan. Back in a bit.

No kisses.

Henry seethed.

Without giving himself time to waver, he snatched up the house keys and headed off along the lane. Juan lived fewer than three minutes' walk away, but Henry made it in under sixty seconds, arriving at the yellow painted door out of breath with the effort of having run. He fully expected Ana to answer, but it was Tomas's face that appeared in the gap. He'd grown up so much over the past year that, at first, Henry barely recognised him, exclaiming with surprise when it dawned on him that this thickset, bearded, almost-man was, in fact, the very same boy he'd known since toddlerhood.

They greeted each other in Spanish, Tomas demonstrably happy to see him.

'Where's your mother?' Henry asked, as he was led through the small, open-plan ground floor, noticing as he passed a number of gaps on the walls where pictures and photos had once hung. The usually immaculate lounge area was cluttered with dirty plates, half-empty coffee mugs, and an ashtray in dire need of emptying.

'She is away,' said Tomas cagily.

'Well, you'd better get this place cleaned up before she gets back, or there'll be hell to pay,' Henry warned, though he saw immediately that the remark hadn't landed well. 'Is everything OK, mate?' he asked, as the younger man's jaw tightened. 'Has something happened.'

Tomas shook his head, but Henry held his gaze, recognising sadness.

'She left?' he guessed.

Tomas nodded, looked away.

'Oh, shit. *Lo siento*. I'm sorry.'

The sound of laughter drifted in through the open patio doors. Tomas threw a glance at Henry, wincing as if an apology was imminent. At the age of seventeen, the boy was wise beyond his years, understood what Henry had tried for so long to ignore, the undeniable closeness that had continued to flourish each summer. It was Violet who was laughing, she who only a short time ago was quivering with rage in his presence, wretched with dread and sorrow. Henry hadn't laughed with his wife for so long that he couldn't recall the last time, nor had she allowed him to hold her, or kiss her, or make love to her. Intimacy had become a shadow, lingering just out of reach.

Struck by a raw and potent fear that he was about to lose something precious to him, Henry marched outside with his shoulders squared, ready to fight for what was his. Luke was there, long pale legs protruding from a deckchair, can of Coke in hand, while next to him, pink-cheeked and disproportionately perky, Violet teetered on an upturned plant pot.

The sensation was one of falling inside a dream. Henry felt suddenly faint and staggered sideways, his arm going out only to be caught by Juan's. His Spanish neighbour had leapt up as if his seat was on fire, and Violet had moved, too, although not nearly fast enough. She would not be able to deny what she'd been doing any more than Henry would be able to forget the fact that he'd been there to witness it, that heart-scouring sight.

Her hand, clasped tightly in Juan's.

43

Violet

'You're doing what?'

Henry's gaze was steady across the table. 'Donating the money – well, as much of it as I'm legally permitted to do, once I've spoken to the tax office.'

A beat of time passed where the ability to articulate anything coherent abandoned me completely. I knew if I attempted to speak, mewls of disbelief would be all that emerged.

We'd come out to eat, the four of us, Henry having offered because he felt bad for dragging us away from Palma. Unusually for him, he'd booked us into Brasserie Número Ocho, which was situated right in the heart of Pollença's main square – a space he habitually avoided on account of it being 'overpriced and overrun'. I couldn't quibble with either of those descriptions, yet the fact Plaça Major was busy did not detract from its charm. Smooth grey slabs were framed by neatly manicured plane trees, their waxy green leaves a welcome splash of colour against the gold stone of the surrounding buildings. Trails of lights had been strung up, riotous food scents filled the air, and the scrape of cutlery was offset by the hum of contented chatter.

Offered the choice of sitting in or outside Brasserie Número Ocho, we'd opted for the former, Luke and I both exhaling gladly as we stepped from the dense heat of the early evening into the air-conditioned interior. My son might have inherited his dark hair and eyes from his Mediterranean-blooded father, but the pale, freckled skin came from me. 'Like two speckled eggs in a basket,' my dad had observed, back when Luke was a baby cradled proudly in my arms, before his mind had been taken over by anxiety. Once it had him in its grip, referring to him as anything other than what he deigned acceptable became too great a risk. Even my dear, sweet, tolerant father had been subjected to the lash of his grandson's tongue. He'd always taken it in good humour, brushing off Luke's disparagement as he might pollen from the sleeve of his jacket. I understood how it felt, and therefore knew how greatly it must have hurt him.

'I was wondering . . .' Henry said now, bringing me back to the table. He cleared his throat and waited until Eliza had lowered her menu before he continued. 'If you'd like to choose a charity. Something you deem worthy of a sizeable donation.'

He'd directed his comment to Luke, but it was Eliza who exclaimed in delight.

'That's so generous of you. There are so many great causes.'

Henry's attention remained on Luke. 'Perhaps a mental health charity,' he went on casually. 'I know we've spoken to a lot of them, and thought you'd be the best person to judge how effective they were.'

Luke couldn't have looked more uncomfortable if he'd tried. He'd pushed his chair back as far as it would go, the struts pressed up against the latticed wall that doubled up as a wine rack. It resembled a giant beehive of sorts, and I'd have been willing to bet that were he physically able, my son would have inserted himself into one of the holes and stayed there.

'Why me?' he said, glowering across the table at Henry. 'It's not my money.'

'No, but—'

'And none of them really did anything anyway, just spouted platitudes at me. The only person who ever helped me out in any real way was Maria.'

Henry pulled a face. 'I thought she was a bit of a charlatan.'

'A hypnotist,' I corrected. 'And Luke's right, she was very good.'

Henry chuntered.

'See what I mean,' Luke grumbled. 'Don't ask for my opinion if you're going to disregard my answer.'

'Your dad's trying to do a nice thing, albeit clumsily,' I said, and Eliza, who had remained quiet until now, agreed with me. When the waiter arrived to take our orders, I heard her hiss, 'He's doing it for you.' Luke, however, remained stony faced.

A youngish couple with a baby had been seated at the table beside ours, and I thought it likely that their arrival had unsettled him. Luke did not respond well to wailing infants, hadn't since he was eight years old and been trapped on a plane with one. Things had become so fraught on that occasion that he'd ended up humming loudly in his seat, hands clamped over his ears as he rocked backwards and forwards in distress. Henry and I had been powerless to snap him out of it, and it'd felt as if every person on the flight was judging us, condemning us, labelling us 'bad parents'.

'It's not a big deal,' said Henry, who I noticed was making short work of his beer. I'd opted for water even though I longed for a proper drink, had been longing for the numbing effects of alcohol too much of late, and it wasn't healthy – nor was it sensible, given how fractious the atmosphere was becoming.

Luke took the straw out of his orange juice and brought the glass up to his lips.

'Whatever, Dad,' he drawled between sips. 'Like I said, do what you like.'

The baby started to cry.

I glanced at Henry, but he was brooding, eyes down and shoulders slumped.

The young mother at the next table reached into the pram and began to make cooing noises, her hand on the infant's tummy but her attention on the menu. The man said something to her, and she laughed, apparently unfazed by the ongoing howl. I'd never left Luke to cry; the moment he screwed up his pink cheeks in preparation, I was there, lifting him into my arms, nestling him at my breast. I had cherished those early months, the moments of togetherness we shared that were ours alone. Henry wanted to help, to try bottle feeding, eager to take over when I was tired, but his efforts had failed. Baby Luke refused to settle with anyone else but me.

'It's a good thing I'm not the jealous type,' Henry would say, trotting out the same remark so often that over time it became not a joke but a barb. He was envious of the bond I had with Luke, and he'd allowed the seed of his disgruntlement to grow.

The tapas we'd ordered arrived, dish after dish of home-cooked Mallorcan delicacies. I'd only wanted some calamari, but Henry had insisted we push out the proverbial boat, and Eliza breathed out a 'whoa' as the tabletop vanished beneath a deluge of food. Patatas bravas speckled with paprika, pescado blanco with thick wedges of fresh lemon, langostinos sizzling in chilli oil, padrón peppers crunchy with salt, several variations of Spanish olive, dense brown hunks of bread, and pots of creamy aioli.

'Tuck in,' Henry said, raising his voice to be heard over the still-bawling baby.

Luke speared a potato but didn't eat it.

I glanced towards the window, saw the rich blue glow of sky behind the clay rooftops, and thought of my mother, her bewilderment when the men arrived to tow away the car I'd failed to pay for, her fear as a letter threatening bailiffs dropped on to the mat.

'I think donating the money is a very honourable notion,' I said, helping myself to some olives.

Henry looked at me suspiciously. 'But?'

'But it's not a practical solution.'

'Go on.'

The pitch of the baby's cry was growing louder, the mother's shushing ineffectual.

'You need to keep hold of the money,' I said plainly, 'so you can afford to buy me out.'

Henry groaned. 'Not this again.'

'We know The Orange House is worth far more than you'll get once you've paid the tax man what you owe, but I'm willing to take what's left and say no more about it.'

I didn't dare look at Luke, but I could feel his eyes on me, laser-like in their focus. I couldn't allow myself to be swayed. I had started, and so I barrelled on.

'You get to keep the house, I get a portion of what I'm owed – which is a very good deal for you, by the way – and everybody's happy.'

'Everybody's happy,' he repeated faintly. 'Jesus, Violet, what is the matter with you?'

I frowned as if I didn't understand the question.

A waiter had approached the neighbouring table; I heard him enquire in Spanish if there was something the baby needed, anything he could warm up for them – some milk, perhaps? It stood to reason that other diners had started to complain about the noise. The woman shook her head. I didn't catch her reply, but whatever it was appeared to satisfy the server, and having topped up their water glasses, he strode briskly away.

The baby, however, continued to protest.

'Since when did money mean more to you than anything else?' Henry asked tersely.

'Since when did pride matter more to you than me?' I wanted to say, though it wasn't as simple as that; not a single slight that had to be forgiven but years of them.

Eliza was casting nervous glances over her shoulder at the young couple. Like me, she was obviously concerned that Luke was teetering on the tip of anger. He'd abandoned his meal and was drumming his fingers against the tablecloth. All of a sudden, it felt like too much. I pushed back my chair and threw down my napkin, poised to stage another restaurant flit and go. But to where? I was exactly where I wanted to be, with the people I cared about the most.

Henry went to stand, his arm already stretching out towards me, but before I could react, Luke got abruptly to his feet. Eliza shrank into her chair, Henry wheeled around, I froze, and then my son did something that none of us were expecting.

Stepping over to the pram, he crouched down and began to make soothing, clucking sounds, before turning to the parents. I couldn't hear what he said, though the exchange seemed friendly enough, and the next moment, Luke had lifted the baby into his arms.

'There, there,' he said. 'It's OK. You're OK. I've got you.'

It took less than a minute for the baby's cries to cease, but when I considered what I'd witnessed, a change in my son so profound and sanguine, it felt as if my own tears could continue to fall forever.

44

Violet

The thunder began its throaty rumble a little after the pinkish dawn, and the rain fell in a torrent that set the cobbled pavements steaming. I watched from the bedroom window as dark clouds emerged from behind the mountaintops and lifted a finger to trace the droplets of water as they skidded down the glass.

I'd heard Henry leave in the midst of the downpour, the scrape of his boots on the drenched stone path, the squeak of the hinge as he closed the gate behind him. We hadn't spoken since leaving the restaurant the previous night, our stuck-record argument about money jolted back into song by the joy of seeing Luke comfort the baby. Our son had managed to push his impatience down, temper his emotions, and take positive action to solve the problem. I could not have been prouder of him and knew Henry must feel the same way.

A flash of the brightest blue tore across the horizon, the rain intensifying as Mother Nature raised her baton, conducting the elements into a cacophony of sound. I was struck by a flippant urge to strip off all my clothes and run naked into the deluge, hands raised, and head tilted back, drinking in the storm until I imbibed its strength. For too long now, I'd sat passively back and watched as life happened to me. The intrepid girl who'd clambered over the wall below me felt like an apparition, so far removed from the person I was now as to be improbable. It was no wonder Henry no longer loved me; I no longer loved myself, no longer much liked myself. If I kept spiralling down at this pace, I was in danger of ending up somewhere so deep, and dark, and lonely, that I might never find a way back.

It was time to stop dithering and do.

Rising stiffly from my hunched position beside the window, I pulled on shorts and a vest, and smeared on some moisturiser. Once downstairs, I slid my feet into flip-flops, found an old baseball cap hanging on the rack by the door, and picked up my bag from where I'd left it slung across one of the dining chairs. There was no sign that Luke and Eliza were up yet, so I scribbled them a note and propped it up against the kettle, before slipping outside into the rain.

Dodging puddles and the few determined tourists who'd ventured out in disposable ponchos, I made my way nimbly down the Calvari Steps into the hub of the town, listening to the myriad chime of bells as first one church and then another marked the arrival of a new hour. My toes were splattered with sodden dirt, the top I'd put on saturated within minutes, but I barely noticed.

There was no queue at the cashpoint, which I took as a good omen until I reached for my purse and discovered that it was missing. Cursing under my breath, I leant awkwardly against the wall, trying my best to root through my bag whilst avoiding the cascade of drips falling off the shopfront awning above.

A crash of thunder shook the sky.

Was it possible that Henry could've taken it? Perhaps I'd pushed him too far, and he'd decided to check the state of my finances himself by trying my bank cards. Ironically, this was exactly what I'd been about to do myself, check and see if my mother had changed her mind and decided to lend me some money after all. Henry knew the pin number for the one linked to my current account, because I'd recounted it to him on my first night here, and he could easily test the others by attempting a contactless transaction. The mere prospect was enough to send a chill through me, and I shivered as the rain continued to fall.

Would Henry really do that? Was he capable of something so underhand? I found it hard to believe, and yet, there was a chance.

I set off with grim resolve towards the part-demolished house on Carrer de la Garriga, not caring about the storm or the perturbed faces of those I passed, and pushed aside the makeshift fence before stalking straight inside and up the stairs. I could hear the radio, bursts of static interspersed with snatches of song, and followed my ears to the attic space, where I found Henry and Tomas in the far corner below the rafters.

'Oh,' I said, faltering at the sight of two people where I'd hoped to discover only one. 'What are you doing here?'

Tomas gave me a bemused look. 'It is my house?' he said, posing it as a question, then, 'I am helping, or trying to help.'

Henry removed a nail that was clamped between his teeth and passed it to him. 'Here,' he said. 'Remember what I said about the positioning – we don't want them too shallow, or the boards won't hold.'

Tomas raised his hammer in a salute. '*Si, señor.*'

'I'll only be downstairs,' Henry said, and then, having looked me up and down, he added, 'Did you swim here?'

'It's raining.'

Making his way to what would one day become a skylight, Henry hooked a finger under the tarpaulin and eased it to one side.

'Just checking to see where you parked your Ark.'

'Hilarious.'

'You shouldn't be up here without a hard hat,' he said, motioning to remove his own.

'Don't bother.' I raised my hand. 'I'm not staying long. I just came to ask if you'd seen my purse.'

Henry frowned. 'Did you check the fridge?'

'That was once!'

Tomas began hammering; short, sharp bursts of noise that went right through me.

'Come on.' Henry ushered me back downstairs and into the shell of the lounge. Sprigs of electric cable burst out from several points along the walls, as well as the middle of the ceiling, which meant the next stage would be plaster-boarding. I wondered what colour scheme Tomas and Carmen would choose, whether they were the stripped-back and modern types, or fans of colour, clutter, indoor plants, and artwork. It was too painful to contemplate the fate of La Casa Naranja, and how much heart a new owner could rip out of her. Then again, I countered, if I was given the choice, I would happily have dismantled every part of myself if it meant I could have Henry back.

'You definitely don't have my purse then?' I asked, turning to find him only inches away.

Henry lifted a hand as if to touch my cheek, then appeared to change his mind. I stared at him, at his contours, those livid scars to which I'd grown so accustomed over the past few weeks. I no longer experienced a visceral clawing sensation in my stomach when confronted with them; they had simply become another part of him.

'I don't,' he confirmed. 'I'd never take away what is yours.'

I groaned, bending my knees, and resting my palms against my thighs. 'It must be at the house. I just thought that— Never mind.'

'That what?'

'It doesn't matter.'

Henry put a hand on my shoulder, steering me slowly around to face him. 'Look at you, Vee – it obviously does matter.'

'I'm a mess,' I moaned, and he tutted.

'Nothing a hot shower and a hairdryer won't fix.'

'I don't mean that,' I said wearily. 'Although, you're right, I do look like a dandelion after it's faced off against a hose-pipe. Fact is, my whole life's a mess, and I don't know what to do about it, Henry, I really don't.'

He released his grip on me, waiting while I slowly levered myself back up to full height, the top of my head level with his chin.

'I'm going to make us a cup of disgusting instant coffee,' he said, 'and then we're going to talk. Properly talk – OK?'

I nodded meekly.

The kettle was in the kitchen – one of the only rooms in the house that hadn't been completely gutted – and I lingered in the doorway as Henry poured boiling water over freeze-dried granules and gave each mug a stir with the handle of a paintbrush.

'Tell me if it tastes like turps,' he said, as I took a tentative sip and choked.

'No,' I spluttered. 'I think turps might've improved it.'

The rain was still coming down, but with less ferocity than before. We took our coffee outside and stood together under the shelter of the half-built porch, watching steam ribbon up into the pale sky. Tomas was still hammering away upstairs, and I could hear the shrill call of the ever-present swallows in the distance.

'We never really talked,' I said. 'Afterwards. Not properly.'

He nodded, staring out across the dug-up front garden. 'I guess I wasn't ready to listen.' He took a sip of his drink, wincing as it burned his tongue. 'Bloody hell, that really is bad.'

'Think of it as medicine,' I said, raising my own mug. 'Do you remember how hard it was to make Luke swallow anything medicinal when he was younger? He didn't even like Calpol, and that stuff is essentially sugary goo.'

Henry smiled faintly. 'Is it any wonder he turned out stubborn, given who his parents are?'

'Poor Luke,' I agreed with a nod. 'He didn't stand a chance really, did he?'

'Him comforting that baby last night.' Henry turned to me, reanimated by the memory. 'When I woke up this morning, I wondered if I'd dreamt it.'

'That's how I felt the other day,' I told him. 'When you and I, when we . . .'

His smile vanished abruptly. 'I'm sorry if I came on strong.'

'Henry.' I let my knuckles graze against his. 'Please, don't say sorry, not for that. Never for that. I'm not sorry. I wanted it to happen. I've missed you, missed us.'

'Us.' He repeated, tossing the word out bitterly, as if the flavour of it offended him. 'Which version of us are you talking about? Because the us that we were when this happened –' he gestured impatiently towards his face – 'wasn't in a great state, if you'll recall.'

'Can't we just forget all that?' I began, only to be cowed into silence by his expression. Henry appeared to be chewing over his words, and sensing that his resolve against me could be weakening, I made myself continue.

'We could start again. People do it all the time. Luke's in a better place now, he's so much more aware of his emotions, and how to get a handle on them. I honestly believe that, and we can be the same as we were before. I know we can if we try.'

He was shaking his head.

'Henry.' I grabbed his arm. 'Please!'

He looked down at my hand, a complicated mix of emotions etched across his face. 'Vee,' he started, and then, just as quickly, 'Forget it.'

He'd looked away from me and was staring across the garden. I turned in time to see Juan push aside the temporary fence, a small, dark-haired girl hitched up on his back. Henry said something that sounded like 'typical', and then a high-pitched scream ripped through the rain-splattered yard. Paulina had spotted Henry, and once again, she had begun to shriek that awful word.

'*Caracortada*! *Caracortada*!'

Juan shushed her angrily, his usual languor thoroughly rattled. 'Sorry,' he mouthed, hopping puddles to reach the house. Paulina's head was buried against her grandfather's shoulder, skinny arms gripping tight, clearly terrified. The two of them disappeared inside without a backwards glance, and a loaded silence stretched out under the porch. I felt as if I'd dry-swallowed a stone, and coughed in a vain attempt to dislodge it.

Henry turned to me. 'It might be easy for you to "forget all that",' he said mutinously. 'But I can't. I don't have a choice. It's here, on my face.'

'I know, I know.' I was starting to become frantic. The brief glimmer of light in his eyes had dulled, the forgiveness I'd dared to wish for dashed away by disgruntlement. 'Henry,' I whispered, but I could tell I'd lost him.

'The us we were,' he said, 'in the beginning? That's gone – destroyed.'

Stepping forwards, he tipped what was left of his coffee into the mud, then turned to face me. 'I'm sorry your life is in a mess, but I don't think I'm the right person to help you, Vee, not any more.'

I felt myself start to crumble. 'If not you then who? My dad is dead, my mother thinks I'm a waste of space, even Ynes is disappointed with me, and Luke is— He can't help me, it's not his job, is it? I don't know whose it is if it's not yours. Tell me who, Henry – who?'

He looked at me pityingly. 'Don't you see?' he said. 'It's nobody's job. The only person who can help you, is you.'

45

Henry

Four Summers Ago

Henry was drunk.

Not in the gentle, slightly fuzzy, everything-is-wonderful way, but morosely. His attempt to drown his sorrows had merely increased their buoyancy, bringing each one to the surface of his subconscious, where they bobbed around, impossible to ignore.

Your son is in crisis.
Your wife is miserable.
You are failing.
You are lonely.
You are sad.

Picking up an empty beer can, he crushed it between his hands before tossing it on to the pile. He'd brought a pack of six down into the clearing among the olive trees and there was only one remaining. Henry cracked it open and brought it up to his lips, spilling a large portion of it down his chin and on to his T-shirt. Even through his inebriated haze, he was aware how pathetic this tableau would look to anyone who happened to pass by. Not that they would, not here, not in his secret place. The only other person who knew he came here was Violet, and she would not risk abandoning Luke for a second. Not even, he thought bitterly, for him – especially not that.

He brushed an angry tear off his cheek.

Where had she gone, his girl? He'd watched her diminish from his position on the sidelines of their marriage, always trying but never quite managing to reach her, the distance between them stretched almost to breaking point, a rope frayed down to a single thread.

He squinted as the sun crept through the branches above him, the blue sky beyond a mocking display of untroubled beauty. The sight of it should have pacified him, the swell of the mountains reminding him how small and insignificant their problems were, when you held them up against the tapestry of the world. But everything had been skewed, his and Violet's life with Luke a cubist painting, all parts recognisable but wrong somehow, a nightmare from which there was seemingly no waking.

He lifted the beer can. Empty. Henry roared, fists pummelling the ground, boots kicking great clumps of earth and twigs into the air. Several birds hurtled skywards, their disgruntled squawks making him laugh – a hard, brittle sound that bore no relation to warmth or humour. Who, Henry thought sadly, was he becoming?

Clambering up, he shook out his carrier bag and stuffed the empty tins inside, telling himself that he must be fine, that if he were dangerously drunk, he would have left them here, traps for unsuspecting rodents and insects, unforgivable. But he hadn't, and so he deemed that he was safe to return to the house, his beloved La Casa Naranja, which glowed red gold on its hillside perch. How he adored her.

Pushing aside low-slung branches that sprang back and lashed across his face, Henry made his unsteady way towards the crumbling wall that encircled El Calvari. The hilltop pilgrimage site was teeming with tourists, some of whom cast a disdainful gaze in his direction as he stumbled past. Two blond-haired females who looked to be in their mid-twenties clutched each other and giggled as he lurched towards them. Henry winked lasciviously. He was used to this, to women eyeing him hungrily, as if he were a morsel they might like to eat. It happened frequently at work, most often with the housewives of rich Cambridge academics, who hired him to put in a new potting shed or build a summer house in the garden of their riverside abodes.

Henry accepted the work, but never the offers to 'pop upstairs and check a problem in the bedroom'. He had learned this lesson the hard way, within the first few months of trading, when he'd turned from examining the supposedly rattling door of a built-in wardrobe to find his client lounging naked across her mattress, a coy finger hooked. On that occasion, Henry had been so flabbergasted that he'd fled and never gone back, but in order to make any money at all, he'd had to become savvier. Taking on an apprentice had helped no end, because having Barney by his side meant he was never alone, no longer vulnerable, less of an easy target for would-be adulterers. And of course, it was even better during the brief time Violet was a part of House-a-Home, but that had all fallen apart when it became clear that Luke needed her with him full-time. Their son would not go to school, and they couldn't force him, but he was far too young to be left unsupervised. This meant one of them had to stay at home. Violet became what was essentially a carer; unable to work through no fault of her own, and yet the system saw fit to turn its back on her. It made Henry simmer with rage.

'Why don't we move to Mallorca?' he'd suggested, as the two of them trudged home from yet another summit meeting at Luke's school. 'Now that they've agreed to home learning, we're free to base ourselves anywhere with an internet connection.'

Life would be better in Pollença, he'd wanted to add. We've always been happier there.

But Violet had shaken her head.

'Why not?' he persisted. 'What are we staying for?'

'Your business,' she said. It had been a long time since she'd referred to it as 'our'.

'I can do the same thing in Spain. I might not generate quite as much income, granted, but we'll be saving a small fortune in rent.'

'We can't. My mum . . . It's too soon after Dad.'

And Henry had felt he'd no choice but to relent. He knew Violet was still grieving the loss of her father; she described it as 'a blockage inside me', one behind which all her joy had become trapped. He didn't say as much, but Henry suspected it wasn't purely the lack of her favourite parent that had hollowed out his wife so completely, but more the ongoing problems surrounding their son. Every time Luke blew up, slammed a door, smashed an item of crockery, headbutted a wall, or made threats of self-harm, another part of Violet seemed to calcify.

Still brooding, Henry took the Calvari Steps at a jog, almost tumbling over as his feet failed to land where he placed them. Perhaps, he considered blearily, that last can of beer had been a mistake after all. Veering off the main thorough-fare, he put out a hand to steady himself only to encounter the hard, sharp spines of a vast cactus.

'You prick!' he swore, laughing at his unintentional joke as he continued to lumber down the lane. There was a song stuck in his head, he thought perhaps by one of those boys who'd been on *The X Factor*, the one with the curly hair who Violet thought was 'adorable'. Henry couldn't remember his name, but he liked the lyrics, how they talked about getting away but not giving up, and he hummed it as he walked,

fingers trailing against walls and fences, the sun's hot breath
on the back of his neck. La Casa Naranja was not far away;
he could see the turret and pictured Luke beyond its walls, a
tightly tangled ball of fear, anger, and mistrust. Henry longed
to free the boy from himself, if only for a few hours, so he
could show him how much more there was to life than skulk-
ing alone in a room.

Tears fell then, and he let them, still humming his sorrowful song, head spinning and skin hot. He was about to cross
to the shadier side of the street for a lie-down when a gate
opened ahead of him, and a familiar man emerged. Juan's
smile of greeting fell away as quickly as he'd plastered it on.

'What the hell is the matter with you?' he hissed angrily,
towing Henry off the road and down the few steps into his
modest garden.

Henry tried to reply but found that his tongue had swelled
up to three times its normal size – or so it felt. Instead, he
laughed helplessly and flopped into a deckchair. Juan stood
staring down at him, arms folded and features stern.

'It is eleven o'clock in the morning,' he said, addressing
Henry in slow, measured English, as if he was incapable of
understanding anything else.

'So?'

'So, you are drunk. *Ebrio*. Where is your wife?'

'Where's yours?' Henry threw back, and for a moment, the
two men glowered at each other. Juan was dressed smartly, in
proper suit trousers and a pale gold shirt with the cuffs rolled
up. An expensive-looking watch glinted on his wrist, paid for
no doubt by the wages he got from Henry's father. The
thought churned unpleasantly, and Henry sat up in his chair,
a hand raised to his mouth.

'If you are going to be sick, use the bathroom,' Juan
snapped, leaping backwards as Henry made a gagging sound.

He only just made it to the downstairs loo in time, and stayed there for what felt like an age, arms wrapped around the bowl, the enamel cool against his cheek. By the time he returned to the garden, Juan had fetched some water and a half-finished loaf of bread.

'Drink,' he said, as Henry lowered himself gingerly into a sitting position. 'And eat.'

'Thanks,' he muttered begrudgingly. 'And don't worry, I've cleaned up after myself.'

Juan nodded in acknowledgement. 'A bad morning?'

Where to begin?

'Try a bad decade.' Henry yawned, exhausted not from physical but mental exertion.

'I am sure it has not all been bad.'

Juan was regarding him seriously. And Henry had to allow that he was right. There had been wonderful times, intimate times, occasions when he and Violet had laughed until their sides ached, kissed until their hearts raced, and held each other close when things got tough. If only those times weren't becoming so much harder to remember.

'He will find his way. You have to learn to trust him.'

'Him?' Henry raised his eyes to Juan's, not following.

'Luke,' he said. 'I know that things are a little bit difficult, but he will grow out of it, this aggression, this –' he waved a hand in the air – 'behaviour of his, it will stop.'

There was a trellis in the far corner turned pink by bougainvillea petals. Violet had planted it there having propagated cuttings from their own garden, using one of her special hormone rooting powders to ensure the fragile stems made it through the first spring, and tending to it during every summer that followed. Her years of careful nurturing had paid off, the flowers now thriving and in full, stunning bloom. Would it one day be the same for Luke? Would he, too, blossom if they kept watering him with love? Violet, he knew, had the patience to wait and find out. It was one of many reasons why she was the better parent. Their argument that morning had been over something petty, the details now so scant that Henry could barely recall what they were, and yet he had walked out and left her, left both of them, because he could. He'd gone, and he'd got drunk, and now he was here when what he should have done was stay, and talk, and be there for her no matter what.

He put his head in hands.

'Are you sick?' Juan sounded slightly nervous.

'No.' Henry rubbed his eyes, blinking as the man's face came back into focus. 'I have to go,' he said, but made no move to stand up.

'Why don't you wait for a while? Until you are sober?'

Henry felt as if a portion of his sobriety had returned during the half-hour he spent in the bathroom, but he didn't argue the point. Much as he wanted to make things right with Violet, going home meant all those sorrows bobbing back to the surface again. He needed a plan first, a way back to being the husband and father he wanted to be.

'How did you know?' he asked Juan. 'With Ana? What was it that made you realise there was no point in trying any more?'

Juan took a sip of water before answering; his tanned hand stroking his stubbly jaw. 'Ana . . . We still loved each other. But we were no longer friends. I did not like her, and she definitely did not like me.' He smiled helplessly and Henry nodded.

'Sometimes, I wonder if Violet feels that way about me.'

He hadn't meant to say it, and the regret he felt was swiftly exacerbated by the flicker of interest in Juan's eyes. He didn't seem remotely troubled by Henry's admission.

'You really believe this?' he asked, to which Henry shrugged. 'If that is true, then I think you should ask her. There is no point in both of you being unhappy. Trust me, I know this,' he added, tapping a finger against his temple.

The piece of bread he'd picked up had turned stale in his fingers. Henry let the crumbs fall to the floor. 'Maybe you should've married Violet instead of me,' he said. 'Perhaps you'd have stood a better chance of making her and Luke happy.'

He expected his friend to disagree, to laugh, to tell him off for suggesting something so farcical, but Juan merely arched a thick, dark brow.

'*Sí*,' he said. 'Maybe I should.'

46

Violet

I began the day of Antonio's wake with a stroll along the seafront. Port de Pollença held so many memories, and as I wandered, I saw glimpses of the past. There was the bar beside the bus stop, where Tomas had accidentally hit poor Luke with his toy car, and here was the patch of shade below the sprawling pine trees, where Henry had brought me for our second official date. My mum and dad, not trusting this strange young man I'd happened across by chance, insisted on accompanying us, and sat up at a table along the promenade, sipping glasses of iced tea and watching our every move. I had complained, embarrassed to have such suffocating parents, but Henry had challenged me on it.

'They care about you,' he'd said. 'Don't ever be cross with them for that.'

It was later he told me more about his own family, the free-spirited mother who'd essentially abandoned him when he turned sixteen, the virtual stranger of a father he'd had no choice but to reach out to, and the bumpiness of their relationship since.

'He must care about you,' I'd argued. 'He gave you a house.'

And while Henry had smiled, there'd been sadness behind it. Antonio had shown his affection through the giving of gifts, extravagant gestures rather than words, and it occurred to me now, as I continued my walk, that the letter we'd found with the black money might have been the first mention of love ever made from father to son.

'I never told anyone I loved them, until I met you,' Henry had said to me, the first time we exchanged those three momentous words, and I'd felt so cherished, as if I was special, when what I should have felt was pity. Sorrow for this boy who'd had to become a man in order to experience love. Our love. A love I was sure would outlast both of us, the remnants of it passing through each new generation, from our child to theirs and so on, its force for happiness only gaining power as the years unfolded.

How could I give up on it?

Stepping down from the pathway on to the pale sand, I sat for a while by the shoreline, elbows propped on bent knees, staring out at a patchwork sea so busy with movement, as waves displaced pebbles, and the surface glittered brightly beneath its halo of sun. Wisps of indolent cloud stroked the distant mountaintops, boats bobbed offshore, and I felt the tendrils of a faint breeze as it drifted across me.

The knot of anxiety inside me began to ease, only to tighten again as panic intruded; thoughts of Corbin McCabe and his thinly veiled threats, of county court judgements and bailiffs, declarations of bankruptcy and frozen accounts, having to admit how far I had fallen, the extent to which I'd let everyone down. My options had dwindled, but there remained a way to save myself, secure enough money to not only pay back my debtors but be free of them for good, cut up the credit cards and cancel the overdraft. I was convinced that McCabe could be persuaded to take a monetary bribe and disappear back into the rat burrow from which he'd crawled. It could all be sorted out, and I was determined that it must be. Henry, I decided, as I stood up and brushed down my shorts, would have to get on board – if not for me then for the tatters of our family. I had to act now, or risk it being never.

Nobody except Ynes knew about my most recent encounter with Malcolm and Mags, and I had sworn her into reluctant secrecy. Henry would be angry that I'd gone behind his back, but I reasoned that he'd left me with little choice. I'd given him the chance to buy me out, and he had refused. The consequences of that decision were therefore on him, not me.

That was what I told myself.

When I slipped in through the front door an hour later, I did so quietly, sneaking from room to room as I plumped cushions, opened shutters, and tried not to dwell too despairingly over the half-destroyed shell of what had once been the dresser. Henry's jeep was missing, but I had no idea if Luke and Eliza were in or out, and preferred not to knock on the turret door if I could help it. My son's mood was a taut string that would vibrate at the slightest touch, and if I wanted my plan to succeed without a hitch, I needed to maintain a serene atmosphere.

When the knock at the door came, I was ready, and opened it with a flourish and a smile. Mags and Malcolm looked bronzed and happy, their week at sea leaving each of them tousled and carefree. When Mags shook my hand, I noticed her immaculate coral manicure had chipped, while Malcolm had swapped his stiff-edged shirt and chinos for a bright green T-shirt with the word 'Mallorca' emblazoned on the front.

'I cannot wait to live here,' Mags gushed, as she breezed through the lounge in a cloud of sickly-sweet perfume. 'I have such a vision for the place.'

'Her mind is a mood board,' put in Malcolm, beaming at his other half as if she was a pearl that he'd popped out of an oyster shell. 'I'm hopeless at all the interiors stuff, but

Mags can visualise the end result, and once she's set on something—'

'Then I always get it,' she trilled. 'It was the same with Malcolm, you know. I saw him across the bar at Raffles and kapow –' she mimicked firing a bow and arrow – 'love at first sight. I sent him an Old Fashioned, and the rest, as they say . . .'

'Is not very PG!' Malcolm guffawed.

I smiled politely and ushered them towards the kitchen. 'Coffee? I made a fresh pot.'

They went out on to the patio as I prepared the drinks, neither one commenting on the lack of glass panels in the door, and I listened as they loudly admired the view.

'I know we said we didn't want a pool,' Mags confessed a second later, accepting her coffee with a simpering 'yummy', 'but now that I'm here, I think perhaps it might be nice. What do you think, darling?'

Malcolm nodded. 'Whatever you think. She's the boss,' he added to me, quite unnecessarily.

The thought of a bulldozer being taken to my beautiful garden made me want to sit down in the dirt and weep, but I continued to smile as if delighted.

'Can we have another snoop around upstairs?' Mags asked, as we made our way back indoors before I had a chance to reply.

Wondering what excuse I could give as to why she couldn't see Luke's room; I went with her into the hallway with Malcolm following close behind and was only a few feet from the front door when it opened to reveal Henry.

The look of horror on his face was met with a sharp intake of breath from Mags.

'Gosh,' she said, hand to her mouth. 'I'm so sorry. It's just, those scars. I had forgotten how awful they lo— You poor, poor man.'

By some feat of extraordinary self-possession, Henry managed not to roll his eyes. Instead, he said calmly, 'That's all right. I'm really not poor at all. In fact, I just became extremely wealthy.'

'Win at the poker, did you?' boomed Malcolm. 'Or what is it they play here? Loteria, that's it. Have you been fleecing the locals?'

He seemed to find this enormously funny, as did Mags, although she was laughing with a fraction less enthusiasm than her other half. When Henry didn't immediately reply, she looked from him to me and raised an enquiring eyebrow.

'Aren't you going to tell us?'

'Sure,' said Henry, folding his arms across the front of his overalls. 'But I'm afraid you might not like what you hear.'

'Oh?' Mags's usually polite tone was cut through with steel.

Henry grinned. 'I'm rich,' he said, 'because I just sold a house.'

47

Violet

'You don't mean this house?'

Mags punctuated her question with a tittering giggle.

Henry shrugged. ''Fraid so. I don't have any others knocking around.'

'But I thought that—' Her face fell as her hand dropped away from the banister. 'We were under the impression that it was still available.'

'It was,' he agreed, making a show of looking at his watch, 'until about twenty-five minutes ago.'

'Who?' I blurted, equal parts furious with him and relieved that Mags's 'vision' for a swimming pool would now never come to pass.

Henry could not meet my eye. 'Someone local,' he said, sounding shifty. 'A guy I know, with a family.'

Malcolm had gone very red. An ugly flush was working its way from his cheeks down to his throat, and his Adam's apple bobbed as he struggled to formulate a response.

'I'm so sorry,' I said to both of them. 'I had no idea. Henry, you should've told me.'

'Probably should,' he concurred cheerfully. 'But oh well, what's done is done. I'm sorry to have wasted your time.'

He stood to one side, the door propped open behind him, the message to leave as loud and clear as if he'd erected it out of six-foot neon signs.

Malcolm made a chuntering sound in the back of his throat. 'Whatever they've offered, we can better it.'

'Too late,' Henry told them. 'Done and dusted.'

'You won't even consider negotiating?' Mags pleaded, fixing him with a doe-eyed stare that had probably worked in her favour countless times before. Henry, however, was unmoved.

'It's off the market,' he said firmly, interrupting her before she had time to say more. 'Now, if you don't mind, I really do have to insist that you leave us to get on with our day. We have my father's wake to prepare for.'

Nobody, I reflected, as a thoroughly put-out Malcolm and Mags made their way from the house, could argue with that.

Henry turned to me, the genial expression he'd fixed across his face for the benefit of our would-be buyers twisting into one of disappointment. 'Nice try,' he said.

'What do you mean?'

'Inviting those parasites back here in an attempt to sell my house out from under me—'

'Our house, Henry. You added my name to the deeds years ago, remember?'

He made a 'tchuh' sound.

'And you're one to talk,' I went on. 'Standing there accusing me of going behind your back, when you've gone and done the exact same thing.'

'No, I haven't.'

'Yes, you have – you've sold the bloody house!'

He considered me for a moment, then stalked past, heading straight up the stairs.

'Henry!'

I went after him, catching the door into the spare bedroom as he tried to swing it shut on me.

'I need to get changed,' he said. 'Are you just going to stand there and watch?'

I folded my arms and leant pointedly against the wall. 'If I have to.'

'Fine,' he said, unzipping the front of his overalls so they fell open to the waist.

I swallowed as my eyes roved uninhibited over his chest, breath catching at the sight and scent of him, dry sweat on warm skin.

'Aren't you even going to tell me who?'

He barely glanced at me as he rifled through a drawer, extracting first boxer shorts, then a balled-up pair of socks.

'Who what?'

He tossed the items down on the bed, crossed to the wardrobe and took out a shirt, smart trousers, a yellow tie. We had decorated this room together, him with a roller and me a brush. I'd worn an old swimming cap over my hair to stop paint dripping on to it, and he'd laughed and called me 'Vee-demort'. My yelps of protest were doused by his lips, kissing me through shared laughter into submission.

'Who have you sold the house to, Henry?'

He stopped, sighed, shook his head. 'Nobody.'

'What do you mean?'

'I mean exactly that. I haven't sold the house. I made it up. Lied.'

The menacing threats from McCabe, the final demands, the repossessed car, the empty bank accounts.

'Oh, for fuck's sake – why?' It was close to a scream. The room seemed to tilt as I glared at him, despair and agony, longing, and self-pity.

Henry stared back, a muscle working in his jaw. 'Why?' he repeated. 'Because you left me with no choice. I thought I could trust you, after everything that's happened. Jesus, Vee

– my dad has only been gone nine days and you go and do this?'

'I needed the money. I told you that.'

'Yeah,' he scoffed, 'you did. You've been like a broken bloody record on the subject ever since you got here. It's why I wasn't in the least bit surprised when I realised you'd stolen from me.'

I was too shocked by this to respond immediately and taking my soundless mouthing as an admission of guilt, Henry threw up his hands in triumph.

'See, you can't even deny it.'

Striding past me, he went out on to the landing, and a moment later, I heard him in the bathroom, the click as the electric shower was turned on. He hadn't bothered to lock the door behind him, but still recoiled when I marched in and yanked aside the curtain.

'What the hell are you doing?' he exclaimed, hands going instinctively to shield his privates as I stepped over the side of the bath and stood fully clothed in front of him.

'I have not,' I said, blinking away droplets in a fury, 'ever stolen from you.'

Henry stared down at me, water cascading over his cheeks, wet hair plastered against his scars.

'I checked the bag,' he said slowly. 'There's thirty thousand euros missing.'

The dress I'd changed into in order to look presentable for Mags and Malcolm was soaked through and clinging to my skin. I opened my mouth, confusion mingling with fruitless desire. Being this close to him again had filled my head with cotton wool, and my thoughts were sluggish as I fought to make sense of what he was telling me.

'I didn't take it,' I said, repeating the denial as he continued to look scornful.

'I wouldn't do that.'

'Then where is it?'

'How the hell should I know?'

Henry dragged a hand through his hair, and unable to bear the scrutiny of his glare, I cast my eyes down instead, past the grooves of his chest to the flat, toned stomach and wet nest of pubic hair, the smooth length of him so enticingly close. It felt wrong to be examining him in this way, but the yearning inside me was untameable, nettles with rope-like roots that spread through every vein. Heat rushed to my head. I could hear his breathing over the sound of the running water, deep and slow and steady, completely at odds with my own racing heart.

'I would've given you the money you needed to clear your debts,' he said. 'You didn't have to steal it.'

Was he right? Could I have taken it? Had the world been knocked so far off its axis by all that had happened that it'd altered who I was, what I was capable of, how much control I had over my own actions? It all felt plausible. I was as positive as I could be that I hadn't taken the money, but Henry seemed sure I had. And which of us, in the end, had proved themselves to be the most trustworthy?

I had to get out of here, away from him, go to a place where I'd be able to ponder all this clearly. I couldn't think straight when he was standing naked in front of me, his body responding to the need I knew must be radiating from mine, even if his heart had closed, telling me there was hope still, that there was passion beneath the cynicism.

I stepped backwards, bare feet slipping on the enamel, and climbed out of the bath.

'How much?' he said, and I froze in the motion of reaching for a towel.

'Twenty-five thousand. Plus a few thousand owing on the car.'

The curtain twitched. I could see him silhouetted behind it, saw him lift a hand as if to move it aside, watched as his arm fell back to his side.

'And there's more,' I added meekly. 'I quit my job, not long before I flew out here. My boss at the estate agency, he found out that I'd been doing something I shouldn't, something awful. I had no choice. He would've fired me if I didn't go first.'

A silence followed this. Henry was waiting for me to continue, but it was so hard to dredge up the right words. Instead of the what or the why, I told him the who, the name little more than a murmur, *Corbin McCabe*.

'That crook?' Henry was shocked. 'What has he got to do with anything?'

'Crook,' I repeated. 'You knew that he was dodgy?'

Henry switched off the shower. 'He tried to recruit me years ago to turn over some properties on the cheap, use below-par materials and pass them off as high-end. When I told him to get stuffed, he said he'd report me to Trading Standards. It all got quite nasty, but eventually he gave up.'

'Bloody hell,' I said lamentably. 'I wish you'd told me.'

'I didn't want to put any more stress on you. Things with Luke were starting to become . . . you know. I thought it was better that I handle it myself.'

'Well, he's clearly been dwelling on it, because he came after me.'

I jumped as he yanked back the top corner of the curtain.

'What do you mean "came after you"?'

I bumped into him at an open house viewing a few months ago and we got talking. He seemed so genuine, and sympathetic. When I confessed that I was struggling for money, he offered to lend me a lump sum, and then refused to accept any kind of repayment from me, told me I could earn it back in other ways.'

Henry looked miserable as he asked, 'Such as?'

'Such as giving him first dibs on new properties, before we listed them online, and encouraging vendors to consider his offers, even if they were below the market value. The longer it went on, the more outlandish his requests became, and then he started demanding that I falsify surveyor reports, or doctor them to include leaks that didn't exist, cladding that didn't meet safety specifications, anything that could shave a few thousand off the asking price. Then he'd swoop in and get himself a bargain, spend two weeks doing each place up, and sell them on again at a huge profit.'

'And you did as he said?' Henry asked, appalled.

'Once or twice,' I admitted, unable to look at him. The shame was such that I was surprised to find the floor still intact below my feet. 'I changed one report and substituted another. I felt so awful afterwards that I refused to do it ever again, but by that time it was too late. My boss had grown suspicious, and McCabe was refusing to see reason. He's still making threats now,' I added desperately. 'He's been at the house, drinking tea with my mum. I'm terrified he'll hurt her if I don't give him something soon, but how can I? I have no job and no money.'

'How much did he lend you?' Henry asked.

'Five thousand.'

He sighed. 'I would have given it to you.'

'I know, but—'

'But you took it.'

'No,' I whispered, shaking my head. 'No.'

'Did you do it out in the lane?' he said. 'Or wait until everyone was out to sneak into the loft?'

'Why would I have invited Malcolm and Mags here if I'd already helped myself to the money I needed?'

A throb of silence filled the room.

'Can you pass me a towel?'

'What?'

'A towel.' The pitch of Henry's voice had changed, the serrated edges softened. As I stood, dripping wet and indignant, his hand appeared around the edge of the curtain.

'Get it yourself,' I snapped, and turning on my heel, I made my way back to the main bedroom. I'd thrown my wet dress on to the floor and was in the process of wringing out my knickers over the basin in the en suite when Henry barged in.

We stood, both in our towels, glaring at each other.

'This has to stop, Henry. I can't keep arguing with you.'

He drooped. 'I know.'

'I didn't steal the money.'

He studied me for a second, then slowly nodded. 'I know.'

'And that means . . .'

I trailed off, unable to finish my sentence, unwilling to articulate what we were both thinking – that if neither Henry nor I had helped ourselves to thirty thousand euros, then we were left with limited options as to who had. And yet, that made no sense to me either. I could tell Henry was conflicted, too; the desperation with which he was looking at me felt like a plea.

When I heard the thud of feet on the stairs it didn't surprise me. I was becoming accustomed to these serendipitous twists of fate, the universe sliding its players into place as if we were pawns in some trivial yet malevolent game.

When Luke appeared in the bedroom doorway, he was clutching something large and rectangular, wrapped in plain brown paper, and lowered it as we approached. The nervous smile that had been playing around his lips fell away as he took in the expressions on our faces, and it was then that I knew.

My son was the thief in this chapter of our story, and I thought I could guess why.

48

Violet

'This is for you.'

Henry made no move to take what Luke was offering, and neither did I.

'Both of you,' he clarified, readjusting the package in his arms. 'It doesn't matter who opens it.'

I cleared my throat. 'Can I, we, open it in a minute? I just need to put some clothes on.'

'Oh, yeah, sure.'

Luke shook his fringe from his eyes, taking in our state of undress. I saw what looked to be the beginnings of a smile as he turned to go and glanced towards Henry.

'Do you think he bought us a thirty-grand painting?' he stage-whispered.

'Not funny,' I hissed back, though his humour had warmed me. 'Go and get dressed. I'll meet you on the landing.'

Instead of my usual shorts, I decided to put on the dress I'd left out for Antonio's wake, which was black with a wrap front and fluted sleeves. One of the many garments I'd splurged on after Henry and I parted ways, each new purchase a small shot of serotonin that kept me going when it felt as if the world was caving in. I didn't need the dress, just as I hadn't needed an expensive new car, so-called 'miracle' face creams, and a bi-weekly appointment to have my nails done – but being able to have all those things had felt freeing. For the first time in my life, it was up to me where my money went, and on whom I spent it.

'You look nice.'

Henry appraised me from the top of the stairs. He, too, had dressed for the wake, the tatty overalls he'd stripped out of replaced by the smarter outfit he'd laid out on the bed. As he raised a hand to sweep his hair back off his forehead, I saw a flash of gold and hope flared. But it was a cufflink I'd seen, not his wedding ring. I still wore mine; had never been able to bear the thought of taking it off.

'So do you,' I said.

He dipped his chin self-consciously, reminding me of the boy he'd been, that gangly eighteen year old who'd no idea how beautiful he was. If only we could've flicked a switch and gone back to that moment, the opportunity to get things right rolled out like fresh turf ahead of us. I would do it all so differently.

'Ready?' he asked, and I nodded, though I almost certainly was not.

Henry went first and I followed him, along the hallway and out through the open back door. A half-empty bottle of white wine had been left open on the patio table, foil scattered around it, and as we made our way down to join Luke and Eliza beside the lemon tree, I saw that four glasses had been lined up on the stone steps.

As they instinctively did whenever I ventured out into this space, my eyes began to roam over the beds, taking in lilac campanula petals veined in black, the tissue-thin poppies, and the gaps between the stone where determined cliffhanger flowers clung, earning their name through sheer tenacity. During our third summer here, I had planted several beds of Spanish love-in-the-mist as a gesture for Henry, and admired the spider-topped heads as I stepped past them. Memories hung in the air out here, as dense and all-consuming as the heat, and I had to make a concerted effort not be caught up in them, to focus, to be present in this, new, moment.

'I thought we should drink a toast to Antonio,' said Luke. 'I was going to get brandy, but I figured nobody would want to drink that.'

'You figured right,' agreed Henry, as the four of us stood in a circle, and sipped in unison. I waited for Eliza to speak, as she usually did in the midst of an awkward silence, but this time she remained quiet. Luke was doing a good job of looking anywhere other than at me and Henry, his trainers disturbing the dust as he shuffled from one foot to the other.

'Are you going to open it or what?' he mumbled, gesturing to the parcel, which he'd propped up against the tree trunk. The fact that I was standing in the exact spot I'd first seen Henry felt significant, as if destiny itself had tied one of life's many strings into a neat bow.

'Of course,' I said. 'Henry, shall we?'

Lifting the large, flat rectangular box between us, we each took a corner of paper and, having counted to three, tore it open to reveal a wooden frame, inside which was an image I recognised.

'Oh wow,' I exclaimed, feeling the sting of tears. Luke had painted an image from the photo album I'd found while clearing out the dresser, the one of me and Henry in the doorway of La Casa Naranja, both of us beaming, his hand placed protectively on the swell of my pregnant belly. The boy that had once been inside that bump had not only captured us perfectly, but the joy of the moment, too, his use of colour, light, and layers of oil adding depth and movement. Henry's eyes shone as he took it in, wonderment softening his features.

'I don't know what to say.' He turned to look at Luke. 'It's beautiful.'

'Exquisite,' I added. 'Stunning. All the superlatives.'

Luke stared at the ground.

'Seriously,' went on Henry. 'This is something else. Thank you.'

'S'all right,' he said, cheeks carnation red.

I pressed my thumb and forefinger into the soft trench below each eye to stem my tears. I knew my son, and this work of art he'd so painstakingly created was his way of pleasing us, making us proud, and demonstrating how important we were to him.

'It's a very special painting,' I told him, leaning in to examine more of the details. 'Shall we take it inside, out of the sun? We don't want it getting damaged.'

'I'll do it.' Eliza stepped forwards, but not before casting a meaningful look in Luke's direction. I caught Henry's eye, and saw that he, too, had clocked this exchange.

None of us said anything until Eliza had moved away. Then, as the back door closed behind her, we all spoke at once.

'You go,' I said to Luke, as he said the same thing.

Henry hesitated. 'I was just going to ask why,' he said.

Luke shoved his hands deep into the pockets of his shorts. 'Why what?'

'Why that photo, of all the photos in that album?'

Luke fidgeted uncertainly. There had been a time when I would've provided a range of responses for him, a multiple-choice list from which he could choose, safe in the knowledge that nothing he said would be wrong. One of my therapists had described it as 'overcompensating'; my mother referred to it as 'suffocating', and Henry merely told me to 'let the boy think for himself'. What none of them seemed to understand was that I'd done it to protect Luke. And far from being a calculated act, it came wholly naturally. Nurturing was what I did; it was the only language I knew by which to parent. I'd had to work hard on quashing these responses when they arose, and even now, the urge to lay down verbal escape routes for my son was a strong one.

Luke, when he eventually replied, did so with his standard air of indifference.

'Thought it was nice,' he said, crunching dirt underfoot. 'A photo of our family where you both look happy.'

'There are loads of those,' I exclaimed, withering at the look he gave me in reply.

'You reckon?'

'Yes. I'm sure there are. Hundreds. Aren't there, Henry?'

He shrugged, screwed up his features.

'There are,' I insisted, wondering why Eliza hadn't come back.

Luke glanced at Henry. 'Sometimes people smile in photos, but their eyes don't match what they're trying to convey with their mouths.'

To illustrate his point, he drew back his lips into a wide, soulless grin.

'I don't do that, though,' I said, more to convince myself than either of them. 'Do I?'

'Mum, come on, it's practically your resting face at this point.'

I responded with a brittle laugh. 'Gee, thanks.'

'I don't blame you for it,' Luke went on. 'I get why you do it, put on a brave face and all that. It's not as if I've given you much choice in the matter.'

'That's not true—' I began, but Henry was nodding.

'When I saw that photo, I felt like I was seeing the real versions of you both for the first time,' said Luke, pausing to swig some wine. He looked deeply uncomfortable yet dogged all the same, and again I had to fight the compulsion to offer him a way out. 'You were happy then, before I came along and ruined it all.'

This time, both Henry and I leapt in with denials, but Luke dismissed both of us with a slow shake of his head. 'You can say it all you want, but I know how difficult it's been for you both, how awful I've been to live with. All the photos I've seen with me in them, you both look different. Like, sad and stuff.'

He'd said all this in a rush, determined to get his point across before either of us had a chance to interrupt him, but in doing so he'd allowed his composed mask to slip. Now, he looked edgy, his skin flushed, and fists clenched.

'We were different,' I agreed gently. 'Having a baby changes you in a unique way, but it didn't make either of us sad. On the contrary, the love I experienced the minute I held you in my arms was indescribable. It was as if life suddenly made sense, the purpose of it all, the reason I was here, on this planet, and had met your dad.'

'She's right.' Henry was smiling at the memory. 'It was the happiest day of my life.'

There was disbelief in Luke's expression. He took another, bigger, gulp of his wine. 'You don't need to lie to me,' he said. 'Especially you, Mum.'

'Me?'

'What Dad said last week, you know, about being angry with me because of everything I'd put you through, because of me being so screwed up?' He'd tapped the side of his head as he said it, and the gesture made me feel as if someone had taken a chisel to my heart. 'At least he was being real,' Luke continued. 'Telling the truth.'

Henry had gone very still. 'I shouldn't have said any of that. It was— I was a mess. I didn't mean it.'

Luke let out a rasp of frustration. 'But you did, Dad – and that's OK. I can take it. I know who I am, and what I've done, all the shitty things I've said to you. It makes more sense that you'd be angry with me than not.'

'But I don't blame you,' Henry insisted. 'I know none of it was your fault.'

'No,' he agreed, 'I know you don't blame me. Instead, you blame each other.'

Eliza chose that moment to come back, bringing the half-empty bottle of white wine with her. She'd changed into a black A-line dress, her pink locks pushed back by a gold hairband, and looked rather apprehensive.

'Everything OK?' she asked, glancing at each of us in turn. 'You told them?' she said, reaching for Luke's hand. 'I knew you'd understand,' she added, with what sounded like palpable relief. 'It came from a good place.'

Incomprehension nudged at me. 'You mean the reason behind the painting?'

'No.' Eliza wrinkled her brow. 'The money – the thirty thousand euros.'

Luke closed his eyes, his head tilted back until it was bathed white by the sun.

The smell of lemons was suddenly overpowering, reminding me of my mother's kitchen, cream cleaner squirted across the draining board, the gusto with which she used to attack the limescale while I sat bouncing a baby Luke on my knees. 'Got to get it gleaming,' she'd say, though never explaining why. I realised now that I knew the answer, understood her need to control something – anything – and tackle a task that came with a satisfying result guaranteed. Watermarks were easier to remove than regrets, plants more straightforward to grow than relationships, and heads simpler to bury in the dirt than stick above the parapet. All the things I'd long accused my mother of doing, I also did, and as I'd observed and learned from her, so, too, had Luke from me.

'It's OK,' I said, as the blood drained from a horrified Eliza's cheeks. 'We'd already worked it out.'

Henry cleared his throat. 'If you'd needed something, you could've just asked,' he said, sounding exhausted. 'We would've sorted it for you.'

'It wasn't for me.' Luke stared at his father. 'It was for—'

'Me.' They all turned in my direction.

'You took my purse, didn't you?' I said, recalling how conveniently it had turned up again the same day I'd misplaced it, sitting on the coffee table as if it had been there all along.

Luke took a deep breath. 'Yeah.'

'You knew I was struggling, money wise?'

Eliza squeezed his arm encouragingly.

'I know you were earning barely nothing at the estate agent, and when I saw the new car, all the clothes, the furniture at Granny's . . . I was worried,' he said. 'I just thought I'd check, you know, to be sure. So, I borrowed your cards. I already knew the pin number to two of them, and the other one was saved in your phone.'

'You should probably delete that,' Eliza put in, with such earnest sincerity that I almost laughed.

'When I saw how much— I mean, how bad things had got, I didn't want to wait until my inheritance came through to sort it – that's years away, and I was worried you'd get into trouble.' He looked beseechingly from me to Henry. 'I was planning to pay it back, all of it. I just thought that if the money thing was sorted then you two could stop arguing all the time about selling this place and, you know, make up and stuff.'

'Oh, Luke.' Henry put a hand on his shoulder.

'I'm so sorry,' I said, appalled at myself and what my stubborn foolhardiness had set in motion. 'This is all my fault. The debt, it could have waited. I was going to sort it.'

There was pity in the eyes of both men as they stared back at me.

'I really was,' I reiterated. 'I had a plan.'

Luke gave into a smile far more wicked than I'd seen him make before.

'So did I,' he said simply. 'Mine was just way better than yours. I took the money to a Western Union place in town and transferred the lot to Granny, told her I'd got some cash from Antonio, and could she put in it my account, and then I diverted it to yours. It's no big deal,' he added, as I gawped at him. 'Did most of it on my phone. And I know you'll want it back, Dad,' he went on, 'and you can have it – as soon as I turn twenty-one.'

'But that's your money,' I said faintly to which Luke made a tsking sound.

'Mine,' he agreed, the flash of confidence making him seem older somehow, for once at ease within the framework of his body. Despite my own shame, I felt pleasure in that moment. Pride for the man who was beginning to shed the petals of his youth. 'And that means I get to decide what I use it for.'

49

Violet

It took some time for the facts to sink in.

Having said his piece, unburdened himself of the worry he'd been carrying, and provided us, his parents, with some titbits of undeniable truth on which to chew, Luke went back inside to get ready for the wake, leaving me and Henry standing dumbfounded in the same spot beneath the lemon tree.

'Blimey,' he said.

'I know. What just happened?'

'I think the cool kids refer to it as "getting owned",' mused Henry. 'He was better at it than me, that's for sure.'

'Better at what?'

'At figuring out exactly what was going on with you. Why you've been so insistent about selling this whole time. I guessed you were struggling financially, but I had no clue how badly – and all this stuff with bloody McCabe. If you'd told me, I promise I would've helped. As it is, I'm tempted to get a flight back to the UK tomorrow just to thump the rotten bastard.'

'I'm not sure you getting arrested for assault would help the situation,' I mused, although I was touched by his instinct to defend me.

'Regardless,' he said darkly. 'He's nothing more than a bully, and this time he's chosen the wrong family to mess with.'

I squinted up at him. 'Can we get out of the sun?'

Henry picked both our wine glasses up off the step, but I had no intention of drinking any more than the single sip I'd had. The beginnings of a tension headache were pressing against my temples; my lips felt parched and tongue sticky.

'I want you to know that I didn't spend all that money on myself,' I said, wincing at the sound the metal chair made as I scraped it across the patio tiles.

Henry lifted the seat opposite and placed it carefully next to mine. Close, but not too close. My hair had dried to a frizz after its shower soaking, and I tried in vain to flatten it down with my hand.

'I didn't think you had.'

'A lot of it went on things Luke needed for uni. I know you sorted out the house for him, but it didn't come with bedding, or kitchen utensils, or a television.'

'You bought him a new TV?'

'I wanted him to feel at home.'

'What about the rest of it? Twenty-five grand is a lot of money.'

I took a moment, closing my eyes briefly as I breathed in for three, then out again.

'You don't know what it was like for me, Henry, having no income of my own, contributing zero, relying on the funds that your job provided. I felt as if I had to account for every penny.'

'We didn't have a choice,' he said. 'One of us had to work, and you wanted to be at home with Luke. I never resented the fact that it was my earnings going into our account, I saw everything as ours, money for our family.'

'Oh my god, how many times? I never *wanted* to be at home, Henry. I had to be. What I wanted was for Luke to be in school, or at friends' houses, not stuck in his bedroom with his miserable mother nagging him about online learning. It was all so stressful and tedious. I was trapped, and watching you go off to do what you loved, all day every day, that was hard. It was really bloody hard. I was jealous of that freedom you had.'

'You were jealous?' He blinked at me in astonishment.

'Horribly. It was why I was so awful to you all the time, so utterly bloody and snappy. And before you say anything, I know that makes me sound completely irrational. I'm well aware it wasn't your fault Luke struggled so much, but he was right in what he said before. I couldn't blame him, and so I blamed you instead.'

'I was jealous, too,' Henry confessed. 'You two were so close. I felt like a bystander a lot of the time, a stranger in my own . . . well, it wasn't even our home to begin with, was it? After the –' he stuttered, shaking his head before continuing – 'accident on the boat that day, it felt as if I stopped being his dad, and that Judas Juan was only too happy to swoop on in and claim that role for himself.'

'I'm not sure that's quite true.' I was havering and he knew it.

Henry appeared stricken, regret spreading like a stain across his features. 'I let Luke down that day,' he said lamentably. 'I let both of you down. I let myself down. I often wonder if this –' he raised a hand to his scars – 'isn't karma for what I didn't do that day.'

'No, Henry.' Without consideration, I reached for his hand. 'Don't say that – don't even think it. It was an accident, that's all, and Luke is fine. He's better than he's ever been. I know there have been a few setbacks since we've been here, but generally, he is calmer, more in control, more compassionate than I ever dared hope he'd be.'

'I used to think it was me,' he went on morosely, as if he hadn't heard me. 'That I'd made him the way he is by wishing he was more like me. I was so adamant that I had to love him better and more freely than my father ever loved me, that I'm afraid I went about it all wrong, tried too hard. I'd watch you with him and wonder how you did it, how you'd managed to figure him out when I just drifted further and further away.'

'I didn't figure him out, Henry. I studied him. Neither of us could go into his head – he'd never let us, couldn't then and wouldn't now, and that's OK. Eliza said something to me the night I arrived, after we'd had that godawful dinner together. I got back to the house, and she was in the lounge and so, of course, I assumed the worst, that they'd fallen out and he'd said or done something to hurt her feelings. But do you know what she said? That she was giving him space to assimilate. Just like that, as if it was the most normal thing in the world. I'd never done that, never understood his need for headspace, that he was downcast and therefore entitled to wallow for a while. I thought making him talk would bring him out of it quicker when all it did was make him angry and frustrated. He didn't know how to tell me to stop, and I hadn't realised I needed to.'

My hand was still in his, and he turned his palm over, wrapping his fingers through mine. We held on to each other so tightly that it was hard to imagine I'd ever let go.

'We have to stop looking at Luke and seeing the little boy he once was,' I said. 'It's not fair on any of us. We need to do our best to see the man he is now, get to know him instead of doubting him. I know I'm the worst culprit, but I'm learning – or trying to.'

Henry tried for a smile. 'You're doing it again,' he said. 'Making all the decisions about Luke, telling me what to do, how to treat him, what I should feel towards him.'

Stung, I went to take back my hand, but Henry tightened his grip.

'Ever since he was born, it's been this competition of who can love him most, who is the better parent, who means the most to him out of the two of us. What happened to us being a team, Vee? We promised each other we'd stick together.'

'And I did,' I burst out. 'You were the one who switched things up. I heard you, Henry, so many times I've heard you say it. "Check with Mum." "Let's see what Mum says." "Only if it's OK with Mum." At some point you decided that I was the bad cop, the sole parent, the one in charge of every tiny decision – especially those Luke didn't like. In trying to become our son's best friend, you pitted the two of you against me. And I'm sorry, but if I became competitive, it's because you pushed me into it.'

Henry went to argue, then stopped, his complexion devoid of all but the mildest colour. My words had struck a chord, and though I was sad I'd made him confront some distressing memories, I also knew it was necessary. If he and I were ever to stand a chance of, as Luke had so aptly put it, 'making up and stuff', we had to cease playing this exhausting game of Mum versus Dad.

I could hear the soft thump of Luke and Eliza's feet as they paced around the house, the sound only just discernible behind the insistent clacking of the cicadas. A plane was passing overhead, its jet trails casting flour-white streaks across the dome of the sky. Henry's hand had gone limp in mine, and I looked round to find him staring at me.

'I wished we'd talked more,' he said. 'Been more honest.'

Leaning closer, I rested my forehead gently against his shoulder.

'I wish we hadn't lost sight of who we were before. Luke recognised it as soon as he saw that photo of us. I think he painted it to remind us of what we stand to lose if—' I sat up, looked at him, willing him to know, to understand.

'If I can't forgive you,' he intoned.

'Henry—'

'No, Vee – don't you get it? Even if we take all the Luke stuff out of the equation, it still doesn't solve the other problems – the parts of us we broke beyond repair. I can't be the man I was before, and every time I look at you, it all comes back. What you did and what I saw, how that became this.' He motioned angrily towards his face. 'The two of you, that night – it ripped away everything from me.'

50

Henry

Two Summers Ago

It was getting dark by the time Henry rinsed out his paint rollers and set them to dry on the balcony wall.

He'd been at the hillside villa since early that morning, layering lining paper on to the walls of the master bedroom before getting started with the first coat of emulsion, and his body ached with fatigue. He was supposed to be on his summer holiday and had only agreed to this job as a favour to his father, who was 'doing important business' with the owner. Henry hadn't asked Antonio to elaborate – what you didn't know, and all that – but he had his suspicions that it was very much a 'you grease my palm and I'll grease yours' type of arrangement.

'Do you think I should refuse?' he'd asked Violet, but she scarcely seemed to hear him, let alone care enough to offer an opinion. It had been a tough few months with Luke, who'd seemed to be on the verge of turning a corner only for things to fall apart when he came up against another boy he didn't like in his sixth-form class. There had been five days – five glorious days – where their son had got up, eaten breakfast, and gone into college without complaint. Then it had all splintered into chaos.

Henry went into the palatial downstairs bathroom to wash his hands, lathering up a good amount of soap and employing the use of a nail brush to scrub the flecks of paint from his skin. He didn't really know why he was bothering, given that he had at least another three days' worth of work ahead. It wasn't as if Violet would mind. She probably wouldn't even notice.

Once outside, he climbed into the driver's seat of the jeep and sat for a while staring out at the view. From his elevated position on the hillside, Henry could see the halo of warm yellow light that emanated out above the old town, its layout of church spires, bell towers and sloping rooftops as charmingly familiar as the face of an old friend. The air was different up here, more fragrant, though with what, Henry could not say with any degree of confidence. Flowers were Violet's speciality. Or, he countered internally, they had been. When she'd had the time to study and focus.

With a yawn, he slid the key into the ignition and fired up the engine. The headlights bloomed on, illuminating a fuzz of insects, the stone wall that ran along the roadside turning from black to the palest grey as he steered his way carefully down and round. Stray cats often darted out from beneath parked cars at this time in the evening, and Henry lived in perpetual fear of hitting one. They'd never had a family pet, much as he and Violet both loved animals – it wasn't fair when they spent such a large chunk of every summer over in Mallorca. Plus, it was difficult when you rented, and even the most lenient of landlords would baulk at the idea of their walls being used as a scratching post. He'd often wondered if a pet would've helped Luke, made him feel as if he had a friend outside of his immediate family. His son had grown fond of telling him, 'You have to like me, you have no choice,' whenever Henry professed his love, and though he knew it came from teenage belligerence and emotional immaturity – Violet was not the only one who read child psychology books – it did little to temper the blows those words struck.

He would have to go back to La Casa Naranja now and face them – the son who thought his father's love was all an act, and the wife from whom extracting any semblance of love left Henry gasping like an underwatered plant. Where there had been affection was now standoffishness, her warmth replaced by rigidity, humour snuffed out by antagonism. It was becoming increasingly difficult to locate the woman he'd fallen for, as if it wasn't walls he'd been papering over all these years but her, the essence of who she was, the joy she'd exuded that had drawn him to her.

They must talk. Tonight. Reconnect.

Henry felt marginally better having made a decision and increased his pressure on the accelerator, taking the final mile at a speed he knew was dangerously close to rash. The lower backstreets that wrapped around this section of the hillside were dark and high-walled, a labyrinth of blind corners and hairpin turns. When he finally pulled up in a screech of dust in the lane outside La Casa Naranja, Henry felt emboldened. He would fix his marriage, no matter what, no matter how long it took, no matter who got in his way.

The clock on the dash told him it was after ten p.m., and a glance towards Luke's turret bedroom confirmed that his seventeen-year-old son was still awake, likely chatting online to one of the friends he gamed with, although Henry used the term 'friend' mildly. When he'd been Luke's age, his mates had been the people he saw every day, not a nicknamed somebody hiding behind a cartoon avatar. But, as he was only too aware, that had been a long time ago. The world had changed, technology was an inherent part of most people's lives, and his son was at least making his way towards being an active participant.

Instead of going in through the front door, he closed the gate quietly behind him and stole around the side of the house to the rear garden, hoping to find Violet sitting out on the patio, moon-bathed and mellow after a few sips of wine. As he emerged from the shadows, however, Henry froze. Violet was indeed in the garden, but she was not alone. Juan was there, too, the deep murmur of his voice like a droning mosquito, and there was something about the scene that made the hairs stand up along Henry's arms. He heard his wife giggle – not laugh, but giggle – a childish titter that sounded as if someone else had taken possession of her. Envy burned inside him, hot and abrasive, and he took a step back, into the darkness.

Juan had been perched on the edge of the patio table, but as Henry watched, he stood up and crossed to the low wall, pointing at something in the far distance.

Violet murmured a reply, and Juan gave a deep, throaty laugh. There was music filtering out from the house, Henry realised. Astrud Gilberto, the track they'd played at their wedding, 'And Roses And Roses'. A song about a girl afraid to love, whose heart is won over piece by piece, petal by petal, as her amour brings her flowers every day.

He watched through eyes now glazing over with tears as his wife started to dance, her bare feet soundless on the tiles as she stepped, spun, and swirled her skirt. Juan turned from the view to face her; Henry could see the flash of his smile, that swarthy grin he so deftly bestowed. He knew he should move, interrupt them, make a joke, rush over and sweep Violet into his arms, dance with her as he had that day in Deià, when they had promised to love, and to cherish – but Henry's feet were stuck fast, rooted in place like the surrounding trees, giving him no option but to wait, to watch.

This was their place, his and Violet's – the garden was where they'd met, where he had fallen so fast and with such a furious sense of rightness into loving her, and now he was watching her defile it, sully the most pivotal moment of his life.

The song ended and another began, the sweetness of Astrud Gilberto's lilting voice so at odds with the melancholy he felt, that exquisite pain of witnessing the inevitable.

Juan's hands were on Violet's waist, the lower half of their bodies pressing together as they moved closer, held tighter, gazed longer. When the second song finished, silence fell, and Henry held his breath as the dancing stopped.

Violet's hair had worked loose from its clasp and fallen between her shoulders, the fiery red of a dragon's roar. She was smiling, lips parted, and chin tilted up. In any other circumstance, Henry would have said she'd never looked more beautiful, and the thought turned his heart to ash. He saw what was about to happen before it did, yet the kiss still landed hard as a mallet against his chest.

With a roar, he ran forwards, his arms raised and thrashing wildly. Violet pulled away from Juan, horror turning her face into a spectre, a black hole into which Henry found himself sucked. He threw a punch in Juan's direction and missed, the Spaniard ducking out of the way, but only by a few scant inches.

'*Bastardo*!' Henry yelled, fists flailing through the air as Juan cowered behind Violet.

'Stop it!' she screamed, as a wine glass fell to the ground and smashed.

'I'll kill him,' Henry snarled, as Violet tried to grab him. 'Get off me,' he snapped, wrenching himself free as Juan jogged out of reach once more.

'I don't want to hurt you,' he said, his palms raised.

Henry scoffed. 'Bit late for that,' he spat, and Violet let out a sob.

'Please,' she said, as broken glass crunched under Henry's boots. 'It was nothing, a mistake, a stupid mistake.'

Henry watched as Juan's face fell, the bruise to his ego wiping away any attempts to be conciliatory.

'What did you expect?' he goaded, as Henry advanced. 'When you treat her so badly, neglect her, make her feel like an afterthought?'

'Shut up,' Henry growled.

'When was the last time you told her how beautiful she is? The last time you danced with her?'

'I said, shut up!'

Violet was properly sobbing; an inconsolable, wretched sound that turned Henry inside out with misery. How could she have done this to them?

'Please, Henry,' she whispered. 'Please don't.'

Turning away with a sob that came out as a bellow of anguish, he stumbled over several plant pots, one of which rolled over and cracked loudly in two. He heard Violet's gasp of shock, followed by a shout as Juan called his name.

'Come back,' they both called, but Henry had no intention of lingering any longer in the murky darkness of his wife's betrayal. He needed to get away, to make sense of what he'd seen, and what it meant.

'Henry, wait!' Violet was gaining on him, her arm outstretched, feet still bare, hair wild.

'Leave me alone.'

He was through the gate and back in the lane, warm night air a suffocating blanket. There was no time to get back in the jeep, she would catch up with him, force him to look at her, to listen, and he couldn't. He felt sick with terror at the thought of losing her, but the strength of his anger frightened him more. He didn't know what would happen if he unleashed it, the sleeping beast inside him liable to tear its way out.

Henry set off at a run, his arms and legs pumping, heavy boots cumbersome on the uneven surface. A darting blur to his left, something small and fast; he swerved, body wheeling round, and collided hard with one of the high walls at the road's edge.

Suddenly, there was light, so much light, so bright that it blinded him. Henry staggered forwards only for his feet to be ripped out from under him, the force flipping him over sideways, the hot tarmac slamming into his face.

And then there was movement, a scream, tearing, agony like no other. Henry closed his eyes, and let the nothingness take him.

51

Violet

He had seen me kiss Juan, and he had run. Straight into the path of a car, travelling too fast around bends shrouded in darkness. The wing mirror had picked him up by the sleeve of his overalls and tossed him down on to the road, dragging him several metres until the driver – a bewildered Spanish woman in her eighties – applied the brakes. A few seconds was all it had taken to destroy one side of his face, an accident born of a choice that I had made, to betray my husband in the worst possible way.

I didn't blame Henry for hating me. I deserved every ounce of it. And yet, I did want the chance to explain why I'd done it. I believed I was worth that much at least. He had refused to listen in the hospital, when his head was swaddled in bandages, eventually sending me a text message that simply read: *It's over. Go home.*

Now, I knew, I shouldn't have allowed myself to be persuaded. I'd ventured down the wrong path with Henry not once, but twice, and I wasn't about to clock up a third.

Taking a deep breath, I made myself face him. We were still sitting on the patio, the same place I had danced with Juan that night, the bubble of happiness around me so flimsy as to be barely there at all. I had been trying to gather up the burst pieces of it ever since.

'It wasn't planned,' I said. 'What happened that night – none of it was premeditated.'

Henry's mouth was a hard line. 'Tell me.'

'You'd been out all day, Luke was shut up in his room as always, and I was bored, I guess. Feeling sorry for myself. I'd had a few drinks by the time Juan showed up.'

'You didn't invite him?'

'No.' I shook my head, half laughing at the ludicrousness of it all, of how much trouble had been wrought by a man deciding to call on a neighbour. 'He actually came looking for you, wanted to talk to you about your father, about some business deal. I can't remember the details. Like I said, I'd been drinking.'

'And?'

'And ...' I exhaled sharply. 'I invited him in. We got to talking, you know, about life, Ana, us, the accident with Luke, how it had changed everything.'

Henry's gaze remained steady.

'I told him I was unhappy,' I said, punctuating the statement with a sad sort of laugh. 'I'd believed it when I'd said as much to Juan, but of course, the joke was on me. I'd known nothing of real misery until after that night.

'Why?'

It was a simple enough question, but I struggled to formulate a reply. The situation was both complicated and precarious, as it had been then, and I considered what to say before I responded. The truth, in the end, was my safest bet.

'Because I was unhappy, Henry, for so many reasons, and Juan cared. Nobody else ever asked if I was all right – not you, not Luke, not my mum. The only people who ever seemed to notice how sad I was were Ynes and Juan. I used to look forward to coming over here to the island partly because I knew there were friends here that genuinely cared about me, who saw me as Violet, a woman, a human being with emotions and limits. At home in England, I was just Mum. That's all I ever was.'

'You didn't kiss Ynes, though, did you?' Henry pointed out.

'No.'

'So, why kiss Juan?'

'It was a stupid lapse of judgement.'

'You're going to have to do better than that.'

'It didn't mean anything.'

'To you, maybe. To me, it meant everything.'

I wrung my hands together in my lap, rubbing at the skin around my knuckles, the shape of them so like the undulating Pollença hills. Luke had told me once that drawing a person's hands was more difficult than capturing a likeness of their face.

'We carry our histories in our hands, Mum. Every story we've had a role in can be told through them; they are the part we spend the most time examining and the one most familiar to us – more so than our features. We get to see our hands, but we can never see a true likeness of our faces, not through our own eyes.'

Luke had shown Henry and me how he saw us, the painting he'd done as clear a rendering as we were likely to get of how we appeared to the world.

'Is it the kiss you can't forgive?' I asked. 'Or the fact it was Juan I did it with?'

Henry flinched as though I'd drilled down and found a nerve.

'Anyone else,' he said. 'Anyone but him, I might have been able to, not overlook, but get my head around. But him? My supposed friend. The man who Luke had hero-worshipped for half his life, who you'd bloody well hero-worshipped ever since that day on the stupid boat. No matter what I did after that day, how much I bent to Luke's will and gave into his every whim, it couldn't make up for the fact that Juan excelled at all the things I was useless at. He saved my son's life when I couldn't, for god's sake. That's why, Vee. That's why it hurt me so much when I saw him doing the one thing that I thought I could still beat him at – making you happy, being the one who made you smile, and laugh and dance. Jesus!' he cried, throwing up his hands then getting to his feet. I watched him pace the length of the patio with his head down and waited for his agitation to subside.

'I wanted you to be that person,' I said, quietly so he had no choice but to come back and sit beside me. 'I kept waiting for him to reappear, but he never did.'

He shook his head in bewilderment. 'I was there.'

'You treated me differently after Luke. The older he got, the more issues that came to light, the further away you pushed me. That's how it felt, Henry,' I said, as he continued to dismiss what I was saying. 'I wasn't even Violet to you any more, I was Mum. Juan wasn't like that – and it was nice to feel seen. He saw as me, Henry. *Me*.'

I expected him to scoff, to tell me I was self-obsessed, that being a parent took priority over everything else – even my sense of identity. It was nothing I hadn't already told myself a thousand times, during a thousand periods of self-slander, and while being a mother meant a lot to me, it was not my sole purpose for existing. I had more to offer, and I wanted Henry to see it, for him to remember who I was.

My hands were still playing an invisible tug of war, and Henry stilled me by putting one of his own over mine. He was completely calm again – almost serene.

'Vee, listen to me.'

I listened.

'I do see you as you,' he said. 'I see that one frown line that shows up whenever you're reading the list of ingredients on the back of a packet—'

'The print is so small—'

'And I see that smile you get when you think nobody is watching, when the sun comes through the trees and turns everything to gold; I see the bitten-down nail of your third finger, the ring you still wear on it, that hope you've never let go of.'

I blinked then, tears threatening.

'I love the way you sing along to radio jingles as if they're another verse of a song, how you'll try to save even the smallest, most shrivelled up of plants. I love that you made me listen when you were worried about my dad, even when I wasn't ready to hear you, and I love how brave you've been with Luke, how many times you stuck up for him, made calls and refused to be fobbed off by those wet blankets at the mental health clinic. If it'd been me, I'd have given up, but you never did, and—'

'Love,' I said, stopping him mid-flow. 'You said love.'

'I know. So?'

I fixed him with a look that could never hope to articulate what I was feeling. There were too many emotions at play, a soup of regret, and sorrow, and adoration.

'Love, Henry,' I whispered. 'Not loved – present tense, not past.'

He started to reply, his words disintegrating as the meaning of my own took root.

'You told me you didn't love me any more,' I said.

Even now, almost two years after he'd done exactly that, it pained me to repeat it. To give it air was to risk reminding him of how he'd felt then, how he might still feel – but I had to know.

Henry didn't say anything, he merely stared at me; perplexity in his expression as he shook his head. There was no way of knowing if he was doing so to dismiss me, or his past self, and the hope – always present, forever a thorn in my side – caused me to shrink in on myself.

'Sorry is all I am,' I told him. 'It's the only thing I have left to give.'

That and love.

Henry looked on the verge of saying something when a clattering sound heralded the return of Eliza, who was stacking her and Luke's empty glasses in the kitchen sink.

'Luke's gelling his hair,' she explained, seeing me peering in through the open back door. 'And Juan's waiting out front.'

I felt myself flush. 'Juan's here?'

Henry took his hand from mine. 'I'll go,' he said, sounding less amenable than he had a few moments ago, and stomped off into the house. Unsure what else to do, I followed him, reaching the bottom of the stairs at the same time as Luke descended.

'Hey,' he said, then, as Henry opened the front door, 'Oh, hi, Juan.'

'What are you doing here?' I blurted rudely. Juan, unsurprisingly, pulled a 'what have I done now?' face.

'The Rosario began forty minutes ago,' he said. 'I thought you had forgotten.'

'Crap, I haven't got my phone,' said Luke, and trudged back upstairs.

Juan was already backing out of the hallway, his attention switching from me to Henry. He could sense that something was going on, that he'd walked into the middle of a discussion, and was clearly trying his best to avoid confrontation.

'I will wait outside,' he said. 'Paulina, she wanted to come with her *abuelo*, but then she remembered about ...' He trailed off, eyes flickering across the scarred side of Henry's face. 'She was too scared to come inside. I am sorry,' he added nonchalantly, registering our stony glares, 'but this is children. If they're not being noisy, they are likely to be misbehaving. You have to watch them like an owl, with a pair of eyes in the back of your head.'

'Got it,' Luke reappeared, shoving his phone into his trouser pocket. 'Shall we go?'

'In a minute,' said Henry. He was looking at Juan, his expression unreadable.

Eliza strolled through from the kitchen, a roll of toilet paper in her hand.

'Thought we might need this,' she said. 'You know, in case we start crying.'

If I cried any more during this trip, I'd need to be placed overnight in a bowl of water to replenish myself like a peace lily.

We trooped outside, to where the midday heat hung damp like a curtain and found the front garden deserted.

'Paulina,' said Juan, with an urgency that sent a chill right through me. 'She is gone.'

52

Violet

Henry and I exchanged a horrified look, and without a word, he headed back inside.

'Can you check the back garden?' I asked Luke and Eliza. 'Just in case she wandered out there.'

They disappeared around the side of the house, and I turned to Juan.

'Don't worry,' I said. 'She can't have gone far. We'll find her.'

He barely seemed to hear me as he began marching around in a circle, swearing in Spanish, and clutching his head with both hands. '*Mierda*,' he grunted. 'I knew it was stupid to let her come. She is very frightened of *cara*— Henry.'

I narrowed my eyes. 'You taught her that word.'

Juan's expression darkened. He was a man who didn't relish being caught out.

'You did, didn't you? You absolute bastard.'

I'd been so consumed with condemning myself for that night, for our kiss, convinced that I'd caused it by putting out the wrong signals, flirting back and encouraging him. But Juan had been the one who kissed me, and he had done so knowing that I was married to his friend, that the two of us had problems, that I wasn't in my right mind.

'Was this whole thing about you and him?' I said. 'Some sort of, what, macho Spanish rubbish?'

Juan stopped pacing and stepped towards me, chin jutting out, hands raised.

'It was all Ana ever said to me. "Why are you not nice like Henry? Why don't you adore me the same way as Henry adores Violet? Why can't you have a good and honest job like he does?" I was never enough for her, she wanted me to be someone else, to be him.'

Shocked into silence, I could only gape at him.

'I do care for you,' he said. 'Naturally, I wanted to kiss you. Look at you, *Pelirroja*, you are very beautiful. Any man would want to kiss you.' He seemed to wilt before me as he spoke, all his usual suaveness draining away.

'But you did it to prove a point,' I said. 'That night wasn't about me at all, was it?'

'*Sí.*' Juan sighed. 'It was about you, and me, and Ana, and I think, perhaps, also Antonio. You all loved Henry more than you loved me.'

I tried to imagine how he must have felt, but all that resonated was frustration. Juan's fragile ego, his need to be viewed as more worthy than anyone else, had corroded his sense of what was right. He'd set out to make himself feel better that night and to hell with the consequences. But even he couldn't have foreseen an accident on the scale of what occurred, when Henry's own bruised pride had lit an unstoppable fire inside his chest, and this horrible nickname he'd come up with could be attributed to nothing more sinister than guilt. Juan didn't want to feel responsible, and so he deflected, made jokes, taught his granddaughter a cruel word, while I had gone the opposite way, and held myself fully accountable for all of it.

There was no time to say any of this to Juan. No sooner had he made his declaration than Eliza and Luke re-emerged, followed closely by a harried-looking Henry, who shook his head as he locked the front door.

'No sign,' he said, as Juan began to swear in earnest.

'She probably went back to the Rosario,' I reasoned. 'Would she know the way on her own?'

He was shaking his head. 'Juan, focus.'

'I'm not sure,' he said helplessly. 'She is never alone, not ever. Tomas, he made me promise to not let go of her hand. *Ay dios mío.*'

The wake was being held at the villa Mateo had inherited, which was situated towards the outskirts of Pollença, around a fifteen-minute walk from where we were.

'Go back there,' I instructed Juan. 'If she isn't there, you can let Tomas and Carmen know, and they'll be able to help us search. Henry, why don't you and Luke head into town, check the gift shops, the ice-cream parlours, anywhere that sells toys?'

They nodded, Henry rolling up the sleeves of his shirt.

'Eliza, can you run up the Calvari Steps, check the view-point behind, maybe the olive groves? She might have spotted a stray cat and followed it.'

'On it,' she said, pressing a kiss to Luke's cheek. 'Shall I set up a WhatsApp chat, too, so we can all stay in touch?'

'Sure, fine, whatever you think,' I said distractedly.

Juan had reached the gate. 'And you?' he asked. 'What will you do?'

My eyes met Henry's, and I knew that, like me, he was remembering the day Luke had wandered off, how we'd discovered him out in the road, small and vulnerable.

'Whatever it takes,' I said.

I watched them go, then hurried back into the house and swapped my black heeled shoes for trainers, kicking the former off with such force that they skidded across the hall-way floor.

'Paulina!' I called, shutting the front door behind me. There was no reply, but I continued to shout her name as I circled the boundary of the house, passing the spot where I'd clambered over the wall all those years ago. A sliding doors moment that saw the path of my life skew in a wholly unanticipated direction. I glanced up at the house, at its peachhued facade and scalloped tiles, and found myself undone by a sudden rush of love. How close I'd come to losing her when all she'd ever done was welcome me. Henry had been right: we could never sell.

I carried on through the lanes, zigzagging my way backwards and forwards as I hurried towards the hub of the town, peering over fences and into the open doorways of shops, asking everyone I encountered if they'd seen a little girl, this tall, with dark hair. Nobody had.

Despite the collective panic we'd all experienced when Juan initially raised the alarm, I'd remained fairly confident that Paulina wouldn't have strayed very far, and that we would find her within minutes once we started to look. But the further I went without so much as a potential sighting, the more trepidation began to take over. Someone could've snatched her, bundled her into the back of a car or into another house. Unlikely, but not impossible, and vile to contemplate. Thinking that I'd check my phone to see if any of the others had struck luckier than me, I delved a hand into my bag only to find it empty, save for a hairbrush and lipstick. My purse, I remembered, was on the kitchen table, and I had a vague memory of plugging my phone in to charge earlier that morning. I was too far from the house to circle back for it now and ground my teeth together with irritation at my own absentmindedness. I had little choice but to head in the direction of Antonio's villa, where I could join up with Juan, and the other guests, and having made my decision, I set off at a run, dodging idling tourists, café tables, and tall racks of colourful postcards as I went. It was only when I caught sight

of the boarded-up windows that I realised I'd come along
Carrer de la Garriga and somehow ended up at Tomas's new
house. Paulina had been here before, not long ago – could
she have come back in search of her papá?

I pushed aside the makeshift fence and listened, but all I
could hear was the screeching cry of the swallows.

'Paulina,' I called, and this time, I heard something. A
whimper, perhaps. I couldn't be sure. The outer door was
padlocked, but I could see a gap between two of the panels
covering what would become a downstairs window. It was
tight, and I swore as I felt the hem of my dress rip, but I made
it through in one piece, calling the girl's name again as I went
and hearing a definite cry coming from above.

There were no hard hats within sight, and no time to locate
one. I ran to the stairwell and took the steps two at a time,
pausing on the first floor, before heading up again to the very
top. The attic was cramped and searingly hot, the dark
tarpaulin no match for the relentless June sun. I stared
around, sweat already starting to prickle, confused as to
where the whimpering was coming from – and then I spotted
it. A tiny hand in a far corner of the space, reaching out from
between the beams.

'Oh, thank goodness,' I cried, hurrying across and falling
to my knees. 'It's OK,' I said, switching to Spanish as I reassured her that everything was going to be fine, that nobody
was cross, that I was going to get her out.

But how?

The space through which she'd squeezed was minuscule,
and no amount of gentle encouragement from me would
convince her to come back through.

'*Me dolió mucho,*' she sobbed. *It hurt me so much.*

Squinting, I peered through the gap, saw the scratches
along her arms, the fear in her trembling lip. She was

pink-cheeked, likely dehydrated, and near hysterical. I required help, needed Henry, but without my phone, I had no way of contacting him, and I knew I couldn't leave Paulina here, not by herself. She was clinging to my hand so tightly that there was a chance my circulation would be cut off.

Casting around for ideas, I noticed a heap of tools a few feet away, and stretching across, rooted through until I found a hammer. If I could prise apart the vertical beams, perhaps I could create enough space to reach through and haul her out. It was worth a try.

I stroked Paulina's hand as I explained in broken Spanish what I was going to do, urging her to move as far back as possible into the space. This she did, clambering over the exposed beams until she reached the wall.

The teeth of the hammer slid into the narrow gap, the wood whining as I pulled it backwards as hard as I could. There was a splintering sound, but the nails didn't budge. I readjusted my position, trying a spot closer to the join, but it was difficult to gain purchase. Sweat ran into my eyes, and my fingers were slick with it. Abandoning the largest, central beams, I crouched and began working on a smaller plank to the side, trying in vain to lever it off. Whoever had bashed in the nails had done so with enough force to half bury the heads in the timber, meaning there was very little I could do to get them out.

Paulina's cries were growing in volume, her chest heaving. If I didn't reach her soon, there was a very real chance that she would suffer a full-blown panic attack, and she was in desperate need of water. We both were.

With a moan of frustration, I returned to the stack of tools, new hope flashing as I spotted a serrated edge. If I couldn't wrench the planks apart, then I would cut them.

The saw slid easily into place, and I let out an exalted breath as I managed to turn it, the timber splitting as the blade got to work. When I had sliced through both, I knelt and repeated the process lower down, kicking out the sections of wood until a small escape route appeared.

I gestured to Paulina, but she refused to budge, her body trembling and eyes wide.

Biting down on my lip, head pounding from exertion, I examined the hole I'd made. It had been a very long time, almost twenty years, in fact, since I'd asked my limbs to bend in the way they had while I was a gymnast, but I thought that if I got the upper part of my body through the gap, then I'd be able to manoeuvre my legs in after me.

Set on my task, eager to reach the little girl and bring this nightmare to an end, I didn't stop to consider how much damage my sawing had wrought.

Not until I heard a loud cracking sound.

53

Violet

It happened a split second after I'd wriggled through.

What was left of the planks cleaved over with an ear-shattering crash, a portion of the roof above falling in and blocking the hole.

Paulina screamed and clamped her hands over her ears. Dust swarmed as I crawled across to join her, my eyes watering, mouth dry.

'I've got you,' I croaked in Spanish, pulling her into my arms, using my body to shield her from any other debris that might tumble in on top of us.

It was so hot, the temperature at a dangerous level, and the lack of fresh air was making my lungs contract.

'Help!' I shouted, though it came out as nothing more than a rasp. Coughing, I tried again, then again, more loudly. Paulina clung to me, whimpering, both of us slick with sweat.

I should have gone as soon as I'd found her; located a phone, called the police. I had done everything wrong. Again.

'Help!' I yelled, the word breaking apart with a sob that sent a fresh tremor through the girl in my arms. I must hold it together. It wouldn't help either of us if I fell apart.

Taking a deep breath, I tried again, shouting on and on, in Spanish and then English, yelling for help, pleading for it, begging to be rescued. After a while, Paulina stopped crying and went limp, her eyes half closed as she continued to nestle against me.

Close to panic now, I scoured the roof above us, looking for weak spots, but there was nothing, only the dark outline of tiles, and the hole I'd made was completely blocked. Untangling myself from Paulina, I ventured across the small space on my hands and knees, peering through the mess of timber in the hope of spotting something I could reach that might help us.

And then I heard voices.

'Henry!' I shouted. 'Is that you?'

'Violet?'

I sat back on my haunches, tears of consolation coursing down my cheeks, and listened to the glorious sound of feet approaching.

'Mum?'

Luke was with him. Kneeling up, I pressed my mouth to the collapsed beams.

'Over here,' I cried. 'We're over here.'

I couldn't see either of them, but knowing they were there, close enough to touch, felt miraculous. It was Henry's voice that came next.

'Vee, what happened? How did you— Jesus.'

He waited while I explained what I'd done, how sorry I was, the state we were both in, and then he took charge.

'Fetch some water,' he told Luke. 'And call Juan, get him and Tomas over here. I need to secure this roof, it's not –' he hesitated – 'it's not safe. You shouldn't . . . stay outside. Don't come back inside until I say, OK?'

'But what if?'

'Go.'

'It's OK,' I said, in as calm a tone as I could muster. 'We'll be fine. Your father will look after us. You go and get the others.'

'All right, but Mum?'

'Yes?'

'I . . . I'm— Just be OK, promise?'

'You don't need to say sorry,' I said, unable to prevent the tears that followed. 'I love you, very much.'

'I love you, too.'

I waited until he was gone before I spoke again. 'Thank you,' I whispered, the wood rough against my lips. 'For keeping him safe.'

'Better late than never.' Henry's voice was thick. 'Now sit tight, I'm going to get you out of there.'

I could hear him murmuring to himself as he examined the mess I'd made, then the scrape of wood as he attempted to move a few pieces aside.

'I'm going to need to fetch some planks to act as support beams,' he said. 'But I'll be back in a minute. They're just one floor down. OK?'

'OK,' I replied shakily, hating the fact that he was going, even momentarily.

Clambering back towards Paulina, I found her slumped against the wall, gaze unfocused, and settled myself beside her again, arms protectively spread.

'Soon, darling. Not long now.'

I'd lapsed into English, but she seemed to understand what I was saying.

'*Caracortada*,' she murmured, upon hearing Henry return, and I squeezed her more closely to me.

'*Sí*,' I said. '*Caracortada es valiente*; Superman.'

She lifted her chin sleepily. '*Superhombre*?'

I smiled. '*Sí, Superhombre*.'

We stayed where we were, crouched together, trying not to flinch as Henry hammered and banged.

'Right,' he said, sounding far more confident than I'd allowed myself to feel in what felt like hours. 'That should hold. I'm going to break through now. Are you clear?'

'We're clear,' I confirmed, bracing myself.

With a grunt, Henry brought down something hard on the tangle of wood. The space shuddered around us, but nothing fell. Another blow followed, then another. I closed my eyes against the swirling dust, and when I opened them again, there was a gap. Henry's face was visible, and it took all my self-control not to rush forwards and kiss it.

'Stay back,' he warned, and I saw a flash of silver as he raised his tool of choice and swung it down into the hole. More of the wood splintered apart, the gap to freedom widening.

'Stop!' I called. 'That's big enough for Paulina. I can lift her through.'

Henry put down his axe just as Juan and Tomas ran into the room, both men puffed out and glistening with sweat. Hearing her father's voice was enough to rouse Paulina, and I carried her carefully across the raised beams towards where his arms were outstretched and waiting.

'She needs water,' I instructed, and Tomas nodded, clutching his precious daughter to his chest as he fought back the tears. 'I understand,' he said, turning to Henry. '*Gracias.*'

Juan was ashen. 'What can I do?' he asked, taking in the scene, the chaos, the fact I was still trapped.

'Go,' I said gently. 'Be with your family.'

'Are you sure that you will be safe?'

'Of course I will.' I smiled at him through the gap. 'I have Henry.'

Juan touched a brief hand to my husband's shoulder, and then he was gone.

'How did you know?' I asked.

Henry looked at me, the way his dark hair was falling across his eyes reminded me of Luke.

'That I was here – how did you know?'

'Truth?'

'Always.'

'I didn't. This road is the quickest route from the market to the villa, and when you didn't answer your phone, I figured that was the most likely place you'd be. It was Luke who heard you shouting.'

My clever boy.

'You should stand back,' he went on, reaching for the axe.

'I will in a minute. But first, can you come here?'

Henry deliberated for a moment, then stepped up to the hole, leaning over so his face was level with mine. 'What's up?'

I laughed at the question, at his nonchalance, at the Henryness of him.

'I thought we could finish our conversation. The one we were having before all this happened.'

'Before you took a saw to my support beams?'

'How stupid was that decision, on a scale of one to ten?'

He frowned as if mulling it over. 'I think I can safely conclude that it makes you a solid, green-eyed, ten out of ten.'

'Hey.' I smiled. 'You stole my line.'

'I bet you wouldn't rate me the same now,' he replied, glancing away. 'What was it you said at the time? Something about symmetry?'

'I'd only known you half an hour then. I was basing the entirety of my decision on looks. Now that I know you, I'd probably opt for something closer to one . . .'

'Why, you—'

'. . . thousand,' I said sweetly.

Henry rolled his eyes. 'Not sure if that makes sense mathematically.'

'I always did hate the subject.'

'You and Luke both.'

'The point is, I rate you. More highly than anyone else. You are gorgeous, Henry – no,' I scolded, as he started to argue. 'I know you have scars, but so do I. We both have them from bringing up our son, from going into a war we never signed up for, and a battle we were destined to lose more times than we won. But we made it – we're on the other side.'

He looked unsure. 'You really believe that?'

'What I think is that we've become so used to the fight that we didn't realise it was over. You've stayed in your trench, and I hunkered down in mine, and neither of us dared move. I don't know about you, Henry, but I wasn't ready to look too closely at the waste ground our marriage had become; I was too beaten down by everything, by life, too shellshocked. I kept hoping things would go back to the way they'd been before, but I never did anything to make that happen.'

He was nodding, and I put my arm through the gap, my hand reaching for his.

Henry took it, his thumb hot against my palm. 'There is no going back,' he said, and I felt as if he'd kicked me. When I tried to pull back, however, Henry's grip grew firmer. 'That came out wrong,' he said. 'What I mean is that the way we were, in the beginning; we'll never be those versions of ourselves again. And that's OK, Vee,' he hastened. 'Hankering after the past makes no sense. We can't go back; we can only go forwards – onwards.' His features softened as he took in my expression. 'What's that face for? You're pouting.'

I pulled in my bottom lip. 'No, I'm not.'

'Out with it, Torres.'

Torres. My married name. His name.

Optimism unfurled and bloomed inside my chest.

'I don't want to go forwards if it means doing so alone,' I said, quietly enough that he took a step closer to hear me.

'The only future I want is you – us. It's all I've ever wanted, even when I was angry with you, even when I thought you didn't love me any more. I would take you, have you, even without that. Do you hear what I'm saying? You don't even have to love me, Henry, you only have to forgive me.'

'I know.' He paused. 'But I'm afraid that simply won't do.'

I took back my hand, and this time he let me, his own dropping to his side.

'You can't move past it,' I said, not a question but a state-ment. 'It's OK. I understand.' The disappointment was suffo-cating, an airless room in a sunken chamber.

Henry frowned at me, and then, with a smile so broad his eyes crinkled, he started to laugh.

I bristled.

'I'm glad you find my utter desolation so amusing.'

He chuckled. 'You are a Nelly – do you know that?'

'Why, because I sawed through your support beams?'

'Well, yes, definitely that, but also because you think our marriage can survive on the strength of your love alone. I mean, your independent streak is always something I've admired, right from the start, when you it took upon yourself to trespass.'

I threw him a sharp look and he grinned.

'But even you can't do it all by yourself. Nobody can – not you, or me, or Luke. We all need each other – don't you see that? We're not a perfect family by any means, but we're the only family I fit into, the only one I want to be a part of.'

My head was beginning to throb. 'I don't understand what you're saying. It's all riddles. Of course you're a part of this family. You always will be, no matter what decision you make about us. You'll always be Luke's dad, and my . . .' I stalled as I searched for the appropriate word, a term that could sum up the vitalness of him, the absolute necessity of his presence in my life, no matter how shallow the dregs of affection he was willing to give. 'Everything,' I said at last, not caring about my tears, nor the desperation that was so palpable it almost brought me to my knees. 'You're everything to me.'

'Oh, Vee,' he said through a sigh, mumbling something else I didn't quite catch.

'What did you say?' I began, moving forwards across the beams only to trip, my foot slipping forwards into the darkness. I heard Henry's shout of alarm as the floor beneath me seemed to split in two, and then I was falling, flailing, grasping at air. I tried to scream, but there was nothing. Pain flared like a struck match, the intensity ripping the air from my lungs. The light dimmed, flickered, and went out.

54

Henry

This Summer

She looked so peaceful.

On the hardest days, those when Luke's anger was triggered from simmering into explosive, Violet had barely been able to sit still, let alone rest, and even in slumber she had appeared tormented, her brow wrinkled and jaw set. Henry had felt as helpless then as he did now and pressed the heel of each hand into his eyes to stem the tears.

The hospital sheets were pure white, the walls of the room an insipid milky yellow, while the artificial lights above made everything feel stark and exposed. Splayed across the pillow, Violet's hair looked like dropped rose petals, her lips a perfect bud.

They were all here, assembled in the waiting room or on hard-back chairs in the corridor. Juan, Tomas, Ynes, Eliza, and Luke. His son hadn't come into the room yet, but he would. As he did when it came to so many difficult things, Luke needed space, and time to assimilate. And that was OK, thought Henry. Acceptance was an open door towards understanding, and he was ready to walk through it now.

A Styrofoam cup of vending machine tea was cooling on the floor by his boot, and he stretched down a hand still covered in dust and scratches to lift it. When Violet had fallen, broken planks of timber had followed her descent, and Henry had clawed his way through it all to reach her, shouting all the while for help, for an ambulance, for someone to do something. He'd always been so capable; a man who could trust in his practical skills and abilities, someone who fixed and restored. But there were some jobs that were past him and, as he'd swiftly discovered, fear was a tough opponent. Nobody could do everything on their own. He'd said as much to Violet, prior to it happening, moments before he'd been about to tell her what he should have been telling her ever since she arrived in Mallorca this summer. It seemed so stupid, now, that he hadn't. What a colossal fool he'd been, how blinded by pride and hindered by ego. Those promises he'd made yet saw fit to break, his vow to look after her no matter what, made not on their wedding day but in a hospital not unlike this one, a tiny baby boy clutched in his arms, the future a warm light on their horizon. Henry had closed his eyes to the reality, but today he saw it, felt it, wanted it.

He looked down at Violet, at his wife, and this time when the tears came, he let them.

'Dad?'

It was Luke, large but impossibly young in the open doorway, shadows dark as bruises beneath his eyes.

Henry wiped his cheeks. His voice, when he spoke, sounded hoarse. 'You can come in,' he said. 'It's OK.'

Luke's gaze flickered to the bed, then rapidly away again. 'Is she . . .?' he began, then appeared unable to finish. Emotion had him in its grip, and Henry watched as he fought to push it down, subdue his own nature.

'I get it,' he said. 'Sometimes, I want to rip it all down too.'

Luke took a step into the room, hesitated, then lowered himself into the other chair.

'How do you stop yourself?' he asked, and Henry thought how simple a question it was, and why he'd never thought to answer it before.

'I tend to think of anger as flowing water. If you dam it, it only becomes more destructive, if you try to drain it, it'll only flood out somewhere else, but what you can do is redirect it. I often find that the thing you're angry about, the thing that pushes you into reacting, is not the root cause of the problem, and if you can find a way to channel that initial outpouring into something else, be it a walk, or hitting a punchbag, or gardening—'

'Or drawing?'

'Yes,' Henry smiled briefly. 'Or drawing. If you can do that, it'll provide you with the calm space you need to figure out what it really is that's bugging you.'

Luke nodded as if working this out. 'I'll try,' he said, and Henry thought it sounded like a real promise.

They passed the next hour mostly in silence, not strained but companionable, Henry watching Violet and Luke's gaze flitting between the two. Presently, he slid a small notebook and pencil from the back pocket of his trousers and began to sketch, the gentle scratch of lead against paper providing respite from the intermittent beeps, muffled voices, and faraway sirens. The windows that had been dark paled into dawn, the sky a hazy silver that shone with the promise of sun. Luke yawned, his long limbs extending outwards like bent pipe cleaners as he groaned and creaked. It was catching, and soon Henry's mouth was agape, the deep exhalation of oxygen making him feel more alert. His eyes moistened and he squeezed them shut, watching the patterns that swirled in the darkness. And then he sensed a change. Movement. A new sound.

Violet's hand, which had for so many hours been clasped in his, twitched.

'Vee?' he whispered.

Jolted by the word, Luke leaned forward in his seat, his nose practically meeting Henry's as both men stared down at the woman in the bed.

Violet's eyelids flickered, her dry lips parting as she blinked, taking them in.

'Hello.'

'Mum?' It was almost a sob.

Violet fixed her gaze on Luke. 'There you are.' She sighed happily. 'My beautiful boy.'

The muscles in Luke's face contracted around his relief, the colour that had drained rushing back into his complexion. She was right, thought Henry. He was beautiful. Talented, complicated, unique, fiercely passionate, and wholly theirs.

Always.

'We've been here all night,' Luke told her, and frowning, she looked past him and around the room. Henry saw the moment clarity struck, the panic widening her eyes as she remembered the events that had led her here.

'My legs,' she said, taking in the canopied sheet. 'Henry?'

'Both broken,' he confirmed, feeling her hand tense in his. 'But cleanly. No surgery required, just plenty of pain relief, hence your long sleep. You took a blow to the head as well, but you're OK.' He'd choked on the last word, his emotion surprising him. 'Sorry,' he said, coughing to mask the tremble. 'It's just that, I was so scared when you fell. I thought that you . . . For a second. It was horrible. You had me really scared, had us both scared.'

Luke was nodding in agreement, and Violet put her hand on his cheek.

'I'm OK,' she said weakly. Then, turning back to Henry, 'Is everyone else all right? Paulina?'

'Absolutely fine,' he assured her. 'She went back to Palma with her mum, but Tomas is here still, as far as I know, along with Juan and Ynes.'

'And Eliza,' Luke added. 'I should go and tell her, tell them, that you're awake, Mum. Shall I get a nurse or something?'

'Sure.' Henry smiled. 'But maybe give us a few minutes, unless you're in any pain?' he checked, but Violet sleepily shook her head.

'Can't feel a thing at the moment. It's wonderful.'

Luke's eye caught Henry's and they grinned.

'I'll be back soon,' he said, standing and crossing to the door. 'And Mum?'

'What is it?'

'I'm really glad you're going to be OK.'

When he'd gone, Violet's demeanour changed, her determined serenity marred by a fresh wave of uncertainty. The peacefulness had gone, replaced by a consternation so acute that Henry felt compelled to reassure.

'What's the matter?' he hastened. 'Does it hurt? Shall I fetch someone?'

He was halfway out of the chair when Violet's fingers closed around his wrist.

'It's not that.' She cast her eyes down to the bedsheets.

'Then what? Whatever it is, you can tell me.'

'I didn't hear,' she said. 'You said something to me, before I fell, and I was trying to get closer, so I could make it out. I wasn't even looking where I was stepping. I need to know. What did you say?'

Henry waited until she'd stilled before reaching across and tucking a strand of her hair behind her ear. He knew the back of it must be matted; stitches and glue mingled with dried blood. She was going to need the tenderest care over these coming weeks.

'What I said was that I forgive you.'

'You do?'

Henry nodded, just once. 'I hate that you kissed Juan,' he said, as the recollection of that night made his fingers tighten into a fist. 'But I understand why.'

Violet glanced away. 'We talked about it,' she told him. 'Minutes before we realised that Paulina had gone missing. He admitted it was all linked to his jealousy of you, how Ana had always compared the two of you. I think he saw kissing me as getting one over on you. Stupid macho idiot,' she added. 'Though not as stupid as me for going along with it.'

'Did you ever love him?'

The question seemed to unsteady her, and she winced as she attempted to shuffle up on her elbows. Henry rushed to assist, but she waved him away.

'I'll do it.'

'Oh my god,' he exclaimed. 'Not this again. Vee, in case you hadn't noticed, you've broken both your legs. I think given the circumstances, it's fine to accept some help.'

'Of course I never loved him,' she fumed, as he plumped her pillow. 'Me, love Juan?'

Henry faced her. 'I assumed that after he saved Luke, that you and he . . . I would've understood,' he said, only to immediately shake his head at the lie. 'OK, no, I wouldn't. That's complete bollocks. It would've destroyed me.'

'Admiration isn't love,' she intoned. 'Gratitude isn't love.'

'So, you really never loved him – not even for a moment?'

Violet flopped back against her pillow. 'No. The only person I've ever loved in that way is you, Henry. You are the one.'

Henry stood up and took her hand in his once again, and then, with his gaze never leaving hers, he dropped on a single knee to the floor.

'What are you?' she started to say, but he shushed her.

'Violet Torres?'

Anticipation danced between them.

'Yes, Henry Torres?'

'I want to tell you that I'm sorry. Sorry for pushing you away when I should have pulled you closer, sorry for hiding at work when I knew you needed me at home; sorry for being jealous of the love you had for our son, and sorry for being a sideline dad instead of running the race along with you. I tried, but not enough. I should've done better.'

She was shaking her head, tears welling.

'You told me before that I was your everything,' he said, and she nodded, smiled. 'And I laughed.'

A small frown. 'I had forgotten that.'

'I laughed because we are so ridiculous, the pair of us. Both so stubborn. We bickered during the very first conversation we ever had, and since then it's been a kind of competition, hasn't it? A contest of who can parent best; who is most like Luke, who is least like him, if it happens to be a difficult day; which of us he loves more, which of us loves the other more. Come on, Vee, we even argue about who loves who more.'

She gave him a sideways look. 'It's me – definitely me. You're a ten out of ten, remember?'

Henry tutted. 'With this face?'

She scrutinised him, a playful smile adding colour to her cheeks. 'There are a few grey hairs,' she noted. 'And you're in dire need of a shave, so let's call it a nine point seven five, shall we?'

'Can I get back to my speech now, please?'

'If you must.'

She sighed, alight now with a joy he hadn't seen for so long. Henry took a breath. He was still on one knee, still holding on to her. He didn't want to ever let go again.

'I think,' he said, fingers snaking through hers, 'that bickering is our love language. It's our fire under the pot, not a flaw but a strength. Luke has it, too – from both of us. He's only just learning how to use it for good rather than bad, and if you think about it, he's got there much quicker than we have.'

She laughed at that, a sound that filled the room with warmth.

'You're not wrong,' she said. 'But I'm sorry, too. For the stuff with Juan, for shutting you out and never letting you help, for getting into debt and lying about it, accepting money from a man like McCabe, for trying to sell our home.'

'You don't need to worry about McCabe any more,' Henry told her. 'I sent him a message, reminding him how far my own Cambridge connections extended, how I put in a new kitchen for one of the chief constables working at Parkside Police Station a few years back and how much we'd hit it off, how I was sure that if I were to have a quiet word, McCabe would find himself at the centre of a fraud investigation. He didn't like the sound of that, unsurprisingly, and has agreed to leave us alone.'

'Just like that?' Violet's eyes were wide.

'Bullies don't like it when people stand up to them.'

'I'm such an idiot,' she wailed, shaking her head only to wince. 'I don't know what I was thinking, Henry; losing you – it changed me. I didn't know how to be any more, how to feel happy. The future felt so empty.'

Henry knew what she meant because he had felt it, too – the loneliness, the bitterness, the despair. And all the time she'd been there, missing him, and he'd been here, wanting her. Twenty long summers and nothing had changed at all. Not really.

'Will you marry me?' he asked. 'I want to make all those promises over again, and this time I want to honour them.

Not a fresh start, but a journey along the same path, only this time I'm bringing a map –' he laughed – 'and a compass, and maybe some of that gross mint cake that never goes out of date.'

Violet had started to cry, the tears running into her smile. 'You want to marry me again?'

'I love you,' he said, knowing as he did so that it really was as simple as that. 'The day you climbed over that wall to steal my flowers, you stole my heart along with them. It's belonged to you since that day and it will be yours for all the days that follow, whether you accept this proposal or not. But I hope you do,' he added. 'I really hope you say yes.'

Violet pulled him forwards until his lips were inches from hers. 'I'll say yes on one condition.'

'Anything,' he said, and he meant it. 'Whatever I have, it's yours.'

She pressed the tip of her nose against his. 'That's good to know,' Violet murmured, her lips parting as Henry stared at her in awe; this woman for whom he'd dismantle the world if she asked him to; take it all apart only to build it over again from scratch.

'But I say we start with a kiss.'

Epilogue

Two Summers Later

He had always thought the house looked at its best in the fading light, when the apricot walls seemed to bask in the doting glow of sunset, its turreted tower raised in salute of another day done. So many hours, and weeks, and months he'd spent here, and yet this moment, he knew, would be the one he recalled with most pleasure.

The patio was busy with people, a blur of voices, of colour, of glasses clinking. A surge of feeling rose, and he caught it in his mind, examined it, searching for anything that might trigger a response. But there was nothing to concern him, no discernible emotion, save for joy. He was in a safe place. These were his people.

Vows had been traded, flowers arranged, a cake cut, and speeches made. His father had talked of strong foundations, his mother of deep roots. To him, however, there could be no better metaphor for life than art. Just as one might gaze at a painting every day and find something new to admire, so his parents found endless things to love about each other. They were a masterpiece not solely on the surface but below it, too, in the layers of oil and light, each imperfection conjuring its own brand of magic.

How lucky he was to have them.

Below him in the village, a church bell began to chime, followed closely by a second, as if one had called out and the other answered. The mountains smouldered in the east and while he could not see it, he knew the water far below would be sparkling.

They had walked along the shoreline that morning, the pair of them, stopping often to scavenge or dig; sand between toes and ice cream for breakfast; flowers picked, and the names of birds taught; her hand holding his, trusting him, needing him, loving him.

She had made him complete.

Moving away from the group, he took the steps down as far as the lemon tree and settled himself carefully on the low stone wall, content to watch from a distance as dispersing slivers of heat danced to nature's song. His eye caught that of his mother, and she came towards him, the limp she'd inherited two summers ago now so slight that it was close to being forgotten.

'Do you want me to take Valentina?' she asked. 'Give you a break?'

For so much of their lives, she had spoken to him staccato; now, her voice was honey.

Luke looked down at his sister, sleeping so peacefully in his arms.

'Don't worry,' he said, and smiled. 'We're both exactly where we want to be.'

Acknowledgements

Novelists are often asked, be it at events or during interviews, what advice they would offer those who are keen to tackle a book. One suggestion that seems to come up an awful lot is this: write what you know.

Here's what I know.

According to the latest statistics from mental health charity Mind, the percentage of men willing to seek help if they feel low is increasing – but there is still a long way to go. Research from Time to Change found that men are less knowledgeable than women about mental health and hold more negative attitudes. They are also less likely to report or discuss their own experiences, and more likely to claim that issues of this kind are the result of a 'lack of self-discipline and willpower'. One in ten men reported getting angry when feeling low, and the Mental Health Foundation found that men who suffer from depression are more likely to exhibit 'symptoms' such as irritability, sudden anger, increased loss of control, risk-taking and aggression. Based on the latest figures, 73 per cent of people in the UK who died from suicide in 2020 were men, and suicide remains the biggest killer of men under the age of 50. Despite this, Mind reports that mental health crisis care services in the UK continue to be 'under-resourced, understaffed and over-stretched', and a survey found that only 14 per cent of those that accessed these services felt they'd received the support they needed in a time of crisis.

Shocking, but not surprising – not to me or my family.

For a long period of time leading up to the writing of *The Orange House*, I have lived amid this storm. I've seen the destruction mental health issues can cause, the cracks that form, the trust that erodes and the helplessness that calcifies when you plead to be heard and are not. But as always during the darkest times, there is also light – a future on which we have focused, a belief I've never lost sight of that somehow, at some distant point, things will begin to heal. It was from this light that Violet, Henry and Luke emerged to find me, battle-weary but determined, and ready, at last, to tell their story.

And so, my first thanks must go to you, dearest reader, for choosing this book and therefore supporting not only this story but all those that will follow. I am so grateful to you all.

To my agent, Alice Lutyens, upon whose bold brilliance (and gentle ribbing) I have become hopelessly reliant, and to the marvellous wider team at Curtis Brown (especially Olivia, Sam and Emma), who do so much negotiating, cheerleading and contract fine-toothcombing.

To Kimberley Atkins, for championing this story from the off and assuring me that, yes, I could – and definitely should – write it.

To my editor, Jo Dickinson, who 'got' this story as soon as she read it and helped me shape it into a book of which I'm extremely proud. I kept waiting for the 'SOS moment' of the edit to hit and it never did – a true testament to your calm positivity. Immeasurable thanks also to my Hodder & Stoughton team, including Alainna Hadjigeorgiou (for publicity), Olivia Robertshaw (for editorial), Alice Morley (for marketing), Kay Gale (for copyedit), Becky Glibbery (for cover design) and Catherine, Sarah, Rich, Iman and Lucy (for sales).

There are far too many authors I want to thank, but key amongst them are Cathy Bramley, Katie Marsh, Kate Gray, Cressida McLaughlin and Kirsty Greenwood (The Castle Crew), as well as Cesca Major and Louise Candlish. Lisa Howells, Chris Whitaker and Tom Wood also fall under the 'author' category, but you three don't help me write so much as celebrate the fact I managed to, and for that I will be eternally grateful . . . even if my liver is not.

To Janie and Mickey at Chez Castillon, where a good portion of this novel was written, thank you for providing delicious food and wine, a stunning setting and the story of Bimbo the monkey. I think about you and darling Rory often and can't wait to return.

The more books I write, the less my poor friends see of me. I'm putting it in writing that I'm aware of this, Sadie, Vicky, Ian, Tamsin, Ranjit, Sarah, Gemma, Chad, Ewan, Kay, SJ, Fanny, Frosty, Tammo and Linds. I promise to do better. Know that I adore all of you.

My final thanks go to my family, who, despite being as battle-weary as me, continue to champion my books, listen while I ruminate over plots and cheer every piece of good publishing news loudly enough to drown out the roosters next door . . . almost. This book would never have been written if it wasn't for you, Mum. Thank you for being so open, and for teaching me what unconditional love looks like. For as long as you need me, I'm here.